Pirate Legacy

Manicato l'naru'

Pirate Legacy
Manicato I'naru'

Pirate Legacy Series, Book One

Frank N Steiner

Salem, Oregon

Cover Illustration and Cover Design by Lee Moyer *(leemoyer.com)*
Ember's Spirit Logo by Rifani Aulia
Broken Wheel Logo by DesignPoint, Inc.
Editing by Josiah Davis and Book Butchers
Editor Alyssa Matesic

Library of Congress Control Number: 2022911303

ISBN: 978-0-9891353-9-9 (Hardcover)
ISBN: 979-8-9864623-0-1 (Trade Paperback)
ISBN: 979-8-9864623-1-8 (ebook)

www.ogfrankenstein.com

10 9 8 7 6 5 4 3 2 1

Broken Cove Accessories
Women's Golf Apparel - Adult Pirate Clothier
Swimwear - Women's Fashion Gloves
Personalized Fittings by Appointment Only
Pasta-de-faria's
Portland's Premier Pasta Place
Roof Top Dining Tuesday through Sunday 10 AM - 10 PM
Broken Cove Country Club
Broken Cove Publishing
Broken Cove Educational Services
Curriculum and training to meet the educational needs of rural communities of the Pacific Northwest.
Broken Cove Industries
Coffee Covfefe
Shiver~me Timbers Rum House
Of course we have rum! We're a pirate organization.
Broken Cove Charities
Pirates' Chocolate

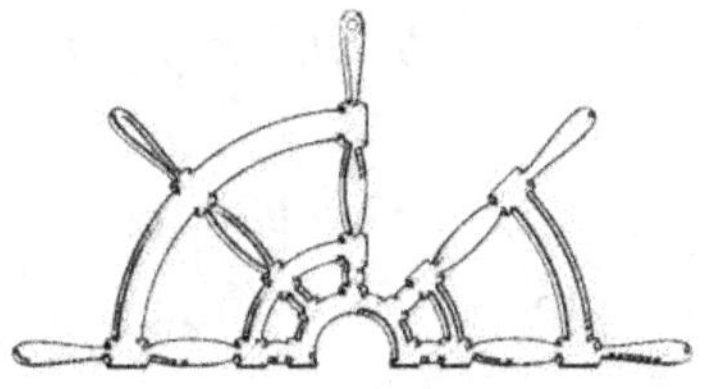

1 - The Shack

A billowing dust cloud rose behind the speeding cab, intensifying Lilith's already heightened anxiety. She fidgeted with her amulet. This job interview forced her to leave her familiar surroundings of home and sent her into the mountainous region west of Portland.

She scanned the dirt road ahead and glanced in the rear-view mirror. The cab driver shifted his eyes from side to side and leaned forward, giving his full attention to the narrow dirt road.

Oh god, my driver doesn't know where we are. I'm going to be late to this interview. What a great first impression, Lilith. They'll see you as unreliable.

"Miss, are you sure about this place?"

Jolted from her self-inflicted mental torture, Lilith said, "It's a hut or shack, or maybe an outhouse for all I know. But it's next to a three-story mansion with a golf course."

"Shack? Do you mean the Velvet Shack? We are headed in the wrong direction to get there."

"What's the Velvet Shack?"

"A strippers' bar. You gonna be a pole dancer?"

Lilith pulled out her phone and cast her most vicious, disgusted face at the cabbie. *Make a move, huckleberry Harry. My blue belt in Brazilian jiu-jitsu can kick your scrawny ass.*

"Sorry, miss. Ain't no cell signals up here."

She peered at the cabbie in the rear-view mirror. *He's watching me.*

"You are a pretty little thing. First of your people in these parts."

Lilith cringed. *Alone in the mountains with Ranger Dick. God, why did I chase this job lead?*

Days earlier, an eccentric little-old woman entered her stepmother's hair salon and chatted with Lilith's stepmother. She understood the casual conversation between the two was about her, but minded her business and kept sweeping the floor. Before she escaped into the break room, the old woman called for her to come closer.

Lilith obeyed her elder and stepped next to the chair. The old woman cradled Lilith's jaw and turned her head to the side for a profile look. The charms dangling from her wrist tickled Lilith's chest. She turned Lilith's head back to face her and nodded with a grateful smile.

After the old woman left, Lilith's stepmother handed her an envelope. Inside it were directions to a job interview in the foothills of the Coastal Mountain Range and two hundred dollars for a cab.

"Whoa." The cabbie pointed to the passenger side of the road. "Look at that castle like mansion."

Trees blocked her from seeing the house in full as they sped along. Far back from the dirt road sat a grand three-story home. Two stone turrets trisected the house. A manicured and expansive deep-green lawn extended on all sides of the Navajo white painted home. The Japanese wisteria was in full bloom and arched over the driveway, creating a tunnel of purple flowers from the road to the house.

The cabbie asked, "Do I pull into that purple covered thing?"

"No. There should be a gravel parking lot with a sign saying, 'Broken Cove Country Club.'"

The pounding in her head dissipated when the sign came into view. Her relief vanished as the cab turned into the gravel parking lot. The amateurish sign—a simple piece of thin plywood—wreaked havoc on her hopes of working for a quality business.

The cabbie pulled next to a cart path at the edge of the gravel.

Lilith paid the cabbie and said, "Thanks for not dropping me off on the rocks."

"It wouldn't be right. Especially for a pretty—"

"Okay-then-thanks-bye," Lilith called back after she launched herself out of the cab.

She straightened her white blouse and tugged the wrinkles out of her navy-blue dress pants. Confident she was presentable, she stepped toward the small plywood building which laid at the end of the cart path. The triple-wide sized mobile home didn't look like the standard clubhouse for a country club. *Is this a job interview, or first-period history in the portable outside my old high school?*

With each step she took, she took satisfaction in her correct choice of wearing her two-tone wedge heel pumps.

Any heel on this blacktop path could send her toppling over. As she walked, something struck her as peculiar. *Only three cars in the parking lot. How bad is this place if nobody is here?*

She approached the glorified shack and questioned which of the two doors to enter. Two large trash cans and a recycling bin sat next to the door at the far end. But the door closest to her had one trash can. It had to be the one she wanted.

The artwork between the two doors captured her awe. A professional had painted a spectacular wall-sized image of the golf course's name and logo on the shack. The white canvas featured the top half of a ship's wheel. A piece of the wheel between the top right handles was missing. *Broken Cove Country Club—and a broken ship's wheel. Cute play on words.*

She slowed her pace to admire the artwork. As she did, the second door at the far entrance opened. A tall blonde woman stepped out. Lilith's eyes bulged at the woman's white bikini top and matching wraparound beach skirt. Huge sunglasses and white gladiator sandals gave the young woman the aura of a runway model during fashion week.

Is she a stripper? Have I been tricked? Ranger Dick was right. I'm the new pole dancer.

Lilith hurried to the door before the woman spotted her. She eased the door shut and turned to face the customer service counter. As cheap and rickety as the outside appeared; the interior was the opposite. Its floor-to-ceiling oak paneling wasn't the inexpensive, discount-bin kind. The interior design style escaped her. *Is this shabby chic, or glorified redneck? Whichever, it ain't what I expected.*

With no one at the cash register, she walked down the

hallway and past an open door to the kitchen. The lights illuminated sleek new kitchen appliances and a spotless floor. She nodded her approval. A professional ran this kitchen.

She continued down the hall and entered a cozy diner-esque lounge with chrome-legged lunch tables and large pine booths. *Whoa. What lamebrain combined a diner motif and a ski lodge?*

A young Latina woman stood on a ladder in the far corner. She was biting down on a pencil as she held a nail in place. With a couple of hammer taps, she secured the nail in the drywall. Suddenly, she whacked the hammer down on the nail, sinking it with one strike. She flipped the hammer up, caught it like a gunslinger, and stepped down the ladder. She squealed with joy at seeing Lilith. "Hola. You're the ten o'clock interview?"

"I am." Lilith found it difficult to overcome her preconceived notion that a tiny girl could wield a hammer as this one just did. "You … and that hammer. How did you learn to do that?"

The young woman pulled her long, dark-brown hair aside. "Dad said I needed a hobby, and boy, was he right? But he came to regret encouraging me into woodworking when my tastes in power tools exceeded his financial resources. The sixteen-speed, two-twenty volt, three-phase lathe with a digital readout was my bridge too far."

Lilith didn't hear a word. She was busy scouring over the young lady's face. *Flawless complexion, perfect facial symmetry. No product in her hair. Damn, modeling agencies would die to sign her.*

"Hey, girl. Whatcha doing?"

She snapped out of her dreamworld. "Sorry. I'm Lilith. Where do I go for the job interview?"

"No further than right here. I'm Charlotte, the current receptionist-slash-cashier. Tayen, the general manager, is up at the old man's mansion and will be here to interview you soon."

Charlotte inspected Lilith's appearance. "Someone my height—just over five feet. And your long locks are gorgeous. What's up with your eyes? Your daddy must have gotten his freak on to give you those crystal sapphires."

Lilith was used to hearing about her blue eyes. If somebody didn't immediately comment about her eyes, they would a few seconds later. She skirted around the topic and said, "We short girls have to stick together. Do you get teased?"

Charlotte smirked at Lilith. "Not when I'm holding a hammer. Any way … You and I will run register and take turns serving tables."

Lilith pointed at Charlotte's clothes. "We can wear that?"

Charlotte waved her hand like a salesperson, showcasing her white ribbed cropped tank top and jean shorts. "This is my day off uniform. And today is everybody's day off."

"Oh … you're closed." Lilith turned toward the window. "That's why there were no cars. And the blonde woman … That's why she wore a bikini top."

"Blondie's name is Talia. She's a physical phenom and someone you'll grow to love. She's street-smart, kindhearted, and a scintillating dancer. You'll learn the best techniques on lap dances from her."

Lilith half closed her eyes. "This is a gentlemen's club?"

"No, babydoll. This is the clubhouse for Broken Cove

Country Club. A small business startup with beer, balls, and a bitchin' awesome golf course. But AJ, our genius owner, doesn't permit stripping or lap dances. Which is a shame, because we could pack this place after dark on the weekends. The money I could make … Mm, and baby, I would too."

Lilith touched the corner of her eyebrow with her fingertip. "After seeing Talia and you, I thought this was a strip club. Her gladiator sandals are fire. You make enough working here to afford Cult Gaia? Or were those Gianvito Rossi?"

"Broken Cove Industries—"

"—or Valentino Garavani?"

"Listen, fashion chick, we aren't paid like they are at the Velvet Shack, where Talia used to dance," Charlotte said.

"Ah. I guessed right; she was a stripper."

"You look relieved to hear you aren't stripping, but you might be upset because you couldn't identify a design by Alexander Wang."

"Wang?" Lilith played with her amulet. "I'd strip for a pair of Wangs."

"Take a seat, Roxy. I'm off to the mansion to fetch Tayen for your striptease audition." Charlotte pushed the kitchen open and hurried out.

Lilith slipped into the wooden booth and picked up a menu. Standard finger foods, nothing fancy. She looked out the window to see the ninth green beyond the gravel parking lot. A blue flag waved atop the pin. The image of a ship's wheel in white leapt off the field of blue.

Right time, right place. I'm ready for the interview. A wave of assurance washed over her. The uncertainty of the morning had sapped her confidence, but the quiet helped restore her centeredness. The lingering scent of apples, nutmeg, and cinnamon reminded her of family and friends during the winter holidays.

A middle-aged couple appeared outside, breaking her moment of solace. The man wore a bright red polo shirt and straw cane hat. His eyes were hidden behind his sunglasses.

Lilith switched to the woman, who stood as tall as the man, but her hair snagged Lilith's attention. The caramel highlights stood out from her sandy brown hair. *That's the work of the city's most prestigious hair designer, Pierre-Yves. What other designers does this woman have?*

Ashamed of herself, she looked away. Lilith's weakness was fashion. Her stepmother's hairstyling business had occupied most of Lilith's life. Hair and fashion dominated her time when not in school. Over the years, she'd become an aficionado of the local designers and stylists.

With her eyes disengaged from the beauty icon outside the window, her ears picked up the couple's faint voices. She scooched closer to the window.

The man said, "The county development officer should use the street layout based on the new survey lines. I don't want the home lots shorted."

He's giving her orders. He's the owner, and she's the general manager, Tayen.

Lilith sensed a tone of impatience from Tayen. "AJ, I have it under control."

"Your neck isn't on the line if plans go awry. My bank account will evaporate if this fails, my dearest Tayen. I could lose it all and end up back on the streets. My fear of going homeless again … Well, I can't put to words that terror."

Lilith rushed her hands to cover her gaping mouth. *Homeless, again? What is happening here?*

Tayen placed her hand on AJ's shoulder. He cupped his hand over hers. "If our plans hold, then I can put aside that fear. But snagging a professional tour stop would really put my mind at ease."

First impressions were everything to Lilith. But first impressions made from secret observations were priceless. She closed her eyes to reconcile what had happened since she arrived. *Spunky Latina, fun to work with. The fashion icon general manager, damn. What can I learn from her? The owner, homeless, again?*

She opened her eyes to find Tayen had disappeared. Lilith rose her butt off the seat and leaned toward the window to find the general manager. If first impressions were important, what impression would she make if the general manager caught her sleeping before the interview?

Unable to find Tayen, she took a deep breath to calm herself. *Relax. This will work if you don't screw it up.* She regained her composure and turned back to the window to watch the owner.

He stared at the far end of the parking lot. She peeked around to see a cumbersome delivery truck stirring up dust as it came toward him. The pops of gravel shooting from under the tires and the rumble of the truck weren't muffled by the thin shack walls.

AJ pointed to where the truck was to back-in next to the cart path. In quick order, the delivery guys dropped off a bulky crate and drove off.

"What did he order now?"

Lilith jumped. Charlotte had returned without her noticing.

"You scared me."

"Sorry." Charlotte grabbed Lilith's hand and tugged.

"We better find out what he ordered without Tayen's permission."

Lilith let herself be pulled out of the booth. "AJ is the owner?"

"AJ de Faria is the grand collaborator, slash owner. He dreams the impossible, and Tayen converts it into reality."

Lilith began, "I saw Tayen. Her hair—"

"I know, gorgeous and goddamn expensive." Charlotte pivoted in front of the door. "She's amazing, and her fashion is dope. I want all her clothes and accessories. I'm not into horse riding, so forget her equestrian gear. But one thing is for sure, you'll start patterning your wardrobe after hers when you get to know her."

"Careful, I haven't even interviewed yet. Let's not put the horse behind the cart."

Charlotte frowned.

Lilith tilted her head to the side. "Cart before the horse. Get used to me doing spoonerisms and total word switches. I specialize in them. So … What is Mr. de Faria like?"

"Never call him mister. Calling him mister … it confuses him. As far as what he's like, he is the human version of the internet only without Wi-Fi. His knowledge base is ridiculous. But say hashtag, and he becomes the stereotypical old fart without a clue." Charlotte rocked back from opening the door. "And for god's sake, don't tell him I called him an old fart. He'll call my dad and send me back to college."

"You were in college?"

Charlotte had her hand on the door and grabbed Lilith by the elbow. "No. I got accepted to several, but I'm not interested in attending."

"Where were you accepted?"

"What schools would impress you?"

"The University of Chicago, Harvard, Yale."

Charlotte winked. "To those add Oxford, Cambridge, and UC Berkeley."

"Accepted to those schools and you're working … here?"

"I graduated high school two years early, and my entrance exam scores were near perfect. But endless homework and studying for the AP exams neutered my social life. If college was going to be more of the same … Screw it, I wanted a social life. I can teach myself whatever I need to know."

Lilith eased her resistance and let Charlotte pull her out the door.

"AJ," Charlotte called out, "this is Lilith, the new cashier."

AJ spun around. "Damn, Tayen was quick with that interview."

"I haven't interviewed yet, Mr. de Faria," Lilith amended.

"Who?"

"I told her you don't know what 'mister' means," Charlotte said.

AJ faced Lilith and held out his hand. His kind and gracious smile exuded his confidence and charm. "Hello, young lady. Lilith, is it?"

Before Lilith answered, Charlotte interrupted. "Look at her eyes. Have you ever seen anything so blue?"

"Forgive Ms. Tavares, Lilith. She is excited about having someone her age working beside her. And yes, her eyes are spectacular."

"The logo will make her eyes pop."

"She's not a shoo-in because of her eyes. The question is, can she make change for a twenty?"

"Twenties are a problem. Fifties and hundreds are much easier," Lilith said with a straight face.

Charlotte blurted out, "Stripper smarts. She's hired."

"Let Tayen do the interview. If she doesn't hire you, I'll have a chat with her." AJ winked at Lilith. "Great answer for the change-making question."

Charlotte tapped on the top of the crate. "What did you buy this time without Tayen's permission?"

"Stop saying I need her permission to buy things."

Charlotte ripped the packaging invoice off the crate. "It came from New Orleans." After a moment, she handed the invoice to AJ. "What language is it?"

"Haitian Creole."

"Not Creole, but Haitian Creole." Charlotte turned to Lilith. "Genius here has mastered a few languages. His list includes Spanish, French, Portuguese, German, Mandarin, Russian, Greek, Japanese, and Koyra Chiini."

"Koyra Chiini?" Lilith asked.

AJ rolled his eyes. "My son, Elliott, gifted me with an ancient book written in Koyra Chiini. Charlotte made the mistake of betting him I couldn't read it. She lost the bet and now she won't let it die."

"Fewer than two hundred thousand speak it, and they're all in Timbuktu," Charlotte retorted.

"Text Manny and ask him to move this into my garage," AJ instructed.

"Why didn't they deliver it to your driveway?"

"The truck wouldn't fit below the wisteria arch. So, I had them drop off here."

"Anything taller than a lowrider won't fit under that arch," Charlotte said.

Lilith enjoyed their playful banter. She sensed Charlotte had permission to test AJ's limits.

"Charlotte," AJ said.

Oops, limit reached. Change the discussion, girl.

Charlotte deflected to escape AJ's wrath. "What's in the crate?"

"It is a personal gift from an old acquaintance."

Yep, his tone just killed their playtime.

AJ spoke to Lilith. "Forgive my young friend's petulance. She believes her striking beauty will sway my decisions so she can get her way around here. We hired her because she is charming and professional with the customers. Not because she has a pretty face."

Charlotte extended her hand to AJ for a fist bump. "Never hurts to use whatcha got."

AJ fist bumped back. "Tayen will officially hire you, Lilith. But the question you must answer is, can you tolerate us? We are high functioning and fast moving. You should expect daily challenges. This will be a thrill ride if you have an inner toughness."

Lilith scanned the area. "What are you doing with your business?"

AJ pointed to the other side of the gravel parking lot. "We broke ground north of the dirt road to construct nine holes for the course and a clubhouse. Broken Cove Country Club is a pirate-themed golf resort based on the Church of the Flying Spaghetti Monster. We are Pastafarian proud and our rooftop restaurant will specialize in pasta dishes."

"And the world's largest rum selection," Charlotte added.

"And the world's largest rum selection," AJ chuckled. He winked at Lilith, and added, "If you told me four years ago this was what I would be doing, I would have laughed until the sun sat." He closed one eye and spoke like a pirate: "But when the gangway opens, ye walk up it, lest ye be shown the gangplank instead. Arrrg."

Lilith smiled and batted her eyes. As adorable as AJ was, she had a serious concern. Rather than let it go, she straightened her back and asked, "You said there would be challenges. Will one of them be me? A black woman in a predominately white neighborhood?"

"And catering to said white population. Good lord, what will we do?"

Lilith didn't anticipate his bluntness, nor did he shy away from her question. She let her hand creep up on her amulet as she began fidgeting with it. "Am I the token black for your diversity check mark?"

"Many intersections meet here, and I stand with those who may be a check mark on other lists. I employ three Latinos. My general manager—Tayen—is First Nations, Chef Dean is black, and my stunning table server is white."

Confused, Charlotte corrected AJ, "Your stunning table server is Latino. I'm not white."

"My table server, who doesn't need a stepladder to punch her timecard."

Charlotte's playfulness returned. "Oh, of course. Tall and stunning means Talia. Smoking hot refers to me."

AJ turned to Lilith and pointed at her chest. "Your amulet, is it an old family heirloom?"

Lilith held it up for him. "Correct. An old family heirloom with a three-hundred-year-old tradition of being passed down through the generations."

"How did you get the honor of receiving it?"

"When I was born, Grandma insisted it was mine. She said my blue eyes had been lying dormant ever since an ancient ancestor had sported them centuries ago. The amulet is said to have come into our possession on some Caribbean Island."

"Three hundred years ago … in the Caribbean." AJ furrowed his brows.

"Shit," Charlotte said, "I can see the gears clicking in his head."

"The Golden Age of Piracy." AJ wiggled his finger, motioning Lilith to come closer. When she stood in front of him, he asked, "May I?"

She unclasped the necklace and handed it to him.

He lifted his sunglasses to study the amulet. For the first time, she had a view of his brown eyes.

He held the amulet up for the sunlight to cast off any shadows. "Strange coloring. A micro-thin layer of copper covers it. And a light layer of a glass-like material. Cool to the touch, and colder still when I pinch it." He handed it back to Lilith. "Is there a story behind it?"

"Not that I've been told. Mom died when I was six, and Grandma died a few short years later. Grandma insisted I wear it always, and Mama-Titi makes sure I do."

"Mama-Titi?" AJ asked.

"Ooh, Mama-Titi," Charlotte said. "Your mother's sister married your father and became your stepmother. Even money says it was a younger sister."

A judgmental uptick of an eye, or the corner of a lip tightening—Lilith received these reactions when people learned about her parents. But AJ and Charlotte's faces weren't showing these microaggressions.

Confident of her new friends' sincerity, she said, "My family is the best, and it doesn't bother me that my dad married my mom's younger sister."

"Nor should it," AJ said.

"So, what is the Golden Age of Piracy?" Lilith asked.

"A time when colonial powers from Europe were at the mercy of pirates in the Caribbean Sea. Were any family stories passed down to you?"

"Mama-Titi heard Mom and Grandma's arguments after I was born. What they fought over seemed silly to her. But there was one knockdown drag 'em out fight about the unfinished business of our great … oh, Lord … don't ask how many greats the woman was. The other fight was about which one of them would return to an intersection of three estates."

"An intersection, or the intersection?"

Lilith froze for a moment. "Is there a difference between the two?"

AJ chuckled. "What other things from the past did they fight over?"

Lilith turned her head to Charlotte.

"Oh, honey," Charlotte started. "Give him a couple of words and in he'll tell you what they were arguing about in details you wouldn't believe."

"The other one she remembered," Lilith turned her head toward AJ, "was something about *the six screaming feathers of the sun.*"

He pulled out his phone. "Six screaming feathers of the sun?"

"Wait, there's a cell signal out here?"

Charlotte held her phone up to show Lilith. "Wi-Fi via his satellite hookup. Use *BCI employees*, not *guests*. And the password is—"

2 – Beagle's Bluff

Tayen performed the official job interview, unlike AJ and Charlotte's 'can you make change' question. No-nonsense, yet personable and gracious, Tayen charmed Lilith with her straightforward professionalism, while Lilith perfected the art of stealing peeks of Tayen's fashion between questions.

As Tayen's eyes fell on Lilith's resume, Lilith whimpered in silence over Tayen's golden-honey, silk blouse and tribal necklace. Her eyes rose as Tayen faced her for the next question. Tayen wrote notes … and Lilith's eyes darted to the black spinel earrings. By the interview's end, Lilith was more obsessed over Tayen's fashion than the prospect of landing the job.

"Congratulations, Ms. Peters. Welcome to Broken Cove Industries. You can start next week, on Monday, when we are closed. Or learn on the fly and start tomorrow."

Lilith accepted Tayen's outstretched hand. "Thank you. Tomorrow sounds like a deal. Can you tell me where the nearest bus stop is?"

"Oh, buses don't come out here."

"How far out do they come?"

"About a half marathon short of us."

Lilith remained calm, not letting Tayen see her panic. "Let me text my mother and see if I can borrow the—"

Charlotte burst through the kitchen door. "Is she officially hired?"

Tayen rested her elbows on the table. Her eyes fogged over, knowing some sort of discussion had occurred between Charlotte and AJ. "Are you saying nothing is official until AJ says so?"

Charlotte nudged into a seat at the table. "When does she start? You know … " She whisked up Lilith's application. "If she lives in Portland, she can carpool with me."

Lilith stopped texting. "If I'm too far out of the way, I can meet somewhere less inconvenient for you."

"Nah. I see where you live. You can take the red line to the Hollywood Transit Center, and I can pick you up there."

"Perfect." Tayen pushed her chair back. "Wear jeans and a white, short-sleeve top. Now, both of you go home. I'll officially see you in the morning."

Charlotte led Lilith to her dilapidated car. "I will have a down payment on a nicer car within three months."

"Where do you live?" Lilith asked.

"Alameda."

"That's an expensive part of town. How come you aren't driving a Mercedes or BMW?"

Charlotte pushed the unlock button on her keyless remote. "I'm working toward one, but I can't get it all at once."

Lilith took her seat. "I still don't understand. You

were accepted at Harvard, you live in a rich neighborhood, and your woodworking tastes are expensive. So why are you working here as a golf course cashier?"

"I gotta make my own way. Predetermined paths and accepted social norms ain't for me. Gone are the days of Miss Goody Two Shoes."

"Ah, your family is conservative."

Charlotte hit the accelerator, grinding pebbles with her tires. "Conservative in keeping with traditional family roles, but they don't expel those who march to a different drum. But enough about me. Why did you come to the foothills?"

Lilith put her phone down. "I don't mind working in Mama-Titi's salon, but I'm ready to experience something new. I haven't experienced Jack-crap in life."

Charlotte turned the car out of the parking lot. "You're a prisoner of the West Coast. San Diego to Seattle to visit family and nowhere else."

"It's not a bad prison. But I have lived nowhere except the West Coast. How about you?"

"Same, but add Mexico, British Columbia, and my whirlwind tour of colleges in New England. So, who told you about this job? I don't remember them discussing it until yesterday."

"A customer told Mama-Titi about it. If that old lady hadn't given her the cab fare, I wouldn't have come. I'm not a girl who does," Lilith pointed out the car window, "trees and more trees. Until I saw Tayen, I thought this was a fashion desert."

"Oh, poor city girl. What will you do without high-end fashion? If there was a fashion desert out here, it's about to disappear. Our fashion designer's shop, Broken Cove Accessories, will produce women's golf apparel and pirate …

outfits." Charlotte cringed. "Kimiko will kill those who call her creations costumes and not outfits. She's a designer, not whatever is below a designer."

Lilith twisted in her seat to face Charlotte. "A country club has a designer fashion line?"

"Oh, honey. You came to a zoo. AJ will steal your imagination. His perspective on the world is unlike anything I've experienced. Ask him a question and be prepared for a journey."

"Like what?"

"Like in a painting. You and I see a person's face. But AJ sees the hill behind the person, where a famous battle was waged. He'll tell you the history of the person being painted, and the painter's frame of mind. When you're impressed with those stories, he'll tell you about the bakery in the background and its two-century history. AJ knows the stories within the stories and you'll never look at the painting in the same way."

Lilith sat still, unwilling to interrupt Charlotte.

"AJ's creativity is boundless and chaotic, but never dangerous. A restraint to his creativity came a couple of years ago. Tayen is the safeguard which keeps his harebrained ideas from flying off the rails. I love her name. In her Native American tribal language, it means New Moon."

Charlotte slowed as they approached the intersection. "She is professional, insightful, and a force of nature. Her business sense paved the way for her stint as a Fortune 500 company's vice president before she turned thirty-five."

"I get the vibe that they are genuine to the core."

Charlotte looked both ways before turning onto the highway. "Without a doubt. And the owner's son, Elliott, is cute. Father and son are very close emotionally, but far apart, geographically. Elliott works a government job in Europe. He's always vague about what he does. I guess he is embarrassed by it, or it's a top-level security gig. When you meet him next month, and if you find him attractive, get to know him."

"What? Date the owner's son?" Lilith asked.

"He's a sweet guy, who will be heir to his father's fortune … should this business get off the ground."

"I'm not here to secure a sugar daddy."

"But if opportunity knocks, open that door," Charlotte said.

Lilith shrugged. "Maybe this is the place. Somewhere I fit in and don't feel out of place."

"Don't tell me you don't fit in. People must be knocking down your door to date you."

"They swipe right, but I'm in a swipe left mood."

"So, how do you not fit in?"

Lilith whirled her hand in the air. "Fitting in may not best describe my feelings. Detached is better. More in the sense of lacking a purpose, wasting time, spinning my wheels. Like a twenty-one-year-old knows what they're supposed to do for the rest of their life after high school."

"That pressure is absurd. You're led to believe if you're not meeting others' predetermined timetable, then you are falling behind and need to get your act together."

"Exactly." Lilith turned her head toward Charlotte. "If you had gone to Harvard, what major would you have done?"

"Psychology. If I got bored with that, I would have headed down to MIT for woodshop."

"MIT has woodshop? You're joking?"

"I never joke about woodworking." Charlotte patted the steering wheel with her palm. "Not to change the subject, but I've done this forty-five-minute drive for over a year, and that's just one way. Me thinks an apartment is in our future."

Lilith lowered her phone and gazed through the windshield. "Working and living in the western suburbs of Portland. I thought I'd always be stuck downtown. It's impossible to rent a place without loads of overtime."

"Or a roommate," Charlotte said.

***

A month later, Charlotte and Lilith moved into their new apartment, which was miles closer to work. Thrilled to be on their own, the two women's enthusiasm energized Broken Cove Country Club. Enamored golfers enjoyed Lilith's girlish charm and generosity, while Charlotte's wit and spontaneous sass left them in tears of laughter.

AJ was hosting staff dinners on Sunday nights at his home. The old shack's days were ending as construction began. Dinner guests entered through the backyard, where they were free to roam the sprawling outdoor Greek-styled courtyard.

Lilith's infatuation with the Greek statues inspired her to wander the courtyard by herself. She couldn't imagine the Gardens of Versailles were more splendid than AJ's stately garden.

As awe-inspiring as the outside was, the house's interior overwhelmed her. Each time she stepped inside, she craned her head back to take in the ornate glass ceiling three stories above. The cavernous atrium was the centerpiece of AJ's home. She found its rustic mountain ski-lodge atmosphere warm and inviting. He had given her permission to take off her shoes when she came in. The heated, natural stone tile flooring amazed her, and her amazement amused him.

The eastern third of the home had receding tiered balconies like Santorini's cliffside houses. A stone turret stairwell connected all three floors.

Sonny and Cher, AJ's two golden retriever puppies, always greeted her with dog toys and wagging tails. She disagreed with Charlotte's incessant teasing of AJ over his naming conventions for pets. Naming the puppies after a singing duo was pathetic, but she forgave him because the puppies were so adorable.

AJ's employees numbered thirteen by the time fall began, and dinners went indoors. His fourteen-chair, solid mahogany hand-carved dining room table fascinated Lilith. She ran her fingertips over the surface, letting her fingers absorb the wood's character and ancient wisdom. Its beauty and sturdiness evoked the sense she had been at this table before. But of course, she hadn't.

A soft four-legged ball of fur forced her arm up. Shazoo, AJ's Himalayan kitten, chose Lilith's lap as the quintessential resting place every time she came into the house. AJ received Shazoo as a gift from an old friend a week after Lilith started work. Tayen joked that Lilith and Shazoo had bonded when Shazoo first looked into Lilith's eyes. Her eyes were the only ones bluer than his.

As dinner wound down and the guests left, Charlotte and Lilith lingered behind with Tayen and AJ. Tayen confiscated her usual chair on the living room side of the atrium. Shoes off, feet up, and with a glass of wine in hand, it was the most informal she ever presented herself in front of the younger ladies.

Lilith captured the end of the couch closest to AJ. She

curled up and leaned on the couch arm as if she was waiting for him to speak. Charlotte mirrored her roommate, only at the other end of the couch next to Tayen's chair.

"I believe we have two daughters," Tayen said.

"Hey," Charlotte protested. "Relaxing in this glorious house after a hard week is a reward worth taking advantage of. I'm sure you visited places like this during your tenure as a corporate officer."

"My visits to majestic European venues with dazzling scenery never let me kick off my shoes. It was always … " Tayen leaned forward in the chair and lowered her feet to the floor. "Don't remind me of those days, please."

She turned her head to check on her purse, which she left leaning against the dining room table leg. Sullen eyes, slumped shoulders, and a tightened jaw; signs of distress which Lilith couldn't ignore.

"Easy, Tayen," AJ said. "Charlotte isn't aware of the crap you endured. International finance—especially at the level you were involved—was high stakes drama."

Tayen leaned back in her chair, but her eyes and jaw hadn't relaxed.

"Lilith."

Lilith snapped away from Tayen with AJ's call.

"I dug into your amulet's history and believe your mother and grandmother were talking about the three estates. It's a reference to pre-revolutionary war France. Does your family's roots go back to France?"

"I'm sorry. What did you ask?" Lilith asked. The sudden shift away from Tayen seemed out of place to her.

AJ dipped his head and winked at her. "Your family, do they come from France?"

Lilith understood why he winked. He was shifting

Tayen's focus to something else. "Yes. We came from the Caribbean."

"Why are we talking about the French Revolution?" Tayen asked.

"Lilith's amulet came with a mystery. Something about an intersection of the three estates."

Tayen leaned back in her chair and looked up at the glass ceiling. "If I remember my history … the church—"

"The Catholic Church."

Tayen stuck out her tongue at AJ. "The Church first, nobility second, and the peasantry stuck in the rear as the third estate. Did I get it right, Professor?"

"Careful, dear. The children will think we are fighting."

"They'll grow up. So, what's with the intersection of the three estates, and how does her amulet fit in?"

AJ placed his cup on the end table. "The intersection of the three estates must be a physical place where church, government, and merchants meet. As for the six screaming feathers of the sun, sounds like First Nations' lore."

Tayen scrunched her nose. AJ's insinuating tone was intended for her. "Do you have any idea how many oral traditions we have? I'm a Northwesterner, and I'm not thoroughly read on Southern traditions."

"But six screaming feathers of the sun can be researched, can't it?"

"Have at it. You don't have to be a tribal member to do research. Besides, I'm busy bringing your premier golf resort to life."

AJ held up his hand in defense. "I thought you might be privy to resources we aren't."

Tayen sat without responding to him.

"Okay. I'll research it later," AJ said. "As for tomorrow, I'm hiking into Wasco's woods with Thom. She printed a topographical map, and we are headed up to what she believes is the cause of the missing lake."

"How does a lake end up missing?" Lilith asked.

"An excellent question which you can help answer when you join us."

"Ah, I'll check my calendar."

AJ waved his hand toward the dining room. "So, at dinner, when you said you weren't busy tomorrow … "

Caught at the start of a lie, Lilith switched course. "My mistake. My calendar is wide open."

"You can use my hiking boots," Charlotte said as she raised a glass to her mouth to hide her from her roommate.

AJ smiled. "Wear jeans and a long-sleeved shirt."

"Jeans for a hike … in the woods?" Lilith asked.

***

The following day, she understood why Charlotte concealed her laughter. Jeans and a long-sleeved shirt were necessary for deep forest exploration.

She stayed close to AJ. Hacking a path through the dense vegetation with her machete was Thom Hua, the golf club professional.

"I'm gonna kill Charlotte," Lilith mumbled.

AJ pushed the chopped brush to the side. "You thought we would be hiking on a paved trail. Not bushwhacking up the mountain, where shorts wouldn't keep your legs from getting scratched to pieces."

Lilith took forever to take a step. Her imagination ran wild with what might be under the twigs and leaves. "How much further are we going before we give up and head back?"

AJ held up the map. "Up around this bend."

Lilith watched Thom hack a path through the dense vegetation. "She is pretty good at swinging that machete. Is that why everyone says she is the club's best golfer?"

Thom stopped and called to Lilith. "Come here. You can cut the last few yards."

Lilith gritted her teeth. Thom swinging a machete was one thing; swinging it herself was quite another.

AJ waved his hand aside, clearing the way for Lilith. "New experiences teach you how to relate to different people. The wider your experiences, the deeper your connections."

Lilith took the machete in her hand and listened to Thom's instructions. She began bushwhacking after her teacher stepped back. Her chopping occasionally missed the mark, which caused Thom to ask AJ in her native Vietnamese: "*Bạn đã chuẩn bị sẵn bộ sơ cứu chưa?*"

"I did. But she's not swinging toward her legs, like you warned her."

Lilith turned around. "What did you ask AJ?"

"Just making sure we are prepared," Thom said.

"You asked about a first aid kit." She peered through the corner of her eye at AJ. "Vietnamese? Add another reason for Charlotte to be pissed."

Once at the stream, Lilith handed the machete back to Thom. "Why not follow the stream from Wasco's property?"

"Mr. Wasco got nervous when I pointed out to our destination on the map," Thom explained. "I suspect he knows about the missing lake. The look in his eye told me he didn't think I could get us here."

Thom dropped her hat and let her jet-black hair fall

over her shoulders. She knelt on her knees next to the rushing stream and leaned over. A sudden flip of her head whipped her hair into the stream. After letting her hair soak for a minute, she snapped her head up, which flipped her hair on her back. "Damn, the water is cold, but it feels great."

Lilith rushed to Thom's side and did the same. Refreshed, she said, "Kneeling reverently before the stream and giving thanks; we just started a new religion."

AJ proceeded up the stream bank, leaving Thom and Lilith behind.

"Poor guy. Bald and unable to hair worship with us," Thom said. "We better follow him."

They chased after AJ, who held up the map and surveyed the area.

Thom stood next to him and pointed out the corresponding points of the map and landscape. "This is where the lake lost its source."

"But by landslide, or mechanical engineering?" AJ asked.

"Who cares about an old missing lake?" Lilith asked.

Thom took the map while AJ explained: "We don't have a sufficient natural water supply for the country club. Pumping city water would cost a small fortune. We have to find another water source. So, as amateur geologists, we pulled up some maps and found a natural streambed headed to this spot. We believe a stream once flowed to the dried-up streambed west of our golf course."

"We need another water source?" Lilith looked around. "Something happened here. That's how a lake goes missing."

AJ stepped forward, away from them. "It looks like a landslide diverted the water. Newspapers from that time mention the lake's vanishing, and shortly thereafter, Wasco's lumber mill became profitable."

Thom lowered the map. "The stream should flow east, not south. This is the area where Mr. Wasco's great grandfather engineered a change to the stream's flow."

AJ jumped into the stream and gritted his teeth. "Damn mountain streams. Cold enough to make an iceberg shiver. But we've got to find evidence of the water diversion." Girding himself with courage to face the icy water, he trudged into the stream with his walking stick.

Lilith followed Thom, who was studying the hillside. Thom pointed out the oddly shaped dirt mounds, which nature didn't form, but a work crew with shovels did. Thom walked further up the river, leaving Lilith to herself. Not knowing what to look for, Lilith shielded her eyes as she looked up at the sun. "It's noon. Say we call it lunch?"

AJ pivoted and lost his balance. He slammed his walking stick into the water. It struck the river bottom, and a heavy ringing sound emanated from below. The walking stick didn't stop him from falling into the turbulent water. Lilith and Thom leapt into the stream and rushed to him. Together, they lifted him and helped him up.

"I'm alright." AJ's eyes told Lilith differently.

"The water is like ice. Let's get you out."

"The cold isn't why I'm lightheaded."

With AJ firmly in Lilith's hands, Thom retrieved the walking stick.

AJ and Lilith stepped onto the riverbank.

Thom spoke over the rushing water. "Streams don't ring when you slam a stick in them. And walking sticks don't stand like a flagpole."

She knelt into the water. After a minute, Thom sprang

up and walked to them. She handed his walking stick back to him. "You punched your stick into a rusted iron platform. I felt around the hole and pulled up this shard." She held out an irregularly shaped piece of iron for them to see.

"Evidence. We got what we were looking for." AJ kept hold of Lilith's arm to keep his balance. "We can eat our sack lunches here, or head back for an early dinner at Tuscano's on the Square?"

Lilith gasped. "Are you serious? I've never eaten there and could never because it's so expensive."

AJ stood. "When we get back to the car, we'll call Tayen and have her join us."

Lilith outpaced them back to the car. Nothing would stop her from eating at the restaurant of her dreams.

***

Charlotte fumed at being excluded for dinner. To settle her roommate's injured feelings, Lilith promised to clean the apartment for two weeks. She had felt sorry that Charlotte had lost out on eating at an exclusive restaurant.

At the end of Lilith's two-week apology cleanings, the old shack was torn down and replaced with a gargantuan party tent. Chef Dean took half the tent and set up an outdoor kitchen for light finger foods and beverages. Lilith ran register, and Talia served tables. The make-shift clubhouse worked well during the summer months.

One scorching summer afternoon, Tayen rounded the tent corner. Lilith couldn't help herself and spot-appraised Tayen's attire. *White mesh tank one-piece ... Smart choice. Floral wraparound beach skirt ... Jesus. Has this woman ever made a bad clothing choice?*

"Lilith."

Lilith snapped back to reality.

"I'm here for the register count," Tayen said.

"Why you and not Charlotte?"

"Sometimes I have to step out of the office for a break. Besides, Charlotte is doing research for a project."

Tayen's sunglasses hid her eyes, but her tight jaw and pressed lips alerted Lilith to her distress.

"Is the heat bothering you?" Lilith asked.

Tayen lowered her voice so Chef Dean and Talia didn't overhear. "Your day trip into the mountains spawned a disaster."

"Oh, crap. Mr. Wasco learned about our discovery of the thingamajig."

"He's not the problem. Our newest headache is Beagle's Bluff."

Lilith squinted. "That's like five miles away. Wasco's woods is way over the mountain pass."

"When AJ poked a hole in the diversion platform, he started the disintegration process. That little hole grew, and the platform broke."

Lilith shrugged; she still didn't understand.

"Without the water diversion, the old stream flowed down to the missing lake, which is filling up fast. The streambed is roughly twenty-five miles long, with all the turns and cutbacks. The critter inhabitants which had made their homes there have been expelled."

"Critter inhabitants? Gross. Mice and rats?"

"No, no. The critters who keep the mice and rats under control."

"Squirrels and rabbits?"

Tayen dipped her head. "Yes, Lilith, squirrels and

rabbits joined forces to evict the mice and rats from their burrows. Not the outdoors type, are you?"

Lilith restrained her urge to snap back, as she would have done with Charlotte. "If not mice and rats—or squirrels and rabbits—what then?"

"Snakes. Twenty-five miles' worth of displaced snakes floated down to the missing lake. The reptilian overcrowding then forced a migration away from the lake. Through the woods and over the hill to grandmother's house they went."

Lilith jerked her feet off the ground and pulled them onto her chair. In a sitting fetal position, she did a full body cringe. "Damn it. Forget about sleeping tonight."

Tayen frowned at Lilith's self-induced paranoia. "The village of Beagle's Bluff awoke this morning to an invasion of slithering reptiles. News crews have rushed there to watch the regional volunteer fire department ferry people from their homes."

"Why don't the people walk to their cars?"

"When snakes outnumber your town's residents ten to one, and the ground moves like you are on an acid trip, you call the fire department for extraction."

Lilith pulled her knees in tighter.

Tayen pulled out her vibrating cellphone and read AJ's texts to Lilith. *"Tree cover repelling news helicopters. Lake is filling, few snakes left there. Thom and I agree, the lake overflows in less than a month. She's reading the map. Headed down path to B. Bluff."*

"Is the lake going to flow down to us?" Lilith asked.

"Thom is reading the map to answer that question." Tayen lowered her phone and closed her eyes. She didn't speak to Lilith, but out loud to herself. "Calm down, Tayen.

Work one problem at a time."

"One problem at a time? What the hell else is happening?" Lilith asked.

"We must contend with water rights violations. In the days of the Wild West, water rights violations carried hefty penalties. Mr. Wasco's great-grandfather violated said laws with the water-diversion platform."

Lilith inspected the ground.

"The snakes are miles away, dear. Put your feet on the ground and stop looking guilty."

Lilith jumped up. "What were the penalties back then?"

"They could be quite severe, depending on the infraction. Water rights were a matter of life and death—not simple infractions or inconveniences. The Johnson County Wars in Wyoming were over water rights. Officially, anyone caught denying others equal access to water sources was subject to punitive fines. A century and a half later, those laws are still in effect."

Tayen lifted her phone to read AJ's texts. "Thom is tracing the likely overflow route on the map."

Lilith waited on Tayen, who sifted through the texts to relay the important information. After a minute, Tayen leaned her head back and groaned. "The lake's overflow is going down to the intersection of the Sunset Highway and Timber Road."

Lilith gasped. "Catalina's produce stand is right there."

"Yep. That nice little bowl like area will fill up to form a lake, making a trip to Astoria impossible on that highway. The state of Oregon will investigate and determine AJ was at fault."

Tayen felt her phone vibrate. She read the text. "They're headed down to Beagle's Bluff from the lake?"

Lilith passed over Tayen's comment and asked her own question. "How d'you learn about the snake invasion?"

"Over morning coffee. The news came on, and we put it together. He called Thom, and off they went."

Tayen raised her phone and summarized AJ's texts. "Thom traced a land depression, which leads to the ridge up the road. Channel through a ridge … And the lay of the land sends the water … I don't know where he's talking about, but it's where we can divert the water to flow through the country club."

Lilith blew a sigh of relief.

"Not out of the woods yet, darling. Wait a minute. These aren't AJ's texts. They're Thom's."

"Thom texting you on AJ's phone? Not a big deal."

"She's hiding behind a tree. They hiked down to Beagle's Bluff, and a news crew ran into them near the trailhead. AJ is being interviewed by a reporter."

Lilith pulled out her phone and tapped furiously. "What TV station?"

"Channel Eight."

A few more taps, and Lilith had the live feed of AJ.

"I've been camping on the ridge back yonder for the last two days, and was headed into town to pick up supplies. Not a snake in sight, but now you're telling me there's a snake invasion down here?

"He is lying through his teeth," Lilith said.

Tayen began texting. "I'm telling Thom to run up to the lake and set up AJ's camp. Should the reporter hike up there, it'll look like he's telling the truth."

Lilith studied her phone. "Damn. AJ should have worn a different shirt. The blue polo in that lighting is totally lit. And the breast logo is clear as clear can be. You wanted perfect marketing. This is it."

Tayen looked at Lilith's phone. "He was dressed for membership interviews. Boy, the broken wheel pops, and the BCP underneath seems to float above the shirt."

"BCP? Shouldn't it be BCI for Broken Cove Industries?"

"He is wearing the shirt from his first business, Broken Cove Publishing. We changed it to Broken Cove Industries when expansion plans came to be."

Lilith tapped her phone. "Oh shi—fizzle. The first of the dirty three are all over AJ's interview."

"He said nothing, and they're reporting his interview as breaking news," Tayen said. "Cable news is desperate to fill their time."

"Oh, yeah. Them too."

Confused, Tayen asked, "What dirty three are you talking about?"

Lilith held up her phone. "The online fashion critique groups who scour the internet to mock bad fashion."

Tayen's incredulity forced Lilith to explain. "They aren't mocking his shirt. He has five stars across the board."

Tayen put her hand over Lilith's phone. "You, and anybody in those groups, have a problem. Fashion critiques at the speed of light means I'm putting you on a twelve-step program."

Charlotte's Memo Pad To-do List

1. Staff directory set up - IT overtime approved?
2. Check contract. Electrician due dates. AJ pissed.
3. Kimiko receipt audit. Over budget--Tayen pissed
4. Chef Dean's appliances-- status on delivery
5. Volcanologist request? WTF? are they jerking me off?
6.
7. Hotel reservations: New Orleans convention.
8. Bakery name ideas: ~~Chocolate Pirate~~ ~~Pirate booty~~
9.
10. Stop eating carryout!! Budget shot :(

Tayen's Notes:
-Call dude Italy, granite floor 4 rooftop restaurant
-Permits on the additional drainage
-Civil engineer: check on parkway bridge and tunnels under parkway
-Broken Cove Charities? interesting

AJ's Notes: (Clear w/Tayen first)
Cantilever styled restaurant

Way ahead of you Tayen.
Paperwork needed to committe boss to psych ward

Staff Attendance:

Manny	Dean	Ladonna	Kimiko	Scott	Talia	Lilith
IN	OFF	OFF	IN	IN	OFF	IN

3 - Invitations

A chaotic and busy spring yielded to the steady construction of the country club complex. Tayen insisted the general manager's office be completed first, so she could quit using AJ's dining room as her office. Too much together time with the owner was driving her batty.

Eager to solidify her competence as the First Assistant to the General Manager, Charlotte made sure she arrived before everybody in the mornings. Her reward was seeing the triumphant sun rising behind Mount Hood, which painted broad strokes of brilliant yellows, inviting oranges, and plush mauves across the sky. Gone was the beast clunker which she traded in for her brand-new electric car. And so was her riding partner, Lilith, who refused to arrive at the early hour of the morning.

She turned down the steep ramp to the members'

underground parking garage and pulled into her assigned spot. She walked tall and proud on her way to the entrance. The painted parking strips and handicap symbols passed her impromptu inspection.

She stepped onto the car lane before the clubhouse entrance. As she did, the clapping of the night security guard echoed through the garage. Ted stood at the foot of the exit ramp at the far end. He applauded and howled at Charlotte's fashion choice.

Her sangria-colored crossover business dress radiated confidence and authority. The turndown neck conveyed professionalism. Low cut and form fitting said she embraced her sexuality; single strap high-heel pumps warned others not to underestimate this five-two force of nature.

She unlocked the entrance door and called out, "Athena, morning lights."

BCI's new voice assistant turned on the lights to Charlotte's delight. The IT guy she hired, Scott, never failed to impress her. Whatever task she assigned him, it was done before she anticipated and always exceeded her expectations.

"Athena, send Scott my hugs and kisses."

A sultry female voice came from the overhead speakers. *"File not available. Are you searching for another file?"*

"My bad, no."

"Similar file found. Say yes to confirm sending 'My Naughty' file to the IT folder."

"Athena, cancel sending any files. Set calendar reminder to rename files. Also, don't pull from my phone without dual confirmation protocols."

She glided up the stairs to the ground floor and glanced at the tiered Greek-styled mini-amphitheater. When

AJ had explained the idea of a Greek amphitheater in the clubhouse, she erupted in laughter. After Tayen tempered back his descriptions with *mini* and *styled*, the idea no longer seemed ridiculous.

Monday's closure likely meant the mail would be stacked high on her desk. Her intuition proved correct after opening the office door. In the midst of her sorting, she opened an envelope which caught her attention. She opened it and pulled out a formal invitation to attend a small business convention in New Orleans. It struck her as odd that a formal invitation was sent, when general invites normally came on postcards.

She shrugged it off and continued sorting.

A few mail pieces later, she came across a postcard. It met her expectations of what a small business convention invitation should look like. "Damn, somebody wants us in New Orleans."

"Who wants us in New Orleans?"

Charlotte—scared senseless by Tayen's sneaking in the door—threw her hands up, along with the mail.

"Engrossed in your work, and you didn't hear me open the door." Tayen snickered as the mail settled on the floor. "What is happening in New Orleans?"

"We're getting tons of invitations to a small business convention. So far there is one postcard and one formal looking letter."

"Two invites don't make a ton."

Charlotte skipped her boss's invite for a verbal sparring session. Instead, she handed Tayen the invitations.

"They always have a convention in New Orleans. I wonder what this one is about?" Tayen read the invitations. "I suspect two different companies sent these. The postcard is a chamber of commerce invitation. You can tell by the generic and general descriptions. But this other one however … ”

Charlotte inched next to Tayen.

"A classy letterhead and wedding invitation quality paper with an outrageous fifty percent discount. In the middle of September? That's less than a month away. Nobody can reserve a room at this premier New Orleans hotel with less than a month's notice."

"So, are we going? And if so, how many do I book?"

Tayen thought for a moment. "Time is of the essence. I'm overriding AJ's objection before I tell him we're going."

"Smart and saves time," Charlotte said.

"Start with AJ and myself."

"Two." Charlotte began a list on her phone.

"Chefs Dean and Ladonna for the staffing refresher."

"Four."

"Ooh, there are seminars galore for our IT guy, Scott. Nice hire, by the way."

"Neither you nor AJ were available to do the interview. Does that make me the supervisor over the IT department?" Charlotte asked.

"Not on my watch. Add Lilith to our convention roster. She needs to be more involved with management."

"Six."

Tayen continued reading the invites. Charlotte waited. Tayen read on.

Charlotte had read the invitations. Together, they didn't contain enough information to justify Tayen's lengthy reading. The protracted silence seemed fishy to her. "Anyone else?"

"I suppose one more, but who … should it be?"

Charlotte wasn't about to beg, and Tayen wasn't

rushing to announce what she had already decided. The duo worked seamlessly in front of customers; while in private, they poked, prodded, and perturbed each other all day long. Tayen held the upper hand in this game, causing Charlotte to maneuver with care.

"One more … " Tayen dragged the torture out as long as she could. "But who would be best served?"

Tayen sensed her assistant was onto her and broke the tension. "I suppose you can go."

"Really? Geewillikers, that would be swell. How can I thank you? A trip to New Orleans will be the greatest day of my life. I'm taking the rest of the day off to celebrate this with my parents. They'll be so happy with their little girl's achievement."

"Over the top and melodramatic," Tayen said as she headed to her office. "You couldn't pull off the sweet girl act if your life depended on it."

"Who needs to be sweet when I get everything I want by being naughty?" Charlotte mumbled.

Seconds later, after Tayen opened her office door, her deep-throated growl brought Charlotte rushing in. Together, they stared at a life-size portrait of AJ, which hung on the wall behind Tayen's desk. His face scowled at the spot where Tayen's head would be when she sat in her chair.

Charlotte bit her tongue and lifted her phone for a photo. Tayen slapped Charlotte's hand. "Damn it. Call maintenance and take this joker off my wall."

"Uh-oh … the bolts." Charlotte understood what AJ was up to the previous day. "Cruel—genius—but cruel."

Tayen looked at the portrait, attempting to understand Charlotte's comment. "Bolts? He bolted this monstrosity to the wall?"

"Without AJ's official order, that portrait ain't moving."

"Fine, help me move the desk. He can stare into open air."

"Yeah—no—not what he did. The pressure sensors and alarm bells are for the portrait. He put the bolts … elsewhere."

Tayen waited for her assistant to explain.

Sworn to secrecy by AJ, Charlotte stood still. However, her eyes kept angling down at the desk, which Tayen caught.

"Oh my God, he did not." Tayen pushed on the desk with her hip and leg. The desk didn't budge or flex with her pushing. "The son of a bitch bolted my desk to the floor."

Charlotte scrambled to exonerate herself for participating in AJ's portrait prank. "He lied to me and said it was for earthquake stabilization. Nothing bad was going to happen to his precious general manager."

Tayen glared at her assistant. "When he calls me *precious*, he's using Gollum's voice."

"Hey, it wasn't to my advantage to question the owner's sincerity, even as the smoke wafted up my ass."

Irritated by AJ's not-so-subtle symbol of perpetual supervision, Tayen lowered her head. "Why did I accept his offer? God, I never stop asking myself that. It's one train wreck after another. We skirt around flooding a highway, avoid detection as the culprits of the snake takeover of Beagle's Bluff, and now this … painting."

"Yeah-but, the painting's stress level ain't as high as the other two," Charlotte said. "Besides, look how things worked out. The channel diversion feeds into our stream, so we aren't paying exorbitant city water bills."

Tayen tried a last nudge of the desk with her hip. "Plus, we own nine properties in Beagle's Bluff."

"Better than the thirty we almost had to swallow. Nine families took the buyouts and moved away."

"Imagine the nightmares they'll have for years to come."

"No more nightmarish than living in Beagle's Bluff." Charlotte raised her phone to snap a photo. "I can't fathom living in a place more depressing than there."

"Put that phone away. No Instagram shots for Lilith," Tayen snapped.

No sooner had the words left her mouth than a beep came from her bag.

Charlotte saw Tayen's phone on the desk. "You have another phone?"

When Tayen didn't answer, she excused herself. "I'm off to confirm our reservations in New Orleans."

"Please shut the door behind you," Tayen said.

Charlotte did so but took one last look at her boss before the door shut.

Tayen sat in her chair and scrambled for her bag. Huddled over it, she glanced at the door, confirming it was shut. She reached into the bag and dug to the bottom. She didn't lift the phone out of the bag, but turned it around to read the display. After an intense reading, she lowered the phone back into her bag.

***

Charlotte received Tayen's permission to tell Lilith they were attending the small business convention in New Orleans. Lilith danced for a month until their departure.

She sat in the passenger van outside the new four-story centerpiece of The Village shopping complex. The smell of fresh tar from the paved two hundred-car parking lot abounded. Tayen sat in the middle bucket seat while chefs Dean and Ladonna pretended to sleep on the back row bench seat.

Scott had his laptop open, working on another IT project. Lilith adored him. Whenever he was within reach, she had to run her hand through his curly hair. His gentle mannerisms, along with his complete willingness to help, had won her over. He was twice her age, and she treated him like a beloved uncle.

The only person not present for the airport departure was the owner, AJ.

Lilith's patience evaporated. The owner's luggage was in the van, but he wasn't. The insufferable idea of missing a moment of her first trip to New Orleans was unacceptable. She catapulted herself out of the van and ran toward The Village complex. The elevator ride up to the fourth-floor restaurant, Pasta-de-faria's, was very quick. She stormed off the elevator in search of AJ and found him atop a ladder behind the restaurant's bar.

"Move it, mister. I would like to stop for breakfast before the airport. If you make us miss our flight—Oh, holy hell, what is that?"

AJ leaned back to view his work. "What? You don't like my decorative pirate's chest?"

Against the wall in the center of the bar, AJ had hung a massive dark wooden chest. Plastic Mardi Gras decorations draped over it. On the top corner, tilting forward, was a pirate captain's black hat with a long, teal-colored feather arching to the back.

Lilith bobbed her head in disbelief. "Every purchase you make is five-star quality. You hire the finest architects and engineers without fearing the cost. Hours of meticulous restaurant planning … And then you hang a two-dollar POS garage sale find above the bar. What the hell are you thinking?"

AJ stepped off the ladder. "Two dollars? The shipping cost more than that." He brushed the dust from his hands. "When I encouraged you to take a leadership role, I didn't expect 'POS' and 'what the hell are you thinking' as marks of your progress."

"I'm learning. 'What the hell is he thinking' is Tayen's favorite phrase. 'POS' is my dad's."

"Your inflection on POS sounded like Charlotte."

"Not telling you her favorite phrase," Lilith murmured.

AJ raised an eyebrow.

She realized her murmur had traveled too far. To pass it by, she asked, "Couldn't you hang your *spectacular* eBay find when we've returned from the convention?"

"I had to put it in before they finished the bar. If I don't finish the overlays before they start the molding, it won't fit. It fits with our Pastafarian theme."

"Whatever. Move it before we miss our flight."

"Look who is excited about this convention."

Lilith explained her excitement as they walked to the elevator. "You've traveled to every state in the United States, but I've been stuck on the west coast my whole life. California, Oregon, and Seattle."

"Washington. Seattle is a city, not a state."

"That tells you how much of Washington I've seen."

AJ entered the elevator and pushed for the ground

floor. "How about Idaho or Nevada?"

Lilith rolled her eyes up at him. "Oh, yeah. Us black folk travel to Idaho all the time."

"I deserved that." AJ squinted to deflect Lilith's disdain. "A state where less than one out of a hundred people are black may not be on your bucket list."

"Seattle, Los Angeles, Portland, and a bunch of places in between are the only places I've visited. Louisiana will be state number four for me, and New Orleans will be unlike anything I have ever experienced. Me, in the French Quarter, not just looking at pictures and imagining what it's like … That will expand my universe infinitely."

"Perhaps not infinitely, but a twenty-five percent universe expansion ain't bad."

Lilith's voice softened. "My family works hard to enjoy as much as they can afford to experience. Vacations are for visiting people we haven't seen for years, not exploring the world. For me, this is a moon landing equivalent."

The elevator door opened, and AJ said, "Then explore to your heart's desire and let me know how I can aid you."

Lilith knew he understood. To hold back a tear of vulnerable appreciation, she switched back to her impatient, excited self. "Charlotte arrives tomorrow on the sixteenth after attending her grandparent's anniversary party. Until her plane touches down, I'm the youngest conventioneer. I want the lay of the land, so we don't waste time figuring out what to do."

"What, you can't have fun with old people like us?"

Lilith batted her eyes and smiled facetiously. "I'm sure my party animal elders will be fun to hang with. What's with the cheesy chest decoration?"

"It was a gift from an old friend. Perhaps the plastic

decorations aren't the best adornments."

"We have an award-winning restaurant if you drop the cheap plastic. Leave the days of the old shack behind to die."

"We had good times in those shacks," AJ said.

"Your teeny-tiny, do-it-yourself over the weekend, insect-inviting shack will not be missed."

Heavy machinery rumbled from across the dirt road. The diesel engine roared, and the vibrations pounded against them. AJ extended his arm around her as she cupped her hands over her ears. "The landscape grading will finish while we are in New Orleans. When we return, the footers for the clubhouse should be done."

"Good."

"Engineers are hopeful about the back nine's drainage. Nobody can believe we are draining an irredeemable swamp crater and transforming it into a golf course. They've suggested I call it Crater Gully."

"Sounds great," Lilith said.

"You have no idea what I'm saying, do you?"

"Nope."

AJ switched tactics. "In New Orleans, you will be introduced to a drink called a Hurricane. Do you know what is in it?"

Lilith's response came out lightning fast. "Light rum, dark rum, lime and orange juices, passion fruit, and grenadine. I've read that O'Brien's is a must stop. I can't wait to try one of them in those tall, decorative street containers. Oh … I didn't stop to think if they would fit in the suitcase when we return home."

When they reached the van, AJ addressed Tayen as Lilith climbed in. "She is ready for the New Orleans nightlife. Put throw pillows on our shopping list. She'll nap through her seminars after partying the nights away with Charlotte."

Tayen pushed her sunglasses up after Lilith's elbow accidentally bumped them off. Lilith's path to the back seat was more brutish than graceful.

"They've been researching the best bars, dance clubs, and shops. They'll never make it to the seminars without adult supervision," Tayen said.

AJ lunged into his seat next to Tayen and shut the van door. "Shopping, dancing, and drinking. Why am I thinking they expect us to feed them?"

Lilith squeezed between Chef Dean and his wife, Chef Ladonna. "I know the restaurants too. With our chefs are gone for three days, I don't want to waste time at stinker restaurants."

Chef Ladonna put her arm around Lilith and hugged her. "Tayen has my stinker proof list of recommendations while we are visiting my parents in Natchitoches. You'll be fine until we rejoin you on the nineteenth."

As AJ cinched his seat belt, the van started. "It's good for me to get away. I think I'm driving the engineers crazy."

"The hydrologists … in particular," Tayen said.

"Am I annoying them?" AJ waited for an answer. In not getting one, he said, "Driver, we're ready. Take us to the airport."

Tayen faced forward in her seat. "Don't think about developments in Portland for a week. I've got everything running on time and in order. Talia has my directions and can manage until our return."

AJ sat and looked out the window at the passing trees. Before they turned onto the highway, he asked, "How did we get a fifty percent discount to a premier hotel during a small business convention?"

"I didn't ask for the rationale from the hotel. And when offers like this pop up, you jump on them," Tayen explained.

"A twenty percent discount doesn't shock me. But half off during a convention? Why would a business shoot themselves in the foot with a ridiculous discount during a money-making event?"

"Would you have said yes with the twenty percent discount?"

"I would have said no thanks."

"With a fifty percent discount on lodging, they snagged our group and pulled us in. If they hadn't, there's money they wouldn't have without us."

"A one-hundred percent discount—"

"—would have made us suspect a scam was taking place," Tayen interrupted. "Quit being paranoid and enjoy our healthy fifty percent discount."

"Three rooms," AJ continued with his skepticism. "Fifty percent off for three rooms. Someone really wants us in New Orleans."

Lilith was listening to music through her earbuds, but her attention was split between the music and Tayen's discussion with AJ.

"The chefs in one room, you and Scott take another, while I get the third room—saddled with babysitting duties of the two girls."

"Babysitting?" Lilith objected.

"Damn, her earbuds didn't block me out."

The chefs on either side of Lilith poked her in the ribs. Through the chef's teasing, she saw Tayen's concern grow as AJ fidgeted with his hands.

In a firm and reassuring voice, Tayen said, "It is a

small business convention. Nothing more. Enjoy the seminars, the food and drinks, but don't search for the bogeyman around every corner."

Lilith knew Tayen and AJ had worked together before she was hired. But she didn't know how well they knew each other. Tayen's obtuse comment couldn't be left alone.

Lilith pulled out her earbuds. "Why the bogeyman comment?"

"It's his first time back in New Orleans."

"And?"

AJ twisted his shoulders around to face Lilith. She noticed the darkness of his face. His furrowed eyebrows cast shadows over his eyes. The seriousness in his eyes was unlike his typical carefree demeanor.

"I may have. Unfortunately, my life's first memories started on a train headed to New England for grad school. I awoke with no memories, but there was a notebook in my backpack, which had a note to help me. I had suffered a head injury and my life's memories were gone. To heal, it was imperative for me to leave New Orleans. Later on down the road, I could return, but if I returned too early, the trauma might be too much for me. The warning proved to be right. Every time I thought about returning, anxiety and fear consumed me."

"Why is this time different?" Lilith asked.

"The anxiety and fear aren't there."

"Wow. The life you've lived. You've earned advanced degrees, went homeless for five years, won a diminished lottery, and now I learn you have amnesia over your entire childhood."

"Don't forget the premier golf resort."

"I included that as part of the diminished lottery."

AJ poked Tayen in the arm. "Would you stop telling people I won a diminished lottery?"

Tayen twisted away from his poking. "A retired librarian wins the billion-dollar lottery jackpot, and three days later you win the next jackpot. Diminished lottery sounds better than depleted jackpot."

Lilith leaned forward, taking a chance on getting swatted by either AJ or Tayen. "What happened to your family?"

"The notebook didn't give me my background, but it did say I was an orphan. That was a bummer to learn. But my backpack held several trinkets that a parent would send with their child who was headed to college."

"Like what?"

"Apples, nut bars, trail mix, a beautiful set of writing pens, a daily calendar of The Far Side—"

"My parents sent me to college with that calendar too," Scott chirped in.

Lilith shook her head. "Must be a nerd thing because I've never heard of it. But those gifts meant you had somebody who cared for you. Why not seek them out before this trip?"

"Did you hear what I said about the fear and anxiety?"

"Well, yeah, but still … I would've worked through it to find those who cared for me."

AJ tilted his head back to see Lilith. "I've learned that carrying forward gives me more peace than dwelling on the past. My gut instinct is telling me the coast is clear; a return to New Orleans is okay. My plans don't include researching my past, but I can't help to think this is a homecoming of sorts."

"What if you run across somebody you know?" Lilith

asked.

"What if the moon is in the Seventh House, and Jupiter aligns with Mars?"

"Then peace will guide the planets and love will steer the stars," Tayen said.

Dean, Ladonna, and Scott sang in unison. "This is the dawning of the age of Aquarius."

Lilith waved her hand to stop. "Old people. Yeah, you'll be fun if I'm drunk off my ass. What I'm getting at—"

"Asking what-if questions isn't my favorite method of investigation," AJ said.

"You can't knock her question down, AJ. It is a valid question in this circumstance," Tayen said.

"If I have amnesia, then I won't know a person unless they walk up to me and introduce themselves. Until then, I'm not working myself into a tizzy by asking a bunch of what-ifs."

Lilith leaned back in her seat. AJ's tone of voice meant the discussion was over.

4 - Wango and Taltz

After they'd disembarked the plane in New Orleans, Chefs Dean and Ladonna headed north for a three-day visit with her parents. They would rejoin AJ and company the day before the convention started.

The rest grabbed a cab and checked into the hotel, where Lilith rushed to unpack. She assigned dresser drawers to Tayen and Charlotte, then she transferred her clothes from her suitcase to the dresser drawers and closet.

Tayen unlatched the connecting doors into the guy's room, commenting on her frenzied roommate. "Gentlemen, let's escort Adorable to dinner before she passes out or drives me nuts."

"Can you tolerate the kids, or will their excitement wear you out?" AJ asked.

"I'll push them out the door if they do."

Lilith responded. "Take a sedative. We aren't noisy. Sometimes we can text faster than we speak."

AJ smiled. "I'm glad I have Scott. Calm, reserved, and without the broad age gap as you have with the girls."

Tayen peeked in the bathroom. "Where is Scott?"

"Out for allergy medicine and a front desk pick-up."

"Pick-up?"

AJ spun around. "Delivery. I meant delivery, not pick-up. I guess it's our convention team shirts. Kimiko was supposed to overnight them."

Lilith listened to AJ and Tayen's conversation as she scurried around the room. She paused when AJ raised his voice.

"Of all the things I confided with you, I wish I could take that one back. Every time those two words are spoken together, you fly off the handle. Every time somebody says 'pickup truck', you shoot me a dirty look."

"I wasn't trying to pick you up," Tayen said.

"It damn well felt like it."

Lilith closed her eyes. *Not the coffeehouse again.*

Tayen and AJ disagreed on every detail of their very first meeting. He'd thought she was coming on to him over morning coffee. She claimed she was looking for an open seat. The phrase 'pick up' was their point of contention.

"We have a card for dinner reservations tonight. Jackets required," AJ said.

Lilith heard him and rushed under Tayen's arm, through the connecting door, and into AJ's room. He stood next to a desk with an invitation in his hand. She snatched the card from him. "Reservations? They never say what a girl's equivalent is for 'jacket required'. There's no time listed. What's that mean?"

AJ swiped the card back. "It means we go whenever, and best of all, it's complimentary."

Tayen didn't believe what she heard. "A jacket-required open dinner invitation … with complimentary drinks—"

"—and a fifty percent discount—"

She ignored AJ's verbal jab. "It feels like we're here for something other than the convention."

Lilith had brushed under Tayen's outstretched arm on her way back to her room. She stopped dead in her tracks upon hearing Tayen's comment.

Scott flung the door open and entered the room with a box. "We checked in half an hour ago and we already have a package."

Lilith scampered back into the room and beside Tayen.

"Slow down, girl. You're moving at a breakneck pace."

Lilith didn't listen to Tayen and reached into the box. Pulling out a shirt, she said, "Oh my, these are really, really blue."

Tayen held one up for inspection. "Blue as blue can be. Pure white lettering and graphics. Wow, these really pop."

She held it to her chest, displaying it for AJ's viewing. "Perfect. A broken ship's wheel with one missing felloe between the handles. And you're right, it pops."

Lilith studied the logo. "The missing part of a ship's wheel is called a felloe?"

"A felloe connects the spokes of a ship's wheel. I named my publishing company Broken Cove Publishing, and the graphic design company gave me a ship's wheel with a missing felloe. Hence, the broken wheel—"

"Awesome job, Kimiko," Tayen interrupted. "The font she chose is perfect."

"Uh-oh, I found a mistake." Lilith held the short sleeve up to show them. "The sleeve has BCP below the broken ship's wheel instead of BCI."

Tayen turned the sleeve over. "AJ, you sent the wrong file to Kimi for the sleeve. BCI is correct on the breast and back logos. But BCP is on the sleeve."

AJ folded his arms. Ridges formed on his forehead as he viewed the shirts.

"It doesn't matter who made the mistake. I still like them," Lilith said.

Tayen frowned at the imperfection. "Well, these are for tomorrow and our time at the convention. Tonight, we have dinner at an exclusive restaurant, so dress accordingly."

"Accordingly?" Scott asked.

"Jacket required."

"A jacket, in this heat?"

Tayen rolled her eyes.

Scott took his clothes bag into the bathroom and shut the door. Lilith vanished into the women's bedroom.

Lilith heard Tayen ask AJ, "What's your problem?"

"Kimiko doesn't have access to the BCP logo, and I know for a fact I didn't send it to her."

The defiant tone in AJ's voice didn't escape Lilith.

"Who else has access to the BCP logo?"

"No one but me. I remember when I sent her the sleeve icon. Shazoo jumped on the desk and spilled my drink before I clicked send. I sent it after I returned with towels." He sniffed. "The construction back home is getting to me. Ever since we walked in the room, I keep getting whiffs of fresh-cut lumber."

Lilith listened from the bathroom as she checked her makeup. What AJ said next startled her.

"Which of us is bringing about this good fortune? It feels like we're about to be trapped in a timeshare sales pitch. Or worse. Is there something I should be aware of? Like why you obsess over your handbag?"

Lilith froze. AJ had confronted Tayen. Charlotte had told her of the mystery phone in Tayen's bag, but no one had ever asked her about it.

"It has sentimental meaning to me."

"Or you check on it to make sure it doesn't catch on fire." AJ shot back.

Tayen's silence was deafening to Lilith.

"Shazoo laid on your bag the other day. When I lifted him, he was warm, and so was the side of your bag. I suspected a battery pack was attached to something in the bag. He found a heat source and camped on top of it. Is it a phone?" AJ asked.

What is Tayen hiding in her bag? Lilith's mind whirled with confusion. While she scrambled to find an answer, she lost track of their conversation. The next thing she heard was AJ's request.

"All I ask is that you keep an eye out for old acquaintances lurking behind the scenes. Hopefully, this is an innocent gift."

Scott exited the bathroom. Tayen spun around, shut the connecting door to the guy's room, and walked to her nightstand.

"Had enough of AJ?" Lilith asked.

"That, and Scott's overdoing the jacket-required request—with a tux."

***

Not knowing how to dress for an upscale restaurant, Lilith followed Tayen's lead. A blue floral print, long summer dress met the 'jacket required' standard for the restaurant. Its off-the-shoulder design met Lilith's minimal standard of utterly sensational. Tayen placed a white sun hat on Lilith's head, which Lilith fawned over with amazement.

AJ rescued Scott from a complete fashion disaster by encouraging him to wear his navy-blue blazer with white pants. Aside from the tux, Scott had nothing to wear for semi-formal occasions.

Lilith wanted to do for Scott what Tayen did for her. She fashioned an ascot from one of her tops and fitted it on Scott. She punched AJ when he said it made him look like a pompous oil tycoon. Scott nodded his approval; for once, he didn't mind looking like a pompous rich guy. Especially with Lilith taking him by the arm as they walked.

Tayen's peacock-colored midi dress was simple, yet regal. Its princess neckline gave her a sensuality which, as general manager of a country club, she shied away from. She knew it was vital to maintain her professionalism at work, but here at the convention, she could relax her standards. When she took AJ's arm to be escorted, Lilith wished the two would stop seeing each other as business partners and start seeing themselves as a cute couple.

At the restaurant, Lilith handed the reservation card to the maître d'. The foursome enjoyed dinner, drinks, and conversation. When they finished, Lilith admitted a day's worth of nervous excitement had worn her out. Scott mentioned that her three cocktails probably helped.

After a brief walk around the French Quarter, they

headed back to the hotel, where Lilith changed into sleepwear and nestled in bed with a tablet. She wanted to reexamine her checklist of things to do.

The next morning, Lilith hustled everyone out of bed and urged them to get moving.

Tayen demanded the team wear the convention shirts. Scott and AJ balked at the blue shirts, but their complaints died when Tayen exited the bathroom in her own shirt. Lilith figured if a distinguished woman wore a shirt similar to theirs, they were okay wearing it too.

Last into the hall, Lilith locked the door behind her. She turned around to find AJ and Scott spinning in the other direction.

Before she had left Portland, she asked Kimiko to make a company crop-top T-shirt for her and Charlotte. Tucked away in the box's bottom—and the reason for her overzealous behavior on its arrival—were the specialized crop tops, replete with logos.

Tayen smiled, winked, and pointed at her exposed midriff. The guys hadn't seen this much of Lilith before and weren't sure how to react to her. Lilith pointed at her white shorts, thinking that those were adding to their discomfort. Tayen whirled her finger and mouthed, 'Who cares?'

Lilith announced the morning's first stop: the Farmer's Market.

AJ walked tall beside her. With an angry dog's tenacity, he stared down anyone whose gaze lingered too long on his gift shop clerk.

Scott remarked about the many people bobbing their heads to get a glimpse of the foursome. Tayen informed him the head weaving and whispers were generated by the dazzling girl in front of them, not their shirts. Lilith turned to

Scott and shrugged her shoulder, accepting the responsibility for their popularity.

They entered the bustling farmer's market and drifted apart. While Lilith handpicked an assortment of fruits and other edibles for the group, she lifted her head occasionally to keep track of everyone's location.

As normal, Tayen mingled with stand owners. *Dear god, she endears herself to everybody, and does so with ease.*

She noticed a group of men behind Tayen. All of them were staring past Tayen and at her. On making eye contact with her, they turned away and continued with their business.

Lilith searched for Scott and spotted him at a rock and mineral stand. He held a geode up to the light. While he studied it, the women on either side of him were staring at her. They averted their eyes when Lilith faced their direction.

Lilith glanced in the street to find AJ talking with a local shopkeeper. As soon as she saw him, the man pointed in her direction. He was obviously asking AJ about her. *Okay, I'm attracting way too much attention.*

More people turned their heads turned her way as she finished filling her basket. She stepped up to a mature woman behind a market stand and pulled the company credit card out of her front pocket.

The woman scratched under her multicolored orange and tan bandanna as she checked Lilith from head to toe. She ignored Lilith's 'hello' and gazed into Lilith's eyes.

Oh, poop. Here it comes. 'Most beautiful blue eyes I've ever seen.'

The woman gently grasped Lilith's wrist and lowered the basket to the ground. She straightened up and said, "Our flower of the sea returns to us, magnificent as the stories of old."

Lilith stood still. *Honor your elders, regardless of how nutty they sound.*

The woman used her finger to trace the breast logo embroidered on the blue of Lilith's top. "The broken wheel and the missing bar beside the mother. What is BCI?"

Lilith not only felt the woman's finger tracing the logo, but also something else was tracing below the woman's finger. She looked down to see the woman's many charms dangling from her leather braided bracelet.

"BCI on your breast logo, and BCP on your friends' sleeves. An unusual way to announce your coming, but we see it," the woman said.

"BCP is a design error that my boss—"

"It is her symbol. Perfect in every way. A child descendant of the great protector of New Orleans."

"I'm sorry. Whose symbol? What is the preat grotector of New French?"

The woman frowned at Lilith.

"I meant the great protector of New Orleans. I'm famous for spoonerisms and transpositions." Flustered, Lilith raised her hand and began thumbing her amulet.

The woman gasped. Her eyes bulged at the sight of the amulet. "Mademoiselle Priestess. Welcome home."

"Ah … k." Lilith released the amulet, letting it drop to her chest. "You must have me confused with someone else. This is my first time to New Orleans."

"Of that, I am most assured, my child." The woman raised her finger to Lilith's chin and peered into her eyes. "You live in a city by Wy'east where lush green forests spread to the horizon, and a mighty river flows to the sea."

"Wy'east? You mean Mount Hood?"

"The child priestess's eyes watched over us for

centuries, and on this day, they walk among us. The single, small emblem warns us that the grave caretaker is coming."

Before Lilith could question the woman, she added, "The full moon marks your journey. May your steps find the roads and not the caretaker's snares. Free those caught in the fog, turning the wheel from daughter to mother. Finish binding the unholy alliance forged in the flames between the rivers."

Overwhelmed by the woman's cryptic words, Lilith's only reply was, "How much for the fruit?"

"No charge, my child. Please keep the basket." The woman lowered her head and stared at Lilith's waist. "With your darling midriff, you're going to receive many, many gifts today."

Lilith twisted around and hurried back to AJ. Panicked by the encounter, she asked, "Am I over exposed?"

"Did someone catcall you?" he asked.

"No, but I just got the 'grandma stare of disapproval.'"

"Are you exhibiting yourself to draw attention?"

"No … not really. I just want to wear what I want to wear without being judged." Lilith turned toward the fruit stand but couldn't find the woman.

AJ glanced over at the stands. "I think you're dressed comfortably, and by this afternoon—when the humidity smothers us—you will be more comfortable than Scott or me. If he or I showed our midriffs, people would gross out. Elliott, on the other hand … "

Lilith searched for the woman behind the stands. "Elliott is in good shape. He'd be able to pull off a great thirst trap."

"Excuse me."

Lilith snapped out of her stupor. "I enjoyed meeting your son. We had fun on the coast and a terrific night at the casino."

"Night … at the casino?"

"Ooh, no, no." Lilith realized she had failed to provide context. "We spent the night at the blackjack table. He was killing it and I broke even. We didn't share a room at the casino hotel."

AJ stroked his chin. "That explains why he went straight to bed. Whew. That better be the last shocker for this trip."

Lilith glared at AJ. "You thought I hooked up with your son?"

***

The morning tour proved the mystery woman correct. Stores declined payment for Lilith's purchases and gifted her with additional tokens of appreciation. Scott wanted to test her popularity with pricier items, but she refused to take advantage of others' generosity.

After a casual and relaxed lunch, the four approached a narrow street intersection heralded by lively music. AJ led them between the packed spectators to an opening, where they beheld a young couple dancing to a jazz band. The two college students danced to the band, enthralling the crowd with their precision and grace.

The young man's hunter-green shirt, drenched in perspiration, clung to his muscular physique, and the summer heat shimmered above his glossy bare arms and shoulders. He mirrored his partner's steps, holding her hand and supporting her as she danced.

As attractive as he was, Lilith gravitated to the young lady. Her frenetic spins and nimble-footed steps captured everybody's attention. Long brown, tightly curled hair whipped with her twists and spins. Beads of sweat zinged away with her head-snaps and hair flips. A hunter-green bandage top and baby-blue shorts hugged her dancer's body.

On the band's final note, applause erupted and whistles ringed the intersection. The dancers bowed and waved as the band continued with another tune. Both dancers circled the intersection with extended hands, hoping for audience participation.

The male dancer held his hand out, expecting somebody would take it as he walked in front of the street spectators. Tayen saw him coming and snatched Lilith's basket out of her hand. Lilith's head snapped back with Tayen's shoving. By the time Lilith's head snapped back, she was in the male dancer's arms.

The crowd oohed at the sight of Lilith in his arms.

Lilith swung her head around and gritted her teeth at Tayen.

"Oh, please. Admit you're happy I pushed you into those gorgeous arms."

Lilith raised her eyebrow, considering if Tayen had done her a favor or not. But with his arm across the back of her shoulders … she wasn't about to complain.

He placed his hand on her hip and asked if she could waltz. She nodded yes, and after he cued the band, off they went.

The crowd burst into surprised applause at Lilith's performance.

The crowd's eruption caught the lady dancer's attention. She had been unsuccessful in luring a partner for a dance. At the applause and cheers, she turned to see her male partner waltzing very well with another woman.

Lilith listened to the crowd moan. Trouble was brewing. She looked around to find the cause of their reaction. In didn't take long to see what the trouble was.

With arms folded and scowling in contempt, the young lady dancer feigned anger at Lilith for stealing the show. And she was walking towards them.

Lilith lost sight of the approaching dancer until the male dancer stopped them in mid-stride. Melodramatic oohs and aahs, along with uproarious laughter, rose from the crowd. The young lady had bumped the male dancer's shoulder, halting the waltz.

He raised his hands in defense, but the young lady snapped her head around. Her hair flip expressed her anger at him. She raised her arm and pointed at Lilith … *that other woman.*

The male dancer bowed to Lilith. Their twist was over. He rose from his deep bow and faced the young lady, expecting her to take him back.

She shook her head no and shooed him away with quick upward flips of her hand.

Disappointed and crestfallen, he huffed into the crowd while holding the back of his hand to his forehead.

Lilith tried to inch away from the feud, but the young lady gripped her wrist, keeping her in the intersection.

The young lady twirled in front of her and placed her hand on Lilith's hip.

Oh my god, she wants me to dance with her.

The young lady asked, "Do you know the tango?"

Inviting hazel eyes pierced Lilith's defenses, warming her to dance. "Yes, Dad made sure I could."

"Is this your first queer tango?"

"Oh, I can tango. I'm Lilith, by the way. Can a jazz band play the tango?"

"They can do anything, and I'm Melody."

"Hold on a moment, please." Lilith jogged to the street corner and plucked a rose from a hanging plant display. She returned and bit down on the rose stem. "Ready when you are."

Melody nodded to the band, and off they danced.

The two danced across the street to the delight of the onlookers. Melody dazzled the crowd with her elegant moves and precise foot work. Lilith gave a respectable performance, but she couldn't match Melody's expertise. She took solace in Melody's encouraging words as they danced. On the last note, the crowd exploded into applause. Lilith tapped Melody on the head with the rose as the male dancer returned and applauded.

Lilith leaned back against Scott, relieved that she hadn't skunked up the session.

Scott arm hugged her around the neck. "I swear every phone in the square was recording it. Somebody will post it on social media before dinner."

She patted his arm in appreciation. "Back to the room to escape this heat, and so I can shower."

AJ smiled. "That, and Charlotte's cab is blocks away from the hotel. I hope her grandparents' anniversary went well."

They hurried back to the hotel where Charlotte arrived in time to greet them in the hotel lobby. She and Lilith chatted like teenage girls as they prepared for the evening's festivities. Lilith's choices altered Charlotte's decision. Charlotte adjusted her choices, which forced Lilith to try something different. Tayen waited for the Wimbledon dress match to finish before finalizing her selection.

Charlotte and Lilith scurried down the stairs to the luxurious lobby, where Scott waited for them.

Charlotte's aura was aggressive and suggestive in her fiery two-piece scarlet party dress with matching ankle-strap net pumps. The carnation pinned in her hair and dangling earrings had Scott's face turning red.

Lilith countered Charlotte with demure playfulness. Her green crochet skater's dress performed as a skater's dress should when she twirled to show it off. Hoop earrings and crisscross peep-toe booties rounded out a stunning look.

Tayen rounded the corner as Lilith stopped twirling for Scott. Lilith was stunned by Tayen's appearance. Her beaver-colored, sleeveless cocktail dress left her speechless. The jewel neckline presented her as a woman of sophistication, while the tribal symbols flowed with its wearer's elegant strides.

Lilith shook her head. *Damn it. Just when I'm killing it, age and grace make me look plain.*

One oddity delayed her from complimenting Tayen. All the ladies worn thigh bands to carry their IDs and credit cards, but the bulge on Tayen's thigh seemed to show she was carrying an additional item.

AJ appeared last, dressed in all black.

Charlotte couldn't resist commenting. "A collarless long-sleeve cotton shirt with dress pants? Add a clerical collar and you're a priest."

Lilith took AJ's arm and escorted him toward the lobby front door. "You never know when we might need a priest. Hurry, this will be our first night excursion on Bourbon Street."

Charlotte rushed beside AJ as they exited the lobby. "Isn't Bourbon Street a bit rowdy for your *delicate constitution*, Father AJ?"

"Careful, or I'll have a chat with your priest."

"How d'you know my family is Catholic?"

"You told me on the day we hired you," AJ said.

"I did not."

"You said your mother was dead set on christening you, Charlotte, when you were baptized. I don't know of a Protestant denomination which christens at an infant's baptism."

Impressed, Lilith said, "Another thing I never knew."

A group of merrymakers approached them from Bourbon Street. Each carried tall plastic to-go cups, common to the French Quarter. One man in the group raised his cup and called out to AJ. "Bayou John. Totally lit, dude."

"Thank you," AJ replied.

Everybody in the group repeated, "Bayou John," as they raised their cups to AJ.

"Who's Bayou John?" Lilith asked.

"I don't know. A local celebrity, perhaps. Why don't you check it out on your phone?"

"Can't. Charlotte and I left our phones in the room."

AJ twitched his head. "You didn't bring your phones? Did hell freeze over?"

Charlotte turned her face toward AJ. "Our clothes don't have room for anything. Attractive young women on Bourbon Street only need a photo ID for drinks. Everything else comes to us with a wink or a smile."

"Where d'you learn that?"

"My cousins came here. They caught on after they doled out a cool hundred on drinks for their wish-night girls."

"Bayou John," a man called out from across the street.

AJ nodded and said, "Tayen, look it up for me."

Lilith looked back at Tayen, knowing there was something else in her thigh band.

When Tayen didn't respond, AJ said, "Scott, you are my last hope."

"Consider your hopes dashed. When Lilith left her phone on the nightstand, I followed suit."

Lilith chuckled.

They stepped onto Bourbon Street, where two women with enormous purple drink containers stopped walking and stared at Lilith. Realizing she was staring back at them, they turned and hurried around the corner.

"What was that about?" Tayen asked.

Lilith wasn't the only one to see the strange behavior. "Beats me."

They continued down the street while people raised their drinks and shouted at AJ. A tall black man stepped in front of them, cutting them off from walking further. He wore a T-shirt with the Pan-African flag displayed on the front. He pointed to the colors on his shirt and matched them to AJ, Charlotte, and her.

Lilith saw it and spoke over the noise. "We're dressed in the Pan-African colors. AJ in black, Charlotte in red, and me in green. Is that why they're calling you Bayou John?"

"I'm not waiting any longer," Tayen said. She released from Scott's arm and approached a man who had his hands in his pockets. "Pardon me, sir. Can I borrow your phone? I would like to see why people are calling my friend 'Bayou John'?"

The man looked at where Tayen was pointing and saw AJ. "Is that a joke?"

"No, sir. It isn't."

The man grinned. "They're calling him that because he resembles a local figure from our past. A vodouisant called Bayou John, the last significant Voodoo Priest in New Orleans."

"He looks like the guy?" Tayen asked.

"No. Bayou John was born in Senegal. The similarity comes from the two girls on his arms. John had fifty wives; all young, all very pretty."

"Thank you for the information," Tayen said as she turned toward AJ.

"Don't blame me," AJ shot back. "I didn't ask for the girls to hold on to my arms on the way to the restaurant."

Charlotte responded before Tayen blamed her. "I just grabbed AJ's free arm, so I felt like I was being accompanied."

"I'm not blaming anybody. We had no way of knowing."

Lilith saw the intensity in Tayen's glare. *She suspects he knew. His past life here in New Orleans? Did he know?*

To change the conversation, Lilith punched AJ in the chest. "So much for our first lesson on New Orleans Voodoo. What else will we learn before the night is done?"

5 - Table of Five

Tayen walked them to the seafood restaurant she'd chosen for dinner. The noise level diminished as they exited Bourbon Street. A gauntlet of people was waiting for tables at the restaurant entrance. Charlotte whittled a path through the crowd to the maître d's podium.

The maître d sneered down at her and returned to the details of his waiting list. Lilith stepped next to her, which caused him to look up for a moment. AJ and Tayen moved in behind the girls … to which the maître d changed his attitude. Scott stepped beside Tayen.

His eyes lit up. "Ah, the party has arrived. The distinguished woman and her elegant daughters. Accompanied by … two guys. Your table is ready. Please, follow me."

AJ raised his hand. "Hold on, sir."

Tayen nudged AJ with her hip. She didn't want him making a scene over the 'two guys' slight.

"You must be waiting for someone else. We are walk-ins, not … reservationists."

She bumped him harder for his goofy attempt at a big word.

"Sorry, reservationist isn't the right word. What I was trying to say is we don't have reservations."

The maître d said in his snobbish way, "I assure you … sir, a table has been reserved for your party."

Everyone stepped forward to follow the maître d, except Tayen and AJ.

"Boy, I tell you. He and I are going to have it out in the back alley if he speaks down to me again," AJ said.

Tayen stepped next to him. "Ignore him. But I would like an explanation on our good fortune for this dinner reservation."

"As soon as you can give me a better explanation for our half-off hotel reservations. I will forgo the obvious joke I could make at your expense."

Tayen nudged him forward with a shoulder bump. "I don't live on a reservation. And yes, I have reservations about our success with dinner and lodging … reservations."

"I think we've wrung out every possible connotation of the word reservation." AJ stepped forward. "Keep this quiet. I don't want the kids tripping out on us."

"Scott's our age."

"I wasn't talking about Scott."

"Oh, that's right. My elegant daughters."

Scott and the girls had taken their seats at the spacious circular table in the center of the dining area. The maître d pulled out a chair for Tayen. The girls had their photo IDs on the table for the inevitable card check. A second table server stood to the side, holding a tray of drinks while the first server checked the IDs. With a quick nod, they were approved, and drinks were placed in front of the ladies.

Scott and AJ shared a glance. "Where are the guys' drinks?" Scott asked.

"Sorry. The order was for the ladies," one server said.

Charlotte turned to AJ, not trying to hide her smugness. "Proof of the truth. Pretty ladies get all the freebies."

"What can we fix for the gentlemen?" the server asked.

AJ opened the drink menu in front of him. "Give us a moment to review the choices."

Scott checked his watch. "Two minutes from the front door to drinks placed on the table. That's a record."

Lilith picked up her drink. "Do you think these are roofied?"

Tayen picked up the glass in front of her. "We have drinks delivered to the table before we sit, and you automatically think somebody has drugged your drink?"

"Our walk here was eventful. Walking in to find we have reservations was an event. These drinks—"

"Yeah, yeah. A flood of drinks is an event." Tayen unraveled her cloth napkin and lowered it to her lap. No sooner had her napkin settled than another server laid more drinks on the table. None in front of Scott or AJ.

"Six drinks, five people. I say we circulate the drinks to the right. That way, we sample all the drinks," AJ said.

Lilith held up her a drink. "What is this lemony-colored one?"

"French 75," Tayen and AJ said simultaneously.

Before she could ask what was in it, AJ said, "A French 75 is gin and Champagne. Your other drink is a Mint Julep. Charlotte has a Pineapple Coconut Mimosa and a Vampire's Kiss. Our lady Tayen has a Bahama Mama and a Sicilian Kiss. And … Oh boy. Look out."

Another round of drinks arrived. This time, the order was doubled.

Tayen surveyed their treasure trove of drinks. "Twelve cocktails, and we haven't ordered yet."

"Hand me the Coconut Mojito." AJ spoke over Tayen.

Tayen addressed the server: "Tell the bar to stop sending drinks. We have plenty."

"Will do, madam."

Charlotte moaned in ecstasy over her first sip. "Mm. The Vampire's Kiss is to die for."

Tayen, leery of inexperienced drinkers, warned Charlotte, "Get something in your stomach before you start gulping. I don't want you loopy before dessert."

Charlotte glugged the Vampire's Kiss, disregarding the warning. "I want to be loopy by dessert."

Lilith snatched away the second Vampire's Kiss from Charlotte. "You didn't let us have a sip of this. You don't get this back until we've all had a sample."

"Oh boy," Charlotte and AJ said in unison.

Tayen pivoted in her seat to see behind her. Three servers dispersed around the table with more drinks.

"I told the bar to hold the drinks."

"Did they send word up to the second-floor bar?"

"Shit." Tayen dropped her head and rebounded at once to add to her previous directive. "Tell every bartender in the zip code to stop making us drinks."

Scott stood and removed the two fresh Vampire's Kisses which had been set in front of Charlotte.

"Thanks, Scott," Lilith said.

"Twenty-one drinks. Pace yourselves." AJ lifted the Sicilian Kiss from Tayen's grasp.

"Very well," Tayen began. "Let's do a little housekeeping before our night of frivolity begins."

AJ pointed at the menu. "Aren't you eating?"

"I chose this place and know what's on the menu. As I was saying, Chef Dean and Chef Ladonna return to us on the nineteenth. We'll have a late dinner and then to bed for the convention on the twentieth.

"Poor Scott's meetings are in a different building several blocks away. We'll see him during lunches and dinners only. The rest of us are at the convention center, albeit in different seminars. Remember, if the presenters are competent, your growth will be commensurate with the effort you put in."

Lilith interjected, "The seventeenth through the nineteenth are for touristy stuff."

"Mornings are best for activities," AJ said.

Tayen tilted her head back. "They never listen to me."

AJ continued, proving Tayen's point. "As you learned from this afternoon, the heat and humidity can be oppressive. Slow-paced, slow-moving activities are worth planning for the afternoons. Don't forget, a little after four, it always storms for ten to fifteen minutes."

"Wait. What?" Lilith asked.

"The sun heats the coast and a moist, warm air mass forms storm clouds. Once enough energy is accumulated, a thunderstorm breaks out. It never lasts long, but be aware of it if you don't want to be caught in a downpour."

Lilith looked around the table to see if anyone else was confused. She turned back to AJ. "Are you saying it rains every day around four? Why?"

AJ frowned. "Did you pass high school science?"

"Science wasn't a strong point."

Tayen interrupted their conversation. "Meteorology is best saved for another dinner. Suffice to say, watch for thunderstorms around four."

Charlotte lowered her menu. "Crab cakes for me. What are you getting, Scott?"

"Cajun jambalaya pasta."

Tayen folded her hands in her lap and glared at AJ. As much as she tried to keep the business trip focused on business matters, she relented from her pursuit. "Moving on to dinner, I guess."

AJ pointed past her place setting. "That Vampire's Kiss, over on your far side. Could you pass it here?"

Tayen reached out and lifted the drink to her lips. Tilting her head back, she downed it in one swift motion, and placed the empty glass next to AJ. She said unapologetically, "Oops." She licked her lips and turned to Charlotte. "Mm, raspberry Chambord, I like."

AJ searched the table for one of the two remaining Vampire's Kisses. Tayen said, "Front right, Lilith. Before he sees it."

Lilith carried out Tayen's directive, grasped the drink, and chugged it, as Tayen and Charlotte had done.

One remained, and it sat between Charlotte and Scott. Like cobras striking at their prey, Scott's dual precision strikes—one to grab Charlotte's wrist, the other to secure the last Vampire's Kiss—won the day. He drank half and stretched over the table, handing the rest to AJ.

"The ladies are scarfing while the gentlemen … will be gentlemen. Well done, Scott," AJ said.

Except for the occasional 'Bayou John' call out to AJ, dinner was a delight for them. The gentlemen remained gentlemanly, freeing Tayen from her role as the mature, responsible one of the party.

Tayen's always present professionalism was diluted by each sampling sip. The girls also found their freedom to do as they pleased. Lilith rotated dinners, much to AJ's perturbance. She snatched his halibut plate and passed her shrimp linguine to Charlotte. Scott assumed a defenseless posture and passed his Cajun jambalaya pasta to Tayen before Charlotte dropped her crab cakes on his plate.

Dinner concluded with the ladies grabbing the three orange-colored drinks, which they had saved for last. Tayen winked at the girls. In a synchronized motion, they drank as much of the drinks as possible before brain freeze set in.

Lilith sprang straight up and said, "I need to dance."

Charlotte shot out of her chair to follow Lilith. But she sprang sideways rather than up, which forced Scott to catch her. Getting her feet squarely under her, Charlotte lasered in and chased after Lilith.

Unlike Charlotte's out-of-control rocket launch, Tayen's standing to her feet looked more like time-lapse photography. Proud of her success, she winked at AJ. "Pay the bill. We're off of here."

"You mean out of here?"

"Exactly." She pivoted, keeping her hand on the table, before walking after Charlotte.

Upon exiting the front door, Tayen watched Lilith scooting down the street, drawn to the music like a firefly pulled to a neon light.

It didn't take long to find a nightclub. Tayen stood inside the doorway when Scott held her arm in a gentleman's fashion. She assumed her questionable stability was the reason for his standing so close.

Charlotte pulled Lilith to the dance floor. Tayen followed and pulled Scott, who reluctantly stepped behind her.

Tayen had her arms in the air, letting go of her administrative persona, when Lilith's yelling caused her to turn. Her gift shop cashier had bent a man's wrist against his forearm and forced him to his knees.

"Do it again—put your hand in another woman's crotch and I will fucking shatter your wrist up to your shoulder."

Lilith released him, letting him scamper away.

"God, what now?" Tayen moved closer and yelled over the music to Lilith. "Are you okay?"

Lilith nodded. She was fine and resumed dancing.

Charlotte yelled back to Tayen, "Her martial arts lessons paid off. I think I should join her dojo."

Tayen nodded as she laughed, but her outward joy was subdued by an ill feeling in her stomach. She pushed her way through the dance club and jogged to the street. Blurry eyed and teetering … She pulled her hair behind her head, bent over, and threw up. After regaining her breath, she yelled at the street. "Damn alcohol poisoning."

Out of the corner of her eye, she saw Scott exiting the door with his arm locked under Lilith's and Charlotte's arms. Once on the street, he wrangled back both girls' hair as they threw up.

Tayen lumbered their direction, amazed that the girls could synchronize their vomits. She bent over to support herself with her hands on her knees. "So, Scott, you have experience with this."

"The antics of a younger sister taught me well."

"How come you're not throwing up?"

With Charlotte standing and Lilith kneeling, Scott's stance was comically lopsided. "AJ and I sipped while you three gulped those drinks. And you drank at least three times more than we did."

AJ had turned the corner and saw the disaster. "Ah, dinner revisited. Charming."

Tayen wiped the corners of her mouth. "I'm calling it a night and heading back to the hotel."

Lilith leaned to her side and clasped on to Scott's leg.

"Steady girl, steady," Scott assured her.

Charlotte struggled to keep her balance, and Tayen looked sturdy with her hands on her knees. Charlotte assumed her leaning on her boss wouldn't be a problem. A misnomer for which both paid dearly. They had tumbled into the spot where Lilith threw up.

AJ helped them to their feet and accompanied them back to the hotel. Scott followed close behind, with Lilith in his arms for most of the way.

Tayen turned around at the squishing sound Scott's shoes made. Lilith threw up on his shoes when he held her hair back. He wasn't complaining, nor did he appear upset. If anything, he was being quite the hero to his coworker.

They turned on their hotel's street, where a dense fog hovered above the street in front of the hotel.

"Someone set off fireworks," Tayen said.

"Unlikely," AJ responded. "Personal fireworks aren't allowed in the French Quarter. And besides, the mist is hovering inches above the street, not much higher."

"Like dry ice," Scott added.

"Is it me," Charlotte rubbed her eyes, "or does it seem darker?"

Tayen looked at the streetlights. "A little, maybe."

"Oh, god." Lilith's tone had Scott turning her head to the side.

"I'm not throwing up," she said. "But that sickly sweet scent might do the trick."

AJ sniffed the air. "Sickly sweet? I find it to be exhilarating, exotic, and stimulating. Ole Willy seems to have awakened—" Tayen's nudge in his ribs stopped him from embarrassing himself. "I'll leave it at exhilarating and exotic."

"The scent makes her sick, but you're inhaling it like you're on a bender. Why is that?" Tayen asked as they reached the valet podium outside the hotel lobby door.

"Ooh," the valet said on seeing them. "Rough night?"

"Too much drinking. Rookie mistakes," Tayen said.

The valet turned to enter the hotel. "Wait here for a minute."

Moments later, he returned with oversized hotel robes.

Tayen grabbed one. "Girls, they don't want our mess walking through the lobby."

"Can't blame them," Lilith said as spun the robe over her shoulders.

Charlotte had the robe over her and began wiggling underneath it. She asked the valet, "Do you have a bag?" No sooner had she asked than her dress dropped to the ground over her feet.

"What are you doing?" AJ asked in shock.

"I'm taking off my dress to get the puke off of me."

Lilith began wiggling under her robe.

"Tayen … stop them, please," AJ said.

"Are you kidding? If I could wiggle out of this dress, I'd be doing it."

Charlotte placed her dress in the bag the valet had handed to her.

"Ma'am, I can have that laundered and returned to your room by breakfast, if you would allow me?"

"Thank you. That would be sweet." Charlotte handed the bag to him.

"Can you add one more?" Lilith held her dress in her hand.

The valet opened the bag for her to drop it in. "I would be delighted."

Tayen checked his hotel badge. "Brayton, why is this fog patch here?"

"It appeared a few minutes ago, but there isn't anything to worry about. Maintenance is checking on it."

"Is it the source of that smell?"

"I suppose." Brayton tilted his head up and sniffed the air. "Fruity … Apricots infused with a spicy pepper."

"Our valet is also a sommelier," Tayen said.

"Indeed I am." Brayton turned his head and stared across the street to a narrow, dark walkway between two buildings. Tayen looked to see what had his attention.

"Apricots and peppers. Good Lord, it's been years."

"Good Lord? Years? Spill it doorman, who's scaring the living shit out of me," Charlotte said.

"A legend of the French Quarter from years ago. She is close, very close, if her fragrance entices and ensnares. Her vengeance is near. But if one is repelled by her scent, safe they will be." Brayton turned his head to them. "But never you mind about our ghosts and the barons who watch over the graves. Go on to bed. I'll have these cleaned and sent to your room by morning."

AJ smiled all the way to their rooms. "I think the employees play a part in promoting the French Quarter's haunted streets. He got us to look down a dark alley, and told us a vague story, which—I'll admit—had a twinge of terror creeping up my back."

"Not funny. If I wake up with night terrors, I'm coming into your room to scream in your face," Charlotte said.

Scott entered his room. Lilith to scampered through the open door, leaving AJ and Tayen in the hall.

"Brayton had me," Tayen said. "Don't count on an early start from us. We may need time to sleep this off."

"Then Scott and I will have the morning to ourselves. Say goodnight to the girls for me."

Tayen shut the door and walked past the closed bathroom door, which Charlotte had taken first. Lilith sat on the edge of her bed; her eyes dulled from drinking too much. Tayen sat on the bed across from her.

Lilith raised her head to look at Tayen. "Sick night, except the actual sick part."

"I hope Brayton gets your dresses clean. It would be a shame if those cute things were irreparably stained."

Lilith reached under her complimentary robe and pulled out her photo ID from her thigh band. "A miracle. I didn't throw up on it. How about what's in your thigh band?"

Tayen put her hand on her thigh. "For everyone's sake, let's not discuss it. It's private and doesn't need any attention. Please, forget about it, and I would appreciate you not mentioning it to anybody, both now and in the future."

Lilith moved next to Tayen on the bed. "I won't. But

give me one reason it is so important, and why your mood changes whenever someone sees it."

"One reason … and we'll never discuss it again?"

"I'll even work to help you out of the corner should anybody bring it up."

Tayen leaned forward, closing the distance between them. "I'll keep this short. This phone has encrypted files, which I gathered from my time in Europe. Information I wish I had never run across, but I did, so I am stuck with it. Others, like me, have identical phones. We are required to enter a response code every twenty-four hours, and if we don't, the others know which of us didn't reply. Those who don't reply might be in trouble."

"Did you do something illegal?" Lilith whispered.

"My only crime was taking good notes at meetings and having the business savvy figure out what was happening. Others, like me, saw the same things. When we compared notes, we had enough information to expose corruption in every part of the world."

"Hand it off to the authorities."

Tayen looked at the closed bathroom door. "We can't share with the authorities. The data analysis hasn't been completed. There is a treasure trove of data for prosecutors. We have cause to believe it points at people who are the authorities.

"Corruption runs deep with those who control vast sums of wealth. We can't hand incriminating evidence over to those who protect the powerful. They'll take it and make it disappear. Oligarchs and corrupt government officials can manipulate their way out of any situation. And for those who try to expose them, they are disposed of."

6 - The First Estate

Early the next morning, the blaring of the alarm jolted AJ from his bed. Scott beat AJ into the bathroom, which forced AJ to consider opening the connecting door to Tayen and the girls' room, so he could use their toilet. He rejected the idea and waited for Scott to finish.

The two men readied themselves for breakfast. Scott chanced physical and verbal abuse by poking his head into the lady's bedroom and asking if they wanted to join them. The lady trio explicitly told Scott where to stick his breakfast invitation.

AJ stepped into the hall. Newspapers were in front of every room's door, except his and the ladies'. He shrugged it off and joined Scott at the stairs. Two police officers passed them as they descended to the lobby.

At the bottom of the stairs, Scott asked, "Why are the police here?"

"A non-emergency call? There weren't any sirens, so I'm guessing it's a minor infraction."

They turned the corner to find more police standing in the hotel lobby, where staff members were answering questions.

"Correction, emergency call," AJ said.

"Should we stay and ask if we can be of assistance?"

"If they need us, they'll stop and ask us."

AJ pushed the lobby door open to find police cars in the street. The flashing blue and red lights caused them to back up against the building. They stood still, watching the activity outside the hotel. Scott elbowed AJ and pointed at the valet podium next to the street, where a bag leaned against the podium.

"Is that the bag—"

"—Yes." AJ interrupted. "The girls aren't getting their clothes back before lunch. Let's move down a bit."

In a few steps, what was taped off came into view. An enormous square field of blue covered the street from curb to curb. To AJ's horror, the image of a broken white wheel sat perfectly aligned in the middle of the blue field.

AJ jabbed Scott on the leg and shook his head for them to remain silent. Across the street, on the walkway between two buildings, a white sheet laid over a body. AJ ducked his head and hurried away. Scott caught up with him, where a group of people gathered at the end of the street.

"What on Earth are they looking at?" AJ asked.

"One way to find out," Scott replied.

They approached the intersection. Gaps between the people allowed for glimpses of a field of blue on the street.

The crowd inched past it one by one. AJ and Scott waited their turn. When they had an unimpeded view, the broken wheel image confirmed their suspicions. Although it was a tenth the size of the one outside the hotel, its impact on them was just as intense.

They stepped aside and listened to the onlookers.

One man said, "There's a huge one of these up by the hotel on Bourbon Street, and dozens of shoebox-sized ones running east on Chartres Street."

Another man asked, "Are these connected to the dead man they found this morning?"

Scott twisted around, keeping his back to the onlookers. AJ gripped Scott by the arm and pulled. They didn't need to be here. As they walked away, they heard a woman say, "The cops said they found two bodies at the hotel. The hotel valet and another one across the street."

"What the hell is going on?" Scott asked.

AJ waved him off, wanting to make sure no one overheard their discussion. He stopped near the end of the narrow passageway and leaned against a black gaslight pole.

"Can I ask now?"

Frustrated, AJ bumped the back of his head on the pole. "You can ask anything you want. Whether I can answer it is the real question."

"Why is our business logo all over the French Quarter's streets?"

"It makes a hell of a street decoration," AJ said.

Scott didn't respond.

AJ watched the onlookers. "The hovering fog last night … It formed right over where our logo is."

Scott turned his head up the street. "Dry ice? Like at a rock concert."

"Fog machine ... dry ice ... but uniformly distributed?" AJ wasn't talking to Scott, but out loud as thoughts crossed his mind. "The fog coming out of a fog machine ... disperses. Or can it hover like last night? If not a fog machine ... what?"

"A chemical reaction," Scott answered.

AJ pressed his fingertips together. "A chemical reagent poured on the street ... and it reacted with a substance that had been there ... before."

Scott's voice rose an octave. "Something was already in the asphalt? There goes my day."

"Why do you say that?"

"I'll have to search city records for contractors who paved the city streets, if you we are to find who did this."

"Brilliant." AJ lowered his head. "My business logo is tied to the city of New Orleans and whatever underground criminal activity lies here. Tayen will love this. She already thinks I'm associated with organized crime because I lived in south Chicago and Kansas City."

Scott shrugged.

"Capone, south Chicago; the mob, Kansas City."

Scott's eyes opened wider.

"Et tu, Brute?"

"You run a pirate-themed organization."

AJ bobbled his head. "And it's called Broken Cove."

"Cool name for a pirate base," Scott said.

"And to speak of the devil, we're on Pirate's Alley, an infamous pirate enclave. The absinthe house behind you is the old pirate bar. It sits a few steps away from a cathedral. Most cities have ordinances prohibiting alcohol establishments within a certain distance from a church. But here—in this teeny-tiny alley—piracy, alcohol, and religion coexisted."

"Are you ranting?" Scott asked.

"My logo is parked in front of our hotel. Two dead bodies were found close by. If I'm ranting, it's justified."

AJ pointed at the buildings. "A public house on one corner, St. Louis Cathedral across the alley, and the old Cabildo next to us. Nice intersection. You couldn't squeeze a badminton court in here."

Scott looked at the building next to the cathedral. "What's the old Cabildo?"

"The old government offices building. I believed the separation of church and state was razor thin, but this is as close as you can get without sharing a wall. This alley doesn't get an hour of sunlight because the buildings are so close together."

Scott adjusted his glasses.

AJ stood and turned in a circle. He didn't blink as his circumstances came to light. His voice wavered between awe and fear. "Oh boy. Strange just went full-blown weird."

"What's the matter?"

AJ faced the cathedral. "Church, the first estate." He pivoted around and faced the alley between the other buildings. "The Cabildo represents nobles and the ruling class on the left."

"The second estate," Scott said.

"And merchants are the third with the absinthe house. The three estates refer to the era before the French revolution. And here we are, where they intersect at the light pole. Lilith's amulet passed through here."

Scott stood with his hands in his pockets. "We've got our business logo on the streets, our valet is dead, the girls' clothes are at the valet podium, and you added Lilith's amulet to this mess. Why?"

AJ heard Scott, but his mind swirled as their circumstances confronted him. He placed his hand on the black enameled light pole. AJ murmured to himself, "If these walls could talk?"

"AJ."

At Scott's call, he raised his head.

"Sorry, Scott. Lilith's amulet was handed down to her with this place as its background. It comes with a riddle. *The return to the intersection of the three estates*, but I don't know what it means. What's killing me is the serendipitous nature of this adventure. The anomalies on this trip … "

"Enlighten me."

AJ released his hold on the light pole. "Last month, we received an invitation to this convention. It included reservations for a prestigious hotel—which is always booked at least two months out. Yet we got in without having to wait two months.

"Our all-evening, jacket-required reservation for four, was paid in full. Restaurants make money by turning tables. Dinner parties are scheduled for ninety minutes. Renting tables by the hour is a losing business strategy. The restaurant had a table reserved for us without knowing when we would arrive."

"A table held indefinitely for four. Why not five?" Scott asked.

AJ raised his head, surprised by Scott's observation. "Our room listing is for five, but dinner reservations were for four. Charlotte wasn't included in the reservation."

Scott turned his head to watch for those who might be watching them.

"Last night, on the sixteenth, you left for the dance club while I waited for the bill. When I asked for it, they told me it was on the house."

"We got lucky with dinner reservations two nights in a row? Is this the homecoming you spoke about in the van?"

AJ looked down the alley. "Somebody can manipulate two restaurants, one hotel, and the street pavement of the French Quarter. What homecoming did I come home to?"

"So, what now? We have a string of mini logos on Chartres Street. Should we follow them, or go back to the hotel and face—"

AJ gasped. "Face the police. The police officers we passed on the stairs. They were headed to our rooms."

Scott bent over, placing his hands on his knees. "Hung over, ill-tempered, half clothed, and a visit from the police … Tayen should get hazard pay for today's work. I better call and warn them."

AJ paced in the alley as Scott texted. "None of them are answering."

"Scott, you don't need to be part of this. I'm likely making a terrible decision, but I'm going to pursue the mini logos. You do not have to follow me. Think about what is best for you."

"I wore the team logo shirt yesterday. Somehow, I think I'm implicated, no matter which direction I go."

AJ waved for Scott to join him.

They reached the intersection at the end of the alley and found a shoe-sized broken wheel emblem. They knelt on the pedestrian-only road to inspect it.

Scott ran his fingers over the pavement. "No paint or plastic layers. No burns or gouges. Rule out lasers and chisels. And no difference in texture between the logo to the surrounding pavement."

"An inlay," AJ added. "Someone baked this into the

street. But who did the inlay?"

"Whoever poured the reagent did it last night," Scott said.

AJ stepped to the bottom side of the emblem. "If I stand here, it looks like it does on the printed page. The missing bottom half of the wheel at my feet, and the five handles pointing away from me."

"It's a pointer. The top handle charts our course," Scott said.

Scott started down the street past the cathedral with AJ in close pursuit. They headed east until they crossed a sixth emblem, which stumped AJ and stopped him from walking.

"What is it?"

"The first five emblems were at street intersections. But number six … is in the middle of the block."

"What about the streets of old?" Scott asked.

AJ pointed at a gate between two buildings. "That gate is wider than most."

"It looks more like an alley than an entrance to a private home."

AJ kicked the ground. "Shit. It's an old street from decades ago. This is an intersection. These emblems were laid over two hundred years ago."

Scott looked at the buildings on either side of the gate.

"The buildings you're looking at have early nineteenth century architecture all over them. Architecture which was employed after the great fire of 1794." AJ turned and continued down the street.

They walked until the ninth emblem appeared. Once again, no discernible intersection presented itself. Scott pointed at both sides of the street. "There's no intersection here."

AJ pointed across the street. "The museum plaque on that side dates the house to 1826. The plaque on this side dates this convent to 1727. Our ninth emblem, at an institution which was established nine years after New Orleans' founding."

"I might stretch the analogy here, but a convent can represent an intersection. The spiritual and the physical," Scott said.

AJ looked at his watch. "6:03 a.m. Nautical twilight in the ninth month. Ninety-nine years between the buildings. Glad I'm not the superstitious type, or the number nine could be ominous for us."

He lifted his head to find Scott, bewildered as ever. "Ignore me. Let's see what's at the convent."

They approached the museum's long-sheltered gate. Stepping inside the opening, they found a priest sitting on a park bench.

At first, the priest didn't respond to AJ and Scott. He closed his book and without looking up, he said, "AJ de Faria, how have you been, my old friend?"

AJ fumbled about to find a reply.

"Not yet. I understand." The priest placed the book on the bench and introduced himself. "I am Father Amare. I bought your book and am finding it refreshing. The internal discussion it has stoked within my soul reminds me of family debates from years ago."

AJ spotted his book on the park bench. "You bought my book? I thought my son made the sole purchase. God, I hate the author's photo."

Father Amare laughed as he stood. "Your photo does you justice. *Historical Preludes to General Church Councils* makes for a tough read for the common eye, but I find it fascinating. And I love your company imprint, Broken Cove Publishing."

AJ placed his hand on Scott's shoulder. "Father Amare, meet my associate, Scott Pullman."

Father Amare shook Scott's hand. "Welcome Scott. I hope you are enjoying our fair city."

"Father Amare," AJ pointed at the street, "what's the deal with our business logo?"

"The image of a ship's broken wheel marks the return of the Voodoo Priestess, and the path which leads her home."

AJ grimaced. "Great. Another mystery."

"I see your angst, AJ. You have questions about your entrance into our world. Not to worry. Tonight, at nine, when you return, I will explain why a vortex of uncertainty whirls around you. Please bring the ladies along. They need to hear of the forces which stalk you from the shadows."

Pinching his nose, AJ struggled to sort through the onslaught of events which had taken place. As courteous as the priest was being, AJ was about to burst. "Forces from the shadows are interested in a golf course owner and his staff?"

Father Amare looked toward their hotel. "Lilith must attend tonight. I will explain what led to the street emblems. They've waited for centuries to point her way home."

"Centuries?" Scott asked in disbelief. "Lilith is barely two decades old."

"She is young. When she is here tonight, I can explain how she could be the descendant of the Voodoo Priestess."

AJ attempted to remain patient. "I could use more of an explanation, please."

"For three hundred years, the broken wheel image marked a community which lived here. Decimated by centuries of misfortune and oppression, few followers of the Priestess remain. Steadfast to the Voodoo Priestess's promises, a remnant continues to uphold her ideals and wait for her descendant to finish the work started years ago."

AJ turned to Scott and said, "He didn't say 'prophecy, messiah, or second coming.' I'm counting that as a positive."

"Yesterday, with your broken wheel shirts beaming brilliantly in the sun, and Lilith leading your march through the French Quarter, forces you never dreamed of awoke. They have waited centuries for the Voodoo Priestess's return. Hidden in our rich cultural tapestry, the wheels of fortune and misfortune have turned. Don't draw attention to yourselves for the rest of the day. The eyes of friends aim to protect you, but the eyes of foes serve to ensnare you."

"Perfect," AJ said. "Us staying off the radar means a day in the hotel room. A full day of room service and porn."

Scott's eyes flew open.

"I'm joking. Room service for an entire day would kill me."

"You're channeling Charlotte, right?" Scott asked.

AJ deflected from answering Scott's question. "Father Amare, do you have any idea about the intersection of the three estates?"

Father Amare didn't break eye contact with AJ. "You were on Pirate's Alley?"

"We were."

"What impressions did you have of it?"

"I think it is too small for a badminton court."

Father Amare closed his eyes and laughed. "A badminton court, no. But a ping-pong table did fit."

"Oh, that would have been a sight to see."

Father Amare's eyes twinkled as he grinned. "My

failed table tennis tournament story will have to wait. But, be assured, many important events have transpired at that intersection. Years ago, the jail opened onto the alley. If a registry had been kept of the individuals who passed through there, it might constitute the most amazing list of *who's who of the modern times*."

"But one in particular is of importance to us, Lilith."

"Tonight, at nine. See you then, AJ."

"Confession … at nine. Wonderful."

"Here," Father Amare handed AJ a card, "take this coupon for an order of beignets. I'll see you tonight." He turned and walked away.

AJ and Scott stood outside the sheltered entrance. With his hands on his hips, AJ said, "Our stroll about town yesterday alerted people to the prophecies of an ancient folklore. I'm burning those shirts tonight."

"I won't lie. It knocked me off-kilter to hear that our little Lilith descended from a Voodoo Priestess," Scott said.

"Yeah, I should have asked if he meant Voodoo Priestess or Vodou Priestess? New Orleans Voodoo doesn't have priests or priestesses. Haitian Vodou does, as far as I know. The difference between them could be important to us."

"He said a community lived here, and they followed a Voodoo Priestess."

"But he didn't say she lived here, only the community." AJ waved his hand over his head. "We'll ask about her tonight. For now, we have a coupon for beignets."

7 - Family Strip Club

The pounding on the door sent Tayen tumbling out of bed. Clothes flew in the air as she hunted for a robe. Lilith's locks draped over her face as she lifted her head from the pillow. Tayen peered through the peephole. Lilith didn't say anything. Her curiosity had been piqued by the sudden morning activity.

Tayen dropped her head, tip-toed backwards, and grumbled in a lowered voice to Lilith. "Damn it, the police are here. Out of bed and get dressed."

Lilith launched from under the sheets in a mad scramble for a robe. "Charlotte, get your ass out of bed. The police are here."

The previous night's drinking left Charlotte paralyzed with a hangover headache from hell. "Ha, ha, ha. The police aren't here. Wake me for dinner, or the first paramedic who passes our door."

Lilith found a hotel robe and hurried to tie the sash. With a whisper-ish growl, she said, "I'm not joking. Out of bed, now."

"Why would the police be here?"

"Your twenty-first birthday is in two days and you were drinking last night."

"They're hunting me down for a three-day underage drinking violation. Whoopee. My orders stand: wake me for dinner."

"Charlotte, out of bed and get dressed," Tayen ordered.

"All right, all right." Charlotte rolled over and flipped up as she wrapped the hotel robe around her. "Jesus, I'm a size zero, and this is still too small. I guess the police will have to accept me in a deep plunging neckline robe."

Lilith struggled with her enormous complimentary hotel white robe. It draped to the floor and doubled over, while the sleeves swallowed her arms.

Charlotte couldn't resist a verbal jab at her roommate's plight. "You're either getting humped by a polar bear, or Bigfoot left it here last night."

"Don't lie, tell the truth, but don't volunteer information not implied in the question," Tayen ordered.

"You're telling us … two women of color … how to interact with the police?" Lilith asked.

"I'm just making sure we're on the same page."

"Thanks for the page check. Glad you caught up to our chapter."

Tayen shot back, "You seem to be forgetting I'm the *I* in BIPOC."

Charlotte tugged on her robe. "It doesn't wrap around and isn't coochie length. Wait until Talia hears about this."

Tayen ordered her into the chair. "Sit and throw a shirt over your lap."

Lilith assessed Charlotte's plunging neckline. "Don't lean forward or twist either, or your girls will pop out."

Charlotte grabbed a team logo shirt and pulled it over her thighs as she fell back into a chair.

Tayen tugged and pulled on her robe. "One more inch is all I need."

"What girl hasn't said that?"

"Charlotte, don't say something like that in front of the police," Tayen ordered before she opened the door.

Two police officers followed Tayen into the room. The first said, "Sorry to bother you ladies this early in the morning. I'm Officer Tim, and this is Officer Angelo."

"Oh, you guys! Male strippers for my birthday."

Lilith slapped Charlotte on the back of her head. "We didn't hire male strippers, you idiot."

"Right." Charlotte tilted her head up and winked at her roommate.

Officer Angelo shook his head. "We aren't strippers, ma'am. We are investigating a disturbance on the street."

He gazed at Charlotte's lap. "Do you see this, Tim?"

Charlotte squirm-checked with her hands to feel if she'd left herself exposed.

"It's impossible to miss that shade of blue. And the logo, a perfect match to the one on the street," Officer Tim said.

Tayen dipped her head. "I'm sorry, Officer Tim. Why

are you here?"

"Well, ma'am, your shirts are why we're here."

"You're here because of our shirts? Are we wearing a gang symbol or something subversive?"

"Ma'am, did you or your associates have anything to do with the graffiti on the street?"

"What graffiti?"

"Could you ladies please raise your hands and show us your palms?" Officer Tim asked.

"I'm wearing an oversized robe," Lilith said, "so I am moving my arms very slow."

Both officers rested their hands against their gun holsters.

Lilith raised her arms and pulled the sleeves back, exposing her empty hands and flipping her palms around.

"Thank you for telling us what you were doing and then showing us."

Tayen held her palms up. "You won't find any spray paint on our hands. We didn't spray graffiti on anything last night."

"We still had to check your hands. The emblem on this young lady's T-shirt matches the graffiti on the street."

Tayen turned to the window but didn't take a step toward it.

Lilith understood. *She wants to look, but that damn robe might ride up on her.*

"Could one of you take a peek outside?" Tayen asked.

Lilith lifted the front of the polar-bear-sized robe so she could walk without stumbling. She inched her way to the window and, upon reaching it, looked down at the street.

A broken wheel emblem covered the street from curb to curb. Crisp, clean white paint formed the broken wheel on a solid bed of blue. It was the exact image of their team's convention shirts. Seeing it caused her to lean forward and accidentally bang her head on the glass.

Knowing where the glass was, she pressed against the window. Across the street, she saw a white sheet at the top edge of the field of blue. She spun around to face the officer. Her mouth and eyes couldn't hide her shock; there was a dead body under the sheet.

"His name was Brayton Colliot. Do you know him?" Officer Angelo asked.

"Colliot?" Charlotte responded with surprise. "I believe the valet's hotel badge said Colliot."

"Do you know him?"

Lilith couldn't move. It escaped her as to why the gracious valet she met hours ago was dead.

Officer Angelo asked again: "Do you know Brayton Colliot?"

Charlotte's voice carried a tinge of protest when she answered. "Not personally, no. He brought us robes last night and told us a terrifying story. But other than that, we never met him before."

Charlotte's forceful reply spurred Tayen to speak. "Officers, please explain what is going on."

"Yes, ma'am. That is him across the street," Officer Tim said.

Tayen slumped and tip-toed her way to the window. With her hand behind her, holding the robe to her butt, she pressed against the window. The white broken ship's wheel on the field of blue shocked her, and after several moments of scanning the street, she saw the sheet covering the body. She stepped back from the window with her chin buried against her chest.

Lilith's phone vibrated.

Charlotte grabbed it from the stand and silenced it. Wanting to peek out the window, she said, "Officers, I'm not wearing anything under this robe. Could you step outside, so I could dress a little less provocatively?"

Officer Angelo stepped forward, picked up a robe, and handed it to Charlotte. "You mean like this?"

In her mad dash for a robe, Charlotte had passed over what she was searching for. "Yeah, like that one." In a blur of standing and twirling, she doubled up the robes over her and raced to the window.

Tayen gained enough strength to turn to the officers. "That mammoth-sized street emblem down below is someone else's doing. This is the first we have seen it. We met Brayton Colliot last night. His death comes as quite the shock."

Tayen's phone vibrated in her hand. She silenced it.

"We need to take your individual statements. Officer Angelo will ask you questions, ma'am, and I'll talk with your friends, one by one, in the hall," Officer Tim said.

Charlotte's phone vibrated on her bed. Tayen tip-toed to the girl's bed and silenced the phone.

Officer Tim pointed at Lilith. "The young girl in the baggy robe. I'll speak with you first. The other young lady, if you would step in the bathroom, I'll ask you questions second."

Charlotte rushed away from the window. "Officer, rather than standing in the bathroom, may I stand in the hall?"

"I'd prefer if you were in the bathroom."

"I'll stand down by the stairs, far enough away from your interview with Lilith. We're wearing robes, so we've got nothing to conceal, and you can keep an eye on all your suspects."

"You think we are considering you suspects?"

Charlotte dipped her head. "Our logo is on your street, and the logo is plastered on our clothing. If we aren't suspects, we are persons of interest. Whichever way you call it, we're under suspicion."

"Would you care to explain why you want to be down the hall?" Officer Angelo asked.

Tayen stood behind the chair with her arms crossed and defended her assistant. "Two women of color questioned by police, and there is a dead body across the street. The brown girl knows the black girl has reason to fear, so she's keeping an eye out for her friend."

"Not all police officers are bad."

"The vast majority are above reproach. But the system is stacked, and not in these women's favor. I'm not white, but First Nations. Still, my white complexion affords privileges Lilith and Charlotte might never experience. Statistically, these women are safer than the First Nations woman standing before you. To understand their fear, walk in their shoes for a day."

Officer Angelo nodded. "No, ma'am, I don't understand. But I have a daughter with many black friends, and I am learning."

"Ladies, if you would, please." Officer Tim started for the door. "I think I have your names correct. Lilith, with me, and Charlotte ..." He stepped into the hall and looked at the landing for the stairs. "Down that way, please."

Officer Tim waited for Charlotte to reach the stairs before turning to Lilith. "Can you explain your whereabouts last night?"

"We had dinner at a French Cajun seafood place."

"Le Cajun Papillon?"

"That's the one. We ate, drank, and ran across the street to dance. We drank heavily. The nightclub owners had to be thrilled we left after we decorated their dance floor."

"Decorated their dance floor?" Officer Tim asked.

"We threw up on the dance floor and our clothes. When we got back to the hotel, Brayton gave us robes, so we weren't an embarrassment. We undressed—under the robes, not on the street—and he put our dirty clothes in a bag. He promised to clean and send them up to our room by breakfast."

"I'm sorry. Why did you undress outside the hotel?"

"Our clothes were drenched. Yuckiness would have dripped across the lobby floor, up the stairs, and—"

"Okay. I understand."

"How did Brayton die?" The softness of Lilith's voice reflected the torn heart beating in her chest.

"A coroner will determine the cause of death. For your sake, I can say we didn't see signs of foul play."

"A heart attack, maybe?"

"As I said, a coroner will determine the cause of death. Unfortunately, our coroner is quite busy this morning. Four other people died in the French Quarter last night."

Lilith stared at the officer.

"After you returned to your room, did you, or any of your other friends, leave during the night?"

"I would say no, but I was dead asleep. If one of us did leave, I was unaware of it."

"Did Mr. Colliot act peculiar in front of you?"

"I'm sorry, peculiar?"

"Did he seem concerned or frightened, perhaps preoccupied?"

"He seemed to be concerned with the tiny alley across

the street, but he wasn't acting strange."

"Did you smell a unique scent?"

Lilith didn't answer. She remembered Brayton's story about the fruity fragrance.

"Ma'am," Officer Tim said.

"Sorry. A scent?" Lilith had to stop and gather her thoughts. "Tayen, the older woman, discussed the scent thing with Brayton. He stared across the street and said if you could smell it … Hold on a minute. He was scaring us with a ghost story, and you're asking about that?"

"What did Mr. Collier tell you about the scent?"

"Ghost stuff. If you can smell it, she dealt it … Whatever. I fell asleep when we got back to the room. I was knocked out cold, dead to the world, until you knocked on our door."

Officer Tim raised his head. "Out cold, and dead to the world? Incapacitated?"

"You could have played the drums next to me and I wouldn't have heard you."

"Who bought you the drinks?"

"I don't know. The woman with Officer Angelo, she snagged the cards which accompanied the drinks. I suppose those would have identified our gift-givers."

"Who else is in your group?"

Lilith glanced at the door to AJ and Scott's room. "Two old guys. Scott is our nerdy IT guy. Gentleman always, kind to a fault, and incapable of any wrongdoing. He's our lovable boy scout. If you dig up something from his past, we'll pay for a peek into that file."

"How about the other gentleman?"

"AJ is the golf course owner who brought us to this convention." Lilith shook her head in frustration. "My first trip from the West Coast and I'm in a robe talking with a police officer. Jeez, not what I planned for."

"You've been nowhere except the West Coast?"

"Nope. A prisoner who can't escape to see the world."

Officer Tim paused. After a moment, he said, "Tell me a little about your boss."

"He keeps to himself and lets Tayen run the business. She takes his fantasies and makes them come true. Me and the other girls are part of his wish-fulfillment. The money is good and the guys at the club tip us well. AJ could've been in our room last night, and we'd never have known."

Officer Tim scribbled on his notepad. "Your boss is a golf course owner who brought you to New Orleans and bought you a bunch of alcohol. You said you were incapacitated last night. You remember nothing after the drinks?"

"We danced after the drinks and dinner."

"And you passed out while dancing with him?"

"Charlotte and I danced while Scott and Tayen danced together. AJ was watching, I'm sure."

"Three women dancing in front of your boss … and his business associate."

Lilith didn't know what to make of his statement. His note scribbling made her nervous.

"Ma'am, did the drinks come straight to you, or did someone hand them to you?"

"I sat on AJ's right and the drinks went from him to me."

"So, he was passing drinks to you."

It dawned on her. Officer Tim thought AJ had slipped her a mickey. "No, no. AJ isn't into drugging young girls."

"You said you can't account for his whereabouts last

night. Ma'am, please be honest with me. Do you feel safe?"

Lilith's tongue abandoned its connection with her brain. "No, no. Forgive me. He is a groping kind of man—gracious, not groping—he is a gracious groper and would never do that with his hands on me."

"He gropes you?"

A shot of adrenaline helped to short circuit Lilith's nerves. "What I meant was I don't know his background very well. This last summer I worked his shack with the other girls."

"Worked his shack?"

"In his shack. We serve food, drinks, and wear these—" Lilith stopped once she realized she was twirling her fingers while pointing at her breasts.

"Talia is—was—the exotic dancer. I serve the drinks and finger the—" Lilith's tongue was tied up tighter than a freeway at rush hour. "I finger the foods—I finger the customers—The foods for the customers' fingers."

Officer Tim clarified for Lilith more than for himself. "Exotic dancers at a golf course, and you serve the customers. Of course, you wear a top when serving the customers?"

"No! I mean yes. It's a golf course, with a topless family restaurant."

"A topless ... family restaurant?"

"We decided to go topless on the top floor." Her frustration grew. "The adults wear clothes on the top floor. And the kids too. The stripper dancers, the server strippers ... they won't strip for families, they strip in the topless restaurant ... they serve—not strip—upstairs. I work the customers down below—I mean, I'm on the ground below where ... Shit, I don't know what we do."

"You don't work as an exotic dancer or remove your

clothing for work?"

She folded her arms. "I might have to if I blow this job."

Officer Tim waited.

Lilith fumed out loud after realizing what she'd said. "Damn it. I can't believe I just said 'blow' and 'job' to a police officer while he is questioning me."

"Ma'am, do you feel safe?"

"Yeppers, I'm safe."

Officer Tim tapped his notepad. "Please, head down to the stairs and send the other young lady back here."

Lilith marched down the hall, furious over her unflattering description of a family strip club. She refused to acknowledge Charlotte as they passed. Once at the stairs, she folded her arms and glared flames on anything her eyes found.

Officer Tim inspected the door to her room as Charlotte walked toward him. He stood back, checked the room number, and checked the guy's door. Once Charlotte reached him, he quit investigating the doors and began questioning her.

Lilith crossed her arms. *Something wrong with our door?*

A maid approached from the opposite end of the hall. She looked past the officer, frowned, and checked her notepad. Then she checked the door next to Lilith's room. She spun on her heels to check the other side of the hall.

Lilith bent to her side, angling for a view of the door to her room. *Both the maid and the officer? What's with our door?*

Charlotte turned her head from the officer and toward Lilith. *What the hell is she looking at me for?*

Then the question rattled down the hall. "What the bloody hell did you say?" Officer Tim had asked Charlotte if she felt safe. Lilith gripped her arms and resumed her eye scorching of the hotel.

The two officers conversed in the hall after finishing with Charlotte. They waved Lilith back and departed.

Lilith entered the room and asked, "What the hell is happening, and where are the guys?"

"Somebody with serious skills in art design painted our logo on the street." Tayen twisted away from the window, perplexed by the events. "This is so far out of my realm of experience. I can't figure out how to unravel this."

"And the guys?"

"Scott called, which is why all our phones were buzzing. I'll text them later. Until then, what can either of you tell me about our street decoration?"

Charlotte blurted out, "Our boss is a pervy strip club owner who's exploiting Lilith and me. We're now a topless family restaurant."

Lilith fell face-first onto her bed. "My words failed."

Flummoxed, Tayen asked, "What words did you say to make AJ a pervert?"

"I described our rooftop restaurant like a whorehouse. Nerves short-circuited my tongue, and I switched 'topless' for 'roofless'. 'Working his shack' sounded dirty. Why did you call the temporary clubhouse The Shack? God, I transposed finger foods with serving customers. My spoonerisms are expanding from words to full phrases and sentences."

"Forget about it. What did you tell him?"

"We danced, vomited, came back to the hotel, and slept until the police knocked on our door," Charlotte said.

Lilith lifted her face off the bed. "You said that?"

Charlotte held up her phone and pointed to Lilith's pocket. "I called your phone, answered it, and slipped it in your robe before we walked into the hall. I muted mine and listened to you. I figured it best for our stories to match—and fortunately, telling the truth didn't hurt either."

Tayen studied her younger counterparts. "So, neither of you had anything to do with our logo on the street?"

"Sorry, mum. We don't have answers to the bizarre appearance of our business logo," Charlotte said.

Lilith popped up from the bed and stormed toward the door. "Speaking of bizarre, the officers and the maid were curious about something in the hall."

Tayen flung her head back. "One mystery at a time, please."

Charlotte and Tayen scooted behind Lilith.

"During Charlotte's interview, the maid kept checking our door." Lilith exited the room and waited for them to join her. "She checked her phone—the housekeeping list, I suppose. She tapped her phone, stared at our room, and then checked the rooms on either side. It looked like our room wasn't on her checklist."

Charlotte stood back, recreating the maid's actions.

Tayen leaned close to the door molding and ran her hand over it. "The molding isn't sitting flush against the wall. A hotel of this caliber would never accept poor quality craftsmanship like this. Do either of you see anything interesting?"

"I'm seeing quite a lot." A male guest staying down the hall stood short of three women in their robes.

Distracted by their investigation, Tayen's caution disappeared and her robe rode farther up her hip.

The lady trio combined forces and produced a wall of

withering scowls at the man. Charlotte said, "I grew up on a farm castrating pigs. Shove off, bucko, before I castrate something else."

The man navigated between them and left.

Lilith winked her approval, to which Charlotte responded, "That's how we do it."

Tayen nodded her thanks and proceeded. "Nothing out of the ordinary here. What upset the maid?"

Charlotte ran her finger down the crease where the door molding and wall met. She crossed the hall to another door and performed the same inspection.

Lilith rubbed the carpet in front of the door. "Did they lay new carpet?"

Tayen dragged her foot over the floor. "I'd say it's halfway to replacement. Why?"

"Well," Lilith stood and walked toward another room, "the wear pattern in front of our door doesn't match the others. Look at the other rooms. The wear pattern goes to the other thresholds, but not ours."

Charlotte stepped forward and bent over. "She's right. The wear pattern doesn't reach. And I smell fresh cut lumber when I get close to the molding."

Tayen bent over and sniffed. "It is fresh cut lumber." She stood straight and folded her arms. "AJ said he thought he smelled fresh cut lumber but attributed it to frayed nerves and exhaustion from the construction. But he wasn't imagining it; he really smelled it."

Charlotte checked the door molding. "Was our room converted into a two-bed room prior to our arriving?"

Lilith snapped her fingers. "Our room is 202 B. AJ and Scott's is 202 A. No other rooms on the floor are numbered with letters."

8 - The Devil's Tears

AJ and Scott rejoined the ladies in their room, bringing with them a dozen fresh beignets courtesy of Father Amare's gift card.

The sweet beignet aroma teased the girls into sniffing the heavily powdered sugar delights. Charlotte sniffed the fine white powder, and it zipped up her nose, causing her to sneeze. A fine white dust cloud flew into Lilith's face. Lilith aimed her beignet at Charlotte for a retaliatory sneeze, but Charlotte darted away and called room service for a juice and fruit delivery.

AJ recounted the trek to the convent museum and the conversation with the priest. It didn't escape Lilith that the conversation wasn't exclusive to AJ and Tayen. In the past, the bulk of these information sessions were between the owner and his general manager. Others were too far behind the senior duo's discussion to make meaningful contributions.

AJ stretched his arms skyward. "Lilith may have descended from a figure in New Orleans's underground history, according to the priest. I'm betting it is a history not recorded in books, but ingrained within the city's culture."

"The broken wheel logo and your book's publication … Is it possible this underground culture is somehow reacting to it?" Tayen asked.

"My book on the history of General Church Councils came out three years ago. I doubt somebody picked it out of a book bin and lured us here. It wasn't destined for the best-sellers list; it was an academic challenge for me to accomplish."

"If not your book, how about the Beagle's Bluff interview? The invitation came less than a month after it aired on every media format."

AJ shifted in his chair. "Damn Beagle's Bluff. Who'd have guessed my walking stick could create so much havoc?"

"You said the emblems are fading?" Tayen asked.

"Scott and I agreed they were fading. The one in front of the hotel was less menacing than when we left. The sun must neutralize or deactivate them." AJ leaned his head to the side. "The images laid dormant for centuries. No modern crossroads created an intersection at the sixth emblem. But there was one decades ago."

"Why are intersections so important?" Scott asked.

"Intersections, or crossroads, are basic to Vodun belief." AJ wiggled in his seat to get comfortable.

"Oh, crap. School is in session," Charlotte said. "Scott asked a question, and now the professor will lecture."

"Vodun," AJ began, "is the religion proper. Vodun refers to the West African variant. Vodou—spelled with one O and a U—indicates the Haitian variety while Voodoo—

spelled with double O's—is the Louisiana, or the New Orleans version. All three are the same religion at their core, but they all have diverging beliefs and practices. Tonight, I'll clarify with Father Amare which one is at work here."

"You're saying Vodun is in relation to our street logo and Brayton's death?" Lilith asked.

"I'm not sure what part Vodun is playing in this. If I had to guess, being in New Orleans means the double O spelling of Voodoo is what Father Amare speaks of when he says Voodoo Priestess. Whoever is manipulating the street emblems, they practice the Louisiana style of Vodun."

A muffled door knock came from the other room. Charlotte scooched off the bed and ran to answer it.

Tayen leaned forward and rested her elbows on her knees. "If street emblems were placed at intersections centuries ago, their locations were handed down too. We need to find those who activated chemical reaction."

Scott spoke up. "AJ, do you want to mention the other intersection?"

"Oh, Lilith's amulet. *The return to the intersection of the three estates* is a place here in the French Quarter."

Charlotte returned and handed out the juice selections.

Lilith protested, "That's the second time they've delivered to your room and not ours. Why not ours?"

"Their room is listed as the room of billing. Our room isn't on their registry?" Tayen leaned her head to the side and looked at the door.

"Sorry, AJ." Lilith took a bottle of orange juice from Charlotte. "What about my amulet?"

AJ didn't respond. He was watching Tayen as she stared at the door. "Earth to Tayen. Is something wrong with your door?"

Tayen didn't respond. She sat on her bed and swiped her foot over the carpet.

Curious, Lilith leaned over to see what had Tayen's attention. Tayen was feeling the carpet with her foot. Lilith lowered her foot from the bed and did the same. She raised her head to find Tayen focused on the guys' room.

Charlotte plumped down on the bed and said, "We haven't told them what we discovered in the hall—"

A flying beignet hit her in the face, stopping Charlotte dead in her tracks. She turned in the direction it came from and found Tayen pressing her finger against her lips.

"Charlotte is happy," Tayen's voice was filled with anger, "in finding a hundred-dollar bill outside our room."

Lilith froze. As much as Charlotte yanked on Tayen's chain, throwing food at Charlotte to silence her was never done. Furthermore, and far more disconcerting, Charlotte's usual witty comeback failed to materialize.

Tayen enunciated her words. "We came to this business convention to learn about best business practices. The street emblems were intended for our eyes." She scribbled on a piece of paper. "Seeing Lilith in New Orleans sparked a folklore about her ancestry, which we have no evidence to support." She held up the paper with her note, which read, *We're being listened to.*

Lilith recoiled with her hands over her mouth. AJ sat motionless, as did Charlotte and Scott.

"If you ask me, we're victims of a case of mistaken identity. I say we skip meeting with the priest and go for dinner. I found a wonderful place up north. Let's take in the city and put this all behind us."

Tayen pointed at Lilith; she was to reply back.

"Sounds like a good idea, Tayen. I will go to the

bathroom and get dressed for our time out on the city."

Tayen smacked her forehead with Lilith's robot reply.

AJ spoke as mechanically as Lilith. "Scott and I will dress in our room. You ladies can dress in here."

Tayen beat her forehead with her palm.

AJ gritted his teeth and tried again, this time sounding natural. "So Scott, what are the Cubs' chances this year?"

"Oh, I'm not into football, so I couldn't tell you."

"You're not into sports?"

"I like baseball, but nothing else."

Tayen fell back on her bed, beating her forehead with both palms.

They hurried to dress and left their rooms. AJ led them to a mall on the banks of the Mississippi River.

Lilith and Charlotte popped into the first clothing store they crossed. They searched for the best headwear, which would change their appearance. Tayen didn't object to their shopping marathon. Wasting time trying on hats was a good way to avoid drawing attention, as the priest had suggested.

With new sunglasses and baseball caps for the girls, they joined the guys in the mall corridor. Scott dragged them into a novelty store where a spacious circular alcove displayed samples of the local hot sauce producers. A narrow counter stretched around the alcove with sixty-six bottles of hot sauce.

Scott stepped up to the first bottle. "Who's with me? Baby sauces until we reach the throat scorchers at the end."

Nobody accepted Scott's invitation.

Lilith cringed when disappointment appeared on his face. She stepped forward. "I won't get very far, but give me a cracker and dab me with number ten."

Scott dripped number ten on a cracker and handed it to her. She put the cracker in her mouth and chewed.

All was well … until Lilith waved her hand at her mouth. "Oh, god. I was right. Ten is enough to kill me." She ran through the store and got a milk from the vending machine.

Charlotte had moved to number eighteen. "I'm not that wimpy, but I'm not going to number sixty-six, *The Devil's Tears*."

She ate the cracker with a good dose of eighteen. Lilith returned with two bottles of milk, the first of which was half empty. It was the bottle Charlotte snagged out of Lilith's grasp.

"Which one made you cry?" Lilith asked.

"Eighteen. AJ's next."

AJ shrugged off eighteen and moved to twenty-seven, *The Cajun Burn*. He licked his fingers and held out his hand to Lilith. She handed him the unopened milk bottle. "Damn. That's ridiculous. Thirty-nine are hotter than that inferno?"

Scott and Tayen tried number forty together. They toasted one another with their crackers and ate.

"It's okay to cry if it's too hot," Lilith said.

Scott winked at her. "It's a good warm up."

Tayen shrugged her indifference.

Scott fixed up two crackers with number fifty, *Blissful Insanity*. Scott wiped beads of sweat from his cheeks. Tayen moved to number sixty, This Shit Burns, doused two crackers with it and handed one to Scott. He bit down on the cracker. Within a second, he stretched his hand out to Lilith, who handed him a milk.

Tayen grabbed the last bottle on the counter, *The Devil's Tears*, and dripped a couple of drops on a cracker.

Lilith wondered if this was where sweat beads would show on her face. Tayen chewed, furrowing her eyebrow in thoughtful repose. "Why do people make sauces that don't enhance a food, but simply burn like the dickens?"

"How can you handle the burning?" Lilith asked.

"My mother loved cooking spicy foods. We teased her that as she grew older, her taste buds burned out. The dishes she served got hotter by the year. But when your mother says eat, you eat. And we ate until our pain receptors burned out."

AJ handed her the last of the milk. "I hope the beignets soak up the hot sauce, or I'm going to have an upset tummy."

"What now?" Charlotte asked.

"I have a stop to make at the convention center. You folks don't have to come. I'll only be a minute," AJ said.

"It's not like we have anything else to do."

AJ poked Charlotte on the nose. "You really don't have to."

"As I said, we don't have anything else."

They filed out of the novelty store and walked to the mall's far end. AJ stopped at a flower store and bought a single white rose. He didn't speak or look at them as he exited the door.

Over the train tracks and down the stairs, they walked.

Lilith whispered to Charlotte, "Where is he going? This is a parking lot."

Charlotte shrugged. She didn't know.

AJ walked to the northeast corner of the convention center. They stayed back, letting him figure out where he wanted to be.

Charlotte held her hands up and shrugged. Lilith reciprocated with her hands. They didn't understand what he was doing, but asking out loud seemed imprudent. A quick glance at Tayen showed she also was in the dark.

Lilith was about to break the silence when Scott handed her his phone. Tayen and Charlotte crunched against Lilith to see what Scott had handed her. Tayen stepped to the side once she viewed the picture. Both girls watched Tayen look away as she shielded her face from them.

Lilith scrolled down on the phone to read the article below the picture of a blanket covering a wheelchair. Lilith's heart skipped a beat. Charlotte pointed at the caption for the picture: Hurricane Katrina.

Lilith raised her head as AJ lowered the flower to the ground. He stepped back, folded his hands together, and bowed his head. It was a memorial.

She couldn't let him do it alone, so she stepped beside him and took his hand. He squeezed back and kept silent. After a minute, he opened his eyes, patted her hand, and turned around to find Scott holding Charlotte and Tayen's hands. They, too, had bowed their heads.

"Thank you. Please, up to the food court for lunch."

Ascending the escalator, Lilith peeked back at the convention center. Another rose laid next to AJ's, but she didn't see who could have placed it.

"I'm paying for lunch."

"Oh, Charlotte," Tayen said, "I'll put it on the business card."

"If you wouldn't mind, I would really like to pay for lunch. It's something I need to do." She added something atypical for her: "Please."

AJ intervened. "Go for it. Surprise me for lunch."

Charlotte pulled Scott by the arm. "I'm taking him with me. Go find us seats."

Tayen slid next to AJ as they walked to find seats. "Why let her pay? Lunch is just a blip on our budget."

"Our memorial sparked her need to participate."

"Participate in what?"

"People often need to participate in some manner when memorials or funerals are performed. They need to contribute something meaningful. It serves as a release, a coping mechanism. How many times have you attended a funeral and sat there like a bump on a log? You feel better if you do something other than take up space."

Tayen pulled a chair out. "I suppose you're right. Even the littlest gesture of help makes you feel useful."

Lilith sat next to AJ. "How did I participate?"

"You held my hand. Don't underestimate how important little gestures can be."

"Oh." Tayen understood. "Scott held Charlotte's and my hand after Lilith took yours. That's how he participated."

Lilith twisted around and found Charlotte standing in line. "She had nothing else to offer, except buying us lunch."

AJ nodded. "I overrode Tayen because it felt like Charlotte was searching for an avenue to help."

"And what about my participation?" Tayen asked.

AJ reached into his pants pocket and pulled out a receipt. "Now, now, honey. I believe I put the rose on the business card and not my personal one. If so—" AJ glanced at the receipt. "Yep, I did. You paid for the rose. There, don't you feel better knowing that you participated?"

"Yeah, actually I do."

Lilith reached across the table and took AJ's hand. "Were you an acquaintance of the woman?"

"I can't say that I knew her. Though I have no memory of living here, when Hurricane Katrina hit, and I saw the aftermath, my gut felt like someone put it in a blender and hit puree. Who amongst the dead were my friends? The woman in the wheelchair with a blanket over her hit me hard."

Lilith squinted. "You may have known her?"

"On to other things," AJ said. "I can't wait to flesh out Scott's Code Purple proposal."

Tayen leaned forward. "You approved Code Purple?"

"Safe transport of domestic violence victims between the courthouse and to the safehouses. Our brand-new facility will work as a transport conduit."

Tayen pulled out her phone. "See, this is what we should be doing on this trip. Working the business, not getting worked by someone else's business."

"Well, this has been a distraction from Crater Gully," AJ said.

"Consulting with geologists, environmentalists, and a volcanologist wasn't in my purview when I accepted this job, but I enjoy it. Who'd have thought draining a swamp hole—"

Lilith waved her hand to interrupt Tayen. "Did you say volcanologist?"

"Crater Gully's insides have the characteristics of a volcano. To be safe, we called in the U.S. Geological Survey to make sure an eruption wouldn't occur during someone's backswing on the thirteenth tee."

"I can't tell if you're joking or not."

Tayen smiled in amusement at Lilith's confusion. She turned to AJ and said, "I'll have Charlotte forward the files to legal and Manny. He can guide the construction crews on digging the underground tunnels and security rooms. But I must remind you, you're chewing up your bottom line. We can't afford additional loans if you create more projects."

AJ winked. "My bank account can stand a nibble or two. Your club membership drives will pull us out."

"If we triple the Captain's Membership fee and triple the members."

"Then let's install a Commodore Membership. Hit up the senior trophy wives club, pitch Code Purple to them, and price the memberships high. Leak the amounts of certain members' additional gifts, particularly Mrs. Holmes, and stand back. Those old gals will jockey for position over bragging rights as the largest charitable donor. By themselves, they'll pay for Code Purple, saving my bottom line from being devoured. Hell, depending on the viciousness of their jockeying, we might get to expand Scott's program."

Tayen drummed her fingers on the table. "I'll have Charlotte crunch the numbers so I can adequately design the Commodore Membership. I could include a once-a-year horse riding lesson as a tiny perk."

Lilith loved it when AJ and Tayen worked through a task together. She beamed as she congratulated them. "You two make a superb team. I don't always understand what you are talking about, but I do get an awesome vibe when your ideas take flight."

"Speaking of which," AJ leaned toward Tayen and clasped his hands, "how'd you know our rooms were bugged? I would have asked earlier, but the fear of a flying a beignet stopped me."

"While you and Scott were at the convent, Charlotte discovered the carpet outside our door—"

Scott and Charlotte arrived at the table, carrying lunch trays. Charlotte said, "After a night of heavy drinking and a morning of confectionery overload, I figured salads were needed. AJ, I got you a Greek salad. I hope it is okay."

AJ accepted the plate from her. "Yeah, it's the best decision for my stomach."

Charlotte handed Tayen and Lilith their salads. "I picked the insalata caprese for you. The red tomatoes and white mozzarella on a bed of green spinach leaves are supposed to remind you of the Italian flag."

Scott took the empty trays and put them on top of the trash receptacle.

Lilith was surprised by Scott's taco salad. "That's one big taco salad. Are you hungry?"

Scott sat at the table. "I didn't drink heavily, nor did I eat three beignets, like the one who is eating the Caesar salad."

Charlotte ignored Scott and addressed Tayen. "I did not find a hundred-dollar bill in the hall."

"I had to say something when the room went dead silent after I threw the beignet in your face," Tayen said.

"Turnabout is fair play. When you least suspect it, I'm zapping you with a doughnut."

AJ formed the time-out sign with his hands. "Enough of the Cy Young throw. Back to what Charlotte found in the hall, other than the carpet."

Tayen rolled her eyes. "I was interrupted and didn't get to finish."

"I was going to say, finding carpet in the hall doesn't rank with the Moon Landing."

"At least I didn't erect two three-story phallic monuments for a fertility cult," Tayen shot back.

"They weren't forty-feet-tall phallic monuments. The contractors had to erect the stone turrets first. That damn stiff wind from the North inflated the plastic caps on top of the turrets, and it looked like two dicks. It took months for people to stop joking about my offering to the golf gods." He added a jab at Tayen. "Pick-up artist."

"There it is," Tayen said. "Whenever you are losing an argument, you resort to bringing that up."

Charlotte intruded and asked, "What happened that day? You two fight like cats and dogs about what happened, but we never hear the full story."

"You want the story to judge for yourselves?" Tayen asked. "Fine, here is how it happened."

AJ stopped her. "Objective storytelling, please. No special pleading of your case."

Tayen sneered at him. "I was tired of my old coffee stop, and I stood outside, debating if I really wanted to go in. An older woman asked me what was wrong, and I told her. She suggested a new place for me and gave me directions, by tracing directions on my palm with her finger.

"The directions were easy. No need for the inordinate amount of time that she took. But I didn't mind because her charms and amulets had my attention. They dangled from her leather bracelet and brushed over my hand. The raw-sienna-colored one was spectacular. I couldn't take my eyes off it."

Lilith sat still and listened to Tayen.

"I drove across town and walked into a packed coffeehouse. One chair was open, and it was in front of AJ."

AJ dropped his head back and closed his eyes.

"He says it wasn't packed and my request to join him amounted to a come-on. We had a lively, engaging two-hour chat in which I accepted his proposal to run Shack One, a food truck and register for his nine-hole golf—"

Lilith interrupted Tayen. "The leather bracelet on the woman who gave you directions. Was it braided and dark brown?"

"Yes." Tayen squinted at Lilith's out-of-place question.

"The charms were gold and raw-sienna-colored—"

"—globe, and the continents were outlined—"

"—in onyx," Lilith finished.

Tayen stared at Lilith. "How would you know that?"

"Was she wearing an orange and tan bandanna?"

"Along with a tan top and chestnut-colored skirt."

Charlotte snapped her fingers to stop the back and forth between Lilith and Tayen. "Both of you encountered the same woman. Awesome. One of you needs to kill the suspense and give us the epilogue to this *X-Files* episode."

They all turned to AJ. "I'm a *Twilight Zone* kind of guy. I'll pass."

"The woman in the market. She called Lilith, Madam Priestess. Is this Voodoo at work?" Tayen asked.

Lilith leaned forward toward Tayen. "You drove across town to a packed coffeehouse. Charms brushed over your hand. Were you enchanted? Destined to meet AJ?"

"The coffeehouse wasn't packed?" Tayen closed her eyes in disbelief. "Was I enchanted? Lured to a coffeehouse on the opposite side of town. Were you enchanted at the French Market?"

"I danced the best waltz and tango of my life. Was I enchanted somehow?"

Charlotte waved her hand in front of Lilith's face. "I haven't seen your tango with that girl."

Scott pulled out his phone. "Let me show you."

AJ said, "This all started with Tayen's guess about our rooms being bugged. What tipped you off?"

Tayen pulled her hair back. "The carpet wear pattern leading to the threshold doesn't match the other rooms. You are in room A, we are in room B. Our floor doesn't have any other rooms listed as A, or B. And we can smell fresh cut lumber in our rooms, which tells us there's been recent construction. Possibly inserts to hide listening devices. And room service never knocks on our door. They knock on yours even though the requests come from our room."

AJ nodded. "Yeah, that would do it."

Scott handed his phone to Charlotte. "Here is the dance someone was kind enough to post on YouTube."

Charlotte took the phone and sipped her drink through the straw.

Lilith tapped her plastic fork on the table as she thought through their predicament. "Dead people, our business logo displayed throughout the French Quarter, suspicious hotel rooms, a woman who may have enchanted Tayen and me, and a priest who read AJ's book. What else do we need?"

"You forgot your amulet. It points to something important on Pirate's Alley," AJ said.

"Oh, thank you. I'm wearing a dangerous trinket around my neck. I'll sleep so much better tonight."

Charlotte dropped her drink on the table.

Lilith scrambled to right it before it trickled out through the straw hole. "Careful, sweetie."

"You asked what else. I think I have your what else." Charlotte handed Scott's phone to Lilith. "This is your dance with …"

"Her name is Melody."

"Okay, with Melody. Look on the street corner, next to the gaslight pole."

Lilith studied the frozen video as Charlotte explained.

"The guy in the white shirt and tan dress pants. He has

two muscular guys with sunglasses behind him. He may not look familiar to you, but I think I can guess who he is. AJ and Tayen might know as well."

AJ choked on the last of his drink. "I gotta see this."

Charlotte flipped the phone around to show them.

Tayen stretched across the table and swiped the phone out of Charlotte's hand. After a brief look, she fell back in her seat and covered the phone. "Shit."

"Confirmed," Charlotte said, "Tayen recognizes him."

AJ leaned over and took the phone from Tayen. "We don't run in the same social circles outside of Portland. Who would fit in both our social circles outside of there?"

"And you're not concerned that I know this individual?" Charlotte asked.

AJ studied the phone. "No clue who he is."

"But Charlotte and Tayen do?" Lilith asked.

"I'm a ravenous reader. That explains how I could identify your dance partner's father," Charlotte said.

"Who the hell is my dance partner's father?"

"Ernesto Cottrell. The most dangerous drug lord in Central and South America," Tayen said.

Lilith waited for AJ. She was at a loss for what this meant. Hopefully he could help her. It was not to be.

AJ had his eyes half closed. He repeated Father Amare's words. "Donning your broken wheel shirts … awoke forces … Hidden behind the rich cultural tapestry, the wheels of fortune and misfortune turned. Don't draw attention to yourselves. The eyes of friends aim to protect you …" The strength in AJ's voice reasserted itself. "But the eyes of foes serve to ensnare you. Shit. Somebody really wanted us here, and they did it with a fifty percent discount."

9 – Candles Revealed

Tayen mandated a strict adherence to disguises and avoidance of open public places. A drug cartel was watching them.

Charlotte and Lilith scampered from the food court to find clip-on sunglasses and ball caps for the guys. After an hour of paranoid loitering in the mall, Tayen remarked on their reflections in a display window. With dark sunglasses, they appeared more suspicious and shadier than before.

AJ solved their problem by hailing a cab and taking them to the Newcomb Art Museum at Tulane University. Lilith's skepticism about the fun they could have in a museum faded once they entered.

Scott lingered in the photography enclave, studying each photo to inform his practice as Broken Cove Accessories' photographer. Kimiko Kijano, designer for Broken Cove Accessories, wanted a catalog for her creations, and Scott had agreed to shoot images for her.

Tayen and Lilith devoured all the collections. They left the others behind as they worked through the museum.

The bookbinding and bookbinding tools trapped Charlotte and AJ into an afternoon of rigorous discussion. The subject fascinated Lilith for a few minutes, but not like Charlotte and AJ, who were like kids in a candy store.

Lilith pulled AJ out of the bookbinding collection and into the museum foyer. "It's dinnertime, nerd boy. Any ideas where to eat?"

"There is an out-of-the-way place Elliott suggested I should visit. Let me see what it was," AJ said as he scrolled on his phone.

Charlotte bounded up next to AJ. "Elliott has good taste. Where is it?"

"I'm working on it. Chill."

Tayen and Scott joined them. "Back to the hotel for a quick clothing change, then we take separate cabs to wherever we are eating," Tayen said.

Lilith swung her bag over her shoulder. "Stagger our ins and outs too. If we aren't in the rooms at the same time, it doesn't sound weird for us not to be talking."

"I found it," AJ said. "It's a two-thousand-foot walk from the convent."

Charlotte threw her head back. "God, I should never have shown you the measurement tool on Google Maps."

***

Four hours later, on the walk from the restaurant to the convent museum, Charlotte blasted away at AJ. "Arrrg! You had the measuring tool on Google maps set on meters, not feet. You extended our walk by a factor of three, giving us a two-thousand-meter walk, not two thousand feet."

Tayen chuckled as she walked beside AJ. "She wouldn't be griping if we weren't as far off the beaten trail as was the lost Roanoke Colony."

"You heard her, folks. Whoever spots the *Croatoan* sign sends up the flare," AJ said.

Irked by the excessive walking, Charlotte retorted, "If no one sees the flare, I'm calling NASA and asking them to retask Cassini-Huygens to locate us."

Frustrated by the walk and their conversation, Lilith said, "Talking with you people requires a master's degree. I never heard of Roanoke Colony, nor their song *Croatoan*, and who is Cassini Huygens? Do Scott and me a favor and don't speak over our heads."

Scott walked last in the group, behind the girls, and addressed Lilith's concerns. "The Roanoke Colony is a lost settlement that disappeared in 1588. '*Croatoan*' was written on a tree was the only clue left of their whereabouts. And Cassini-Huygens was a space probe around Saturn."

No one spoke after Scott's clarification. AJ, Tayen, and Charlotte strained to keep straight faces. Lilith refused to speak a word, nor would she thank Scott for his answer.

AJ halted their march. "It will be nine soon. After we turn left at the corner, we'll have half—"

Lilith bumped AJ's elbow. "Why is it so dark?"

"The streetlights are out," Tayen said.

"This is how procedural shows start. Unsuspecting victims walk into a situation where the audience obviously knows is dangerous. Normal, intelligent people leave in these circumstances," AJ said.

Lilith waited for someone to leave. When no one took a step, she said, "So much for any of us being normal."

She led them forward, with Charlotte and Scott close behind.

"Weren't we leading the entire way?" Tayen asked.

"With our destination in sight, youth and stupidity's courage grew—"

"Youth and stupidity didn't measure the map in meters," Charlotte said.

"Fine. The bold and valiant of heart finally had the courage to take the lead," AJ said.

"The bold and valiant of heart … *manicato*. A fitting designation for Lilith," Tayen said.

"I'm not bold or valiant of heart. I'm tired, pissed, and looking for who wrecked our day."

They reached the sheltered gate and entered the courtyard. The moonlight shone on the shrubs, which formed little paths for them to walk. Lilith stopped before they passed the gate entrance. "I say we wait for the priest. Entering without a clear invitation—" She growled at Charlotte's hand in the small of her back. "Stop shoving me."

"This is your invitation. I'm just helping you along."

Lilith spun around with the next push. She attempted a wrist lock on Charlotte, but her roommate was quick to escape. They struggled until Lilith changed tactics. Before Charlotte knew it, Lilith had flipped her and pinned her to the ground.

"You're only a blue belt?" Charlotte asked.

"I had the wrist lock, but you slithered out of it."

Dust fell in Charlotte's face, causing her to close her eyes and scrunch her nose. Lilith saw the sneeze coming and rolled away. She bounced up as Charlotte sneezed.

Tayen brushed the dust from her shoulder. "Just wonderful. We are covered in dust." She watched AJ wind up for a sneeze. When it seemed he snuffed it out, Scott sneezed behind her. Like falling dominoes, AJ, Lilith, and Tayen sneezed in quick succession.

Father Amare stepped out of the shadows. "Oh no. Not the dust."

"Is that an Ash Wednesday gag gone awry?" AJ asked.

"I'm afraid not. Let me get something to clean you off."

Charlotte rose from the ground and brushed the dust off her shoulder. "Father Amare, I'm Charlotte. If you would like, I can find a service to clean your gate."

"How polite, young lady. But time is of the essence." Pointing to the far end of the courtyard, he said, "Enter the side door to the church. Once inside, lock the door behind you and wait for a candle to light. I'll join you in a few."

Father Amare retreated into the dark.

Down the courtyard and to the side door, Scott pulled the door shut and locked it once they entered.

Lilith held up her phone to shine her flashlight. "Crap, my battery is dead." Four other phone lights came on. "Smart phones, the twenty-first century's version of the Swiss Army knife."

"Here we are, in a church disguised as a semi-trailer."

Tayen's thick sarcasm didn't escape AJ. "We're supposed to believe we are in a trailer."

Charlotte tapped on the wall. "It's background paper used in photography. Somebody painted it to look like the inside of a trailer."

"Do you trust this guy?" Tayen asked.

"Not yet. But my gut check says he is okay. Scott, how about you?"

"I'm neutral."

Charlotte passed Scott to the other side. "We're trusting two neutered males. Yeah, this will end well."

Behind the paper wall came the sound of an engine starting.

Tayen held her arm out and pointed at the wall. "A truck engine coming from tiny speakers. Pathetic. This has to be the world's worst carnival ride."

AJ shone his light on Lilith, who clenched her fists at her side. "I should be dancing, exploring the world. But no! I'm standing in a fake trailer waiting for a priest."

"Not the worst porn plot line," Charlotte said.

Scott shone his light at AJ. "Now she's channeling you."

The floor rocked and swayed. The sound of tires running over wet pavement and splashing puddles came from behind the wall.

"Foot pedals," Scott said. "Step on the pedal, and the plywood we are standing on rocks like we are moving."

At the other end of the simulated semi-trailer, a trapdoor swooshed open. A candle on a pedestal rose to one side of the opening. Father Amare popped up from the hole and shoved the pedestal against the wall. "This way. Use the brush to dust off before descending the stairs."

Tayen led them toward the pedestal. "I'm countering the neutered males' gut check and calling this the lamest carnival ride ever."

One by one, Tayen brushed the dust off them and sent them down the narrow spiral stairs. Lilith was first down the hole, but she waited for Tayen to enter.

"This is a stone turret stairwell, like in AJ's house," Charlotte said.

"It's going down a long way," Lilith said.

"Below ground stairs, in New Orleans?" Scott asked.

Charlotte stopped on the steps. "Plus, we are below sea level. Who the hell would put this here?"

AJ bumped Charlotte's shoulder. "Keep going. We'll ask Father Amare."

Moments later, they huddled close together at the bottom of the stairs. A short, narrow hallway was visible in the dim light.

Charlotte bent over with her hands on her knees. Lilith did the same after she took a single step forward. She looked to the side and saw Tayen pressed against the cobblestone wall.

Lilith rubbed her forehead. "Are you all feeling like if you threw up, you would feel better?"

AJ pinched the bridge of his nose. "Yes, and add a flashing headache too."

"Let's get this meeting over with as soon as possible." Lilith stood straight and led them down the hall, where a soft flickering light shone through an open door. Father Amare was lighting candles and didn't see them.

Lilith entered a half-moon-shaped room. With each passing moment, her eyes adjusted to the dim light, allowing her to see more. An enormous antique map of the Caribbean Sea and the Gulf of Mexico covered the flat wall from floor to ceiling and end to end.

Charlotte squared up next to the flat wall and reached out to touch it. "This is one big ass map."

"Careful. Please do not touch. This is a three-hundred-year-old map," Father Amare said.

She retracted her hand. "Alrighty then, no touching of the old sea map."

Tayen couldn't hide her astonishment. "Exceptional work. For a three-hundred-year-old map, the cartographer did an exceptional job. They look fairly accurate to me."

"Except the northern coast of South America. The coastline is too far back," AJ said.

Father Amare held out his hand to Lilith. "Welcome, young lady. If you are who we think you are, we can learn about the artist and what she left behind on this map. The map and its painter are why you are here."

Lilith shook his hand. "I'm the sweet girl next door, not a talented painter. My only exceptional trait is my eyes."

"Oh, tonight, we may discover that you have more to offer than you think." Father Amare hopped up to sit on a crate. "Please, everyone, take a seat. We have much to discuss, and I fear we won't get to cover everything."

Tayen hopped up on a crate and wiggled into place. "Tell us, Father Amare, why is Lilith of such interest?"

"AJ's TV interview awoke ancient forces. His blue shirt, with the white broken wheel, matched Jade Péchette's pirate insignia. We've waited centuries for the Voodoo Priestess's return."

"One shirt emblem broadcast in the French Quarter and I become the darling of an underground's fantasy quest?" Lilith asked.

"Legend says the Voodoo Priestess's ethereal blue eyes stole countless hearts and minds. One look into her eyes and a person's soul was submitted to her will forever. The Voodoo Priestess was a short woman who led a community of displaced individuals. They rallied behind the broken wheel, her symbol. Her accomplices included an older white man, who wrote her biography, and a tall French-speaking woman, who served as her confidant."

Lilith dropped her head. "AJ wrote a book, and I have the eyes."

Father Amare added, "Also, she kept frequent company with a short, sassy companion."

Charlotte asked AJ. "When they said 'companion' in the days of yours, did it mean lover or good friend?"

"In the days of yore, it meant lover. And don't think I didn't catch your exchange of 'yours' for 'yore' as a jab at my age." AJ turned to Tayen. "A tall, French-speaking woman?"

"I'm five-eight. That's not tall," Tayen said.

"Compared to Charlotte and Lilith, who slip under five feet if they slouch, you're a giant."

Tayen didn't answer, but she did glare at AJ.

He turned his head from her. "Father Amare, when you say Vodun, which one are you talking about?"

"All three. West African, Haitian, and Louisianan, but not the Hollywood version."

Charlotte and Lilith blurted out, "Hollywood?"

"Indeed. Your beliefs about Voodoo have resulted from decades of misrepresentation. It started with whites observing ceremonies at Congo Square or the summer solstice at Bayou St. John. Their false assumptions resulted in the Hollywood version, a Frankenstein religion, which would be unrecognizable to those from centuries ago."

"Which—if any—wishes us harm?" Tayen asked.

"The Hollywood incarnation." Father Amare pressed his hands together. "As you learn Vodun, you will learn to spot the Hollywood version, as well as how people use it to scare others."

"Are we being monitored in our hotel?" AJ asked.

"Most certainly. Ernesto Cottrell is here in the city.

His drug cartel takes direction from a shadow organization called the Bennington syndicate, and they have long sought the descendant of Jade Péchette. Ernesto works apart from the Bennington syndicate, but with Jade Péchette in the mix, assume both are interested in Lilith and her friends."

Lilith pointed to herself. "What makes people believe I'm related to this Voodoo Priestess?"

Father Amare rolled his shoulders back and took a deep breath. "Jade Péchette was born Chitimachan, the indigenous tribe of this land. She was taken to France as a very young child, became a pirate, and returned to New Orleans after its incorporation in 1718. Those who still follow her teachings and ideology, the Péchettes, live in New Orleans and throughout the Caribbean. They operate below the surface, hidden and ready to act once the descendant returns and the treasure is recovered."

Lilith opened her mouth to ask about the treasure. Father Amare raised his hand and answered before she asked.

"Jade's War splintered her community. The Benningtons are opposed to the Péchette's mission, and they are a lethal criminal organization. Their reach is long, and their influence runs as deep as the Medici family of Italy. Ernesto is part of the Benningtons, but not its leader."

"A physical description, a business logo, and a drug lord have pegged Lilith as the Voodoo Priestess's descendant. Circumstantial evidence rules," AJ said.

Tayen kicked the crate she was sitting on with her heal. "Prove she isn't a descendant, and we are off the hook?"

"No." Father Amare slipped off his crate. "Proving she isn't a descendant won't dissuade Ernesto. Your currency is convincing him you know everything, and he needs your help. He values people according to their usefulness. If you are of no value to him, killing you is of no concern. If you have value, at least you stay alive."

"At least? What does that mean?" Lilith asked.

"He disfigures people and sends them back to their villages as a message to never interfere with his business."

Lilith fidgeted with her amulet. "Disfigures sounds horrible."

"Okay," Charlotte interjected. "To keep from being stuck in this nightmare, what do we do to keep this asshole from burying us with Hoffa?"

"Who's Hoffa?" Lilith asked.

"He was part of the Roanoke Colony."

Father Amare spoke before Lilith could lash out at Charlotte. "This map room was constructed by the Voodoo Priestess three centuries ago. It lay hidden until two young boys discovered the old tunnel which connects to this room. The boys ran home and had their mothers return with them. One mother remembered the stories from her childhood about a lost map room. She had the boys cover the entrance and when they returned home, she called to Haiti, where the woman's sister lived. The sister was a Vodou Priestess, and she came to New Orleans to confirm this was the lost map room left by Jade Péchette. That Vodou Priestess was Priestess LaTonya."

AJ rolled his head back as his face turned white. Lilith couldn't recall seeing him in such pain. She turned to Father Amare, who stood as still as still could be.

"Who is Priestess LaTonya?" Tayen asked.

AJ rocked forward and rested his hands on his knees.

Charlotte hadn't taken her eyes off of AJ. "The name on the crate in the parking lot. I couldn't read Haitian Creole, but I could make out the name."

The air hung heavy, and the candlelight illuminated little. They waited on AJ.

He closed his eyes. "I began grad school alone. She befriended and helped me adjust. She was a lifelong pen pal, my anchor, the eternal fixture I turned to. God rest her soul. Priestess LaTonya died not too long ago."

"Why didn't you tell us about her?" Lilith asked.

"LaTonya preferred our relationship to remain on the down low. She informed me that if she and I met in New Orleans, it could bring trouble to my children and myself. The day she died was the day I stumbled and poked that hole in the rusted iron platform in Wasco's woods."

"What?" Father Amare's voice faltered.

"I stumbled in a stream, which led to the flood of snakes into Beagle's Bluff."

Father Amare bent over and dug his fingers into his calves. "At what time did you stumble?"

"Close to lunch," Lilith said.

Father Amare placed his hands on his hips and tilted his head back. "Priestess LaTonya died in the early afternoon, around two."

"Lunch time in Oregon is two in the afternoon New Orleans time," Scott said.

Charlotte squealed as she crammed her legs together. "Oh God, not now. I'm not pissing my pants."

"Settle down," Tayen ordered.

"I can't. When I freak, I pee."

"That's why you don't watch horror movies with me?" Lilith asked.

Tayen had had enough. "Father Amare, explain why AJ's stumbling and Priestess LaTonya's death have three people down here upset and the remaining three confused."

Father Amare tilted his head down. "Priestess LaTonya placed a protective spell on AJ. When she died, so did the protection, leaving him exposed."

"Voodoo is real?" Lilith's voice rose with her growing disbelief. "We're in this because a Voodoo enchantment ended?"

Tayen asserted herself to gain control. "Before we go blaming Voodoo, let's hear more about the Priestess. Father Amare, please."

"Priestess LaTonya, a Péchette, and her sister kept this room's location a secret from the Benningtons. After her death, I assumed the role of the tunnel guardian. I am the only one who knows where the map room entrances are."

Tayen fidgeted with her shirt. Beads of perspiration had formed on her forehead. "Forgive me, Father, but do you have a heater on?"

"No, there are no heaters down here. Breathe deeply and think happy thoughts."

She flapped her shirt on and off her chest, pushing air through her shirt. "I'm okay if we leave soon."

"This won't remain a secret forever." Father Amare looked around the room. "Since Hurricane Katrina, the Bennington syndicate has scoured New Orleans and the surrounding vicinity to find the map wall."

"Our hotel reservations came with a fifty percent discount. Would you, by chance, be the entity who gave it to us?" AJ asked.

Father Amare frowned. "Fifty percent? No business would shoot themselves in the foot by giving a fifty percent discount during a convention."

"What exactly is the treasure?" Tayen asked. She refused to look at AJ.

"Gold, diamonds, the traditional treasure findings. But there are many more nontraditional riches. Items which are rumored to be more valuable than the gold and diamonds. I assume these treasures are scientific discoveries, or perhaps works of art. Whatever they are, this map wall has their location."

AJ looked at the wall. "How do we reveal its secrets?"

Lilith slid off her crate and jumped upright, holding her arms up like a genie. "Abracadabra. Ah shucks, it didn't work."

Not amused, AJ pushed Lilith's arms down. "Father Amare, what words—what actions does she need to perform?"

Father Amare shrugged.

"Beetlejuice—"

"Not funny, Charlotte," Tayen rebuked.

AJ cupped the back of his neck. "This candle lighting isn't getting the job done. Is there another light source?"

"Jade Péchette didn't have electricity three centuries ago and look what she created with minimal lighting." Pointing at the crate below her, Tayen said, "Dig through these crates and find how this woman worked her magic."

Everyone hopped off their crates and opened them. An assortment of crinkles, clangs, and Charlotte's cursing came from inside the crates.

Lilith pulled out a cylindrical device made of wrought iron. "I don't have the foggiest idea what this is."

Tayen joined Lilith and scratched the top of the device with her fingernail. "This flat area is covered with a thick layer of red wax. Perhaps it's a candle holder?"

Lilith snapped her fingers. "A candle holder wall ornament."

They looked around the room, but nothing on the wall presented itself as a place to hang a candle holder.

"How many holders are there?" AJ asked.

Lilith bent over the crate. "I see five."

"Father Amare's candles aren't positioned well. They're sitting on crates, but the five outcroppings on that wall are better spots for candle lighting."

Lilith looked at where AJ was staring. Five wooden outcroppings were evenly spaced along the circular wall, which gave the room its half-moon shape.

"She set candles on the outcroppings. These are the candle holders." Lilith poked Scott in his ribs, asking him to join her at an outcropping. He took the iron candle holder and placed it on top. The rounded top prevented it from sitting. "A perfect candle positioning, but an imperfect pedestal."

Charlotte stood next to them and felt underneath the outcropping. "There are slots underneath." She took the wall ornament from Scott and flipped it upside down. "These are connecting nodes." She raised it into the grooves on the bottom of the outcropping.

Lilith squatted to see if it worked. "Perfect, it fits."

"But it isn't locking. When I release, it drops." Charlotte stepped to the next outcropping, pushed the wall ornament up, and twisted. It remained in place. She stood back and frowned. "Who burns a candle upside down?"

"Those things rotate," said Tayen. "These rounded tops are the bottoms. Find the locking mechanism so we can rotate them. I'll lock the wall ornaments in place while everyone searches for the locking mechanism."

Lilith studied the outcropping while Scott searched the wall. Charlotte jumped up on an outcropping, trying to force it to spin.

AJ said, "Searching the floor holds more promise than your swinging from—"

Charlotte slipped off the outcropping and crashed on the floor. "Ouch, my back. That'll hurt tomorrow." Before AJ could add insult to injury, she said, "Hey, I found …"

They waited for her to finish.

"Does anybody see a fireplace poker in a crate?"

Scott pulled a tool out of his crate and walked it over to her. "FYI. A fireplace poker is called a fireiron. And FYI to everybody else: I'm betting whatever we need for this adventure, we'll find in these crates."

Charlotte took it from him, and with all her weight, she stabbed it into a small iron ring lodged in the bottom of a thick wood beam, which ran from floor to ceiling. A clank came from behind the wall.

Scott spun the outcropping around until another clank sounded. "Rotate the outcroppings for the candle pedestals."

Charlotte used the fireiron to unlock the outcroppings, while Scott and Lilith matched the iron candle holders with their corresponding outcropping.

Tayen returned to her crate and pulled out two candles. "This red candle matches the red wax under my fingernail. That outcropping had red wax on it, so that's a match. Check the wall ornaments for green's position."

Scott stopped an outcropping's rotation halfway up for AJ's inspection. "There are two wax colors: a red one and a metallic white. Two candles for this place?"

"I hit the mother lode." Lilith rose out of her crate with three candles. "A blue, a lavender, and a brick red."

AJ stopped his inspection and looked at Lilith. "Tayen has a red candle."

"I'd call Tayen's a violet red with its bluish tint,

where yours denotes an intrusion of a rich brown."

AJ raised an eyebrow. "And you wonder why we want you in a twelve-step program for fashion obsession?"

"Does it matter where they go?" Father Amare asked.

While Lilith matched the candles with their counterparts, AJ answered. "The candle holders match specific outcroppings. We have to match the wax residue with the corresponding candles. But what I am finding curious is how pristine this room is. Three hundred years and no dust?"

Father Amare ran his finger over a crate. "You're right, AJ. No dust."

"And where's the water damage?" Charlotte asked. "Hurricane Katrina flooded this area. Yet, no water damage."

"LaTonya sealed the entrances with a material she mixed." Father Amare strained in looking at the map. "But you're right, there is no water damage."

"The candles are in position," Lilith said.

"Hold on." Tayen held up a pale-yellow glass globe. "I have five candle globes, and none are the same color."

Charlotte thought for a moment. "Candles emit light, and globes could transform the light through polarization."

Scott adjusted a candle above an outcropping. "The Voodoo Priestess understood how light works. Different candles with different globes yield different light waves."

"That's a lot of combinations," Charlotte screeched. "We'd be here forever. I say we use magic words. There's fewer of them than combinations of globes and candles."

Tayen rolled the globe in her hands while Scott lined up the other globes on the crate.

"Tayen, would you describe the pale-yellow globe as yellow, or champagne?" AJ asked.

"Champagne works."

"How about the olive-colored one?"

Tayen pointed at the pale-green globe.

"Call the gray one nickel, teal for the one on the corner, and indigo for the last one."

Lilith approached the crate with the globes. "Champagne, olive, nickel, teal, and indigo."

"Conti," AJ said. "Our first avenue into an ancient mystery. And New Orleans's first avenue: *Conti* Street."

"Oh, boy. An in-depth knowledge of New Orleans history will be essential for this treasure hunt," Scott said.

Charlotte sprang past Scott. "Conti leaves us with two combinations for the globe order. Right to left, or left to right? Either way, two choices are better than trying magic words."

Lilith stood on a crate and took the first globe from Charlotte. She lit a match and held it to the blue candle's wick, waiting for it to flicker to life. She turned her head when AJ gave her an order.

"Lilith, stop right there. Keep your head in place. Please do not move."

She froze in place. "What's wrong?"

The room grew darker by the second. With the single blue candle burning, they moved along the circular wall, so Lilith's face was visible to them. They huddled close together and stared at her. The shock on their faces terrified her.

"Father Amare," AJ said, "there is your confirmation. Those are the eyes of the Voodoo Priestess. Her descendant is our gift shop clerk, Lilith Daisy Peters."

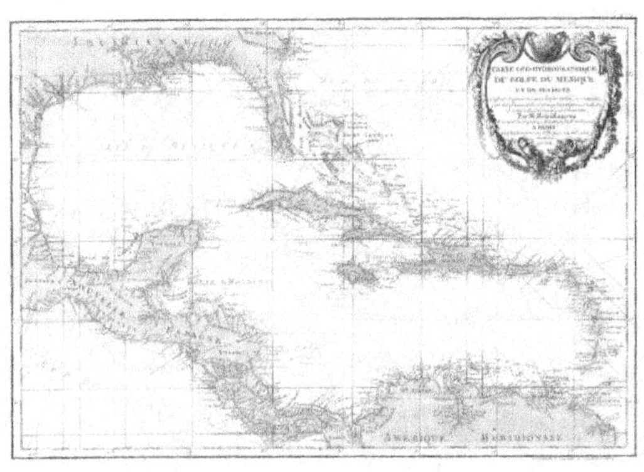

10 - Writing on the Wall

Had a comet streaked between the Earth and the Moon, nobody in the map room would have noticed it. What was happening with Lilith's eyes was no less shocking than an unparalleled cosmic event.

The unbroken attention directed at Lilith left her feeling vulnerable. "Stop looking at me like I'm a freak."

Charlotte raised her phone to snap a picture. "Nuts. My phone is dead."

Scott raised his phone. "Same here."

AJ pointed to his eyes as he described what was happening to Lilith's. "Your eyes are putting on a show of amazing light blue streaks, like the swirling arms of a spiraling galaxy. It's unnerving because we can't see your natural eyes. I can't explain just what we're seeing."

"Should I move? Or am I stuck here forever?"

"Where's your amulet?" AJ asked.

"Where it always is, on my chest."

"I think it fell off."

Lilith held up her hand to show the amulet between her fingers.

"Why are you holding your hand up?" Charlotte asked.

Lilith looked at her hand to find the amulet gone. "Holy mother of … Why can't I see it?"

"Are you holding it?"

"I'm pinching it with my fingers."

AJ turned to Scott. "Jade Péchette having mastery of light waves? You may have understated her abilities over the laws of physics."

"Mastery of light waves," Charlotte said as she lifted her black T-shirt over her head. "One candle and things turn invisible? I'd say she skipped mastery and went straight to owning it."

She adjusted the spaghetti straps of her teal-colored crop top. As she did, it became apparent she had done something wrong from the look on AJ's face. "Why are you staring at me?"

"A little warning next time when you're taking off a shirt. Your top didn't come into view until late. For a second, I thought you were stripping, and I wondered if I had any ones or fives."

Charlotte gave him a dirty look. "It's hot down here and I'm getting lightheaded. I took off the T-shirt to cool down."

Tayen pointed to the wall. "The map is gone."

Lilith spun around. "Where did our map go? AJ?"

"My guess is we're using elemental candles. Burning an element produces a particular light wave."

"English, please."

AJ scratched his head. "Whatever is burned to produce light gives us different tones and atmosphere. Our eyes pick up subtle differences, which we describe as soft and warm, or harsh and brilliant. However, when a scientist uses a spectrometer, they can break down a light source and tell you things you'd had never guessed possible. The read out of light will tell you if a planet has an atmosphere where life may be found, or if the planet is just a barren rock."

Lilith whirled her hand around for AJ to continue.

"This room's creator understood the principles of light well enough to manipulate what we can—and I have a feeling—what we cannot see. Adding the globes will change the lighting."

Charlotte studied the flame from the blue candle. "That's a sic flame. Has anyone seen a pure blue flame?"

"Arsenic burns pure blue," AJ said.

"Arrrg," Tayen growled. "This damn lightheadedness is irritating me. Light the candles and put the globes on. I'd like to get out of here."

"Are you sure your irritation is from your lightheadedness, or that AJ knows arsenic burns a pure blue?" Charlotte asked.

"Light the candles."

Charlotte wasn't challenging Tayen again. Her boss's tone of voice carried the threat of death.

Lilith lit another candle. "Whoa! A brick red flame."

AJ stood with his hands in his pockets.

"What's the matter, Professor?" Charlotte taunted. "Can't name—"

"Calcium."

She frowned. "I'm checking your guesses when my phone's charged."

"Scott's flame is lilac?" Lilith couldn't believe her eyes.

Charlotte didn't ask; AJ didn't tell.

Scott lowered the last globe, and the room turned black—save for the candles and globes, which glowed their respective colors.

"Okay. Wow. What happened?" Lilith asked.

"The candles? Are they floating in midair?" Charlotte added.

Scott rubbed his finger on the wall. He turned to Lilith. "It's there, but it refuses to let me see it."

Amazed, Charlotte said, "Light hits the wall, and the wall refuses to reflect any light. Black is the absence of light, and this is absolute pure black. That bitch knew how to paint a perfect pure black?"

Tayen leaned forward. "My feet are missing."

Lilith turned to see Tayen's legs had faded into the darkness below her knees. The crates were dark gray, and the floor hid in the darkness.

As they panned around the room, the map wall glowed, like a light from another world. The map's antique yellow vanished, and the old spotty brown lines transformed into solid boundaries. The sea and rivers flickered into multiple shades of blue, while land formations took on forest greens, mountain browns, and flatland beiges.

"Is this LED technology?" Charlotte asked.

Scott studied the walls. "No way is this three-hundred-year-old LED tech. It's an advanced reactive surface, but this isn't possible, even with today's tech."

AJ rocked from side to side. "If you move a bit, the water twinkles and rolls like an ocean."

Two curved lines faded from obscurity on the map. They grew darker and more pronounced with time.

"Those are ship's courses, if you ask me. Blue and brown lines ... and dates below them," Tayen said.

AJ read the dark blue lettering out loud. "1712, that's the earliest date on the blue line, and the latest ..." He searched the map, and when he found what he was looking for, he scratched his chin. "1724."

Tayen's impatience leapt out. "Just tell us."

Lilith was growing worried at her boss's worsening behavior.

AJ cocked his head to look at Tayen, while seeing the map out of the corner of his eye. "All these dates fall within the accepted dates of the Golden Age of Piracy."

"Jade Péchette was a part of the Brethren of the Coast?" Father Amare asked. "I suspected she was connected to pirates of old, but did she work with the likes of Bellamy, Bonny, and Blackbeard?"

"Not unless they sailed south to meet her. The Brethren of the Coast swarmed over the central and northern regions of the Caribbean. This map shows her domain was in the southern Caribbean."

"The brown line is shorter than the blue," Lilith said.

Charlotte mirrored Lilith and traced the blue line. "It came from, and then returned to, Europe. But while in the Caribbean, it sailed much further than the ship in brown."

"There has to be a heater on down here," Scott complained.

"Your physical exertion has warmed you. Relax. Breathe deeply to calm yourself," Father Amare said.

Lilith stared at Father Amare.

"What now?" Tayen asked. "We have five candles, nothing more."

AJ faced the center outcropping. "Before we reverse the globe order, let's cut the candles down to four at a time. Lilith, blow out the candle with the champagne globe."

Lilith crawled onto a crate and blew out the candle. With the flame extinguished, the room brightened. The wall's eerie eternal darkness became a cozy navy blue. Amazed by the change, she said, "Willy Wonka, eat your heart out. This room's quirkiness is better than the chocolate factory."

"Change the candles; change the wall coloring," Charlotte said.

The map's land formations didn't change, but the water turned a darker shade of blue.

"I'm gaining the impression this is Jade's nighttime template. Isn't this how a sea looks at night?" AJ asked.

Charlotte raised her hand and pointed to the far left, top corner of the wall. They followed her finger to where a foreboding dark lettering faded into view.

Impervious to Demons
If you know how

"Demons?" Lilith's voice crackled. "We have to deal with demons?"

"From Oompa Loompas to demons in one candle. So much for Willy eating his heart out," Charlotte joked.

"Father Amare, is your phone charged so we can record this?" Tayen asked.

"I didn't bring my phone," he replied.

"Wonderful. I'll have to memorize what we find."

"What's wrong with your phone?" Charlotte asked.

"No charge. Let's hurry up and try the other candles."

Lilith followed Tayen's order and lit her candle. When Charlotte blew hers out, the walls transformed from navy blue to plum, and the map no longer gave a nocturnal impression. The first message vanished. No sooner had it blinked out than another message appeared on the top center-left of the map: *DARE FROM ALL.*

"What's the dare, and who is the all? And I won't mention that it's in all caps," Charlotte said.

Scott pushed his glasses back from the edge of his nose. "How did this woman emit wavelengths and double … Nope, that wouldn't work. This is crazy advanced. I can't figure out how not to conclude she canceled—or masked—certain wavelengths. But that's fringe science."

"Can't the globes add wavelengths?" Lilith asked.

"Globes aren't a light source. They can block, or polarize, but this is something else. With four light sources, she … I'm babbling. AJ, what do you think?"

"I'm as lost as you. Light the next candle."

They did, and the walls changed again.

"Purple," AJ said.

"Plum," Lilith corrected.

"Yeah, okay. Oh, look, there's our third message: *Midnight's Royal Eye.*"

"Hey. I just thought of something," Charlotte said. "Not only did the artist configure the candles and globes, but they also had to adjust for the paint on the walls."

"Fascinating." Tayen wasn't about to entertain any more of this. "Next candles, please."

Scott and Lilith achieved a rhythm of changing out the candles and globes. Before he could ask what to call the color, Lilith said, "Hunter green."

"Here comes the next message. *Victor Visibly Vanquished.* Commit that to memory, Tayen."

Father Amare had sat and watched quietly. But he stood when the message appeared. His steps toward the map wall were measured and cautious. Lilith and AJ exchanged glances; this meant something to him.

"Father? Are you okay?" Lilith asked.

He didn't respond as he stood below the message.

Charlotte swirled her hand like the cursive writing of the message. "The writing is different. The other writings were beautiful, skilled calligraphy. This one doesn't have the elegance of the others."

AJ held his hands behind his back. "The clues have appeared from left to right with exact interval spacing. Not so for *Victor Visibly Vanquished.* It's off to the side, with different handwriting. Father Amare? Are you with us?"

"I am." He turned around and faced AJ. "I don't know what this means, but it is familiar. I'll have to research it."

"It seems to have rattled you to the core."

"Jarring is a better fit. But don't mind me. Please, continue with the lighting."

Scott and Lilith took care of the last candle change. "Christmas red," Lilith said.

Charlotte read the last message. *"Revenge for Cortes Delayed.* The writing has returned to the fine calligraphy." She turned around to see the circular wall had taken on a brilliant orange. "Wow. That's orange."

"No. This is an intense shade of orange. That is the color they call … Tiger." Lilith bit her lip, expecting a comment from AJ. When it didn't come, she turned around to find him, along with Scott and Father Amare, shielding their eyes.

"What is wrong with you guys?"

"Change the lighting, please. It is making me sick." AJ had closed his eyes.

Charlotte lit the fifth candle, returning the circular wall back to its invisible black.

Scott rubbed his eyes. "That was unbearable."

Tayen had placed her hand on Scott's shoulder, checking to see if he was okay. "The guys had physical pain, but we found it warm and soothing. Is that what the color tiger does to people?"

"The guys were in pain?" AJ asked.

Tayen nodded.

"It felt like a burning dagger. From my eye to the center of my brain," Scott said.

AJ peered over his glasses. "This is a weapon against men?"

The question silenced everybody, except Charlotte, who summarized what they were thinking. "Absolutely wicked."

Lilith blinked her eyes. "Any way. We have five messages, or clues. How are they going to help us find the treasure?"

AJ wiped the perspiration from his forehead. "It must be late. I'm feeling the heat you girls have been complaining about."

"Relax, focus on the calm and the steady," Father Amare said.

AJ turned back to Lilith. "Five messages … No, you're right. Five clues were hidden for centuries, and on our first night, we have all five. Lucky for us, we have the third clue, *Midnight's Royal Eye*. Lilith is a Babylonian name which means in praise of things which come in the middle of the night."

"Royal is a shade of blue," Charlotte added, "and we have someone with ethereal blue eyes. Lilith is midnight, royal is blue, and she has blue eyes. She is *Midnight's Royal Eye*."

"Perfect." Lilith removed her black T-shirt. "The woman in the market said the next full moon would mark my journey. Tonight's full moon was visible during our walk here."

AJ stood with his hands on his hips. "You and Charlotte need to warn us when your T-shirts are coming off. You just gave me the second titillating event of the evening."

Lilith tugged on her fuchsia strapless bandage top. "It's hot down here."

"What the old woman in the market said is coming true. The full moon marks your journey," Charlotte said. "But what makes September seventeenth unique?"

AJ cleared his throat.

"Other than it's Constitution Day."

AJ nodded. Her answer was correct.

Father Amare tapped Lilith on the shoulder. "Who talked to you in the market?"

"An elderly woman who helped me with fresh fruit yesterday morning."

"Can you describe her?"

"She was way taller than me. An amazing head wrap, light brown eyes, sturdy, not fragile by any means, light Creole accent, strong hands, and she smelled like cinnamon, nutmeg, and apples. Do you know her?"

"She doesn't resemble any living soul I know."

"That leaves dead souls," Charlotte teased.

Father Amare didn't laugh. "However, your description is reminiscent of a long-celebrated lady from New Orleans's history: Marie Laveau."

AJ laughed. "Charlotte opened her mouth and got it right. Marie died over a hundred years ago."

Lilith gulped.

"Did anyone see her besides you?"

Lilith's gaze drifted from Father Amare to AJ, who rolled his eyes. "That's a big fat no, Father."

"Who is Marie Laveau?" Lilith asked.

Father Amare rolled his head to stretch his neck. "She was a kind woman who many associate with Louisiana Voodoo. Her generosity made her a central figure in the French Quarter. Outsiders, white journalists, assigned her the title the Queen of Voodoo. A legend was born and has been propagated ever since."

"So, this Queen of Voodoo—"

AJ spoke over Lilith. "Back to why this journey starts tonight."

Charlotte countered AJ. "She didn't say 'starts'; she said 'the full moon marks' the journey. Too bad we didn't wait a couple days for the full moon. A full moon falling on the equinox … What a dope mark that would make."

Tayen flipped her head back. "Ghosts talking to Lilith on a day with equal parts night and day. I don't get paid enough for this."

"About this ghost—" Lilith started.

Father Amare addressed Charlotte's previous comment. "Equal day and night occur on September twenty-sixth for New Orleans, not the twentieth."

Charlotte batted her eyes. "Excuse me?"

"Those who look to the mystic day of equality know

the correct day of equal halves. However, the difference between the twenty-sixth and today is nine days. Vodou numerologists attribute the number nine to the Barons, guardians of death and the grave."

"This ghost queen—"

Charlotte spoke over Lilith. "September is the ninth month, and equinox is nine days away. Nines and cemetery guardians? Am I getting punked?"

Scott stared at AJ. "Nine emblems from the cathedral to the convent. The difference between the two plaques is ninety-nine years."

"Oh, Scott. Nautical twilight, the time we arrived here this morning, gives us another set of nines."

Tayen had had enough. "Get me to a bar. You can tell me all about nautical twilight over drinks."

"Alcohol isn't a solution."

"Tonight, it is," Charlotte said.

Father Amare led the way up the turret stairwell and reminded his guests: "Control your breathing. Slow your pulse. Find peace in the quiet—"

Lilith shouted, "Yeah, we got it, relax. But back to this ghost lady Queen of Voodoo who spoke to me—"

11 - Unleashed and Untamed

AJ stumbled and fell against the convent gate. The sudden swirling in his head had come out of nowhere and tripped him up.

Tayen struggled to keep from losing her balance. Her legs wobbled underneath her, making it difficult to place her foot where she wanted. She stretched out and leaned on the sheltered gate wall. It kept her from falling, but she couldn't right herself. She kept tumbling and rolling along the wall until she bumped into AJ. He and the wall formed a corner which stopped her from falling to the ground. Clutching onto his shoulder, she asked, "What the hell happened?"

He placed his hand on the small of her back. The moment he did, she pressed her body against his. From her knee to her shoulder, she didn't leave a gap between them.

Every nerve in his body fired with pleasure. All he could think of was kissing her neck.

Tayen swung her head around. "I haven't had a drink, but fuck. I'm drunk off my ass."

AJ took a deep breath. He struggled to shift his attention off of Tayen's neck. A slight turn of his head gave him a view of his IT guy.

Scott plastered himself to a light pole. He wrapped his arms around it, like a river was about to sweep him away.

"Girls?" Tayen called out, as she placed her hand on AJ's chest.

Her touch sent a pulse of euphoria through his spine and down to his groin. The girls' safety was paramount, but his body craved something else.

Charlotte answered Tayen's call. "I'm okay, but somebody better explain what the hell happened?"

Lilith had been crouching on the street. She straightened up and said, "Food poisoning. Our off the grid restaurant just laid our asses out. Damn. I feel horrible."

"This isn't food poisoning." Tayen leaned her head so far back she was looking upside down. "This feels like ecstasy or something else wonderful."

Charlotte rose off the street. "Mollys don't make you clear-headed, and at the moment, I'm as focused as the James Webb telescope. If you got a molly, blame the idiot who led us down Roanoke Colony."

"What's Roanoke Colony?" Lilith asked.

"It's not a rock band, darling."

Surprised, Lilith squinted and asked, "How d'you know that's what I was thinking?"

"Intuition." Tayen kicked her leg out and stepped forward. "Find an EDM club and let's get our rocks off."

"You mean rock on? Get our rock on?" Scott asked.

"Hell. Why not do both?" Tayen winked at Scott as she pulled AJ by the hand. "I'm ready for both."

Scott blushed with Tayen's seductive leer at him.

Lilith rubbed the back of her neck. "Were we talking about an EDM group earlier? Cassini Huygens?"

AJ couldn't resist Tayen's pull. "Damn, déjà vu is beating the hell out of me. Lilith said Cassini-Huygens, but she has a science avoidant personality disorder."

Charlotte put her phone in her pocket. "Eleven o'clock, and no priest. Looks like he ghosted us."

Scott released himself from the light pole. "Weren't all of our phones dead a few minutes ago?"

Charlotte spun around. "Talk about déjà vu. That's what I was thinking."

Scott pointed at her chest. "When did you and Lilith take off your T-shirts?"

Lilith raised her hand to her chest. "I think they came off at a strip club? I remember a wild light show. Some old guy gave me hell for exposing myself."

Charlotte rubbed her lower back. "The old fart smacked me in the back."

"Is anybody else confused?" AJ asked.

Tayen turned around and grabbed AJ's hand with both hands. "Who cares? The priest didn't show, we took a long walk. Screw it. Find a bar and drink until we die."

Scott put his hands in his pockets. "So much for relaxing and slow breathing to find our center."

Lilith pointed toward Bourbon Street. "Charlotte, take point. You know where the best dance spots are."

Charlotte marched up the street with Lilith several steps behind her. Scott walked behind Lilith. In the back of the line, Tayen held AJ's hand like a love-struck teenager. He was quiet to a fault.

Tayen swung her arms with abandon. She bumped AJ with her hips and brushed her arm against him at every chance. She unabashedly unbuttoned her blouse low enough to make her intentions undeniable.

AJ had never felt an attraction to Tayen. But with her hip swaying, coy glances, and caresses to his torso, she had ignited a burning ember of passion inside him. She smiled at him, knowing her flirting had aroused him.

Scott peeled off half-way and rushed toward a quaint bar. It didn't faze Lilith or Charlotte; they marched on.

Tayen daintily waved goodbye to Scott, who didn't even look back to the people he was leaving. She opened her mouth and clicked her tongue. AJ had trouble determining if she was angry with him or if she was trying to get his attention. When Scott entered the bar, she flipped him off and slid next to AJ. Her arm around his waist sent more waves of euphoria through him.

Charlotte marched ahead. Alert and unafraid, she nudged people aside, clearing a path for Lilith. They turned the corner, where Charlotte slowed their pace. Lilith nodded her respect to the Voodoo store on the corner. With her respects paid, they continued down Bourbon Street.

Gone was the shy girl from Portland. In her place was a confident, self-assured woman, who strode with authority and certainty. Sounds, which had made Lilith flinch on the first stroll down Bourbon Street, no longer intimidated her. Instead, they empowered her, causing her to throw her shoulders back. She held her head high and walked like a queen, surveying her kingdom and subjects. No trace of timidness or indecision.

A man approached her and offered his drink to her. She ignored him and walked away.

Several blocks down, Charlotte rushed away from the group and entered a dance club. Lilith waited for AJ and Tayen to join her, and together, they entered.

Tayen and AJ searched for seats. Lilith took AJ's hand and led him to the top tier of the multi-leveled club. He followed her to an occupied table, where she stepped in front of the two couples and told them to leave. The couples grabbed their drinks and ran from Lilith.

She pointed at the bench, which Tayen scrambled into as she pulled AJ with her. He scooched close to Tayen and saw their table had an unobstructed view of the dance floor.

"How d'you scare those people away?" AJ asked.

Lilith winked and turned to watch the dancers.

In a flash, Charlotte appeared with drinks for Tayen and AJ. She placed them on the table and took off her jeans. Below her jeans, she wore bodycon shorts to match her top. Lilith took off her jeans as well. They'd come to dance and had dance clothing under their jeans.

Charlotte tossed their jeans on the bench seat next to Tayen, then she grabbed Lilith's hand and rushed with her down to the dance floor.

Tayen wiggled against AJ, forcing him to put his arm around her shoulders. With his arm out of the way, she pressed her shoulder, hip, and thigh against him. Shyness didn't stop her from resting her hand on his inner thigh.

AJ's eyes sprang open. The electrical current running from her hand to his groin stole his breath. Every muscle in his body tensed.

Charlotte danced with a tall Latino man first. As the song changed, she switched to a young white woman of her height. Each new song meant a new partner, and Charlotte's line of waiting partners was unending.

Lilith danced. After a while, she returned to their table for a drink and a rest. Her eyes burned and flickered with a burning light. Those who glimpsed the celestial flames of her eyes lost interest in their friends. They lowered their drinks to the tables. Table after table, dancer after dancer, they all turned toward Lilith.

Tayen threw the girls' jeans over AJ's lap and snuck her hand underneath. With her hand between his legs, he tensed up and froze, letting her have her way with him.

Lilith winked at him. She didn't have to guess where Tayen's hand was. She stretched across the table. Tayen leaned forward and rose off her seat a bit. Lilith hooked her hand on the back of Tayen's head and pulled her in for a kiss. Tayen didn't resist and gave Lilith a deep, impassioned kiss.

Lilith released Tayen, leaned back, and left them to go to the dance floor.

A minute later, the lights dimmed, and a foreboding drumbeat transformed the club into a chasm of calamity. Side conversations ended, and faces turned to the dance floor.

Lilith stood in the center. Her appearance dominated the club, with every gaze glued on her. Two young men pranced around her. They towered over her. She coyly raised her shoulder to her chin as she rubbed one of the young men's biceps. The dim lighting found her eyes, igniting their mesmerizing glow. Men circled her, sending the faint of heart away. Two women strode beside Lilith and mimed washing her like a bathing queen.

She rolled her hips, brushed against the men, and danced erotically with the women. She didn't move to the music; it moved to her. Wherever she stepped, someone was there to protect her. Whenever she dropped to the side, she was caught. If she strode wildly about, nobody was in her way. Each dance move was choreographed to her wishes, even though she didn't speak a word or point in a direction.

As the dance ended, Lilith rolled over a table and whisked a candle into her hands. She stole a drink and took a large gulp. With her mouth full, she spit-misted the fuel over the candle and gave life to a brilliant stream of fire. In the midst of the flames, a woman danced as provocatively as Lilith had. The woman's hair burned the purest red.

The flame lasted a moment, and then vanished. People snapped from their trances and began talking.

AJ lurched forward and gasped for air. He spotted Lilith leaning over a table, exhausted from her erotic dance. A steady stream of sweat dripped from her face onto the table. She raised her hand to her top, which was soaked through. The domineering, unflappable dancer Lilith had presented on the dance floor was replaced by a terrified and trembling young girl.

Tayen and AJ raced to Lilith, but Charlotte reached her first and grabbed her by the arm. "Easy now. Follow me and let's get you back to the hotel."

"What did I do?"

"You danced the lights out of this place. Totally dope. Where d'you learn to dance like that?"

Lilith held her hand out to AJ. "My jeans. I think I should wear them."

"That's alright." AJ dangled both girls' jeans in front of himself. "I'll carry them back to the hotel."

Out on the street, Lilith said, "Something forced me to lose control. When I fell to one side, someone caught me. If I ground my hips, someone's leg was there for me to grind on.

Hands touched me where I wanted and whatever I wished for; it came to me."

Charlotte steadied Lilith by the arm as they walked. "I know. I need to get you in bed after your performance."

"Why am I about to pass out? I didn't drink anything."

"It's been a long day. You're tired, and a good night's sleep will do you good."

"Thank you for caring for me, Charlotte. You are the best girlfriend I could have. I promise to pay you back."

"Payment is coming sooner than you think."

AJ and Tayen rushed behind the girls. Tayen continued flirting. She tried taking the jeans away from AJ. She whispered to him, "If they ask, say you spilled a drink." She leaned against him and bit his earlobe.

"What has gotten into you?"

"Nothing yet. But when the girls fall asleep, you can change that."

AJ knew better than to succumb to his impulses than he did in the dance club, but his body was screaming for Tayen. After a torturous walk to the hotel, AJ handed Tayen the girls' jeans and rushed to unlock his door. He grabbed a pair of underwear and entered the bathroom. Upon walking out, he found a trail of tossed clothing stretching from the connecting doors to his bed. Tayen was under the covers, with one leg over the bedsheet.

"If Scott walks in, your plans are ruined," AJ said.

"He is passed out in our tub, so we will be alone."

AJ stepped toward the door to the connecting room.

Tayen raised her leg under the sheets. "I wouldn't open that door. The girls beat us to it. Charlotte had Lilith seduced and half-undressed before I could escape the room."

AJ turned around to face Tayen. "Where did all this sexual energy come from?"

"I don't know and don't care. All I want is to burn it off as fast as we can."

AJ walked to the side of the bed. "What if Scott wakes up and comes in?"

Tayen pulled the bed sheet back for AJ. "The more the merrier. I can do both of you, or … both of you can do me."

***

In the morning, AJ woke to a single brilliant ray of sunlight reflecting from the wall mirror. Groggy to the point of falling back asleep, he wasn't immediately concerned with Scott in the adjacent bed. He ran through his wake-up checklist while lying on his back.

What time is it? Early, too damn early. Where am I? New Orleans. Jesus, why is my stomach screaming at me? I wonder if Tayen is as hungry?

Panicked, he swung his arm at the far side of the bed, where Tayen was. But his arm didn't hit her, it crashed onto her pillow. He sprung up to find her. She was gone. But AJ's panic didn't subside. A trace of her clothing had to be visible. Scott would have had to move her bra from his pillow when he went to bed. If he didn't, it had to be under his sheets.

He rolled out of bed and landed with a thud. Scott stirred at the sound and vaulted into sitting upright. He strained to focus on AJ. "Jeez. I'm so hungry I'm sick."

AJ struggled to stand.

Scott grabbed his vibrating phone and glasses off the nightstand. "Somebody is up. Let me see who it is."

AJ tested his balance by lifting his foot. "I'm sore and stiff, like I didn't move during the night."

"Lilith just left and went for breakfast." Scott scrolled through his messages. "Charlotte left half an hour ago. She will meet us at noon when Dean and Ladonna arrive from visiting her parents. Uh-oh. Their family visit must not have gone well if they left a day early."

AJ listened, but he was eying Scott's bed in search of Tayen's bra.

"Tayen left an hour before Charlotte."

Scott's mentioning of Tayen forced AJ to brace himself. He wished Scott wouldn't ask about Tayen being in AJ's bed, but if Scott asked, how would he answer?

"Strange. They all said they're taking personal time. Could it be our 'together time' is driving them bananas?"

AJ remained nonchalant. "Possible. Hey, when did you get to bed?"

"It's hard to say." Scott reached for the nightstand and grabbed a slip of paper. "I had a couple of drinks at that out-of-the-way bar. But this receipt indicates I had six."

AJ noticed the troubled look on Scott's face. "You don't remember the drinks?"

"I don't. Nor how I got back here. I dreamed I fell deathly ill. And the girl Lilith danced with the other day. She cared for me until I was out of danger."

"Ah, every guy's dream, being cared for by a beautiful woman. Say, let's go for breakfast before I faint. We can try the one you were curious about."

Scott jumped out of bed and ran to the bathroom. "I'll be ready in a jiffy."

When the door shut, AJ rummaged through Scott's bed sheets. Tayen's bra wasn't there. He reversed course and rearranged the sheets so it didn't look like he ransacked Scott's bed.

They scurried to the restaurant. Two additional side orders of ham were required to satiate their appetites. Afterward, they proceeded down Pirate's Alley to survey the intersection which had engrossed them the day before.

Scott impressed AJ with his knowledge of the types of stone used for the streets. He identified the sections of granite and dolomite before proceeding to the slate and brick areas.

Tears formed in AJ's eyes. "My IT guy and my club professional share my geeky hobby of geology."

"Thom Hua? She's an amateur geologist?"

"She's closer to a professional than an amateur. Have you met her?"

"Not yet," Scott said. "She's busy with the course, and I'm buried in a closet with computers."

"You'll love her. But hey, I must confess I was wrong about the emblems," AJ pointed at the street. "Their placement was in recent times, not centuries ago."

Scott balked. "There was no priest to confirm yesterday's events, so let's chalk it up to life's oddities which defy explanation."

AJ pivoted on his heels and led them back to the hotel lobby. They entered the hotel and took seats. AJ took a single chair and Scott sat at the far end of a couch.

Lilith entered shortly thereafter, followed by Charlotte. Neither spoke. Charlotte plopped in the chair opposite AJ, and Lilith sat in the middle of the couch.

"So," Scott asked, "how was your morning?"

"Fine," came the girls' synchronized response. Neither of them looked up from their phones.

Scott glanced at AJ, who nodded to leave them alone.

Tayen hustled in through the front door. She took one look at AJ and dipped her head as she walked to take a seat beside Scott. Like her younger counterparts, she focused on her phone rather than speaking to anybody.

Scott slow-nodded AJ away from saying a word.

AJ ignored the advice. Upon opening his mouth, he learned women's intuition was not an urban legend. The three women lowered their phones and cast death stares at him. Had it not been for the synchronization of their death stares, he might have spoken.

With AJ's silence secured, the ladies returned to their phones.

Chefs Dean and Ladonna had walked into the lobby unnoticed. Hearing Dean clear his throat, Tayen jumped up and hugged Ladonna. "Welcome. Your room will be ready in a few minutes, but I'm surprised you managed to arrange an early check-in."

Ladonna said, "Early check-ins aren't a big deal. Who's the joker who persuaded them to give us room 644?"

"You aren't next to us?"

"Not even close."

"Is something wrong with the room?" Lilith asked as she stood.

Ladonna side hugged Lilith. "It's the haunted room. We are checking into a ghost room on International Talk Like a Pirate Day. What a way to start this convention."

"International Talk Like a Pirate Day?"

Dean poked Lilith's shoulder. "You didn't read the clubhouse charter. She works at a Pastafarian facility and isn't aware that September nineteenth is International Talk Like a Pirate Day. Time to find a plank and make her walk it. Arrrg."

After a group laugh, Charlotte said, "September nineteenth is tomorrow; today is the eighteenth."

Ladonna said, "Boy, what did you folks do to lose a day?"

Charlotte checked her phone.

Dean said, "We spent three full days with her parents, and we left before Franklin's theorem on visitors kicked in this morning."

"What's Franklin's theorem?" Lilith asked.

"Visiting guests and fish have one thing in common: on the third day, both begin to stink."

Everybody was too consumed with their phones to laugh at Chef Dean's joke.

"Wow. This is a tough crowd."

AJ stammered as he checked his phone. "We slept through an entire day? Drinks on the seventeenth … and the eighteenth disappeared? No wonder we were so hungry."

"Mother fuck." Charlotte shot out of her seat and ran out of the lobby toward the stairs, dropping her phone as she ran.

Shocked by Charlotte bolting from the lobby, Ladonna asked, "What's wrong with her?"

Tayen lied to hide the real reason for Charlotte's flight. "She has a UTI, and when you gotta go, you gotta go."

"Oh God," Ladonna said. "I've had my fair share of those. We better check on her."

Tayen slid out of her seat and followed Ladonna up the stairs, tapping Lilith on the knee as she passed.

Tayen made sure Lilith saw her pointing discreetly at the seat. Lilith spotted Tayen's phone and scooched over the couch to pick it up. After reading the screen, she lowered the phone and whispered to AJ. "Tayen's flight itinerary lists our departure on the sixteenth, not the fifteenth. I know for a fact we left on the fifteenth."

AJ leaned back in his seat.

Scott held up his phone. "Lilith's dance in the street, the YouTube posting date is the sixteenth. At the same time, our flight itineraries have us over Colorado."

Lilith squeezed her legs together. "Who knew Charlotte's UTIs were contagious?"

Dean returned. "I have our room keys. When I return, there's an old acquaintance of mine we should visit."

"Hurry back. I'm looking forward to meeting your friend," AJ said.

Watching Dean turn the corner, Scott announced, "I found a video of Lilith dancing a second time on TikTok. Apparently, while I drank in my little hotel bar, Lilith burned down the dance floor on the seventeenth. Two dances in two days on two social media outlets?"

AJ squeezed the chair's arm. His anger came through his voice. "Things got funky on us after we arrived at the convent museum."

"On time at nine," Scott said.

"Nine o'clock, but we left from the museum at eleven."

Lilith ran her thumb over her amulet. "We stood in the street for two hours? I have no memory of doing that. Then, we were panting like dogs, exhausted, and experiencing déjà vu, at eleven?"

AJ leaned forward in his chair. "Two hours and one day, missing. Did a Voodoo Priestess get to us?"

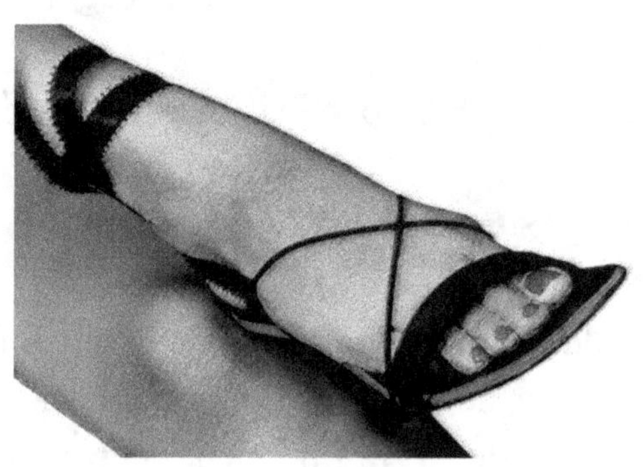

12 - Who Wore What

Five weeks later, after returning to Portland, the emotional upheaval from the small business convention still weighed on the group. Any useful information they'd learned in the convention was overshadowed by the events beyond the convention.

The team's open sexual activity made Lilith uncomfortable. The intrusive recurrence of seeing her bosses in bed together—while she and Charlotte did the same—sent her into hiding in solitary carve-outs in the construction. One positive coming out of the convention was her deepening relationship with Charlotte.

The roommates' intense physical intimacy had turned into an authentic love. Their shared open displays of affection warmed everyone's hearts. Talia defended the girls whenever someone teased them about dating. Broken Cove Accessories designer, Kimiko, was the primary instigator of the teasing.

Lilith took her lunches at the rooftop restaurant to limit her contact with AJ and Tayen. With grand opening four months away, she would never have the magnificent place to herself once they opened.

The elevator door opened, and two excited golden retrievers wagged their tails upon seeing Lilith. Her 'aw' of delight at seeing Sonny and Cher soon became a groan of protest. If the dogs were here, so was AJ.

The golden retrievers' noses switched from happy greetings to nosing her lunch bag. She maneuvered around them to the upper-level railing. The upper tier bar area afforded her panoramic views over the golf course. Tables and chairs were scheduled to arrive in early February, which meant the railing was the only place to sit.

Jumping and twisting onto the railing, she took a carrot from her little brown bag. The dogs sat and gave her their best beg-stare. As 'no' formed on her lips, dog biscuits sailed past her shoulder.

She knew one day she'd have to face him, but she still had to talk herself through it. *Calm down, relax. It is AJ, the kind owner and your friend.* She took a deep breath and asked, "How can you sneak up on me with these tiles?"

AJ leaned on the railing with a half-eaten sandwich in his hand. "Because my dogs distracted you."

She spun around to face the bar. *Discuss anything, but don't let it devolve into a discussion about New Orleans.* "I love this flooring. The gorgeous dark chocolate marble … and the gold veins. You're transported to an ancient royal palace the second the elevator door opens."

"Thanks to Tayen's connections. When they cut it from the quarry, her friend set it aside and called her. She pounced, and we have a one-of-a-kind floor," AJ said.

Lilith held up her hand and rubbed her thumb over her fingertips.

"Yes, very expensive. It almost broke the bank. Had she not persuaded her friend to discount it … " AJ paused. "Funny. Have you noticed she does a lot of 'persuading' when she wants something?"

She avoided his question and steered the conversation away from discussing Tayen. "A million-dollar floor with a million-dollar view better work. I'm afraid to ask how far in debt you've dug yourself, especially since you're expanding the stores."

"The addition of more business units meant the outer ring had to expand. A single floor around the center building has turned into a four-story shopping ... Mall isn't the word, is it?"

"Shopping complex is best. I wasn't thrilled about naming it The Village, but it's better than the shack you started in. From a cheap plywood shack to a mini-Vegas casino." Lilith turned to AJ. "I've never been to Vegas or in a casino. Is Mr. Davidson's comparison right?"

"Not far off."

"Casinos are expensive to build."

AJ dipped his head as he turned to face Lilith. "You're preoccupied with my finances. Why?"

"Because Charlotte is stressed over it?"

"She shared my financial picture with you?"

"I observed her. She didn't straight out tell me."

"You poked, prodded, and cajoled her into telling you."

Lilith bit her lip. "Don't all girlfriends?"

AJ didn't answer.

"Is a forty-year mortgage—"

"Damn it. That was Tayen joking around. I'm not saddling myself with an impossible monthly payment for the rest of my life."

"So … I probably misunderstood the turbo solution."

AJ pulled dog biscuits from his pants pocket. "Turbo doesn't mean converting golf carts into mini-Lamborghinis. Turbo means our club pro and her friends."

"Thom and her friends are turbo? Urban dictionary?"

AJ flipped the biscuits to the dogs. "I see Charlotte's taught you a thing or two."

"Then what's turbo?" Lilith asked.

"Thom's professional golfing buddies love the front nine. After Thom showed them the back nine layout, they contacted tour officials. She believes tour administrators will be impressed and will evaluate the course to find its slope and rank ratings. If the ratings are super, women's professional golf may have a new tour stop, and we'll have tour revenue."

"A lot or steady revenue?"

"A women's tour stop is steady. A women's major tour event, a lot. However, a men's tour stop would be a lot and steady. A men's major, like the US Open, that would be enormous carrying forward."

Lilith frowned. "Why do the men's events bring in more money than the women's?"

"Popularity. Unfair, but that's how it works. Ounce for ounce, women golfers are as good as the men and should be rewarded for it."

Lilith smiled. For the first time in weeks, it felt like she and AJ weren't estranged from one another. She wanted to keep it going. "Charlotte tells me Thom's friends have bought up half of the lots behind the front nine."

AJ gazed at the area Lilith was referring to. "I can't say I'll enjoy the noise of luxury homes being built over the coming months. Lumber crashing, nail guns shooting, cement trucks rumbling. I have from Halloween's Eve through St. Valentine's Day without construction noise. However, an April vacation may not be out of the question."

"What will people think when the owner leaves a month after grand opening?"

"Better a scoundrel than a frayed-nerved, agitated, nutty owner who never escaped months of construction."

Lilith understood. "You live here twenty-four-seven. You may have cause to vamoose."

AJ stretched and twisted at the waist. "Pasta-de-faria's needs tables and lighting. The second-floor employee locker rooms need lockers and toilets. Electrical and plumbing contractors are everywhere. The kitchen is waiting on appliances, and we gotta find a rum supplier. God, what a to-do list."

"How about my spot?"

"The first-floor gift shop and reception areas are the easiest to finish, so it's last on Charlotte's Memo Pad To-do List." AJ's phone vibrated in his pocket.

Lilith tilted her head to the side. "I suppose. It's just shelves and a greeting desk."

"Uh-oh. Tayen wants us in the office, now."

"What happened?"

"Tayen's text said Charlotte is in trouble, but she didn't elaborate."

They ran to the clubhouse across the road and entered through the front doors. Talia stood behind the reception counter and pointed them at Tayen's office.

Lilith rushed to Charlotte's side. Sitting in Tayen's chair and sipping water, Charlotte said, "I'll be okay."

Lilith knelt close for emotional support. "What happened?"

Tayen said, "Mrs. Ferreira chatted with Charlotte about our trip. The Ferreiras left for Europe a day after we got back. Upon their return, Mrs. Ferreira was itching at the chance to discuss our trip. The Ferreiras are regulars and visit New Orleans every spring. Their consistent patronage has earned them a regular spot in the same room at the same hotel."

"The hotel we stayed at," AJ said.

Scott burst into the room and rushed to Charlotte. He knelt and held her hand.

"I'm okay, Scottie. Now that you are here, I'm better than okay." Charlotte squeezed his hand.

Tayen continued: "Mrs. Ferreira was comparing her two-story luxury suite to our adjoining rooms when I overheard their discussion. I rushed to her side—"

Lilith finished for Tayen. "Something scared her and she pissed her pants." Charlotte was sitting on a towel, which told Lilith everything she needed to know.

AJ sat in the chair next to Charlotte. "What did she say?"

"Mrs. Ferreira knew where we stayed by Charlotte's description of the stairs, the elevator, and even the wallpaper color. Her ridiculous knowledge of the hotel brought to light some troubling details. Did I mention they are regulars?"

AJ held up his hands in defense. "What did she tell Charlotte?"

"First, our wing doesn't have connecting rooms. Yet

you and Scott were in 202 A while we were in 202 B. The police officers knew something was amiss, and the maid was bewildered. 202 B doesn't exist, according to Mrs. Ferreira."

"Don't forget the bathrooms," Charlotte said.

"Oh, yeah. How could I forget? Mrs. Ferreira said if you stay in a connecting room in our hotel, the bathroom has showers, not tubs, unless you are in a luxury suite."

Worried about Charlotte's state of mind, Lilith pleaded, "Can we discuss this later?"

"Don't worry, I pissed everything out with Mrs. Ferreira. I'm dry as a bone on the inside, but," Charlotte pointed to her lap, "I nailed my pants real good."

Tayen rolled her eyes. "Mrs. Ferreira knew the carpet was replaced two years ago."

AJ waited.

"Hell no. I'm not rehashing that conversation. So, I saved the best for last. Charlotte's precise positioning of our door put our room in front of the Ferreiras' luxury two-story suite. Our room—202 B—doesn't exist. Yours and Scott's room supposedly occupied what was the suite's living room."

Charlotte responded to AJ's raised eyebrow. "My pants-pissing was justified. Don't ya think?"

"Fresh cut lumber," AJ pressed his hands together, "someone constructed two rooms for us inside a larger suite."

Lilith blurted out. "Nothing absurd in weeks, and with one discussion, we're back in the convention's chaos. I'm flying back to New Orleans and hunting down that priest we were supposed to meet."

"What happened to the balcony bedroom?" Scott asked. "If we were in a suite, there was an upstairs balcony bedroom with a full bathroom."

"We never received the complimentary morning

newspaper," AJ said.

"Nobody cares about a missing morning newspaper," Tayen huffed.

"We didn't get a newspaper because of the dates," AJ said. "The eighteenth disappeared. Removing any source with a date on it would reduce the chance of us discovering it was the nineteenth. They didn't account for Chef Dean and Chef Ladonna. Had we not looked at the flight itineraries right then, we might have attributed a missing day to a faulty memory."

Charlotte stood. "I am going to change."

Lilith stood with her.

"Oh, bless you, honey. But I have jeans in my desk drawer. I'm not headed home."

Lilith gave her hug and stepped back.

"With Charlotte on the mend, I'm going back to the workshop. One GPS system to perfect," Scott said.

Lilith tilted her head.

"Golf ball Positioning System, not global positioning system," Tayen said. "AJ wants an app for golfers to mark yardage and strokes for data collection. The information will determine our slope and course rating."

"Oh … I see."

"You have no idea what she said, do you?" AJ asked.

Lilith snarled her lip at AJ, refusing to answer him.

AJ shook his head. "I had hoped the convention was a practical joke. Something that was one and done."

Tayen removed the towel from the chair. "I wish it never happened."

"Do you care to clarify which one of the *its* you're talking about?"

Tayen looked at Lilith and back at AJ.

"Are we going to discuss the *it* thing?" Lilith asked.

AJ grimaced while Tayen closed her eyes.

"I'm sorry about the thing we did. The barrier between all of us is taking a toll on me. I'm so embarrassed by my actions."

Tayen leaned forward. "Honey, no. We're sorry. AJ and I shouldn't have done what we did."

"It's not like we were unwilling. We participated without reservation," AJ said.

Tayen threw the towel at AJ.

Charlotte entered the room. "Clean undies and jeans, done. So, what are we talking about?"

AJ leaned back in his chair. "We are confronting our acts of intimacy from last month."

"About damn time." Charlotte sat on Tayen's desk corner. "At least none of us fell on the floor with all that rocking and rolling. Who knew the queen bed in AJ's room could fit four?"

AJ folded his arms. "A queen bed in my room?"

Charlotte skipped AJ's question. "Look, Lilith and I have been dating since the convention. You and Tayen have my utmost respect. For one night, our inhibitions fell to the floor as fast as my panties did. The old folks did their generation proud."

Tayen sat in her chair. "Sexual encounters with subordinates, and young ladies like you two, grates against my standards of professional behavior. And in discussions with AJ, it doesn't sit well with him."

"It was an orgy. A one-night extravaganza with you and AJ," Charlotte said.

"You are right. One night of unbridled ecstasy. But can you see that AJ and I are uncomfortable that it happened?

We share your respect and utmost admiration. But it feels like we made a power move on you two."

AJ waved his hands. "A queen bed, in my bedroom? My room had full-sized beds, not queens."

"Four active people in a full bed?" Lilith asked. "Four people in a queen is a feat, but in a full? They would have to be Cirque du Soleil performers."

"What size beds were in yours?" AJ asked.

"Fulls," Tayen answered.

Charlotte held up her hand. "AJ, whose room did we frolic in?"

"Scott's and mine."

Lilith and Tayen looked at each other in surprise.

AJ squinted. "Okay, my turn. Why did you and Lilith bring fishnet stockings to a convention?"

"I didn't have fishnet stockings," Lilith said.

Charlotte squinted back at AJ. "I didn't bring or buy those. So how did we get them?"

"You weren't wearing fishnet stockings. Nobody was wearing anything," Tayen added.

AJ and Charlotte's eyebrows shot up.

"Okay, hold on just one minute." Lilith held her hands out. "We frolicked in our room, not the guys' room."

AJ twirled his thumbs. "I remember it in my room."

"Were there whips and chains?" Charlotte asked.

"No," Lilith and Tayen retorted in unison.

AJ stopped twirling his fingers. "You know what this means?"

"You and I are kinky as hell, while Tayen and Lilith are pillow queens," Charlotte answered.

Lilith placed Charlotte in a headlock.

AJ rocked forward and jumped to his feet. "It means

our orgy never took place. Someone hypnotized us to make us believe we did."

"Where was Scott?" Tayen asked.

"He split off to the hotel bar."

"When we got to the room, he was fully clothed and asleep in our tub," Lilith said.

AJ scuffed his feet on the floor. "Two hours outside the museum. Two hours gone on the eighteenth. Were we hypnotized more than once?"

"Dual mysteries at a time. Not how I work." Tayen crossed her arms and leaned back in her chair. "Perhaps we were hypnotized for the priest's meeting, and another hypnotism implanted our orgy. But why sexual fantasies?"

"To hide any traces of a second hypnotism."

Lilith whirled her hands in the air, encouraging AJ to explain.

"Say we met with Father Amare. With clues in hand and suspecting Ernesto Cottrell's men were waiting to nab us, he hypnotized us to hide the meeting. The second hypnotism, in our hotel room—"

"—Where did the first happen?" Lilith asked.

"I'd say at the convent museum, where we had a two-hour meeting with Father Amare."

"And the second hypnotism in the hotel?" Tayen asked.

"The second, performed by Ernesto's men, hoped to learn the secrets of our meeting with Father Amare. To mask any traces of their operation, a third hypnotism was done. It concentrated us on sexual fantasies. Our fixation on an orgy would distract us from any memories that might escape their purview."

"Did we use candle wax on one another?"

"Ooh. There's your kinky side," AJ said.

Tayen refused to let him under her skin. "It was under my fingernail. When we awoke on the nineteenth, I scraped red wax from under my fingernail."

AJ looked at her finger that she held up. "Lighting a candle in a hotel is illegal, and the French Quarter's history is littered with devastating fires. Open flames are strictly forbidden. However, red wax under a fingernail point to a meeting with Father Amare."

"The candle evidence alone isn't enough. How do we verify?" Tayen asked.

AJ pointed out the window. "Time to bring our New Orleans-born Vodou trained Voodoo practitioner into the loop. Kimiko Kijano."

"You didn't tell us this until now?" Charlotte yelled.

"I thought this would pass. She already thinks I'm half off my rocker, so keeping her out of the loop was my survival instinct kicking in."

***

Half an hour later, Broken Cove Accessories' fashion designer sat in Tayen's office, listening to the tale of their adventure. "I was out, and they dragged me back in. Which lunatic sent you? The Péchettes or the Benningtons?" Kimiko asked.

Tayen looked around the room at her colleagues. "We heard the name Jade Péchette, but we don't know who she is. Can you break through the hypnotisms, if indeed we were hypnotized?"

Kimiko closed her eyes. "Let's set things straight. I practice Voodoo. It's my belief system, and I can't talk to you about it because y'all are not from there. Only natives of New Orleans can understand the ways of the motherhood. The first person who calls me a Voodoo Priestess is getting a one-way trawler trip to Pirate's Bay."

Before AJ could ask, she answered, "I don't know if Pirate's Bay is real or not, but the East River is getting full."

Tayen fist bumped her for shutting AJ down. The girls dipped their heads so he wouldn't see them laughing.

"I am not a Vodou Priestess. I am well-versed in Haitian Vodou and West African Vodun thanks to a brilliant teacher, but please, don't call me a priestess." Watching AJ, she made her intentions clear. "Mention gris-gris bags or Voodoo dolls and I'll bring them to life on you."

AJ shied away from his original question. "Where do we start?"

Kimiko pulled out bags from the pocket of her rose-colored paper bag culottes. Lilith was engrossed with Kimiko's culottes and didn't see the bags.

"What are those?" AJ asked.

"Gris-gris bags to hang on Tayen's head."

Lilith sensed AJ was about to strike with a wiseass comment. Thankfully, Tayen intervened.

"Why do I have to go first?"

Kimiko tapped Tayen between the eyes. "If you had a choice, whose head would you want to peek inside: his or yours?"

"You're right; me first." Tayen reclined in her seat, letting Kimiko tie a braid around her head. She laid the gris-gris bags over Tayen's eyes.

"AJ," Kimiko commanded, "text me the questions to ask her."

She spoke softly to ease Tayen into a hypnotic state.

"Relax and breathe deeply. Enjoy the scents circling and soothing your soul. I'll count backwards from sixteen. Breathe out with each number I say, and in, between the numbers. Relax, concentrate on your breathing."

Still as still could be, she gestured for AJ to text her with the questions for Tayen. "After dinner, you walked from the restaurant to the museum. Tell me about the sheltered gate. What happened there?"

"We passed it," Tayen said.

AJ shook his head no and texted the next question.

"You went inside the sheltered gate to the convent museum courtyard. Tell me about it."

"Best carnival ride ever."

Kimiko batted her eyes. AJ shrugged.

"What was the name of the carnival ride?"

"The Devil's Tears."

Lilith and Charlotte leaned forward.

A flurry of texts explained the hot sauce tasting Scott had enticed them into at the mall.

Tayen trailed-off on endless strings of incoherent tangents no matter what Kimiko asked. Tayen began singing *Oklahoma*, which Kimiko shut down instantly. "Okay, honey, where will we find The Devil's Tears carnival ride?"

"After the moon landing."

Kimiko dropped her head; it was going nowhere.

AJ wasn't as dismissive.

Kimiko waited for a text. He tapped his phone and flipped it around for her to see. He wasn't sending her the text, but flashing the message on the screen.

Kimiko read it and proceeded. "Tayen, what happened after the moon landing?"

"Two gigantic dicks were erected as an offering to the

golf gods for picking me up."

Half-closed eyes signaled Kimiko was done. "Tayen, at the count of five, you will awake and feel refreshed."

Tayen awoke to find Kimiko taking the gris-gris bags off her eyes. "Did it work?"

"Nope, afraid not." AJ handed Tayen his phone.

Tayen read it and nodded. "Back in the dark. How sad. I am leaving for lunch. I shall return later."

AJ mouthed *ha-ha* as she smirked at him. He said, "I too shall leave this office and check on our progress for the grand opening."

Charlotte and Lilith knew what they were doing, but didn't speak as they left the office.

Kimiko shook her head at Tayen and AJ's obtuse statements. Following their lead, she said, "I am leaving for the Bahamas on Thursday for my refresher on tantric sexual practices."

An hour later, Tayen led the girls in the back door to AJ's house. They eased their way into the eastern stone turret stairwell to find AJ seated halfway up the stairs. Scott stood behind him wearing headphones. A long cord extended to a shoebox-sized case that he held under one arm. He was sweeping a hand-held device over the steps in the turret stairwell.

AJ motioned for them to gather closer. "Those who placed listening devices in our New Orleans hotel also hid them in my house. The office, your homes, and all our cell phones have been compromised. Scott's toy has located the one in this stairwell, and he muted it. We are free to talk in this turret."

"Did Kimiko break the hypnotisms?" Tayen asked.

"No. You spoke gibberish, and she never cracked the

shell someone installed in your head."

The congestion in the stairwell included two happy golden retrievers and one diva-esque Himalayan cat, Shazoo. A button on a wire dangled from his mouth.

Charlotte wrangled the button and wire from Shazoo's playful grasp and held it up for them to see. "I bet this is what a bug looks like."

Scott scanned it. "Yep, dead bug. Attaboy, Shazoo. How did he find a bug?"

AJ rubbed under Shazoo's chin. "Are poor kitty's ears sensitive to bug frequencies? Best I check with your vet."

He lowered Shazoo to the step and said, "Kimiko told me in the parking lot before she worked on Tayen that breaking a hypnotism requires a point of familiarity. If we are hypnotized—as I believe we were—we need points of familiarity to unlock the blocks placed in our subconscious. Tayen's answers were gibberish unless her gibberish had context which someone could decipher."

"You understood her gibberish," Lilith said.

"Tayen sampled The Devil's Tears in Scott's hot sauce challenge. To Kimi, it was nonsense. To me, along with her mentioning of the moon landing, her answers had context. All of Tayen's answers related to events we experienced in New Orleans, except one. The one which took place here, in Portland.

"When I built this house, the stone turrets had to go up first. For weeks, people joked about the windstorm and the tarps popping up. They looked like two giant phallic monuments. Then she said 'for picking me up.' Tayen and I discussed this on the first day we met in Portland—not when we were in New Orleans."

Lilith's eyes were fixated on AJ. "That's the argument

you and Tayen always have. It's the shared point of commonality."

"Precisely." AJ smiled. "We're supposed to be in this turret. This turret is the key to unlocking our blocked memories. Our point of reference lies in these walls. No one except me would suspect the key to the hypnotic block was outside of the events in New Orleans. I suspect one last point of familiarity will break the block."

"What do we need, a magic word?" Lilith asked.

AJ nodded.

"I was joking."

"I'm not. You said something in our missing hours and it will unlock our hypnosis."

Incredulous, Lilith lifted her arms and layered them in front of her chest. "Here goes nothing." She snapped her head forward and said, "Abracadabra."

Charlotte's Memo Pad To-do List

1.   Go to Seattle?
2.
3.   Assist with special delivery?!?!
4.
5.   WHY go w/Manny to Seattle?
6.
7.
8.
9.
10.

Tayen's Notes:

Last week's interviews w/Talia's friends.
They'll be here ... while I'm in Seattle???

AJ's Notes: (Clear w/Tayen first)

He agreed w/Tayen. without arguing. wtf?

Staff Attendance:

Screw this. I'll be in Seattle.

13 - Broken Cove Accessories

Ominous swirling shadows materialized on the turret walls. They gathered strength before stretching their vengeful claws at the rays of light. Like a hunter, they chased the light from the turret stairwell.

Lilith doubled over. The muscles in her pelvis contracted, giving birth to a wandering phantom below her ribs. It surged upward from her pelvis, stealing her strength as it ascended. It streaked upward through her chest and out of the top of her head. Her head snapped back, which let her see the swirling shadows race through the turret ceiling. Stunned and shaken, she fell against the wall.

Cher licked Charlotte's face, and Sonny did likewise with AJ.

Tayen sat with her arms extended out, placing her hands on her knees. Scott sat, seemingly unaffected. But when he spoke, Lilith could tell he was tired. "When we are done here, I'm going home and die in my bed."

"Why aren't you slumped over ... like me?" Lilith asked.

"I choose to not show my suffering."

"This too shall pass." Lilith lifted her head and turned toward AJ. Her strength grew in proportion to the anger which had begun to simmer in her veins.

"Son of a bitch. I didn't know," AJ said.

"I don't know your mother, so I'll leave her out of this," Charlotte retorted.

AJ held his hands out to defend himself. "I didn't know about the turret stairwells in New Orleans."

"Give it a shot, old geezer, before one of us shoots you."

"You have identical stone turret stairwells to the ones in New Orleans. And you want us to believe it is a coincidence?" Lilith asked. Like Charlotte, her credulity had been stretched beyond her capacity to believe AJ.

"You've got to believe me; I didn't know. Can't we be glad the hypnotic block was broken?"

Tayen bent her head from side to side, stretching her neck. "Father Amare hypnotized us in the turret stairwell. He saw the dust covering us after we passed through the sheltered gate. With the interrogations coming at the hotel, he had to protect us through individual hypnotisms. Our memories were blocked from ... "

"From whom? Ernesto or the Bennington crime syndicate?" AJ asked.

"How about both?" Charlotte added.

Lilith had been massaging her lower back and listening to the discussion. Before she realized it, she had murmured her thoughts out loud. "Raised body temps and lowered inhibitions. No wonder why we were amorous."

"Earth to Lilith. What are you saying?" Charlotte asked.

"The individual hypnotisms he did on us in the turret."

Charlotte's eyes sprung open. "I was first to the top. I thought it was a group hypnotism."

"Nope. We stayed at the bottom of the stairwell and one-by-one, he did us at the top. The second hour of our meeting was our individual hypnotisms."

"What does that have to do with raised body temps and lowered inhibitions?"

"Father Amare told me before my hypnotism that the dust used under the sheltered gate is called Demon's Breath. Its side effects include raised body temperatures, lowered inhibitions, and sleepiness."

"The buildup of heat," AJ said. "Tayen doesn't tolerate heat and got snippy at the least provocation. The girls removed their T-shirts, and Scott and I were—"

"Sweating with the oldies," Charlotte said. Before AJ lit into her, she added, "Someone was in our rooms, all day on the eighteenth. They had access to our phones and laptops."

Tayen's face turned pale.

Scott bobbed his head to shake the fog away. "Assume all electronic communications are monitored. That was his warning to me. Give me a week. I'll have tablets and phones secured, but I need an expense account for purchases."

"I'll give you whatever cash you need." Tayen's voice lacked its usual strength.

Lilith didn't fail to notice. "Is everything okay?"

"I ... " Tayen struggled to form her thoughts. "When we return to New Orleans, when we meet Father Amare again, I owe him an apology for doubting his sincerity. He returned my handbag to me on the morning of the nineteenth, after our missing day."

Lilith handpicked her words to not betray Tayen's secret phone. "He returned the bag your tribe gave you, *and* all the contents inside?"

"Yes. I went for breakfast before anyone was awake. A priest passed by my table and placed my bag on the chair next to me and walked away."

"Mm-hmm," AJ said.

Lilith's eyes popped open. *He doesn't believe Tayen.*

"Since Scott and Shazoo found bugs," Tayen wasn't about to let AJ ask about her hidden phone, "we know they are listening to us. Assume they have access to our social media and bank accounts."

"Hey, what was the semi-trailer about?" Charlotte asked.

"It was part of the protective hypnotism, a false lead," AJ said. "When they interrogated us, all they heard was the same story about driving away in a truck."

Charlotte squinted as she pieced it together. "We share the same truck ride story, and they search elsewhere, not on the museum grounds. But why the orgy hypnotism?"

Scott's eyes bulged.

"Ah, 'strong stimulus remembered, mild stimulus forgotten.' That was my individual hypnotism warning," AJ said. "An orgy would be a strong stimulus to cover up anything we might remember from the day-long interrogations."

"Scott," Lilith sensed he was about to lose it, "we

didn't have an orgy. Those dreams were implanted to mislead us."

Scott breathed a sigh of relief.

Lilith turned to AJ. "Why wasn't he included in the orgy?"

"Stop calling it an orgy," Charlotte said. "Orgies start with five. We followed golf etiquette and had a foursome."

AJ ignored Charlotte. "Scott stopped at a bar for a few drinks—"

"We didn't drink; we went dancing," Lilith interrupted. "They were concerned about killing Scott because Demon's Breath and alcohol don't mix?"

AJ stood. "His death would've complicated their work. They released us with tracking devices on our phones and are waiting for us to find the treasure. We're alive because they believed we know something."

Tayen spoke with her administrator's voice. "AJ, talk with Kimiko and learn about the history of the Péchettes and Benningtons. Lilith, dig into your ancestry. Scott and I will set up a secure communication system. Charlotte, become a spy. Know everything about our employees, our vendors, the contractors, and members."

***

Days later, Scott delivered secured tablets and smartphones with his security features. Charlotte received two tablets: one for business and one for Scott's new video cameras. Two dozen camera feeds captured every moment that transpired anywhere within the entire country club complex.

AJ's attention turned to shit. Cleaning up after Sonny

and Cher, he found bugs in the dogs' poop. One morning while standing on his third-floor balcony, Shazoo scratched a bug out from under a living room chair. Cher sniffed at it, but Sonny immediately slurped it up.

Charlotte discovered a new development. Random newspapers began arriving at the clubhouse. Stamped with the greeting: *Courtesy from Adela Frontera*, they always arrived three days after their publication date, and from a wide range of cities. She showed them to AJ, but he didn't know who Adela was. But he did explain the feminine form of Adela meant *serene*, and the masculine meant *favor*. She rolled her eyes, amazed at the loads of useless trivia he had.

Tayen scoured the papers, hoping to understand why they were receiving them. The lead stories featured an eclectic assortment of random individuals. Perhaps that was the point, Charlotte joked. It was a collection of people, nothing more. They came to the same conclusion: the newspapers were giving them persons of interest to watch for.

Charlotte created a database of people and places. She labeled it the Bennington file, in accordance with Father Amare's warning to her. 'Ernesto's personnel will fail to hide themselves, but not so with the Benningtons. Use that genius intellect of yours and keep tabs on those who seek you harm.'

The five gathered routinely in AJ's turret stairwell to devour the newspapers.

A week before Christmas, an overnighted package arrived from Tampa. The newspaper was dated from one day earlier, breaking the three days rule. Charlotte texted the news and ran to AJ's house. She hurried into the turret stairwell and handed the sports to AJ. Shazoo had become accustomed to their meetings and demanded somebody open their lap for him.

Lilith raced in the back door and entered the turret stairwell as Charlotte snapped the paper. "A-ha. Here it is, a chest washed ashore last week, and a Tampa museum has it. The photo shows our broken wheel logo carved into the lid."

Scott and Tayen entered the turret and heard Charlotte.

"How do we travel to Tampa without someone spying on us?" Tayen asked.

"I'm more concerned by who floated the chest," AJ said.

"I don't have any Benningtons in Tampa. We'll be safe to travel after New Year's in a couple of weeks," Charlotte said.

Tayen weighed the possibilities. "It may be impossible to fly to Tampa without someone tailing us. They had access to our New Orleans flight itineraries. How do we sneak past people who have access to the TSA?"

AJ posed a question to his general manager. "Would a Bennington work for the TSA, or would they buy off a TSA employee?"

"They had our New Orleans plans, but Tampa isn't on their radar," Charlotte said.

Tayen slowly acknowledged Charlotte could be right. "If we go, it has to be before the second Monday in January, before interviews begin. We will be hiring two hundred plus soon, and five department head positions haven't been hired. In particular, the pastry chef position has to be filled soon."

"You four go. If I'm not here, they'll search for me and find this Tampa museum. If none of you are here, it fits with the *being on vacation* misdirect," AJ said.

"You'll have to take my place in the pastry chef interviews."

Lilith laughed. "He's the tiebreaker for the bakeoff. Oh, goodness, gracious me. How will he ever master those skills? Relax, Tayen. The chefs have it covered."

Tayen sneered at Lilith. "Fine. Charlotte, buy the airline tickets and tell Talia she has the front desk while we are gone."

***

After New Year's Day, Tayen and company flew to Tampa, leaving AJ to the pastry chef interviews.

As expected, the executive chef, Dean, and sous chef, Ladonna, carried the bulk of the interviews and let the owner handle the softball questions. The last interviewee ran late, giving the chefs and the owner time to compare notes. They agreed on the top two but failed to come to a consensus on a third for the following day's bakeoff.

Talia took a break from working with Kimiko's clothing line and assumed Charlotte's role as the receptionist. She peeked around the corner into the new kitchen. "You folks ready for the final interview?"

"Bring her in," Chef Ladonna said.

Talia held on to the wall and kicked her leg out as she slung her head back and pointed to the lobby.

Chef Ladonna leaned over and whispered to AJ. "Was she showing off her pole dancing skills on the wall, or was she warning us about the next candidate?"

"I never saw her dance, but if that's what … holy … "

Chef Ladonna waited for AJ to finish, but he didn't. He was engrossed with the next interviewee.

A tall young lady entered the room. Her sparkling green eyes and flawless tan complexion were framed by thick, silky-brown hair. Her cream-colored long-sleeve silk blouse didn't take one's eyes from the angelic face. A camel-colored belted-waist suede skirt and matching pumps completed her ensemble.

AJ nearly knocked the table over as he sprang to his feet. A chaotic and eager introduction gurgled out. "Hello, I am Father … Sorry, I'm the homer, owner, AJ de Faria. Glad you could make out with us—I mean, make it out here."

Chef Dean jumped up. "I'm Dean, the ex-chief—the executive chef, and this woman is …" Dean swept his arm around to introduce his wife, but Ladonna's name had vanished from his vocabulary.

Embarrassed by her husband's and the owner's tongue-tied introductions, Chef Ladonna leaned on the table and pushed herself up. "I'm Ladonna, the sous chef, and his soon to be ex-wife if he doesn't pull it together."

The young lady extended her hand and shook hands with the interview panel. "I am Lydia Calveiro. Sorry for my lateness. My car threw a hissy fit."

Chef Ladonna sat. "Please, take a seat. The extra-curricular activities you list on your resume are unusual. Dance and fencing?"

Lydia giggled. "Because of my height, people think I played volleyball or basketball. But my sports were dancing and fencing. I was homecoming queen senior year, and on homecoming court the three previous years. American Student Government junior and senior years, humane society volunteer, art critic for the student newspaper, and I've done Habitat for Humanity since I was old enough to swing a hammer."

AJ and Dean sighed.

Chef Ladonna's comment was unambiguous. "If the

idiots on either side of me can't pull it together, I'll handle this interview while they go take a cold shower, together."

Dean regained his focus. AJ stood, but realized Dean wasn't joining him, which forced him to retake his seat.

"Lydia, you understand we are interviewing to find our top three candidates for a bakeoff tomorrow?" Chef Ladonna asked.

"Yes, I am aware of tomorrow's bakeoff."

***

Half an hour later, the interview concluded. They thanked Lydia for her participation and watched as she exited. Ladonna's sole vote for the third bakeoff participant didn't matter. Dean and AJ agreed Lydia was their choice.

The next morning, the three bakeoff participants stood outside the kitchen. AJ and Chef Dean had dressed far more professionally than the previous day, prompting Chef Ladonna to repeat her threat of doing it alone if they didn't act their age.

The bakery would specialize in chocolate. Therefore, the bakeoff would test the chefs on three chocolate desserts.

The three chefs worked on the assigned categories: chocolate cakes, brownies, and free choice, where they could create anything they wished so long as it was made of chocolate.

At the last minute, Chef Ladonna changed the bakeoff to a blind taste. She didn't trust the guys' judgement with a cute cook in the ranks.

Talia brought out the desserts. Chocolate cakes varied in presentation, but not significantly in taste. It took several tastes before they made their decision and moved on.

Brownies came next. Talia licked her fingers after she placed the plates on the table. She held up three fingers to AJ, which he interpreted as her favorite.

The free creations were last. The chocolate chili tart with lime, while delightful, was unbalanced with a skosh too much heat for Chef Ladonna and AJ. A chocolate, peanut butter, avocado pudding sounded intriguing. For Chef Dean, however, only the right ratio of peanut butter to avocado could win his vote.

The final dish was a layered triple chocolate mousse tart. One could eat it a layer at a time, or push a fork through all three layers, which combined to make a fourth flavor.

Talia, still licking residual brownies from her fingers, tallied the judges' scorecards and announced the winner.

Lydia Calveiro took the top scores in every category. Chef Ladonna restrained the men's enthusiasm by slapping down their energetic congratulatory fist bump.

AJ departed to handle construction matters on the ground floor bakery while the chefs handled the closing formalities of the bakeoff.

Minutes later, AJ was approving a contractor workup as he stood in the hollowed-out shell of what would become the bakery. When he finished, he turned to see Broken Cove Industries' pastry chef standing behind him.

"Congratulations Lydia, or should I say Pastry Chef Lydia Calveiro?"

"Lydia, please. I wanted to thank you for the opportunity to prove myself as your pastry chef."

"You interviewed well, and we judged your work objectively, thanks to the blind taste test."

Lydia couldn't hide her disdain for the dangling electrical wires and construction dust. "This is the bakery?"

"Unfinished, but it's getting there. Behind us will be the coffee shop. You'll have both under your wings. If you want, our general manager will hire your baristas. Did the chefs explain your schedule for the next six weeks?"

Lydia dipped her head. "Yes. Six weeks on the road, seeking the best chocolate practices here and in Europe."

"In two days, you fly to New England. Dean has mapped out half your trip with some acquaintances of his. Learn from them and then map out the rest of your search yourself. Do not be afraid to ask for whatever you need."

AJ felt a tap on his shoulder. Before he completed his turn to see who it was, Kimiko asked, "Can I take her now?"

He finished his turn and said, "Lydia, this is Kimiko Kijano, Broken Cove Accessories' fashion designer. Her shop will be on the second floor, above the gift shop."

Lydia extended her hand. "Pleasure to meet you."

"Five-eleven, size eight to ten—"

"Kimiko," AJ scolded. "She isn't on payroll yet and you're measuring her?"

"I'm doing the pirate catalog photos, and she was made for the *Bella Donna Long*."

"She's the pastry chef, not a—" AJ stopped to consider what Kimiko had said. "Did you say she was made for the *Bella Donna Long*?"

"Well. Look who listened at the staff meeting."

"It's impossible to ignore your sketches for adult women's pirate costumes."

"Not costumes; fantasy wear."

"Expensive fantasy wear."

Kimiko poked AJ in the chest. "Women won't think twice about the price tag of their custom-designed sexy pirate outfit. And once their significant other sees it, they will dole out whatever price we list. If you're worried about your pastry chef being the T and A model in *Long*, we're doing chin down shots only, no facials. Which is tragic. Her skin tone … darker than the typical Spanish woman."

Kimiko held Lydia's chin like a grandmother inspecting a grandchild's face. "Your green eyes would stop an Ussuri brown bear from charging back in Japan."

AJ corralled Kimiko's hand and asked, "Do you have a supernatural power to envision your designs on people with one look?" Rethinking what he said and to whom he said it, he retreated. "Okay, that was stupid. That *is* your superpower."

Kimiko pulled her hand from AJ's grasp and pointed at Lydia. "This body was created for me to clothe. My designs, her body, and sales skyrocket, making you tons of money."

"Not with your forty percent cut off the top."

"My contract is signed, and I'm not renegotiating down to the twenty-five percent you proposed."

"Lydia," AJ said as he stared out of the bakery. He was never sure if he or Kimiko were in charge. "If you would like to dress in Kimiko's creations, it is your choice. It will not be expected of you as part of your job duties. Beware, her pirate fantasy wear is quite risqué."

"Kimiko's creations," Kimiko mused. "And we rename it Kimiko Kijano's Kreations. All K's."

AJ placed his hands on his hips. "You have five seconds to figure out why I'll never let that happen."

Kimiko thought for a moment. "Oh, no, no. I told you I am horrible with marketing and branding."

Lydia raised her hand. "Why does a country club have a fashion designer?"

Kimiko dragged Lydia from the unfinished bakery. "I served tables before he learned I sewed. My custom-made golf gloves led to a line of women's golf apparel, and finally to the adult pirate outfits. I dressed Talia and Charlotte in the *Pirate Queen Tall* and S*hort*, squeezed Lilith into the *Bohemian Pirate Captain*, and paraded them across Pioneer Square. Since then, requests for adult-themed pirate costumes haven't stopped."

"Is Talia the receptionist?" Lydia asked.

"Second assistant to the general manager and the lead server for Pasta-de-faria's." Kimiko pointed up the bus lane toward the road as they proceeded to the elevators. "Here she comes from the formal clubhouse across the street."

AJ tagged behind them. He called out to Talia as she jogged down the bus lane. "I should have guessed you would be in this photo shoot."

"Kimi threatened me with great physical harm if I didn't," Talia said.

AJ waited for Talia as Kimiko and Lydia disappeared behind the closing elevator door.

"Did Snow White accept the job?"

"Talia, don't call her that."

"I swear to God," Talia's jog turned into a walk, "the squirrels brought her nuts, the birds adorned her with a scarf made of leaves, and the damn raccoon pack got all starry-eyed when she exited the car. It must be her eyes."

"Talia," AJ warned, "she doesn't have your street-savvy style, but it's no reason to call her a naïve princess. After all, Kimiko has her in the *Bella Donna Long*."

She stepped in front of AJ and pushed on his chest. "*Long?* Damn, she'll kill in *Long*. I'm sporting *Bella Donna Short* for the shoot."

"Praise be to God." AJ raised his hands to the heavens. "A person I can trust in *Short*."

"I'm not sure how to take that."

"Please take it as a compliment. *Short* is the most risqué in the line. It comforts me to know you have the experience to handle the job. Your professionalism means the world to me. Last year, if you had told me I'd own a business selling women's fantasy pirate wear—"

"Pirate fantasy wear," Talia corrected.

"Imagine if people learned she was the one in *Short*. The bus lane outside the coffee shop would be blocked by gawkers."

"But *Short* is okay for your lead server in the rooftop restaurant?"

"You're not wearing *Short* while serving tables."

"I might." Talia squared up to AJ. "You said staff chooses the uniform. You weren't forcing us into something we didn't feel comfortable in."

"You … wearing *Short* when a family takes their seats with their nine-year-old—"

"Not on family nights," Talia said.

AJ saw a spark in her eye.

"But—"

"Here comes my headache."

"—the second Thursday night of the month would be for ladies only. Guests would need a special invite, which they get with a fitting in the store. Oh, better include a purchase, too. It'll be the hottest legal ticket in town."

AJ pointed at the parking lot. "Who owns the six cars I don't recognize?"

"My friends are helping with the photo shoot. Tayen prescreened them last week."

"Prescreened? They'll be table servers?"

"And models, for whenever Kimi needs us."

"Six cars, six friends." AJ mulled over the situation. "Where did they work prior to here?"

Talia's playful tone disappeared. "The Velvet Shack."

Wrinkles formed on AJ's forehead, which was followed by his rising eyebrows. "Are they as cute as you?"

"And what if they aren't?"

"Work with me. Picture family night when the entire Velvet Shack dancers are serving tables. A family man is with his wife and children, when bam! The server, who stripped for him, is taking his dinner order with the wife there. His bugged-out eyes will give it away every time, and Pasta-de-faria's will be known as 'the cheaters revealed' restaurant."

The elevator door opened. Talia shrugged and stepped in. AJ joined her. "Kimiko better do a great job with you seven and my pastry chef. Please don't call her Snow White ..."

AJ finally understood, which precipitated Talia's response. "This is a fashion catalog—"

"Seven of you, and a pastry chef is Snow White."

"When the purchaser wears the clothing—"

"—That's how Kimiko starts her sales pitch to me when she knows I will object."

The elevator door opened to the second floor and Talia rushed out. "She suspected you'd object."

AJ followed her. "So she designed the line and hid its name from me until it was too late to cancel. Did Tayen approve Kimi's line?" AJ palmed his forehead. "Nope, she couldn't. She's away on vacation."

Talia faced AJ. "Do you trust me in *Short*?"

"You know I do."

"Then trust me, there's nothing to worry about."

AJ held out his hand. "Show me where to stand. Eight women in Kimiko's outfits make me nervous."

Talia opened the studio door and peeked inside, making sure everyone was robed. She announced their presence, introduced her friends to AJ, and disappeared into the fitting room.

Minutes later, she escorted Lydia out to the photo stage. *Bella Donna Long* was a scarlet-colored satin cold shoulder bodysuit, which featured an O-ring below Lydia's breasts. The satin material hugged her body, but exposed little skin. White puffed sleeves covered her arms from the off-shoulder line. A large black pirate captain's hat looked natural on Lydia's head, and the miniskirt came close to reaching down to the top of the black thigh-high leather stilettos.

Bella Donna Short was made with a third of the satin material as *Bella Donna Long*. The O-ring centered between Talia's breasts, which were shoved up by the tight-fitting scarlet crop top. While Lydia was covered, Talia's décolletage was exposed. Black fishnet stockings and stiletto heels substituted for the black leather thigh-high boots.

"Do I just stand here for the pose?" Lydia asked.

Kimiko turned on the dance music. "Dance, ignore the camera, and face the lights. Slow, sensuous motions and enjoy the moment. Pretend we aren't here."

Lydia closed her eyes and let the music guide her. Taken by Lydia's angelic face during the interview process, AJ had failed to notice the master's degree in dance on her resumé. Controlled yet natural hip rolls oozed from a Master of Dance.

AJ winked at Talia and gestured to tell her he was leaving. He had to leave for the airport to pick up Tayen and the Tampa crew.

***

An hour later, AJ pulled a white minivan into the pickup lane at the airport. He received Tayen's text that they were coming to the exit. With the side door open, he waited.

A woman wearing dark sunglasses exited the wide automated revolving door. Her fire-red, short-bobbed hair penetrated through the dull colors of a dimly lit airport terminal. The red micro skirt, fishnet stockings, and deep plunging neckline were perfect for a red-light district in Amsterdam, but not for Portland in winter.

The woman walked up and leaned her body against AJ, giving him an open-mouthed kiss. Tilting her head back, Tayen said, "Get in the goddamn van and don't say a thing."

AJ complied.

Tayen slunk into her seat, strapped her seat belt on, and ordered him to drive to the next door. He stopped where she had ordered. The side door and back hatch opened. A nun entered the side door, and a long-haired guy, who looked like he was from a religious cult, threw bags in the back.

After the cult guy entered and shut the side door, Tayen said, "Drive us out of here."

"Why is Charlotte dressed like a nun and Scott like a cultist, and where is Lilith?" AJ asked.

A pounding came from the side door.

Scott opened the door and let Lilith in.

"Sorry, Lilith. Flaunting my body in front of three-thousand air travelers distracted me," Tayen said.

Lilith banged past Charlotte on her way to the back, where she slammed herself against the seat.

"Economy class sucks, doesn't it?" AJ asked.

No one answered.

AJ tried again. "Hippie Scott, Sister Charlotte, and hooker Tayen. Did y'all lose a bet to Lilith?"

Dead silence.

"Someone talk or I'll continue to make things up—"

"I had to carry twenty pounds of quarters through airport security," Charlotte yelled. "That's why I am dressed like a nun."

"Twenty pounds of quarters?"

"We'll get to that," Tayen snapped.

"Did you run into a Bennington?"

"The Benningtons weren't the problem. Currently, we're hiding from the Tampa police. When our shipping crate crosses the Florida state line, the feds will be involved too."

14 - The Tampa Heist

Tayen's apparel worked for the Gulf Coast in January, but not for the Pacific Northwest's wintry subfreezing temperatures.

"Somebody get in my bag and grab a shirt."

AJ couldn't help himself and kept sneaking peeks at his half-dressed general manager. And she noticed.

"Eyes on the road, not my thigh, you dirty old man."

"Please finish the joke: why a hooker, a hippie, and a nun got in my van?"

Tayen punched the dashboard heat console, cranking the heat to the highest setting. She turned every vent on her.

"You might get warm, but you'll burn the rest of us out of the van," AJ said.

"I laid the airplane blanket down thirty minutes ago. Since then, I've been freezing. This outfit doesn't retain heat."

"Or hide nipples," Charlotte said.

"Shit. Where's my—" Tayen's winter coat crashed onto her shoulder. Before she wrangled it around her torso, a nun's habit hit her on the side of her face. "Charlotte!"

"Cover your red hair. No one looks at a nun, but that red is loud enough to start a riot."

Tayen pulled the habit on. "I know this is your payback for my beignet throw in your face. When we get home, you're dyeing it back to my natural color. How the hell I let you talk me into crotch-rocket red over moral-abyss black is beyond me."

"Bubba's Convenient Store didn't offer high-end fashion choices. You live with what they had, and besides, I thought we agreed on the pink coloring," Charlotte said.

"No reputable company names a hair color after a woman's body part."

"Oh, get over it. Your Victorian virtues were a liability. Crotch-rocket red was the least pornographic name of the bunch."

Tayen ignored Charlotte. "Our excursion didn't go according to plan. For god's sake, I hope the news in Tampa didn't make it up to Portland."

"Excuse me? You made the news in Tampa?" AJ asked. A quick glance in the rear-view mirror showed him Lilith was banging her head on the headrest.

Tayen wrapped her arms around herself. "Let's start with the weather screwing over our flights. If I learned anything from this, it is to never fly in winter after a major holiday."

"You didn't know—" AJ stopped, realizing he was about to piss off his general manager.

"Charlotte scheduled four different flights in case someone was on to us. Better safe than sorry, so I approved the bookings. Scott left at 4 a.m., and the rest of us departed at one-hour intervals thereafter. His flights were diverted to other airports, where he got lucky and took flights which put him in Tampa three hours earlier than his original arrival time. Best freaking luck of the entire trip."

"Murphy," Tayen thumbed at Charlotte, "delayed, diverted … hell, even dissected. Whatever could go wrong, wherever it could go wrong, it did. Her cab pulled into the hotel twenty-four hours after taking off from Portland.

"I escaped all troubles and arrived on time. My bags, however, toured North America and greeted me at the departure gate this morning when we left.

"Meanwhile, at Denver International, Lilith spent thirty hours straight in the terminal, waiting for the blizzard to dissipate. She arrived at the hotel when we returned from the first museum trip."

"She could have driven from Denver to Tampa in less time than it took for her flight to clear," Charlotte added.

Lilith raised her hand for a backhand to Charlotte's noggin.

AJ rapped the steering wheel with his thumbs as he watched Lilith restrain herself. "First trip to the museum. There were two trips?"

"On the first trip," Tayen resumed, "I posed as an antiquities professor, Scott was my assistant, and Charlotte was the aspiring student. Congenial and professional, the staff charmed our socks off more than we did theirs. They didn't let us view the chest. Charlotte spotted a closet to hide in while we were there. Before closing, she and Scott re-entered, locked themselves in the closet, and waited for them to leave. Lilith and I waited outside for Scott to bypass security and let us in. We underestimated their security systems."

"Systems?" AJ asked.

"They had a security system, and businesses around the museum had theirs. Too many freaking security cameras."

AJ looked in the mirror at Scott, who returned a blank stare back to him.

"A couple of hours later, Scott opened the door, let Lilith and me in, and began scuttling the other business's security cameras. Again, too many systems could have recorded us. He had to erase them. Hacking a bank's cameras is a felony, but what the hell—we were just starting our felonies list."

"Felonies … list?"

Tayen pulled out her phone. "We pored over the chest in their processing room and dug through their findings. The museum curator suspected somebody planted it in the sand, giving the impression that the chest mysteriously washed ashore. Nobody accepted his claim, and his notes amounted to nothing more than a footnote in their investigation."

She read from her phone:

Carbon dating results: 18th century. Lack of water damage. No degradation. Chest undisturbed for centuries.

She lowered her phone. "Very few contents were in the chest. The few materials remaining were secured in three thick, brown plastic-bag-like pouches. Inside were an assortment of papers written in French and English. All their dating matched the chest's. Document analysis is expected back from Oxford by the spring. Until then, they refused to speculate on what they contained."

"Oxford? We have to go to England?" AJ asked.

"Wrong Oxford, genius. Oxford, Ohio."

"Oh. That is a shorter trip."

"Documents sent to a Dr. Newcomb," Tayen read.

"Sophie Newcomb?"

"Mother puss-bucket. Don't tell me you know her?" Charlotte yelled.

"Not personally, no, but she is a world-renowned scientist." AJ's head bobbed from side to side. "They carbon dated the artifacts, so why send ancient papers to an astrophysicist?"

Stunned, Charlotte swung her head toward Scott. "Shit, no one had that in our betting pool of 'who the hell is Dr. Newcomb?'"

"Wait a minute," AJ said, "you folks didn't figure that out even though I took you on the tour of the Newcomb Art Museum at Tulane?"

Dumbfounded, nobody replied to AJ's question.

Tayen rubbed her eyes. "Okay, on to the less underwear-soiling revelations."

"First, the chest wasn't used to haul gold or gems, but to carry art. Two portraits, protected by the brown paper, plastic-like stuff, were inside. One was a landscape of the ocean shore, and the other was a beautiful haze-filled estuary with two valiant looking ships moored to a wooden dock."

"Our two ships from the map wall. You saw the pirate base?" AJ asked.

"I believe so. However, the paintings presented an unusual dating problem. An experimental photoscopic dating technique produced some rather obtuse results.

"The paints were dated to different eras. Multiple artists painted the *Ocean Shore* canvas over a two-century span. The *Estuary* paints covered five centuries."

Charlotte tapped AJ on the shoulder. "I skedaddled

into the lady's room after this next bit of information."

"The paints used in *Ocean Shore* ranged from 1725 to 1900. They discredited the *Estuary* results because of the high variance yield of about five hundred years."

"What about the frames?" AJ asked.

"They were dated to within this millennium."

"This millennium? This millennium is less than two decades old."

Tayen turned to Charlotte. "Told you it didn't matter if I said century or millennium."

Charlotte checked her seat belt. "Imagine this passenger van catapulting us through the windshield had you told him the truth and said this decade."

The van jolted. AJ's knee-jerk reaction to Charlotte's news caused him to hit the brakes.

Tayen reached back to loosen the seatbelt strap, which was strangling her. "Moving on. The chest contained a hidden compartment in the upper lid. An antiquities professor was scheduled to open it in the morning. We took action.

"Charlotte jabbed a kitchen knife into a slit in the lid. It splintered into a thousand pieces, but we found another brown paper bag thing. We dismantled the chest to bring it home. That was when we heard coins dropping into a pop machine. Charlotte was getting a can of soda. We couldn't leave fingerprints, so we destroyed the vending machine to retrieve the quarters."

"Twenty pounds of quarters? Nowadays vending machines run on credit cards and dollar bills." AJ looked at Charlotte in the mirror.

Charlotte held up a wad of dollar bills. "Destruction of public property, theft, breaking and entering, and whatever you call hacking a bank's surveillance system."

"Scott found an auxiliary security system in the staff break room." Tayen paused. "Do you want the abbreviated version of what happened next?"

AJ nodded yes.

"He traced the auxiliary system to the secret room. We broke into it, downloaded the security video footage, and found footage of the manager spying on the lady's bathroom. That footage went to the police after he scrubbed recordings of us in the museum. Then he scrubbed the bank and the surrounding stores, loaded the chest in the rental van, and may have accidentally burned the museum down."

This time AJ didn't hit the brakes, but he did punch the accelerator for a brief second.

Tayen said, "It wasn't his fault. The manager left a space heater on in the office, and Scott may have kicked it on his way out."

AJ read the faces in the mirror. The two young ladies' detached demeanor didn't fit them. "An inadvertent kick by Scott, or an intentional kick by someone else?"

Lilith and Charlotte continued to be nonchalant.

"Their lips are sealed," Tayen said in frustration. "Their story of 'Scott kicked the space heater' changed to 'he might have kicked' when I confronted them. They didn't look too upset when the building burst into flames."

Charlotte gave a single shoulder shrug.

"We sped out of the parking lot and searched for a place to crate the chest for shipping to Portland. Twenty-four-hour lumber stores aren't in vogue, so Charlotte had us drive into a home construction site. I wasn't aware of her expertise in woodworking. Were you?"

"Yes," AJ said. "If psychology was too boring for her at Harvard, woodshop down at MIT was her next option."

"MIT doesn't ... Never mind." Tayen flipped the heater's fan down a notch.

She continued her story. "Lilith used her phone to give Charlotte some light to work in while Scott and I held up shirts to hide Lilith's light. We drove around Tampa and found a place to ship Charlotte's crate."

"MIT doesn't have woodshop," Scott said.

AJ bobbed his head, unsure what to ask next. "The Benningtons ... weren't a concern?"

"We feared that if anybody was onto us, they would nab us when we returned to the hotel. Call it paranoia induced by sleep deprivation. So, we drove around Tampa for eight hours and passed our hotel repeatedly to ensure we weren't tailed."

AJ held his hand low enough so only Tayen saw it. He thumbed towards the back, where Lilith sat quietly.

Tayen jettisoned any pretense of social decorum. "Oh, she's pouting."

"I'm not pouting."

"Oh princess," Charlotte barked, "get over it."

"It was a Halston," Lilith cried.

"No credit card use on the trip to keep us off the Bennington's radar, sweetie. Limited cash, and the unanticipated expenses of crating and shipping—"

"Hair coloring and disguises too," Charlotte added.

Tayen flung her hand at her hair. "—and little Ms. fashion sees a dress—"

"It was a Halston, not a dress."

"—and she's been pouting ever since."

Charlotte's voice rose. "In twenty-four hours, we created one hell of a felony list, and what is she upset over?"

"Scott, what's your take on the trip?" AJ asked.

"I'm passing on this one."

"Okay, Scott's out. So that leaves the disguises."

Charlotte blurted out. "If you were caring coins in an airport, what better foil than a young, naïve nun? I said, 'Coins for the children. Coins for the children, please,' with my best girlish charm, and nobody questioned it. I didn't get any coins, but the twenties were appreciated."

"Which you're donating to your church," Tayen snapped.

"How about the hooker and the cultist?" AJ asked.

"Remember when I told you I posed as an antiquities professor? She had an assistant, Scott, and an aspiring student, Charlotte. The museum curator remembered us and did a bang-up job of describing us to the police sketch artist."

She took the newspaper Scott handed her and flipped it open for AJ. "Front page center, above the fold, and listed as persons of interest."

"Oh boy. Lifelike sketches. But why a hooker and a cultist?"

"They're searching for the drab, boring university types in the paper. Not a stoned, long-haired cultist, or a flashy, middle-aged hooker with no inhibitions toward public displays of affection."

Charlotte added, "And whose nipples stuck through her blouse."

***

Days later, Lilith was hunkered down in a woodshed between the parking lot and the four-story village complex. Contractors, job applicants, and visitors saw her first when they pulled into the snow-free parking lot.

Over two hundred positions needed to be filled, and at least twice that number of applicants relied on Lilith for directions. Her activity, plus a whining space heater, kept her warm in one of the coldest Januarys in Portland's history.

She developed standard replies as the winter concierge: *Back of house interviews, third floor. Front of house interviews, fourth floor. Clubhouse interviews across the street. No, you can't have my number. See Charlotte in the clubhouse.*

There were far fewer interviews during week two. Department heads hired as fast as possible, but many positions were yet to be filled.

Lilith enjoyed meeting new people, but detested the burdensome accumulation of new snow. Steaming hot chocolate sent by Charlotte, and the sight of AJ's golden retrievers romping in the snow, was fun for the first week. However, when howling winds and below zero temperatures invaded, Lilith vacated the woodshed and went to AJ's house.

Since the Tampa fiasco, AJ had become a permanent fixture in his third-floor office perch. The office was a small circular platform which jutted out from the western stone turret. A narrow walkway large enough for two people connected the turret to the platform. Low handrails heightened the sensation that you would fall if you weren't careful. Cushioned benches sat four guests around the outer rim of the platform.

Scott loved the Cerebro vibe each time he worked there. But most of all, he appreciated the lack of hiding places for listening devices. The third-floor office was an easy scan for him. Next to the turret stairwells, it was the most secure room in the house.

Lilith and Charlotte never stopped teasing AJ about

his missing second floor on the western side of the house. During the home's construction, he couldn't decide on what to do with the second floor. The contractor laughed when AJ told him to skip it, and that's how the western side was completed; a house with a third floor, but no second floor.

Lilith entered through the back door and brushed the snow from her boots. Disappointment hit her when Sonny and Cher didn't rush to greet her. A quick peek into the kitchen explained why. Scott and Charlotte had the refrigerator door open.

She walked up the three flights to AJ's office, finding him hard at work at his desk. She took a seat on the padded bench behind him. "Find anything, Professor X?"

"Hey you, Scott and Charlotte just left," AJ said.

"They're in the kitchen raiding your fridge with the dogs."

AJ spun his chair around. "Your girlfriend has a cruel sense of humor. Poor Scott got a shock when he reached the top of the stairs. She had hiked up her skirt under her … "

"Oversized cream-colored boat neck sweater."

"Boat neck. I learn something every day. As I was saying, with her skirt hiked up beneath the sweater, she looked like a one-night stand leaning against my chair with her just-out-of-bed hair."

"Poor Scottie. She's evil."

"My word choice didn't help. I told her to pull down her skirt and his face turned four shades redder."

Lilith jabbed his shoulder with her finger. "I'll hear about it tonight. For now, tell me what you have."

AJ spread his arms over his desk like a child who didn't want to share. "Since the crate came, everyone has bugged me for details. I told you, not until the meeting."

Lilith poked harder, knowing he'd cave-in to her persistence.

"Fine, let me introduce you to Captain James Andrews of the British Royal Navy. The pouch hidden in the lid of the washed-up chest contained his journal. It details an exhaustive sixty-mile stretch of defenses on the South American coastline. Quite the achievement for a group which wasn't a colonial power.

"British archives list James Andrews MIA in 1713. He played a central role under Captain Jade Péchette, who I guess promoted him to pirate captain."

"Finally, headway."

AJ flipped to the back of the journal. "There's the image of a broken wheel and the name of a place."

Lilith leaned forward. "Broken Cove Palisade? They named their pirate base Broken Cove? And our company … Broken Cove Industries. Whoa, bruh."

"When we cruised the French Quarter in our convention shirts, our backs didn't draw the attention. The shirt sleeve with the broken wheel emblem and the BCP lettering underneath is what stirred the cauldron."

AJ leaned back in his chair. "The pirates on South America's north shore controlled two cities, five lighthouses, and one mammoth-sized pirate base. They pirated a wealth of war materials and other valuable items. The estuary portrait, with the two warships docked in their pirate base, is Broken Cove Palisade."

Lilith leaned back on the bench. "Péchette, Andrews, and Bennington?"

"Andrews took care of the defenses, Péchette led, and one Bill Bennington served as an adviser, but nothing tells me about Andrews."

Lilith pressed her hands together. "B for Bennington, P for Péchette. Do we have a candidate to fill the C word?"

"She's raiding my fridge."

"Not that C word."

AJ chuckled. "There is another person Andrews mentioned. A tall Spanish woman who spoke several languages, including French. Captain Morena Calveiro."

"You hired—" Lilith jumped up, and immediately sat back down. "Our new pastry chef is a Calveiro."

AJ let Lilith piece it together.

"A Calveiro? Was she with the Péchettes, or the Benningtons? When does Chef Calveiro return from her six-week chocolate tour? I want to meet this bitch."

"Lilith, keep your voice down. Knowing her name will affect how you interact with her. You need to be your usual charming self, not an interrogator. If our new chef is an innocent bystander, we might lose a talented chef. Scale back your suspicion; make an organic assessment of her."

She squinted her eyes and wrinkled her nose. "What is an organic assessment?"

"Hell if I know. Organic is a hot word to use in writing, so I'm trying it out."

Lilith dismissed him with a wave of her hand. "In less than a week, a Calveiro chef and a Calveiro pirate have entered our lives."

"She returns in four weeks."

"Charlotte better re-run another background check."

"I did," came a voice from the stairs. Neither of them had heard Charlotte climbing the stairs to the office.

"Damn it, Charlotte. Pull down your skirt. I'm not Scott."

Laughing, Charlotte lifted her sweater and her skirt

fell into place. "Why the attraction—I mean interest—in Ms. Calveiro? God, her catalog photos are sensational, and those long, silky legs are perfect for the *Bella Donna Long*. Why the second background check?"

AJ frowned at Lilith.

"We ain't married, so she's free to admire other women," Lilith said. She stood and pointed at the journal. "Look for yourself, troublemaker."

Charlotte bent over to inspect the journal. "Snow White is a spy? Talia called her Snow because she is a total princess, not because of the photo shoot. If Lydia can hoodwink Talia, she's dangerous."

Lilith began fidgeting with her amulet. "Talia is the human lie-detector. She can read faces and body language like no one's business. Well, except Scott's natural poker face."

"Ladies, if Ms. Calveiro is a spy, she is a concern for us. Lilith has a point. Two Calveiros coming into our lives in the same week is suspicious," AJ said.

"Did you share the other pages with her?" Charlotte asked.

"Just the journal."

"If I may, Professor."

"Quit calling me professor. I didn't intend to recreate Cerebro when I designed this office," AJ said.

Charlotte smirked and spoke to Lilith. "The back pages of the journal were left incomplete. Not whole pages, but selected words and sentences were omitted. We are guessing the missing pages lie over the existing pages to fill out the text. Without the missing pages, all we have is an incomplete puzzle.

"However," she poked on AJ's head, "our ancient

literary analysis expert believes the notes came from a person who had a clear mastery over chemistry. This pirate organization, this Voodoo Priestess—which you descended from—unlocked the science of chemistry a hundred and fifty years before anybody else did."

"Are the nontraditional pieces of the treasure the discoveries of chemistry?" Lilith asked.

"Our pirate-chemist synthesized a drug which suspends long-term memory formation, and puts a person in a heightened state of suggestibility. A person breathes this in, and they become a willing, but mindless, personal servant. The pirates used this dust to incapacitate sailors on passing ships. The legend Father Amare spoke of was real. A Voodoo Priestess stole a person's thoughts and soul with her breath."

"Functional zombies." Lilith said.

Charlotte sat on the bench across from Lilith. "This dust of theirs must be the same substance which got us at the convent museum. It blocked the formation of our memories during our missing day. We were at the mercy of those in our room. If not for Father Amare's personal hypnotisms protecting us, we would have blabbed everything we learned from the map room."

Lilith curled her legs up on the bench. "Where does that leave us?"

AJ said, "If we can find the missing pages to the journal and analyze Demon's Breath, we might crack the first clue on the map wall; *Impervious to Demons, if you know how*."

Charlotte's Memo Pad To-do List

1. Weir flow rate -- nominal. Crater Gully not draining. It's winter. Relax.
2.
3. Sort job applications, create hiring lists, EEOC training modules, payroll accountant in-house or
4. contract outside agency?
5. Pastry chef returns from world chocolate tour. See what she needs. (Talia says she's a looker.)
6.
7. Social Media campaign. Not me. Get somebody else.
8. Cool!!! I'm the director of the social media crew who are made up of the clubhouse receptionists.
9.
10. Hey. If I'm overseeing the social media ... Cleaver. They backed me into the job :(

Tayen's Notes:

Database set up: Ask AJ for help.
New employee orientation: grab T's notes D:drive
Map D:drive Scott's job.
Map all drives !!!

AJ's Notes: (Clear w/Tayen first)

Elliott's homecoming.
Borrow Lilith's flats and jeans.
Casual top, fuzzy, cute, dainty ... gag not me.

Staff Attendance:

Manny	Thom	Dean	Ladonna	Kimiko	Latrice	James	Lydia
IN	IN	IN	IN	IN	IN	IN	1/2

Scott Talia Lilith: always here, never gone.

15 - Gold Digger or the Spy

In the snowiest of winters, Portland snow lasted up to two weeks. But not this winter. After six weeks of unending snow, people were cursing its existence.

Lilith grew tired of staffing the woodshed next to The Village complex. Thoughts of Valentine's Day had her wondering what Charlotte would have planned had they not quit dating. Her thoughts changed with a sudden gust of wind blew snow in her face.

Angered by another icy blast, she stomped and kicked her feet, trying in vain to kill the snow. There was not a soul within screaming distance, so she didn't care if she looked like a two-year-old throwing a tantrum. Exhausted by her outburst, she slipped and fell on her butt. She sat up, crossed her arms, and screamed.

To add insult to her injury, the sound of galloping paws rushing toward her came from behind. AJ's golden retrievers routinely ignored the slowdown-on-ice protocol. Lilith laughed when they barreled through people. But this time, they were barreling toward her.

She braced for impact, but her tiny frame was no match for two rushing seventy-pound golden retrievers.

Boom!

A plume of snow poofed on contact.

Sonny licked her forehead, and Cher sniffed her chin. She pushed them away. "Cute and stupid, both of you."

AJ stood yards away, laughing so hard he doubled up. She raised her mitten-covered hand. *This mitten may cover my hand, but he'll be able to tell I'm flipping him off.*

She pushed herself up and waited for AJ.

A glance around the grand intersection stoked her imagination. She imagined it was summer and The Village's normal routine had taken root. Golf carts headed to the first tee, minibuses from the clubhouse rolled down the Village corridor, restaurants were full, and the kiosk listed golfers' tee times.

Her daydream ended with dog paws on her chest. Cher didn't like her human standing with her eyes closed. However, Lilith's stability on ice was more tenuous than Cher's. She stepped back and slipped. Laying in the snow, she refused to move or push the dogs aside.

"If you don't like the snow, go inside," AJ said after he reached her.

"I like Portland snow. But this Swiss Alps shit never goes away."

He helped her up and brushed the snow off her coat. "This too shall pass, my dear."

"Grand opening is in two weeks. The back nine—"

"Crater Gully. Learn the names for this facility."

"Fine. Crater Gully ain't draining 'cause of the snow."

"I don't have power over the weather."

Lilith raised her mitten-covered hand. Her true feelings were hidden in her mitten. "Golfers don't golf in this."

AJ squeezed her mitten, having guessed which finger she aimed at him. "Trust me. It's no secret how far from ready we are. The snow in Crater Gully will delay us, but there is a bright side. The clubhouse personnel are in place, and the front-of-house staff is almost filled. Back-of-house staff is coming along—"

"Blah, blah, blah," Lilith interrupted. "Charlotte and Tayen are scared you will run out of funds before opening. Staff training and contractor bills with no cash flow in? You'll have to default on the loans before long."

AJ side-hugged her. "You either took a course in management, or you listen very carefully to Charlotte."

"She and Tayen are working all angles for cash flow."

"If cash flow becomes a problem, Manny can empty the maintenance barn for Talia and company's exotic dancing."

Lilith slapped him on the arm. "How can you not be anxious?"

"Would it help if I stomped in the snow and screamed my lungs out?"

"It'd make you seem human."

AJ laughed. "I hate to tell you, but it'll get worse. I'm delaying the grand opening to May first."

"Two months' payroll for over two hundred employees?"

"It's getting tight, but not impossible."

"Charlotte said you're stretched like someone on a medieval torture machine. Your diminished lottery winnings are dwindling," Lilith said.

"If we don't have all associated businesses running by the grand opening on May first, then you can panic. Reservations for Pasta-de-faria's are set for the first two weeks. I'll open the front nine in late April … if I'm desperate. Kimiko's BCA orders are through the roof. What else can I do?"

"What about Crater Gully? It isn't draining," Lilith said.

AJ's confidence wavered as he peered past the clubhouse to the back nine. "Trust in nature and engineering."

"When do the lady golf administrators come?"

AJ gritted his teeth and shook his body. "May first."

Lilith grabbed his hand, unsure if she had heard correctly. "Did you say May first?"

"Grand opening on May first. It will be grand in one of two ways. Spectacular opening, or same day closing. I didn't do myself any favors by agreeing to the May first tour inspection."

Lilith didn't know what to say. Whatever she thought to say never felt adequate to share with AJ. She had her head up, hoping to find something to encourage him with. A car zooming down the road caught her attention. It slowed and pulled into the parking lot and headed toward them. AJ and Lilith were both watching it in curiosity.

The door opened, and a woman stepped out.

"Uh-oh. You be nice. You hear?" AJ warned.

Lilith zeroed in on the car. Her eyes betrayed her distrust.

"Lilith. You were in Tampa when Ms. Calveiro was hired. I don't want you choke holding her before we open."

"Where the hell did she get that tan? My god, those are knee-high calf-skin Valentino's. The girl's got style."

Lydia tugged on her coat lapels as she trudged through the snow on her way to them.

"Moose Knuckles, damn bitch," Lilith grumbled.

"Don't punch my pastry chef."

"Moose Knuckles is a designer parka and expensive as hell."

AJ called out, "Lydia , this is Lilith."

Lilith mumbled low enough, so only AJ heard her. "I hate this bitch."

AJ elbowed Lilith in her shoulder.

"Lydia Calveiro. AJ has told me about you."

AJ mumbled. "Lilith, stop acting like Charlotte."

Lydia stared into Lilith's eyes. "Are you wearing blue contacts?"

"No." Lilith's contempt faded as she caught a glimpse of Lydia's eyes. "Wow. Your eyes are as green and brilliant as the Chalk Emerald. You wouldn't happen to speak French, would you?"

AJ shoved Lilith in her back.

Lydia laughed. "English only. Not speaking Spanish is my fault. I guess fourth-generation immigrants lose the mother tongue."

Lilith twisted around to AJ. "Why do Tayen's hired girls—except Charlotte and me—have to be six feet tall? Almost every table server is tall enough to be a small forward in the WNBA."

"Kimiko and Thom aren't six feet. Nor are any of the girls on the greenskeeping crew."

"Maybe 'all' was over stating my point."

"She won the bakeoff fair and square." AJ nudged Lilith forward as he stepped away. "Lilith, give our pastry chef the full tour. Then send her to Tayen for keys, codes, and the like. I'm headed to the clubhouse to discuss this six-foot-tall job requirement with my general manager."

The thumping of galloping dogs came from behind them. Lilith wrapped around Lydia, bracing them for the imminent impact.

Lydia reciprocated the embrace. "What's this for?"

"The owner's dumb hounds are going to hit us."

The galloping dissipated as it reached them. Lilith turned Lydia around to see why a crash didn't occur. Sonny and Cher stood feet away, unsure of the stranger wrapped around Lilith.

Lydia squealed. "Oh, they're so cute!"

The dogs wagged their tails at Lydia's excited greeting.

Lilith grumbled at the dogs. "Losers. You think twice before careening into somebody bigger than me."

Lydia stood from petting the dogs to see Lilith beckoning her with a finger wave.

"This way. You've got to see the catalog."

Lydia stepped behind Lilith. "Did it turn out okay?"

They reached the elevator, where the door was already open. They stepped in, and Lilith pushed the button for the second floor.

"You wore Kimi's designs. What do you think?"

"If the photos are half as good as her designs, watch out. But I don't understand. How hasn't she been discovered in the fashion industry?"

The door opened, and they walked the few steps to

Broken Cove Accessories. "She doesn't like the limelight, but she loves sewing and designing. AJ gave her the forum to design while we handle the day-to-day business for her. The catalog is on the counter when we first enter."

Lilith held the door open, and Lydia marched into the finished store. Mannequins showcased Kimiko's pirate outfits and women's golf wear. Hats, tops, shorts, and gloves filled the shelves and countertops. A far cry from the empty store Lydia had stood in when she was hired.

She picked up the catalog from the counter and pulled it against her chest.

Lilith laughed. "You beat out strong competition for the front cover, and page four is all yours."

Lydia pushed the catalog from her chest and thumbed through it. "Wow, I guess I can model." She flipped it around and pointed at page five. "Is this Talia?"

Lilith nodded.

"I didn't expect to start here as a model for pirate costumes. I was hired as the pastry chef, and moments later, I entered this shop to the shock of a lifetime. High-quality clothing with professional models. And Talia, why is she here? Modeling agencies would die to have her."

"She does ratchet up the sexual fantasy bracket of Kimi's clothing. She likes us, and we like her. It seems to be enough to keep her here."

"Are you a basketball fan?" Lydia asked.

"What makes you think that?"

"You just said fantasy bracket, and earlier you compared the servers to small forwards in the NBA."

"Oh. The members are wearing off on me. March's college basketball tournament is around the corner, so that's all I hear nowadays."

"Ah. An occupational hazard. Your customers' interests whittle into your interests after a while." Lydia peered out through the glass door. "I am curious, though. I have only met two guys, AJ and Chef Dean. Are there other men working here?"

"Are you working on your MRS degree?"

"No, definitely not."

"Definitely not?"

"I'm not in the market for a husband or boyfriend."

"Forgive me. That was rude of me," Lilith said.

Lydia whirled her hand above her head. "I asked about the male population because this is a golf course, typically a male-dominated arena. I've met and talked with more women than men. The vibe I'm getting is that this is a woman-centric golf course. That is weird, isn't it?"

"Weird is the first and last item on the menu around here." Lilith blinked as past events ran through her head. "We stand at a crossroads, with unparalleled success down one path, and unmitigated failure down the other."

"I had the feeling everybody was under the gun."

"We are. We're concerned for AJ, who is the sweetest boss. He cosigned my roommate's car loan and paid for three of our department heads to move from Missouri. If you fit into his business model, he lets you do as you please. He has crazy ideas, and our general manager, Tayen, makes his dreams come true."

Lydia raised an eyebrow.

"Tayen heads him … Damn it." Lilith held up her hand, stopping a catastrophe of word-twisting . "She takes his exotic dreams and … Shit, no, that's worse."

"He's idealistic, and she's pragmatic?" Lydia suggested.

"Praise Jesus. Exactly what I meant."

Lydia smiled and continued thumbing through the catalog.

"What are your dreams, Lydia Calveiro?"

Lydia's eyes flashed from doe-eyed innocent to suspicious combatant. "That feels like the sort of prying question one gets in an interview."

Lilith had failed to disguise her suspicion of a Calveiro's appearance after the events in New Orleans. She scrambled to regain the upper hand. "Just as you find it strange that Talia works here, I, too, find it hard to believe you haven't modeled. These catalog photos are professional grade. And I'm not referring to the clothing or photos. Why aren't you modeling in Milan?"

Lydia laid the catalog on the counter. "I don't dance in a G-string like the stripper dwarfettes. Nor professionally for a dance company. Dancing is my passion and joy, but living a dancer's life would kill the rewards dancing gives me. My senior year in college, I switched to another passion: cooking. Modeling never entered my mind. I'm the type who spends a week in the Metropolitan Museum of Art, not wandering down Madison Avenue."

Lydia placed her hands on her hips. "Did I pass?"

Lilith smiled to disarm the encounter. "Grand opening had to be delayed, and I'm protective of him. He has risked everything he owns on this business, and it would kill me to see his efforts fail."

"You think I'm here to submarine his plans?"

"Knee-high calf-skin Valentino's and a Moose Knuckles designer parka. And this is your first job as a chef?" Lilith's suspicion was out of the shopping bag.

Lydia studied Lilith's face. "Why such devotion from

an employee? Or are you more than an employee?"

"I don't consider him my boss, but a friend with benefits." Lilith was proud of herself for sticking up for AJ and clarifying their professional relationship. But when Lydia's jaw dropped open, she realized what she had said.

"Goddamn it. That's the second time I've screwed the pooch in describing our relationship. Back in the fall, I led the New Orleans police to believe he was my pimp."

Lydia's rapid blinking told Lilith her clarification did nothing to assuage Lydia's perception.

"God, that morning grows worse with each retelling." She pointed to the door. "Your bakery and coffee shop await you, Chef Lydia—" Lilith paused. "I was going to use your full name, but I didn't catch your middle name."

Lydia took a catalog and walked to the door. "Well, if you're trying to be formal, my full name is Lydia Morena Calveiro."

***

AJ returned home from the contentious meeting with Tayen. She produced job application filing dates to prove she wasn't singling out women taller than five-ten. Her explanation of 'we grow them tall on the West Coast' did little to appease him.

He returned home and stomped the snow from his shoes. Through the house garage and down the hallway, he heard dishes clanking in the kitchen. He rounded the corner where Charlotte was unloading the dishwasher. Not expecting this, he asked, "Who else has keys to my house?"

"No keys. But the code to your garage door is general knowledge among the senior staff and trusted subordinates."

Charlotte paused for a moment. "Come to think of it, I can't think of a person who doesn't have the code."

He snarled at her. "Why are you unloading the dishes?"

"I'm helping you on the day of Elliott's homecoming. I can't wait to see him after his stint at The Hague."

AJ wasn't buying it. "Dress jeans, low heels, and an adorable peach-colored fuzzy sweater, diamond stud earrings from Tayen … You're shooting for the domestic housewife look."

Charlotte spoke with uncharacteristic passivity. "I dress casually when not in the office, and I wanted to help you clean the house."

"Lilith cleans your apartment. You refuse to touch the vacuum cleaner."

"I want your house neat and tidy."

"Gold digger. You want to appear adorable so Elliott doesn't suspect you are balls-to-the-wall fashion and makeup."

Domestic Charlotte disappeared, and shameless Charlotte spoke. "So what if I am? He is cute, and I'm applying for the trophy wife position. Imagine me as your darling daughter-in-law."

"Quit pouting your lips. They don't work on me. He's ten years older than you, and besides, I thought you and Lilith were an item?"

"We're best friends, but a long-term relationship would result in a murder."

"Should I offer my condolences for the breakup, or congratulations on the mutual conscious uncoupling?"

"Well, Gwyneth, mutual conscious uncoupling works. We are best friends, so congrats are in order."

AJ frowned. "Manny said you've spent more time in the maintenance barn—"

"I went out with a greenskeeper on a few dates. Carlos was a good time, but not what I'm looking for."

"What are you looking for? Other than one-night stands?" AJ asked.

"What makes you think Carlos was a one-night stand?"

"Forgive me. Two nights."

Charlotte had her middle finger extended, but she didn't have time to raise her arm. The sound of the garage door opening brought the conversation grinding to a halt. Elliott was home.

AJ stood with his arms folded. Charlotte held up her hand and pointed at her ring finger, where an engagement ring would go. A car door shut, and the garage door opener hummed as the door lowered. AJ shook his head and sneered. Charlotte wet her lips with the tip of her tongue. The door opened, and Charlotte relented. "Father first." When AJ took a step forward, she added, "For now."

Elliott opened the door and entered the hall. AJ stepped from the kitchen and embraced his taller son. "Good to see you. Sorry for the mountains of snow."

Elliott pushed back to see his dad's face. "It looks great, and so do you." His glasses fogged up, but not enough to hide his hazel eyes. Taking off his gloves, he turned around and found Charlotte. "Whoa! What's with the June Cleaver look-alike?"

Charlotte held out her arms, expecting a hug. "Elliott."

A foot taller than Charlotte, Elliott had to lean over to hug her. She clung to his neck as he straightened up. Her feet dangled above the floor while she taunted AJ with her tongue close to Elliott's ear.

Elliott twisted her to the side and searched the atrium. "Where are the dogs?"

"They're with Lilith. Let me text her to send them home."

Elliott sniffed Charlotte's neck. "Nice perfume, and you're wearing jeans. Why not your typical skirts or dresses?"

With her feet back on the floor, she twirled around, making sure he got a good look at her waist and hips. "These things? I threw these on to help your dad in the kitchen."

"You learned to cook?"

"I'm better at cleaning than cooking."

Elliott took off his jacket. "Peanut butter between two double chocolate pop tarts covered in chocolate isn't cooking."

Charlotte quit acting and squared off at AJ. "Blabbermouth. Is there anything father and son don't talk about?"

"Wait until I tell him what you were doing with your tongue a second ago."

Charlotte flipped AJ off. "I don't cook or clean, but there isn't an alcoholic beverage I can't make. Name your drink, Elliott."

"Tequila Sunrise, if you would." Elliott felt his ear as he took a seat next to the kitchen island. "The snow can't be good news. Will Crater Gully dry out before spring?"

AJ sat next to his son. "The March opening ain't happening."

Charlotte opened the refrigerator door. "The decision to delay the grand opening to May first is for the best. I'm heartbroken we couldn't get the ball rolling, but every business sector is lining up for a delayed grand opening."

Elliott asked, "Did you get a new general manager? Just listen to her. Tayen has her on the fast track to upper management. She sounds like me when I was doing oral arguments to defend my MBA."

"She assumed the role of the Wikipedia of Broken Cove Industries," AJ said. "It can be scary how much info she houses between those ears. Employees, deliveries, contractors, schedules, and whatever form is needed for whatever you're doing. Charlotte knows without having to pull up a spreadsheet. Go ahead, ask her anything."

"Okay," Elliott shot out, "What are Pasta-de-faria's occupancy rate on Fridays, and how does third quarter the employee turnover rate look?"

Charlotte slid the Tequila Sunrise and her phone on the kitchen island over to Elliott. "Four scenarios planned with strong confidence on scenario two. It projects one hundred percent occupancy with an hour's wait for table openings, and less than three percent employee turnover."

Elliott didn't bother to look at her phone and slid it back. "I believe you."

"On days with her by my side, I don't have to pick up the phone," AJ added.

"How about the convention in New Orleans? No one has said much about it."

Charlotte spun around and faced the liquor bottles on the counter.

AJ stammered and looked away. "Ah, well, it had moments. More headaches than it was worth, if you ask me."

"Dad, I am asking you. What happened at the convention?"

"How long are you staying?"

"Two weeks."

Shazoo sprang up on the island, surprising Elliott. He lifted the cat off the island. "Shazoo, you shouldn't be jumping on the kitchen counters. Hey, what have you got in your mouth?"

Charlotte spun around, fearing the worst. Before AJ could grab Shazoo, Elliott had pulled the bug out of his mouth. Holding it up to the light, he took a long look. He bent over and placed Shazoo on the floor. Without saying a word, he pointed at the bug.

AJ winced as he spun out of his seat and motioned for Elliott to join him. Charlotte waved goodbye; she was leaving. AJ's demonstrative finger-pointing overrode her departure. Conditioned by silence and people moving toward the stairwell, Shazoo bounced behind them.

Elliott sat on the steps in the turret stairwell. Charlotte nuzzled into his lap and picked up a purring Shazoo. AJ refused to address her shenanigans.

"We had difficulty in New Orleans."

"Ernesto Cottrell type trouble?"

"How did you know?"

"I'm government, Dad. It's my job to know."

AJ rolled his eyes shut.

Elliott lifted Charlotte off his lap and placed her next to him. "My work keeps me in Ernesto's sphere. It didn't take me long to run across the YouTube video of Lilith and Ernesto's daughter."

"We were blissfully ignorant. Their dance was totally innocent."

"And a favorite with my coworkers. They hid it whenever I stepped in their cubical."

"Are you investigating us?" Charlotte asked.

"I'm not investigating you. But others in my office—and a growing list of nations—are interested in your business. They reassigned me a couple of times to different investigations. Whatever I delve into, it comes back to your country club."

Elliott held up the bug Shazoo had brought him. "With the possible exception of an unidentified entity in Amsterdam, no one knows why Ernesto Cottrell is interested in you."

"What is in Amsterdam?" Charlotte asked.

Elliott skipped her question. "What happened in New Orleans, Dad?"

"Ernesto thinks we are privy to info concerning a pirate treasure."

"Are you?"

"Did you know Priestess LaTonya?" Charlotte asked.

Elliott's eyes popped open. "Oh my God, why mention her?"

"She died last summer. If you believe in Voodoo, her death lifted a protection spell and exposed your dad to the underworld in New Orleans."

"You mean Ernesto Cottrell's underworld?"

"Him, or the Bennington Crime Syndicate," AJ said.

Elliott hemmed and hawed for a moment. "Yeah, not too far off. The BCS doesn't interfere with Ernesto's dealings, and if they do, they push him out of the way. But hey, I changed jobs. Maybe they changed their methods."

"A series of coincidences lined up against us," AJ said. "We have the clues to find this pirate treasure, and we're working to understand them. I am under no illusions. Once we give Ernesto what he wants, he will kill us."

Elliott nodded. "A realistic expectation. I'm glad to hear you aren't deluding yourself. So tell me, what is the treasure?"

"The usual pirate treasure of gold and gems, but also nontraditional items, which haven't been divulged to us. Evidence … " AJ bobbed his head. "Forgive me, oral traditions, not evidence, indicate scientific findings and possibly artwork."

"What treasure could draw a drug cartel's attention? There aren't enough remaining huge finds left in the world."

"Limit the treasures to the Caribbean or the Gulf of Mexico, and we have two candidates: the Montezuma Treasure, and Blackbeard's Treasure."

"Why not the Treasure of Lima?" Elliott asked.

"Stop." Charlotte waved her hands. "Explain these treasures before I lose it."

"They are the big ones left to find, dearest," Elliott said.

AJ wrung his hands together. "Our time frame eliminates the Treasure of Lima, and the location makes me lean away from the Montezuma Treasure. Our pirate map was created by a member of the Brethren of the Coast, and the dates on the map correspond with Blackbeard."

Elliott leaned against the steps. "Brethren of the Coast, Blackbeard, and the Golden Age of Piracy. Great. But Blackbeard was notoriously unreliable. His claim to have hidden a legendary treasure is dubious."

Charlotte beat Elliott's leg in frustration. "Don't become a freaking data geek like your father."

AJ didn't acknowledge Charlotte's slight. "Why are you here, in the dead of winter?"

"As I said before, I'm not investigating you."

Charlotte pressed her finger over Elliott's lips. "You have an MBA. How d'you learn about lost pirate treasures?"

Elliott kissed her finger and pulled her hand down. "My job led me away from business management. For the last three years, I've been earning another master's, this one is in art history."

"You work in The Hague for the US government with advanced degrees in business and art history." Charlotte was piecing it together. "You investigate crimes pertaining to, but not limited to, art. Drug cartels have a rich history of dealing in stolen artwork."

"With a mind like that, why did you decline Yale and Harvard?"

"Make me your wife, and I'll share all my secrets."

Elliott turned his head to dodge the kiss aimed at his lips. "Dad, what do you know about Tayen's past?"

AJ fell back against the turret wall. "Don't tell me she is dirty."

"Her name comes up at the strangest times and places. When it does, people disperse faster than if they smelled a skunk."

Charlotte didn't like hearing this. "Tayen left her job as vice president of international finance because shit happened wherever she went. The angst on her face when we talk about business dealings is real. She was not involved in the criminal underworld."

"That's one theory," Elliott said. "The other is she has a repository of information which could indict many, many people. We aren't aware of how consequential her info is. Is it widespread but shallow, narrow but deep, or widespread and deep? None of her activity came to me until the last couple of weeks."

"Elliott, she is a guardian angel to me. Charlotte suspected her past, but dug up nothing. Are you telling me I can't trust the person who organized Broken Cove Industries so it can succeed beyond my wildest dreams?"

"Dad, if you trust her, continue to. But if you suspect anything, tell me. What should worry you is your new hires. You have scores of new employees, and some could be Ernesto's people. Trust your inner circle and no one outside of it."

"That's easy," AJ said. "Us, Lilith, Tayen, and Scott. Well, Kimiko too. Hey, let's walk over to The Village and give you a quick tour. I want my dogs back from Lilith."

They hurried out of the house and down the ramp to the underground tunnel leading to The Village. At the end of the tunnel, a hundred yards away, two women had just reached the bottom of the Village ramp with two dogs behind them.

Elliott called out, "Sonny, Cher." The dog's ears perked up. He called out again, and they galloped up the tunnel with all deliberate speed. Elliott greeted the groaning and jumping canines, laughing at their uncontrolled joy.

"Are you seeing that?" Charlotte whispered to AJ.

AJ strained to see down the tunnel. "Add lighting for the house tunnel to Manny's list. I'm either hallucinating—"

"You're not hallucinating. Lilith's eyes are glowing."

AJ braced himself.

Elliott stood from petting the dogs. "You two really need counseling. It's freaky lighting that's reflecting out of their eyes." Raising his voice, he called out, "Is that my Lilith Daisy?"

Charlotte whispered, "Let him think it's freaky lighting and not the freaky thing from New Orleans."

AJ pointed down the tunnel. "But Lydia's eyes are glowing too."

Lilith rushed down the tunnel and threw herself at Elliott. He growled his excitement as he caught and spun her around. He didn't recognize the other woman and lowered Lilith to the ground. "Forgive me, who is your friend?"

Lydia stepped from the shadows. Her eyes sparkled as the light radiated from her green irises. She inched closer to Elliott, not realizing the deep red blush on her face betrayed her first impression of him. Her fingers spiked out from rigid hands as she stood silent.

Elliott failed to speak. His blushing face said more than his gaping mouth.

AJ and Charlotte breathed easier. Halfway down the tunnel, both Lilith and Lydia's eyes stopped glowing. Lilith took notice of their relief. Together, the three witnessed Elliott and Lydia's failure to act like adults. It looked like love at first sight to Lilith. AJ and Charlotte smiled; they saw it.

Lilith broke the silence and made the introductions. "Lydia, this is Elliott de Faria, son of AJ. Elliott. Meet our new pastry chef and coffee shop manager, Lydia Calveiro."

Elliott held his hand out; Lydia held hers out; but they were too far apart to shake hands.

Lilith turned to AJ and Charlotte, and repeated Lydia's name. "Yes indeed, Lydia … *Morena* … Calveiro."

AJ and Charlotte's smiles vanished.

16 - Admin Meetings

A frenetic surge of activity swarmed through the general manager's office on the last Monday before the grand opening.

Charlotte nudged the burnished bronze-framed roll-a-cart against the corner wall. Fresh pots of steaming coffee overshadowed the wondrous aroma of the cart's cedar inlays. She wanted the atmosphere of the first official administrative team meeting to equal the splendor and sophistication of a Manhattan executive office.

Tayen carried her laptop and giant coffee cup to the oval conference table, which occupied the southern half of her office. Her coffee cup depicted a horse from her teenage years. Whenever asked about her cup, she reminisced about her first and favorite horse.

Department heads took their seats and set up their

laptops. Kimiko held her USB cable up as she searched for a connection. On cue, small ports popped up from the conference table. Amazed, Kimiko looked at Charlotte, who winked and placed a remote on the coffee cart.

Tayen started the meeting. "Welcome everybody. I am pleased to announce we have filled all department head positions. Dolly Hightower has accepted the director of Broken Cove Charities position."

Light applause rose as Dolly nodded her hellos.

"Good to have you aboard, Dolly. I need to share one other informational piece before we start the first full admin team meeting. AJ will fill the position for Broken Cove Education."

"He got it so you'd get some peace?" Kimiko asked.

Tayen ignored the question. "Onto the first item of business: the grand opening is moving back two months."

"Don't tell me he gets two votes. One as the owner and one as BCE director."

"Kimi. Quiet," Tayen said.

Lilith straightened the beverage cart and listened. She tapped her chest to find her amulet. It had popped from under her top, and she couldn't feel it for a moment.

"The strategic business unit names were approved by the owner. Pirate's Chocolate wins because of its resiliency against double entendres. I won't recount the many dirty names generated by our pirate-themed chocolate bakery. Pirate's Chocolate Booty describes our business. However, it's not the image we want meme'd to death in the first week after opening.

"The coffee shop name, Coffee Cove, had universal support at our last meeting. The owner," Tayen took a deep breath, "chose an alternative spelling. Coffee Cov*fefe*."

Admin members displayed looks of confusion. They were poised to ask why the change in spelling, but Tayen's dead eyes and cheerless disposition warned them not to.

"As you know," Tayen continued, "Crater Gully is an impact crater formed millions of years ago. Bowl shaped, it holds enough water to form a swamp, but the eastern flank is too low for a lake to form. A drainage system was constructed to dry out the crater and give us the back nine. In the center of Crater Gully, we have a large shallow, lake. By far, this was the most ambitious and expensive project we've tackled.

"However, this record-cold winter has affected Crater Gully's drainage. Our head groundskeeper, Manny, informs me that the back nine won't be ready until late April. To secure a tour professional event, we hit the ground sprinting, not simply running. Our staff needs to perform flawlessly under a variety of stressful situations. Proficiency comes with sufficient training. For more details, our Assistant General Manager, Elliott de Faria, can explain."

"Good morning. Thank you for the intro—"

"Thpppt."

"Charlotte," Tayen shouted, "shut the door and take Lilith with you."

Lilith walked to the door, confused by her inclusion with Charlotte's banishment.

"Elliott, sorry for my assistant's childish behavior."

"Thank you. I want to say—"

"Why did she raspberry Elliott?" Kimiko asked.

"She's pissed she didn't get the Assistant General Manager position. Elliott, continue."

"What I—"

Kimiko interrupted Elliott. "The owner's son gets the job, and the one who fits naturally into the position is denied?

Nepotism. No offense, Elliott. I like you, but appearances are everything. And since my business is appearances—"

"Kimiko, not now." AJ raised his index finger to his lips. "Elliott, you have the floor."

"Thanks, Dad—"

"I needed someone with experience to fill the position," Tayen interrupted. "Charlotte is talented, but Elliott has the requisite experience. Elliott."

"My plan for—"

"You quit your job with the government in The Hague? Without two weeks' notice?" Latrice Williams, Broken Cove Food and Beverage Manager, asked.

AJ spoke before Elliott could. "He liked what we were creating here, and he wanted to be a part of her."

Tayen corrected AJ. "He wanted to be a part of our world-class golf resort and professional golf tour stop."

It was too late for Tayen to cover AJ's verbal miscue. Heads had turned toward Lydia.

Embarrassed by the attention, Lydia said, "I'm just a pastry chef who's dating the owner's son. I didn't persuade anybody to hire him as the assistant general manager."

Chef Ladonna said, "Good thing we don't have a by-law against admin members dating or being married, otherwise Dean would be out of a job."

Tayen feared the meeting was running off the rails and raised her voice. "We are a dynamic and talented group of individuals. But I guarantee it won't take long for this admin team to learn how we act in meetings."

"Ha-ha, ha-ha." The closed office door couldn't block out Charlotte's laughter.

***

Tayen had a smoother start for the next week's admin meeting. She reported, "Devices left by the hydrologists are helping us monitor the progress of Crater Gully's drainage. No increase in the flow rate over the weir. AJ, all yours."

"Thank you, Tayen. The cold weather froze Crater Gully and slowed the drainage. Which leads to my idea for next winter. I would like—"

"Yeah, no." Tayen cut him off. "I demand we ban AJ from making any further modifications to the existing plans."

"Oh, come on. It wasn't insane."

"Freezing the lake in Crater Gully in the winter months for ice-skating is outrageous," Tayen growled.

AJ retorted. "You didn't know what a hectare was until Charlotte searched it for you."

"Yeah-well-now we have 2.95 of them in the lake."

"What's a hectare?" Kimiko asked.

"Ten thousand square meters. Genius here wanted to freeze the equivalent of six football fields into one massive skating rink. All those in favor of banning the owner from future modifications, say, aye."

In unison and unanimously, the motion passed.

AJ leaned back in his chair, pissed. "How does an owner get banished from making decisions about his own business? Hell, I even lost the girlfriend vote. It was her chance to score some brownie points."

"On to the next item." Tayen's tap on her laptop resounded throughout the room. "We need a Gertie alert."

Lydia raised her hand. "What's a Gertie?"

"Something we don't have 2.95 of down in Crater Gully."

A snort came from the other room.

"Charlotte," Tayen knew her assistant was laughing at AJ's comeback, "shut the door."

Elliott began, "Gertie is our resident—"

"Why do we need a Gertie alert?" asked Kimiko.

"Because news of a golfer killing a thousand-pound moose by an errant nine-iron isn't something I want to discuss with a news reporter," Tayen said.

"Gertie is a moose?" Latrice asked.

"The country club sits on the edge of the wilderness. The fifth and seventh holes have wildlife intrusions, and the moose was our first incursion. Our golden retriever ambassadors, AJ's dogs, played with Gertie next to the seventh green, and led her back into the woods. A couple of days later, Gertie reappeared, and they repeated their play-therapy, which was enough to send her away."

Elliott said, "Gertie alerts—"

"Who named it Gertie?" Lydia asked.

The office door opened, and Charlotte poked her head around the door. She batted her eyes and smiled.

"Shut the door, moose lover," Tayen ordered.

***

Tayen ran the next week's meeting with a firm hand and shut down distractions before she lost control. Her rigid tone of voice informed the admin team not to cross her path.

"New security cameras are being added. Gertie and the other wildlife are one reason. Another is for basic security. We have a sprawling multi-million-dollar complex, and security is required by our insurance."

Lilith straightened the beverage cart. She knew Tayen wasn't sharing the real reason for the added security. In the turret stairwell meetings, Scott had reported the abrupt appearance of multiple strangers with binoculars. Elliott warned these strangers were likely Ernesto Cottrell's operatives, who were asserting a more robust surveillance.

Tayen explained, "As you have heard, strangers have popped up on the edges of the premises. Staff reports out-of-place individuals in unusual locations. We don't know their intent or purpose, but AJ and I agreed to install cameras, which will give us better monitoring of our complex."

AJ and Elliott sat uncharacteristically still.

"The security system allows us to implement Code Purple: the domestic violence protection transport for battered women. We'll transport victims from courthouses to safehouses."

Tayen surveyed the room to gauge their reaction.

"AJ and I believe the twelve sitting here want to participate in this nontraditional job responsibility. But we shouldn't make assumptions and will not compel you. If you don't want to be a part of Code Purple, please let me know."

Kimiko said, "Just as we banned AJ from future project changes, I can say we are all onboard with Code Purple."

After hearing his admin team say 'aye,' in unison, AJ leaned forward. "Scott created the program. We secured independent funding and recruited a small army of personnel. Talia runs point and is the face for Code Purple. Both individuals have loved ones who have undergone domestic abuse. Your response to this magnanimous service—" AJ choked back his pride. "Well, hell. I have no words."

He nodded to Elliott. "Tell us your news."

"Thanks, Dad—"

***

The following week at six a.m., Elliott picked up his father in the new four-seated golf cart, *The Mini Black Pearl*. Painted navy blue with white lettering, *The Mini Black Pearl* was designated the queen of the new golf cart fleet.

AJ hurried out of the garage door and took the passenger seat. "Wonderful. Fog to start the day."

Elliott drove the cart across the pickleball court. "Orientation day for new hires. What—"

AJ's cell rang as they descended the ramp to the underground tunnel connecting AJ's house to The Village complex. "Tayen's upset that we're late."

"She has a full day scheduled, so don't screw with her timetable," Elliott said.

"Charlotte will keep her on schedule. As for you, where will you be during orientation?"

The motion detectors turned on the tunnel lights, and Elliott no longer strained to drive in the darkness. "I can hear the disappointment in your voice. But my decision is final and you need to let it go."

"You quit a high-paying government job over a cute girl," AJ said.

"Lydia is intelligent, a talented chef, a gifted dancer, and not afraid to join me at the gun club."

"You forgot stunningly beautiful, which I'm guessing was the ultimate deciding factor."

"Attraction brings the customer into the store to browse. But once in the doors, it's the quality of the product that matters. Her looks got me in the store."

AJ surveyed the rows of golf carts in the cavernous underground garage. "You just commodified your girlfriend."

"Don't tell her." Elliott zoomed the golf cart up the ramp into The Village. "The past month has been all marketing and sales. I'm inclined to a reductionist frame of mind."

Elliott took a sharp turn onto the bus lane, which almost jostled AJ out of his seat. "She joins you at the shooting range?"

"Lilith said building a relationship means taking an interest in the other person's hobbies. I am learning dance, but she's faster at learning firearms."

Elliott sped them across the street and down the ramp to the clubhouse's underground parking garage.

"Dad, I know you're concerned with Captain Morena Calveiro, but this is pastry chef Lydia Morena Calveiro. She is nothing but a hometown girl without connections to organized crime." He parked *The Mini Black Pearl* in the reserved parking spot next to the members' entrance.

"All I ask is if you see anything incongruous with her, dig and find out if it negatively impacts us," AJ said.

Elliott opened the door. "Listen to us. I'm preoccupied with marketing and commodified my girlfriend, while you're using geometry and math terms. I take it you filled the math position in Broken Cove Education?"

"The product—damn it, another math term. Yesterday's interviews gave us a leading math candidate and two language arts folks."

Moments later, they entered the general manager's office, in which the meeting was already in progress. Tayen did not pause at their entrance.

"We have two hundred and thirty new employees for today's orientation. After my first hour presentation, division heads will take their subordinates on their respective tours of the complex. Except for Coffee Cov*fefe* and Pirate's Chocolate, most of you have multiple positions to fill."

"Ahem."

"Sorry, Kimiko. You have one position to fill. Fitting food and beverage personnel in pirate regalia will keep you busy for the next month."

"After today, we will have more daylight hours than night," Kimiko said.

"The vernal equinox is two days away," Tayen said.

"Equinox is a science term for the day and night of equality at the equator. But other cities have the mystic day of equality before or after the equatorial equinox. Portland's day of equality comes two days before the equator's."

Tayen's eyes sprang open, and the blood drained from her cheeks. She darted her eyes at AJ to find him as shocked as she was. Father Amare's forgotten words had returned to them.

Tayen stood. "Elliott, take over, please." She hurried out of the office with AJ on her heels. She ran through the office waiting room and burst into the elevator lobby. AJ rushed up to her side and grabbed her arm.

Rather than stumbling, Charlotte kicked off her high heels as she ran after her bosses. Lilith scooted behind, picking up her roommate's shoes along the way.

"Focus on today, not what happened in New Orleans six months ago. This is a coincidence, not divine providence," AJ said.

Tayen didn't resist AJ's wrist grab. "Six months ago, we had our orientation to the map room on the mystic day of equality. Six months later, we have another orientation with the same words Father Amare used."

"What can I say? Big events hit us on the equinoxes.

At least we are avoiding the solstices. Don't let superstitions around astronomical events drive you insane," AJ said.

"I hate to bring this up, but we received the newspaper with the Tampa chest on the winter solstice," Charlotte said.

Tayen pulled out her phone. "When's the damn summer solstice? I'm resigning the week before."

Lilith bumped Charlotte and mouthed her question so as not to interrupt. *'What is a solstice?'*

"Hold it together for today. Employee orientation can't be delayed," AJ said.

Charlotte turned to Lilith's side and whispered, "Summer solstice is the longest day and shortest night of the year, which happens in June. Winter solstice comes in December and gives us the shortest day and longest night."

"One more incident with this treasure hunt on a day with an astronomical event and I resign," Tayen said.

***

An hour later, orientation in the Greek-styled mini amphitheater began. A podium stood dead center in the concentric tiered rows. The stained-glass dome glowed with the sunlight and illuminated the podium. Charlotte's short video, illustrations, and masterful slides were executed flawlessly.

As the hour neared completion, Tayen gave glowing individual introductions of the division heads and key non-management personnel. New employees applauded as each division head stepped forward and waved their hellos.

Lilith squirmed to the side, wishing she didn't have to accompany the division heads. She was the lead gift shop clerk. There were not enough subordinates in her area for her to meet the requirement for management. She was okay with not shouldering more responsibility. But the lure of a significant raise caused her to rethink her position.

Tayen's gracious introductions ended with Lilith. "Last is the woman who will lead the gift shop and welcome center. She is the heart of The Village complex, not because of her central location, but because of her winning personality and willingness to help whenever asked. Our lead gift shop clerk, Lilith Peters."

Lilith stepped forward to applause. It stopped as the new employees swooned with oohs and aahs. Several people said, "My god, look at her eyes."

Tayen smiled at their amazement. "Yes, Lilith has magnificent blue eyes. Don't crowd her to get a look at them." A glance at AJ informed Tayen something was wrong. His face had turned a ghostly white, and his eyes bulged. She turned to see the cause of AJ's panic.

Lilith's eyes were glowing as they had in the map room. Twinkling blue streaks revolved like a spinning galaxy. Employees had dropped jaws and gaping wide eyes. Some rose from their seats as they leaned forward.

Unsure of what was happening, Lilith found AJ standing near the back of the amphitheater. He motioned for her to step back, which she did to a chorus of disappointment from the employees.

"Sometimes the light hits her eyes just so," Tayen said, "and it's crazy when it does. Now, let's move on to—"

Tayen continued with orientation, and Charlotte rushed to AJ, who stared at the dome. He belayed his orders. "Grab Scott, find the glass manufacture and everyone associated with our stained glass. Find out if this is coincidental, or if somebody is trying to expose Lilith."

Charlotte scurried off.

Elliott stepped beside his dad. "Why is everyone who went to New Orleans losing their composure and panicking for the second time today?"

"You saw Lilith's eyes as we encountered them in the map room. Plus, other details are coming to life."

"What's coming to—"

AJ cut his son off. "Shadow Tayen. Keep her on task and on her feet. Charlotte, Scott, and I are on this."

He tapped Elliott to go as Lilith approached.

"Stay away from the stained-glass dome, please. Don't ask what is happening and fulfill the tasks assigned to you for today. We'll talk later."

Lilith twirled away.

AJ turned to the podium, finding Tayen in control of orientation. Beyond her, on the other side of the mini amphitheater, he caught Lydia glancing at him. She turned away when they made eye contact, but he kept watching her. After a few seconds, she glanced back at him.

***

That evening, a meeting took place in AJ's atrium. Scott finished scanning the house for listening devices and cleared them to speak. Tayen collapsed on the couch and drank from her water bottle.

"I wouldn't be surprised if that water bottle was filled with alcohol," AJ said.

Tayen held up the water bottle. "Then you're not surprised. It's filled with thirty-two ounces of margarita."

Charlotte lifted her water bottle. "I'm way ahead of you. This is forty ounces."

"Sit up. I don't want spilled margarita on my couch," AJ said.

"It's tequila, so I'm good."

Lilith burst through the back door. "It's later. Spill it."

The suddenness of Lilith's entrance caused Charlotte to spill her water bottle. Sonny and Cher sniffed the tequila, but didn't lick it. Charlotte rolled off the couch and ran to the laundry room for towels.

Perturbed, AJ watched Charlotte run away. "We can't pin responsible for this morning's eye show on anybody."

Lilith flopped onto the couch. "My eyes did their thing? Like in New Orleans?"

"That they did," AJ said.

Shazoo leapt into Lilith's lap and nudged himself into her stomach. "Do you mind if I take one of your bedrooms? I'm tired and would prefer not to drive home."

"Charlotte has your stuff upstairs. She suspected the both of you would be exhausted."

Charlotte knelt over the couch with a towel, pat drying her tequila spill. "We have the Moulin Rouge room."

Lilith clapped her hands. "Yay."

Tayen lowered her water bottle. "I'm taking the Victorian bedroom and saving myself the half-hour drive home. Nice planning, Charlotte."

"Elliott in the pirate bedroom, the girls in the Moulin Rouge bedroom, and Tayen in the Victorian. I have a full house," AJ said.

Lilith asked, "Why did a bachelor design a Moulin Rouge bedroom? It's all frilly, girl stuff."

"I gave my interior designer free rein. She did it to spite me, kind of." AJ thought about it. "We had killer consultation meetings."

Charlotte folded the wet towel and laid it aside. "You need something at the hallway entrance on the second floor. It's too bare and feels like empty space."

"I've felt the same way about that." Lilith lifted her head and pointed up the second-floor walkway balcony. "You should place Greek statues on either side. Muses. You've got several outside, so why—"

Elliott said, "Not to spoil the interior design session, but we should discuss our progress."

"Leave it for tomorrow," Tayen said.

"I meant your progress with the treasure clues."

AJ leaned forward to pet the dogs. "What can I say? Captain James Andrews's journal describes a hidden pirate base. Broken Cove Palisade was well fortified and in a strategic position. Its location isn't mentioned."

"Then why abandon an impenetrable pirate base after a decade?" Lilith asked.

"I don't know, but Andrews's journal showed their chief weapon was Demon's Breath."

They sat quietly.

AJ leaned back from petting the dogs. "Anesthesiologists work off the principle of twilight amnesia. Patients don't remember pain during their operations because their mind is in a twilight, where memories don't form. It takes strong stimulus to break through. If we find a sample of the dust, chemical analysis could lead to a counteragent."

"Something for later. Orientation day two is less than eight hours away. I want to share something," Tayen said.

"Something happened at the kiosk today. Scott's baby sister, who accepted the website design/developer position, had a black eye. Talia and company surrounded her like a wolf pack. One greenskeeper saw it, as did Charlotte … "

"Charlotte," AJ said in his fatherly voice. "What did Talia's crew and the greenskeepers agree to?"

"There wasn't any verbal discussion or agreement between the two groups."

"How about nonverbal?"

"How can you have an agreement without words?"

AJ growled. "You're evading my questions. And let me remind you, young lady, we don't take the law into our own hands, even if it is justified. Retaliation is not the purpose of Code Purple."

"Understood. I agree whole heartedly."

AJ squinted. "There will be absolutely no news reports about a torched car."

"Never." Charlotte paused for a moment. "Nope, torching cars isn't in our repertoire."

"I don't want to read about any of my employees who forgot to eliminate a home security camera and got caught doing whatever they might do."

"Oh, yeah … excellent reminder."

"Paintball guns are the darnedest things," AJ said. "They can disable a security camera from an unbelievable distance. Elliott, what do paintball guns cost?"

"Ah, top of the line runs about $500?"

AJ pulled out his wallet and placed $500 on the end table. "No Oregon store owner's security camera should record any of our employees purchasing a paintball gun."

Charlotte repeated AJ's warning. "No Oregon store owner's security camera. That means … I'll need tomorrow off. My aunt, up in Seattle, is under the weather and needs my help. Poor thing is so fragile."

"Well then, you give her my best when you see her in the state of Washington."

Tayen and Lilith stood. Tayen spoke for them both. "We weren't here for this conversation, and Charlotte, leave an email about you taking the day off to visit your sick relative in San Quintin."

"Seattle."

"Not if you get caught."

Charlotte passed by the end table and picked up the money. "Ni-night, AJ."

As the ladies marched up the stairs, Elliott said, "I don't want to hear my father ordered a hit on a car."

"You won't."

"Nor about his step-by-step instructions for a retaliatory strike on a guy who beat his girlfriend."

"Charlotte follows instructions, and I believe her when she says torching a car is beyond their comfort zone."

"Nor do I want to hear my father—"

"Tell me when they can't hear me."

Shocked by his father's change in tone, Elliott looked at the second-floor balcony walkway. "They're in the hall."

AJ faced his son. "I took the Adela Frontera newspaper from the office this morning. With Tayen freaking out, I figured it best she didn't see it on Portland's equinox."

Elliott tilted his head back.

"I devoured every word and scoured every photo. A gentleman's obituary picture stood out. It was taken in front of a church. The half-moon-shaped transom window in the background contains our broken ship's wheel. Unfortunately, it doesn't show where the picture was taken."

"Where did the newspaper come from?" Elliott asked.

"The Dominican Republic, one place the ships' courses showed on the map wall."

"You want to head there?"

"I do." AJ leaned forward. "Scott and Tayen are too hot for a trip anywhere near that area. The Tampa papers' fugitive portraits have circulated to a wider audience, and I don't want to chance their exposure. I'll take the girls with me in early April."

"At the same time when we present Code Purple to the district attorneys?"

"Yes. The last two weeks of April will be cram-packed with preparations prior to grand opening. It isn't ideal, but what has since this journey started?"

"Early April it is then." Elliott leaned back in his chair, satisfied with the plan. "Well then, the only thing left for us to discuss is the ex-wife warning system."

"The ex-who … what system?"

"What was your side meeting about this morning?"

"I don't know what you're asking about," AJ snapped.

"The ex-wife early warning system."

"Never heard of it."

"Ex-wife early alert system."

"Nope."

"The ex-wife early alert warning system."

"Oh, that."

Elliott wasn't laughing.

"Hey," AJ swung his arm around. "Two minutes of conversation around here can stretch pretty far down the road. I said one thing and before I knew it, we are talking about a laser light show on Mt. Hood, sixty miles from here."

"What did you plan for my mother when she comes to visit?" Elliott asked.

"Nothing. Besides, Tayen would have killed any of the big-ticket items we planned for EWE-AWS."

"You assigned it an acronym?"

AJ dipped his head. "You're not aware of the creativity this staff has?"

"What about the small-ticket items?"

"EWE-AWS didn't have any small-ticket items."

Elliott threw his hands up. "Whatever. But if I see skywriting or billboard graffiti or anything unimaginable to a normal person, it's up to Elkhorn Cliffs Retirement for you."

"Elkhorn doesn't have a retirement center," AJ said as he tried picturing the area Elliott was referring to. "It's a cliff … overlooking a canyon river valley."

Elliott smirked at his father.

17 - The Second Estate

With the grand opening delayed, training had an abundance of wiggle room until Tayen assigned Elliott to oversee Code Purple. Scott had designed Code Purple and its technical aspects. Talia fronted the program as spokeswoman and point of contact. Their first meeting with Elliott resulted in program enhancements.

After two weeks of training, the new employees of Broken Cove Industries attended another orientation. Elliott introduced Talia and Scott. Scott simply waved hello and took a seat in the front row. Talia's silk chiffon purple blouse was tied into a bow below her chin. She shared her past with domestic violence.

Her mother had suffered from the violent tirades of her husband, which he justified through his religious beliefs. She escaped the beatings thanks to her mother's persistent interventions. Feeling she caused her mother's beatings, she ran away from home. With a forged ID, she began stripping, which gave her more money than a fifteen-year-old knew how to manage.

But the strip club owner intervened and guided her days to steer her clear of drugs, alcohol, tobacco, and prostitution. Her clean appearance and nightly performances brought in a steady flow of customers. With her being so young, he chose to protect his long-term goldmine production over a short-term cash windfall. He kept her from the vices that would tarnish her natural beauty.

Talia pointed out the irony. A strip club owner was more concerned for her body than her father's concern was for her eternal soul.

Sniffs from sorrowful listeners were the only sounds heard. When she outlined how Code Purple would transport domestic violence victims to safe shelters, the sniffs turned into affirmations of 'yes, we'll do this.'

Elliott concluded the presentation, informing the BCI employees that participation in the program was voluntary and not compulsory. Those wishing to stay out would be excluded from further program details. This would keep the program's practices and procedures secret among Code Purple personnel only.

The staff's overwhelming response shocked Talia and Scott. Two-thirds of the employees stood in line to fill out confidentiality agreements when the meeting ended.

Training began a week later. Tayen secured a meeting with four district attorneys, which gave Code Purple four weeks to prepare.

Training was broken into halves. Mornings were for Code Purple, while afternoons were for the traditional jobs.

Until Charlotte's observation switched it around. If back of house staff trained on food preparation, why not test their results on front of house staff? Free lunches, no wasted food, and honest feedback for the chefs. Tayen and Elliott were amazed by her idea and approved it on the spot.

As the days passed, the ranks of employee participation in Code Purple swelled. On April tenth, the district attorneys arrived at the clubhouse for the Code Purple presentation. In the second-floor executive dining room, reserved for small gatherings, the Code Purple admin team greeted the district attorneys, the local county sheriff and his plain-clothed deputies.

Elliott greeted them. "Thanks for coming to hear our proposal for safe transportation of domestic violence victims. While your record for keeping victims safe is solid, we want to improve your percentages and reduce stalker retribution attacks. We are privately funded, so Code Purple won't add to your budgets."

District Attorney Miller scratched his chin. "Anytime something is added to our docket, our budgets take a hit. As you outlined this program for me last month, I see the need to add two liaison positions: one in my department, and one for the sheriff's office."

Talia spoke. "The liaison you currently use makes two calls. One to the shelters and one to the sheriff's office. We will coordinate the calls so you only contact us. We cut your phone calls to one by assuming the coordination between the other two calls."

"Alright, young lady, get us to the core of the matter. How does your program work, and how is it more secure than what we already provide?"

"Sheriff Musgrave," Talia pointed to the sheriff and

his deputies, "has agreed to assess our setup. They have not been told on how our system works, but they're aware of how domestic abusers operate."

District Attorney Miller rubbed his eyes. "I need an inside evaluation, not just an external one. A test without both perspectives is useless."

"Deputy Olivia Castillo will provide your insider's test. She will pose as the transport."

Miller nodded his approval, along with the other district attorneys.

Talia continued: "A domestic violence victim, which we'll call the transport, leaves your court rooms and travels here in a van. They will be dressed in a white top, blue jeans, sunglasses, and a head covering. Once they arrive at Broken Cove Country Club, they'll disappear into the complex with our help. A short time later, they will arrive at their protective shelter, free from any stalker."

Miller waved his hand back and forth. "You left out the key details of what happens once they are here."

"Correct, I did. Sheriff Musgrave and his three remaining deputies are tasked with finding the transport, Deputy Castillo, while she passes through our complex. We are confident she'll disappear from her stalkers' detection, which is the purpose of Code Purple."

Miller laughed. "Let's see it. Fool Musgrave and his deputies and you'll have our confidence that the program will succeed."

"I'll escort the deputies downstairs and let them get ready," Talia said. "Enjoy the breakfast from our bakery, Pirate's Chocolate. Elliott and Scott will guide you once we start the trials."

Fifteen minutes later, Scott displayed the camera feeds

on the executive dining room monitor for the district attorneys, and Elliott narrated what they were seeing. "Deputy Castillo is in the white van coming down the road. Scenario one has the van stopping at the clubhouse's front door. As you can see, two stalker-deputies are in the car across the street. We will position the third deputy in areas which will be crucial for your inside evaluation."

The van stopped at the clubhouse entrance, and Deputy Castillo exited wearing a white top, blue jeans, sunglasses, and a head covering with Talia by her side. As promised, she was unrecognizable from the disguise. They entered the clubhouse.

Minutes later, a woman led Deputy Castillo back out. At the same time, another woman accompanied a second decoy out of the east door, while a third decoy exited the west exit. A fourth came out the front entrance. Scott used his mouse to point at a fifth coming out of the north side of the clubhouse. All five decoys were transported away on golf carts headed in five directions.

"The shell game. Simple, yet effective." Miller tapped the table with his hand. "I take it these golf carts drive to a waiting vehicle to complete the transport?"

Scott said, "We chose cart paths with natural choke points where other vehicles can't pursue, should a stalker decide to go off road. Plus, somebody will always work the monitors to report a stalker's whereabouts or identify potential stalkers."

"What if the stalker is already in the clubhouse?"

"Unknown persons in the clubhouse will direct the van to an alternate location. Let me send the all-clear, and we'll run scenario number two."

Minutes later, the van came down the road as before.

But this time it turned right into the bus lane, which proceeded into The Village complex, instead of turning left and going to the clubhouse.

Elliott stood behind District Attorney Miller. "Deputy one is outside Pirate's Chocolate, and deputy two is at the kiosk outside The Village bus lane. The van will stop at the elevator lobby and drop off Deputy Castillo."

Miller watched the van stop. Talia and Deputy Castillo ran from the van into the elevator lobby. The two deputies rushed in, but the door to the first elevator had closed. One deputy stayed there; the second raced out to the stairs on the backside.

The door to the second elevator opened, and two women walked out. Both wore white tops, blue jeans, and sunglasses, but no head coverings. The deputy who stayed in the elevator lobby ran out to the main entrance into The Village complex. Upon reaching the kiosk, five decoys were once again on golf carts, speeding away in different directions.

"Four decoys and two in-your-face taunts, Sheriff Musgrave," Miller said.

"If the monitor-caller," Scott pointed to himself, "sees the need for additional decoys, we can push up to ten per building. If need be, the transport can sit tight in our facility while five to ten decoys flee in just as many directions. We have dozens of strategies to confound and confuse any would-be stalkers."

Miller swiveled in his chair. "Sheriff Musgrave, do you see any holes?"

"I do." The sheriff stood and pushed his thumbs under his gun belt. "The Code Purple people know where our deputies are. I want to try more people where Scott and that young lady's team won't know who the stalker is."

"Throw your best at us. If we can't pass your test, we don't deserve to earn your trust," Scott said.

"Very good. I'll need the district attorneys and their assistants. Plus, I'm calling in five additional plainclothes deputies, giving me sixteen people to break your system."

District Attorney Miller stood. "What's the plan, sheriff?"

"Not here. We'll huddle by that airport screen thing by The Village entrance—"

"At the Kiosk," Scott corrected.

"The Kiosk, and I'll give instructions there. I don't want Scott overhearing our operation and advise his people."

"Head down to the kiosk. I'll stay here and notify my team. Afterwards, we'll meet at the kiosk and discuss the results," Scott said.

The formal dining room emptied, leaving Tayen, Elliott, and Scott.

"Good work," Tayen said. "Your preparation is well done, but can the Sheriff outwit you on this one?"

Scott typed on his laptop. "Have those contracts ready. You'll be signing them at the kiosk."

Half an hour later, Sheriff Musgrave had the district attorneys, their assistants, and eight deputies spread throughout the country club complex. Six of them stood outside the clubhouse. The remaining ten spread out in The Village. Standing by the kiosk, Sheriff Musgrave waved to the camera above the kiosk, giving Scott permission to start the simulation.

The white transport van sped down the road. Talia explained to Deputy Castillo. "We have sixteen suspects, but we don't know which one is the stalker. Scott made the call for a village complex strategy."

"I'm back in the elevator?" Deputy Castillo asked.

"Not this time. We will pass the elevator lobby on the right, but we are exiting the left side of the van and entering our coffee shop. The floor will be wet, so we are going to slide across the floor and smack into the wall. Then we'll run into the storage-room hallway."

"You're hiding me in a back room?"

Talia snapped her fingers. "Thanks for the suggestion. Now we have a third option for this strategy. However, this time we are executing Option A: the emergency chute and ladder next to the pastry chef's office. I won't have time to follow you down, but someone will meet you at the bottom and lead you away. Get ready, we are turning onto the bus lane."

The van passed the raised gate arm and drove down the bus lane. Deputy Castillo lowered her sunglasses for the Sheriff to confirm she was in the van. The elevator lobby came into view. True to Talia's word, the van continued a few yards further and stopped in front of Coffee Cov*fefe*.

Talia yanked the door open and launched herself out of the van with Deputy Castillo in close pursuit. With Castillo out, two other women zoomed into the van. They dressed identical to her in the same jeans, T-shirts, sunglasses, and head coverings.

From the corner of her eye, Castillo saw two decoys running down the hall from Coffee Cov*fefe* to the bakery.

Coffee Cov*fefe*'s floor was wet, and two baristas stood ready with mops in hand. Talia and Deputy Castillo ran in, slid across the floor, and slammed against the wall. Talia helped her into the storage-room hallway. The baristas mopped the floor, hiding their slide marks.

Lydia waited by her office door. The floor next to the pastry chef's office was open, and a ladder descended into the dark below. Lydia helped Deputy Castillo onto the ladder. "Chutes and ladders. Hold on for dear life."

Deputy Castillo clung to the ladder and closed her eyes. Lydia tapped her phone, and the ladder dropped. A trapdoor slid into position, hiding the exit hole.

Talia yanked off her T-shirt and head covering before dropping her jeans to the ground. Underneath, she wore a blue and white one-piece cycling jumpsuit. Lydia poured a pitcher of water over Talia and used her foot to shove the jeans and T-shirt into her office. Talia took the pitcher and gulped the remaining water.

A deputy entered the back room as the baristas yelled for him to stop. The wet spots on the floor and Talia soaking wet in her cycling one-piece convinced him of the deception. At the end of the back hallway, a decoy set ran into the bar: Broken Cove Rum House. He ran back the way he entered to chase the decoys.

Lydia high-fived Talia. "He never questioned your biker's outfit. Did he not know who you were?"

Talia wiped her face with a towel. "He wasn't in the clubhouse meeting before these scenarios, so he wasn't aware of my status as program director. I was just a dumb blond in biking gear. Now the fun begins. Watch our decoys."

The deputy ran through the coffee shop to the bus lane. There, he found another set of decoys rushing into the gift shop. He took one step in their direction when another decoy set dashed out of a different gift shop gallery and toward the pro shop. Before he could take a step, he looked up to see a decoy set on the second-floor terrace and another on the third-floor terrace. The deputy held up his hands and yelled, "I quit, you win."

The decoys and their escorts stopped and high-fived one another. More decoys and escorts exited from Pirate's Chocolate and the Rum House.

Everybody gathered at the kiosk. Sheriff Musgrave laughed at the number of employees who had attended. Tayen, Elliott, and Scott didn't hide their smiles as they approached from the clubhouse. The gathered employees parted as Manny drove his extended greens-cart next to the kiosk.

Talia wrapped Lydia's jacket around herself to stay warm. Cheers rose as she and Lydia reached the sheriff and district attorneys. She asked, "Did we pass?"

"I'm not saying until you return Deputy Castillo."

Talia nodded to Manny, who lifted the extended seat in the back of his greens-cart. Deputy Castillo popped up with hers extended like a magician's assistant. BCI employees helped her out of the secret compartment.

Everybody applauded … including Sheriff Musgravc.

District Attorney Miller smiled. "Olivia, you had the inside view. How do you assess Code Purple?"

"Pity the fool who enters Broken Cove Country Club. They do not know what waits for them."

BCI employees yelled and cheered in celebration.

Deputy Castillo continued after the celebration died down. "While Talia and I waited before the third run, she showed me the multiple schemes and variations ready at their disposal. I was shocked at the chute and ladder next to the pastry chef's office. The ladder dropped below the floor and a trapdoor slid in place. I climbed down the ladder to find this grand old gentleman, Manny, waiting for me. He opened the seat, and I squeezed into this secret compartment."

"What about the other runs?" Miller asked.

"The decoys and escorts knew what to do, and where they were headed. A single stalker has no chance here. A team of stalkers? Well, stalkers are single creatures, so a team of stalkers won't happen." Deputy Castillo turned to Talia. "But why do this?"

Talia pointed behind Deputy Castillo. "I'm the face of Code Purple, but Scott is the designer and inspirational lead."

Deputy Castillo pivoted and faced Scott.

He squared up to her. "I have a relative who was a victim of domestic violence. Before that, a dear friend of mine died when her husband killed her in a drunken rage. She endured years of abuse. This area has a good record in transporting domestic abuse victims to safety. But we want to do better. My little sister … "

Scott's voice gave out. District Attorney Miller surveyed the hundred-plus who were listening to Scott.

"I had an opportunity and shared my vision with the senior management team, AJ de Faria and Tayen. They told me to draw up the plans. Talia came aboard, and damn … no one says no to her when she asks for their help." Scott raised his hand in Talia's direction. "Not because they can't, but because they see her commitment and drive to make it succeed."

Scott's face turned red. "There is a second reason nobody said no. The reputation of our First Assistant to the General Manager, Charlotte Tavares, is not a secret here. When she says, 'I know where you live,' she really does. And nobody wants that flaming torch on their front door, questioning why they weren't participating."

Somebody yelled out, "That's for damn sure," which spawned an uproar of laughter.

Elliott stepped forward. "District Attorney Miller, we have the contracts. There is nothing new in them since we negotiated the terms last week. I believe we have passed your tests. We are a secured facility and can effectively transport victims to the safehouses without incident."

"I'm not signing it here," Miller said. "However, back in the formal dining room with that spectacular view, and after the lunch you promised, I'll sign."

Tayen turned and started walking toward the clubhouse. "I'll call in the order. Our chefs have a treat in store for you." The district attorneys and their assistants followed her.

Elliott winked at Lydia. "It worked. How do you feel about our secret passages and tunnels now?"

Lydia winked back. "Dope. This is strange for a group with no ties to law enforcement. I must second Deputy Castillo's conclusion: God pity whomever enters here looking for trouble. Defending this place is easy."

"You are one sick puppy. This isn't one of your gaming fantasies, DeathStingofTsetse. You need to cut back on the war gaming. Get back into your hobby of picture framing."

She batted her eyes and smiled seductively. "We all have our habits. And my user name is TsetseStingofDeath, not whatever you said."

Elliott turned around to find Sheriff Musgrave shaking Scott's hand.

"Well done, Mr. Pullman. You have a winner here and you have my full support."

"Thank you, Sheriff."

Sheriff Musgrave continued to shake Scott's hand. Elliott noticed their handshake wasn't the typical greeting or congratulatory shake. He slowed his approach to them.

"I remember that horrendous day, and you … standing by the roadside when we found her body."

Elliott stopped. Musgrave's comment knocked him for a loop.

"I cannot thank you enough for not outing me, Scott. No day passes where I am not haunted by her memory. My failure to protect Deana from that monster—it rips me apart every day."

Scott squeezed the sheriff's hand. "Together, we can make sure other victims don't meet Deana's fate."

18 - The Mansion

Before Code Purple's audition with the district attorneys, AJ, Lilith, and Charlotte had flown to the Dominican Republic. AJ's logo design had appeared in a photo from a local newspaper. With no further leads, the picture of a transom window with the broken wheel was their best chance of unraveling the map wall in New Orleans.

AJ drove the tiny rental car toward the mountains on day two of their travels. Their matching dark sunglasses, broad straw sun hats, and white shorts marked the trio as tourists.

Charlotte sat in the back seat with her feet on AJ's headrest. "Funny. You would think a tropical island had palm trees everywhere. But this place is half desert."

Alert and studying the passing scenery, Lilith said, "It's all about imaging. Suck the consumer into the fantasy with glitz and glamour. Reality pays the rent, but the fantasy pays for the private jet."

She bumped AJ's arm with her elbow. "How did you pick these places to visit?"

AJ reached over his shoulder to poke Charlotte's foot. "The newspaper with our church photo is distributed in the southern and western provinces. Our stops so far have been look-see visits, but to make sure we didn't skip something important, we needed to stop at them."

Charlotte took AJ's poking as a game and tapped his hand with her foot. "What's our next look-see?"

AJ pinched her big toe. "Why spoil the surprise?"

Lilith ignored their goofing around. "I'd be lit if this was a vacation. But with my growing felony list in Tampa, I'm not in the mood for surprises."

The country road took a broad, elongated turn. In the middle of the arc, a clearing yielded to an outdoor patio, which was tucked off to the side of the road. Spacious wrought iron tables with wicker chairs were shaded by white cantilever patio umbrellas. The light-gray natural stone patio had been swept perfectly clean.

Lilith lowered her sunglasses. "Adorable and wildly bizarre. Put this in downtown Portland and it'd kill. What is this place?"

"The Caribbean version of a Cracker Barrel, minus the crackers," Charlotte said.

Lilith laughed as she turned to AJ, expecting him to chastise Charlotte. He smiled and pointed next to the patio.

Both girls read the sign. Its contents caused them to shoot out of the car and scamper up the sidewalk. Lilith couldn't contain her excitement and kept asking Charlotte if this was the place.

"This is the name on the anonymous newspaper, right?"

"Yep, Adela Frontera. Although, if you think about it, a name on the delivery kind of nullifies the anonymity aspect of the whole thing."

"Hey." AJ called out. "Wait up for this cracker to get in the barrel."

Off to the side of the patio stood a small one-room building with no doors. Lilith walked in it and found empty shelves on all the walls. "This is set up like a gift shop. But why is it here in the middle of nowhere?"

An elderly man emerged from behind the gift shop wearing a cobbler's apron. The stains on the apron and the faint wafting of smoke showed he was attending a barbecue pit. His muscular physique hid the years of his experience, as did the faint streaks of gray in his hair. He carried a cane with him. He yelled, "*Hola mis amigos. Bienvenido Bienvenido. Tome asiento en una mesa, por favor.*"

A Great Pyrenees dog trotted behind him.

"*Hola.*" Charlotte led the conversation, letting AJ interpret for Lilith.

The enormous sized dog watched Lilith.

AJ took a chair and sat. Lilith sat across from him, never taking her eyes off the dog. He translated for her.

"This guy is the caretaker. He's insisting on listing our lunch choices. Barbecue shredded pork or blackened chicken breast sandwiches. Oh, he has mangú with eggs and salami."

Lilith's interest wasn't in the food. "What about this place?"

"You're not curious about the mangú?"

She lowered her head and peered over her sunglasses. "I don't care if they are fried bananas. I want to find the place with the window."

His eye rapid flutters informed her she had just said

something dumb. "What? Is mangú fried bananas?"

He turned his head around and continued translating for her. "This is an open market between the city dwellers and the mountain folk. People trade, barter, and sell here. And this guy is the social lubricant with food and drink."

The man held up three fingers and turned away. His dog sat, never once taking his eyes off of Lilith.

"Three drinks for his new friends. When he returns, he'll explain the name," Charlotte said as she took a seat.

AJ surveyed the patio and one-room building. "He must do alright. Look at the stone inlay and the craftsmanship in this place. This guy is a true middleman. Halfway between the city and the mountains."

The caretaker returned with glasses and a pitcher of water.

AJ took the lead and let Charlotte translate for Lilith. "Adela Frontera died here centuries ago. This area is protected by Oungans and Mambos, Vodou religious leaders. The Oungans, male priests, consecrate the area, then eight years later—the Mambos, female priestesses—consecrate it as well. Each sixteen years, the cycle of male and female consecrations is completed. No evil may transpire on this land or the curses come to life."

Charlotte leaned toward Lilith. "He's saying it doesn't matter if you believe in Vodou or not. This oasis has the respect of the locals, and they know not to come here with the intent of deception or dishonesty. Adela Frontera is the place for equal exchanges."

The caretaker hurried away. Lilith kept glancing at the dog, who hadn't taken his eyes off her.

"He's evading my questions, but when he returns, he promises to tell us about the transom window," AJ said.

Charlotte leaned back and strained to see where the caretaker had gone.

AJ answered her question before she asked. "I guess there's a little setup on the other side of the gift shop."

The caretaker popped from behind the building, balancing a tray on his arm.

"Holy crap, that was fast. How did he—" Lilith couldn't finish. The caretaker traversed the ground like a gazelle and reached the table with stunning quickness. He placed the plates and tableware in front of them.

AJ was about to ask about the transom window, but stopped when the caretaker gave him the stern grandpa look.

"Ah, you just got owned. Grandpa wants you to eat before he answers your questions," Lilith said.

No sooner had she spoken than she received the caretaker's authoritative stare. She drove her spork into the mangú and lifted a small portion to her mouth.

"What do we do if we don't like it?" Charlotte asked.

"Oh, poor baby. This time you don't get to choose between spitting or swallowing."

AJ grabbed Charlotte's wrist before she could threaten Lilith with a spork.

As lunch proceeded, the caretaker told them where to find the transom window in the next town. He couldn't hide his fascination with Lilith's amulet. She held it up for him to see. "*Tempest, hija de Tristao. Atado en la niebla y la eternidad,*" he said.

Lilith faced the caretaker and waited for a translation.

"Tempest, daughter of Tristao. Bound in the fog and eternity," Charlotte said.

Lilith turned to AJ, who sat motionless as his face lost its color. She placed her hand on his, but he didn't respond.

"AJ." She squeezed his hand and repeated, "AJ. Are you okay?"

He blinked and answered. "Thank the caretaker for lunch. Let's be on our way."

Lilith looked at Charlotte, hoping her roommate knew why AJ had gone limp.

Lost, Charlotte stared back at Lilith, hoping her roommate had an answer for AJ's behavior.

Lilith shrugged and shook her head.

Charlotte expressed their appreciation for lunch and the information about the transom window. Lilith was consumed with finding out why AJ had become as white as a ghost. She only gave a cursory wave goodbye to the caretaker. Rather than letting AJ drive, she took the keys and drove them to the town.

AJ sat motionless in the front seat, with Charlotte leaning as close to him as possible from the back seat.

The small town buzzed with activity. News agencies from the capital were swarming the town. Forced to park because of halted traffic, they toured the town on foot. AJ wasn't speaking, but at least he was walking.

Charlotte explained what she heard from the townsfolk as they walked. "Local authorities have cordoned off the road ahead. We'll have to walk around. I can't say for sure, but it sounds like a body was found. Police are on the scene."

Lilith held AJ's hand while Charlotte led them through the streets to the church. Shade trees lined the sides of the church's cramped parking lot. Charlotte flashed her phone at Lilith, confirming it was the church in the newspaper photo.

"Cute little church for a cute little town. But why

here? Why is this place of importance?" Charlotte asked in hopes of stirring AJ out of his doldrums.

When he didn't respond, Lilith gave it her best try. "Why is a landlocked church sporting a ship's wheel over the front door?"

AJ pointed at the transom window. "The missing felloe. It isn't between the one and two o'clock position."

Charlotte jumped on his observation. "It's between two and three. The wheel turned to starboard."

Lilith and AJ bent over to stare at her.

"Pirates and ships. Get with the program and learn the terms, folks."

"Hmpf," AJ said. "She's got us there. If we're chasing a pirate, sailing terms could prove helpful."

As they returned to studying the transom window, the church door flew open, and three muscular men ran down the steps. A van screeched up behind them, and its panel door slammed back. Two men dove out and grabbed the girls.

Lilith's attempt to flip her assailant met sheer brute strength. He easily corralled her into the van. Charlotte rolled up into a ball, forfeiting her capture without a fight. AJ's punch connected but failed to deter the man who grabbed him.

Taller than Charlotte and Lilith, AJ didn't pass under the top of the door frame as the girls had. His forehead slammed against the door frame, snapping his head back. He fell on the van floor, unconscious and bleeding from the gash above his eye.

The door slammed shut, and the van sped out of the lot.

"Shit. First aid kit, now. This is a deep cut," one abductor said.

Another abductor threw the first aid kit at him and addressed a frightened pair of women. "Sorry for this, but you were in danger, and we had to get you off the street. Where are the keys to your rental car?"

"You expect me to hand over the keys after you kidnapped us and knocked him out?" Lilith barked.

"I'm sorry about AJ. As your host, I feel horrible about his injury."

"You know his name?" Charlotte growled.

The host held up his left hand and traced the outside with his right index finger, from thumb to pinky. "You're Charlotte and this is Lilith."

Charlotte flipped him the bird. "I know a hand gesture too, fuck face. Why abduct us?"

He looked at his fellow kidnappers with disappointment. "Oh, no. Father Amare didn't show them."

"Start explaining," Lilith yelled.

"You know about the Péchettes. They created a hand signal. If you trace your left hand from thumb to pinky, that shows you're safe and a friend. If the trace is from pinky to thumb, you are saying you are under duress and in danger."

Lilith whirled her hands in the air. "We're safe. So why the—"

"A drug cartel is on the lookout for unknown people. There is a meeting occurring on the mountaintop mansion, and strangers are being questioned, and killed if it is deemed they're a threat. We had to reach you before someone pointed you out. Time didn't allow for formal introductions at the church."

Lilith and Charlotte shared a glance. Not hearing Charlotte voice an objection, Lilith turned her attention to the man working on AJ's gash. She sighed in disgust at AJ's wound. It gave comforted her to see that his caregiver seemed to know what he was doing. "Is your friend a nurse?"

"Yes, he is. What else can we do to prove our sincere intentions?"

"Take us back to Adela Frontera."

"Excellent choice, but who do you think contacted us?" the host said.

Charlotte pounded her fist on her leg. "Lunch … the caretaker kept us there until you were in position to nab us. The keys are in AJ's pocket."

The host fished out the keys. "We'll take care of the car. In the meantime, we'll drive you to our base. Despite the rough introductions, we are honored to have you, Madam Priestess."

"Oh, Jesus Christ," Charlotte blurted out. "Her blue eyes show she is a descendant of a pirate, and you folks are ready to coronate her. I'm hotter than her. What does that get me?"

"Whatever Madam Priestess wants you to have."

"I was hired before her; I'm not kissing her ass … Well, not like I did when we dated."

Lilith didn't know what to do. She relied on AJ for direction, but with him out cold, she had to make this decision. "Where are you taking us?"

"We have a home, a base of operations for the Péchette faction of the Voodoo Priestess's organization."

Not having a better option, she said, "Take care of AJ, and drive us to this place of yours, please."

An hour later, they turned onto a dirt road. The long drive through a thick canopy of trees ended at a barn-like home. They rushed AJ inside and placed him on a couch.

Charlotte took in her surroundings. "This was one hell

of a big barn. Wow. One kick ass renovation."

Lilith glanced up from AJ. "Nice. It could pass for a wilderness resort. But why are we here? Where is Father Amare?"

"This is an independent cell of the Péchette faction. We have many cells throughout the Caribbean and Gulf Coast who serve at the wishes of the Voodoo Priestess from New Orleans," the host said.

"Hold on. We learned New Orleans Voodoo doesn't have priestesses."

The host said, "There was one Voodoo Priestess in New Orleans. But never again. However, the daughters of the Voodoo Priestess—Lilith's mother, grandmother, and woman ancestors—do bend our ears to their wishes. Not because of spells or enchantments, but by duty to finish her mission."

Lilith closed her eyes. "What is my pirate ancestor's mission?"

"Uncovering the purpose of the mission is why you are here."

Charlotte raised both hands over her head. "Goddamn circular reasoning. Gotta love it."

The host continued: "This barn was connected to the mountaintop mansion, which is up the road. But since the Haitian Revolution, we have remained independent from the influence of the mansion."

"These were the slave quarters," Lilith said.

The host nodded she was correct. "Father Amare notified us about you and your friends. We are pleased to host you and are ready to help retrieve the items left in the mountaintop mansion, the Bennington Mansion."

"Shit, where's the bathroom?" Charlotte squeezed her knees together.

"Hold it in, sister," Lilith ordered. "Did you say the Bennington Mansion?"

"Keep saying Bennington and I'll pee right here."

"Show her to the bathroom before she pees on the floor."

The host had another cell member take Charlotte to the bathroom. "The Benningtons originated from here centuries ago. While they have dispersed to other regions, they maintain the mansion for one of their division directors."

AJ groaned as he regained consciousness. Lilith spent the next half hour recounting their trip to the Péchette barn and explaining what she'd learned.

AJ sipped from a water bottle. "The owner must use a helicopter to access the mountaintop. The drive up there is for commoners and servants. Their security has to be tight. Is there a layout of the mansion?"

"Give me a moment."

The host excused himself and entered a room down the hall. A minute later, he came back with a cardboard tube. He opened it and pulled out a large sheet of rolled up paper. He laid a sketch on the table. "Blueprints don't exist for the mansion. However, years ago, general labors made this sketch from their observations when they worked there. A gardener, a maid, and an electrician did their best to step off distances. It shouldn't shock you if the measurements aren't precise."

"At least it gives us an idea," AJ said.

"Over time, a lot of building materials have been taken up there. All we have are anecdotal accounts of their construction and expansion. This sketch could be meaningless for all we know," the host said.

AJ twisted the drawing for Charlotte's inspection.

"Your spatial acuity is better than mine. This is gonna be like the transom window. We won't know what we're searching for until we're on top of it."

Charlotte took time to read the drawing. After a while, she said, "There's nothing remarkable here. But this wall, the one which faces the lake, it's weird. This wall is wedge-shaped, or severely mismeasured."

AJ bent over for a closer inspection.

Charlotte pointed out what she saw. "This inside wall measurement is longer than the outer wall. Over a thirty-foot span, the wall gets much thicker at one end."

The host peered down at the spot Charlotte's finger was on. "That's the old section of the mansion. Word is they barely use it."

"Old section?"

"The further you go to the northwest of the mountaintop, the older the building is."

Charlotte rubbed her finger next to the wedge-shaped wall. "We want the oldest section of the mansion. If they haven't discovered this anomaly, that's where we'll find what we're looking for."

"What do you think is there?" Lilith asked.

"Chests." AJ said. "Chests, or a map that points to the chest's location. The question is, how do we get into a crime syndicate's mansion?"

The host rose from bending over the sketch. "Their annual meeting is in two days. Bennington's do their business in the afternoon and have a party in the evening. This meeting is taking place on the same night as the monthly party for local VIPs and invited guests. Charlotte can enter with the caterers. The mayor from the coastal town takes a pretty young lady as his arm candy to these events. If Lilith can wiggle into his—"

"Yep, she can wiggle it, grind it, or whatever else—" Charlotte stopped upon seeing Lilith's death glare.

"Two in, one to go. But what about me?" AJ asked.

"An elderly honored guest attends these parties. She has a nurse around the clock, so we can substitute you for the night," the host said.

"I'm a nurse, Charlotte's a caterer, and Lilith's a vicious trollop."

Lilith fiddled with her amulet. "Are these parties formal?"

The host frowned. "The local sex workers claim these monthly parties are their biggest nights."

"Local sex workers?"

"People not from the Roanoke Colony," Charlotte said.

***

Early the next morning, the host of the Péchette cell escorted Lilith to the coastal town. If she secured the mayor's affection, she wouldn't be with AJ or Charlotte until the following night.

To her shock, wearing a white bikini top and floral beach wrap-around skirt was all it took. The mayor couldn't take his eyes off of her at the bar. She had hooked him. Not wasting time, she invited herself as his guest to the mountaintop party. He was all too eager to take her. She fought off his advances all the way back to her hotel; promising good things came to those who waited. After she closed her hotel room door, she jumped in the shower to get his paw prints off her skin.

Late the following afternoon, the mayor arrived at Lilith's hotel in an extended limousine. She jumped in and was forced to roll down the windows. His cheesy cologne started her gag reflex. She was certain its lacquer-thick application constituted an environmental hazard.

Atop the mountain peak, overlooking Lake Enriquillo, sat an expansive and venerable mansion. Gallant mahogany trees formed a canopy of seclusion, making the mansion feel like an organic outgrowth of the timber. The Italian marble driveway wound from the main gate to the Champs-Élysées-styled avenue, which led to the mansion's front door.

The fountain, which was the length of a football field, partitioned the avenue in two. Lilith didn't blink as the mayor's car glided past the golden-lighted sparkling fountains. Statues of exotic fauna decorated the outskirts of the avenue like a king's court. The car pulled under the pergola, and a formal valet attendant opened the door.

Lilith launched out the door, away from the handsy mayor. Her sapphire haven-cut strapless dress had aroused him all the way up the mountain.

Thank God this is the tropics or I would freeze, she thought. If not for the narrow strap wrapping around her upper ribs, she was bare from ear to ankle on one side.

She double-checked the dress to make sure it covered her. She was formally dressed, yet she felt like she had nothing on. A quick glance at the other women guests strengthened her confidence. The sober ones looked as uncomfortable as she felt. The ones at ease appeared to have been drinking. Her sixth sense spun her around in time to catch the mayor's attempted grope. She might be his trophy for the night, but this trophy was for display only.

Holding his hand and smiling like a good girl should,

Lilith led them inside. The host described the mansion as cavernous and decadent; something akin to a numb-nutted God Emperor's liking. She couldn't disagree with his description.

Lilith pushed from one room to another in search of AJ and Charlotte. *Why is every other room is a parlor? The serving staff ... treated like shit, and these poor women have a hand on their ass at all times. I want to burn this place to the ground.*

She spotted AJ standing behind an elderly woman in a wheelchair. He stood against the wall, keeping out of the way but close enough to assist.

Lilith pivoted and held the mayor's hand up to prayer level. "Can you go back to the room where they served the caviar and get me a sampling? Pretty please."

The mayor moved in for a kiss, but it landed on the back of her head.

Eager to talk with AJ, she stepped toward him, but he nodded her off. She realized it would appear suspicious to the mansion-full of guests if she conversed with the hired help. But if she pretended she was reviewing the bookshelf to his left, they could exchange information secretly.

She reached the bookshelf when a cocktail waitress brushed her side.

"Drink, *señorita?*"

Lilith's reflex was to decline, but the voice was Charlotte's. Her jaw dropped open when she turned around to find her roommate had dyed her hair platinum. A quick peek down at Charlotte's scarlet corset and black garter belt caused her eyes to bulge. She lifted her head. "That's so radical it's out of your comfort zone."

"Intimate apparel in the workplace ain't my thing.

Kudos to Talia for doing it."

Lilith took a champagne glass. "Platinum works on you. Why did you stuff dollar bills in your corset?"

"I didn't stick them there."

Lilith choked on her champagne.

"They're Benjamins and Grants. Not Washingtons, Lincolns, or the prick on the twenty." She turned her hip around. "Grab the one they stuck up my ass. If it ain't a Benji, I know the asshole who stuck it there and I'm off to teach him a lesson."

Lilith peered from the corner of her eye. "I'm not touching it."

"Great. Where's AJ?"

"Behind you. I'm going to the bookshelf beside him."

The two took different courses, but reconvened next to AJ near the bookshelf.

He took a glass from Charlotte's tray. "Pardon me, *señorita*, is there a fireplace in this mansion with a solid oak mantle? I heard some other guests speaking about it and was hoping for a chance to admire it."

"Forgive me, no, *señor*. This wing was added over the last decade. The old wing, beyond the courtyard, might be the place you are looking for?"

AJ sipped his champagne and asked, "Across the courtyard?"

"This is my first time here, *señor*. I haven't made it over there yet, but my break is coming soon."

AJ whispered as he surveyed the half-clad women in the room. "My apologies for getting you into this jackal arena. You can see the angst on these women's faces. How can you look so cheerful?"

"*Mira mi trasero y verás por qué.*" Charlotte turned

around, allowing AJ to see the back of her outfit. She came about full circle, and he stuffed two Benjis down her corset.

"Yes," AJ smirked. "I see why you're upbeat with cash stuck up your butt. If my fingers touched you, forgive me. I was aiming for the two hundred-dollar bills, not a sexual harassment lawsuit."

"He gave me two Benjis?" She batted her eyelashes and looked around the room. "I gotta pass that guy again." She walked away, ignoring people who were looking to her for a glass of champagne.

"Leave it to her to make a buck in this cesspool," AJ murmured.

He looked forward, avoiding eye contact with Lilith. She backed closer to him and looked the opposite direction. He turned his head so it wouldn't be obvious he was speaking with her.

"Your dress is fabulous, but you look as uncomfortable as Peter Venkman's male ESP research subject."

"No shit Sherlock. The female research subject didn't have a thing to worry about. But the tables are turned in this place. Every woman here is in danger."

"Is the mayor giving you trouble?"

"Handsy is expecting me to dominate him later. He misinterpreted my intentions when I pinned him in the back seat on the ride up. Sex with me ain't in his future. Broken fingers, though, might be."

AJ sipped his champagne. "Careful, tiger. Charlotte is working over to the other wing. The corridor branching off from the hallway behind me has some artwork I should explore."

"Go and be safe. I'll wait for handsy before we slip

upstairs for a tour," Lilith said.

AJ moseyed around the corner and disappeared.

Finished with the bookshelf inspection, Lilith sipped her champagne and watched the partygoers.

Natural facial expressions, relaxed body posture, smooth flowing conversations: completely absent. Jesus. These people aren't here because they want to be. They're here because they're afraid.

A woman Tayen's age eased into the room from the hallway. Lilith recognized the dark jungle green cocktail dress as Louis Vuitton. *Her décolletage would make any twenty-something envious. She projects strength ... and confidence.*

Lilith worked her way down to the woman's single-strap pumps, but the designer of origin escaped her. *Turn to the front, gorgeous. I want to see who you have on your feet. Attagirl, pivot toward me. Step toward me ... Shit. She's coming at me.*

A quick glance up confirmed it; the woman was walking toward her. Lilith exaggerated her inhale when the woman was in conversation range. "Your Vuitton is breath-taking, but the shoes ... also Vuitton?"

The woman smiled and pirouetted. She landed in front of Lilith and said, "The lady knows her fashion. I can't blame you for not knowing Missoni's shoes. They'll debut at fashion week in Milan."

Lilith gasped. *She's wearing Missoni six months before Milan. Who the hell is she?*

"You are pretty. My niece would ... Who escorted you here tonight?" The woman asked.

Lilith felt trapped. This charming brown-haired woman's appearance had disarmed her, but her question was like a gun aimed between her eyes.

"Handsy—I mean the mayor—from the coast brought me."

The woman glided beside Lilith and faced the partygoers. "No, handsy is accurate. Where are my manners? I'm Patty. And you are?"

"Estella. Pleasure to meet you, Patty. Forgive me for asking, but is this your place?"

"My name isn't on the title, but I run every square inch of it. Except for Ernesto's office."

Lilith's heart skipped a beat, then returned with a concussive blast. This was Ernesto Cottrell's home. She raised her hand to her amulet; certain her heart had sent it popping off her chest with her heart explosion.

A phone vibrated inside a hidden pocket of Patty's dress. "Duty calls, Estella. Enjoy yourself, and hopefully I'm not so busy that I may rejoin you later. Here comes handsy—I mean the mayor."

The mayor stepped beside Lilith. Before his hand slid down her back and headed lower, she grabbed it. "Take me upstairs. I'm ready to tie you up and start your night of ecstasy."

Excited at his dominatrix's willingness to begin, the mayor pulled Lilith by the arm. She wasn't having it with his yanking. With a quick wrist flip and twist, she pinned his hand behind his back. "I'm in control now, not you, moron."

As they passed an adjoining hall, Lilith saw AJ had made his way down the corridor he wanted to explore. He held a picture frame and stood eerily still as he faced a young, brown-haired woman. Every drop of blood seemed to have drained from his face, and he wasn't blinking.

19 - The Ill-fated Ship

Lilith hooked the mayor's wrist and spun around him after she closed the bedroom door. She jerked his arm up to the middle of his back while she bent his wrist down. He arched backwards, which allowed her to keep him off balance. She run-shoved him forward until he fell face down on the bed.

"My god. If this foreplay, I can't wait for the rest of your domination," the mayor moaned.

Lilith leapt off the bed, grabbed a brass lamp off the nightstand, and smashed it on the back of his head, knocking him unconscious.

"Consider that your climax, asshole."

She dragged him to the bathtub and hog-tied him with the cord she'd yanked from the lamp. The devil within convinced her to plug the tub and turn on the water. Moments later, the angel told her differently and had her returning to the bathroom to turn off the water.

The second floor was empty, so she could reconnoiter the rooms unhindered. Bedroom after bedroom yielded nothing except appreciation for the interior designer. She entered the last room and stopped dead in her tracks when the door shut.

Fishnet stockings, draped over carmine-painted walls, evoked the spirit of a French cabaret. Long tassels and feathers lay over the edges of mirrors and window frames. The impressionist paintings weren't those of street artists, but by the grand masters of Impressionism.

She inched her way into the room, stunned by its grandeur and beauty. She opened the closet door to find dozens of shoes lying about in chaotic disarray.

Above the mosh pit of shoes, she found scores of dance costumes on hangers. An exquisite selection of designer dresses, skirts, and tops filled the closet. She stepped out of the closet and found the room's owner standing in the doorway. Neither she nor the woman spoke, and introductions weren't needed. They had danced in the sultry heat of New Orleans's French Quarter six months earlier.

Sizing up her dance partner, Lilith said, "This doesn't have to go badly, Melody. Ignore me and I'll walk out of your life."

"Hard to ignore you, Lilith. Your dress is … titillating, but not tawdry."

Lilith eased out of her heels, one foot at a time. Melody held a knife by her side.

"I didn't come to fight you," Lilith said.

"You have no idea what you've waltzed into."

"Don't I know it? We weren't aware this was Ernesto Cottrell's home. Had we, we wouldn't have come."

"Why are you trying to drown the mayor?" Melody asked.

"I thought I turned it off."

"It was off, but you started to fill … Never mind."

"Step aside, Melody. Ignore us and we'll leave."

"It won't be that easy. I won't expose you, but you really don't want Dad or Nico finding you."

Lilith didn't respond. Melody's motivation seemed awry to her. "In New Orleans, you were in our rooms. A soothing, caring, compassionate voice in our darkness while the interrogations took place."

Melody tilted her head in shame. "For the day you were hypnotized, I was an intimate and integral part of your lives. I walked you to the bathroom and fed you before you went back to bed. We couldn't afford to have you waking up because you were hungry."

"You sat in the chair beside the bed … *My* side of the bed. You were angry?"

"A couple of Dad's goons figured since you were asleep—"

"You don't have to finish." Lilith waved her off. "You stopped them from raping us."

"Strong stimulus remembered. Dr. Harrell was right. My anger imprinted on you when I stopped them."

"And you sat on the bed next to me … The whole time. "

Melody looked away from Lilith. "Dr. Harrell had me help you folks up to the second-floor bedroom, where she did the interrogations. AJ's session lasted over six hours. Everybody else was about two."

Lilith added on her fingers. "Fourteen hours. But we were under for over twenty-four hours?"

"We took time between each of you to plan our strategy." Melody's voiced cracked as she asked, "Are you and your friends human traffickers?"

"Goddamn … sex …" Lilith waved her hands in front of her before she regained her composure. "What twisted mind gave you the impression we were human traffickers?"

"Do you traffic women to the US for prostitution?"

"We never did, and never will."

Melody turned her head. "Dr. Harrell interrogated you under the direction of the FBI's regional director. Dr. Harrell recruited me to assist in the sessions. We were searching for a hidden room which facilitated human trafficking at the behest of Broken Cove Industries and its owner, AJ de Faria."

"No, girl. They twisted it. AJ is setting up a domestic violence survivor transport program. The redemptive form of human trafficking," Lilith said.

"Goddamn it." Melody blurted out. "They lied to me."

"When you and I danced—"

"It was the first time I met you. Two days later, I was in your hotel room, aiding in the interrogation."

Lilith pointed to the door. "You were the young lady speaking with AJ downstairs."

"Yeah, I scared the hell out of him. To be fair, seeing him here scared me, too."

"Just what the hell happened to us in New Orleans?"

"You stayed in the Empress Suite, which Dad reserves when he goes to New Orleans. They converted it into typical hotel rooms and monitored your visit," Melody said.

"The smell of fresh-cut lumber was our first clue that something was off."

"You were taken, one at a time, to the second-floor master bedroom, and hypnotized. I didn't understand what room they were after." Melody searched Lilith's face for an answer.

"They're after a real room, but not one where women and children are trafficked. But why the orgy dreams?"

"To hide any traces of our day-long intrusion. Dr. Harrell, my psychology adviser, said strong stimulus would focus your mind away from our extended visit. We were supposed to be out by morning, not a day later. Someone got to you first, and that messed everything up."

"You learned about us," Lilith said.

"Little personal details, but nothing insightful. They were pissed. Someone shielded you with a previous hypnotism. They said it was a priest named—"

Men yelling at the top of their lungs came from the floor below, forcing Melody to step to her bedroom door. No sooner had she opened it than three rapid gunshots came from downstairs. Lilith slammed her hands over her mouth as another three-round shot rang out.

Melody opened the door and motioned for Lilith to leave. "Head back to the party. If you are caught up here, they'll do horrible things to you. Listen to what I say."

Lilith inched her way to the door, unsure if she should believe Melody.

"When Aunt Patty blows dust in your face, don't inhale. Sneeze, then pretend to fall asleep. The dust is to put you in a light, hypnotic state. Act passive, vacant, and if you talk, ramble. Tell her you are following my directions."

Melody escorted Lilith to the stairs. "Tell your friends what I've told you."

With Melody's gentle push, Lilith descended the stairs

and returned to the room she'd left AJ in. Before she reached him, she and the other partygoers were shoved against the walls. Several men aimed submachine guns at them.

Lilith stood on the opposite side of the room, apart from AJ. She mouthed for him to follow her lead. Gunmen pushed four of the catering staff into the room. They clung to one another and lowered their heads. The fourth caterer was Charlotte.

Spotting Lilith against the wall, Charlotte intentionally stumbled in Lilith's direction. A gunman caught her by the hair and yanked, slamming her against the wall. Charlotte sobbed while Lilith consoled and whispered Melody's instructions. Lilith pulled Charlotte's hair back and was greeted by a tearless face. Charlotte faked her hysteria.

Charlotte whispered to Lilith, whose jaw clenched tighter with each shared detail.

A woman screamed in the hallway, but the scream never finished. The sound of a three-round shot from the submachine gun silenced her. A moment later, Patty marched into the room.

Lilith had failed to put it together until now. The charming woman she spoke with earlier was Melody's aunt, Aunt Patty.

Patty entered the room and marched in front of a terrified young woman. A gunman stood behind her, who lifted a perfume spray pump in front of the young woman's face. "Breathe in the dust," Patty said. The young woman did as instructed, and a split second later, she sneezed.

Satisfied, Patty moved to the next person.

Lilith mouthed '*Demon's Breath*' to AJ.

Further down the wall, a man inhaled the dust, but didn't sneeze. The gunman pressed his gun on the man's forehead. "Can I shoot?"

Patty pushed the gun away. "I get two tries before you can shoot."

She squeezed the spray pump, and again the man didn't sneeze.

Patty shook her head.

The gunman placed the gun between the man's eyes and pulled the trigger. A circle of blood on the wall behind the man's head marked the exit wound. He dropped to the floor, dead.

Aghast at seeing a man killed in front of her, Lilith fell back against the bookshelf, with Charlotte pressed against her. All colors faded into shades of gray, and sounds blended into indiscernible muffles. She forgot how to breathe, and her hands and knees quivered in fear.

Other shots rang out from the hallway.

The woman next to Charlotte panicked and wept. The gunman didn't want to hear her sobbing. He jammed the barrel of his gun under the left side of her chin and pulled the trigger. A three-round burst decimated her head, sending the woman tumbling against Charlotte.

Patty yelled, "Stop shooting. Ernesto can't question dead people. And for my sake, stop with the three-round bursts. More bullet holes mean more repairs."

While the gunman reloaded, Charlotte struggled to stand. Lilith sensed her difficulty. She pulled Charlotte's arm onto her shoulder to keep her from falling. The gunman pointed the gun at Charlotte.

Lilith only saw the gun. Her mind blanked out. Not until the gun swung away did she take a breath. She couldn't tell if she was shaking or if it was Charlotte trembling, but either way, combined or individually, they were having trouble standing.

Charlotte twisted toward her. The terror in her eyes was overshadowed by the blood-splatter, which drenched the entire side of Charlotte's face. Lilith raised her jittery hand to wipe the blood from Charlotte, which drew the gunman's ire.

He returned to pointing his gun at Charlotte's head. "Stop, or you'll be the one wearing her blood on your face."

She stopped and faced forward, as did Charlotte.

Patty worked around the room to Lilith. "Oh, Estella. Sorry about your first visit to hell. Inhale and sneeze, pretty girl."

"Yes, Aunt Patty. I am following Melody's instructions, just as she told me to tell you."

Patty hesitated to squeeze the spray pump. Lilith turned her head to Charlotte and returned to face Patty.

"Then follow what she said to the letter," Patty said. She sprayed, and Lilith sneezed.

After Lilith wiped below her nose, she grabbed Charlotte's hand. "Repeat what I did, for Aunt Patty."

Patty looked at Charlotte. "The companion? It can't be."

Charlotte sneezed and righted herself.

Patty continued down the line to AJ. She raised the perfume spray to AJ's face and stopped on hearing Lilith's sudden outburst.

"Oh my God. This is fantastic, Aunt Patty. Blow that guy like you blew me, for Melody's sake." Lilith swayed her head and smiled like she was drunk. "Whoa. Hell yeah. This feels good."

Patty looked into AJ's eyes. "You know what to do?"

"Yep, as per Melody," AJ said.

She squeezed, and he sneezed.

Patty moved to the next man, but he didn't sneeze. The gunman didn't wait for Patty's second dusting. Lilith closed her eyes and held onto Charlotte. They both flinched when a single shot rang out.

One by one, people slumped to the floor, asleep or dead.

Lilith pretended to sleep through the parade of individuals rising on command and disappearing into the hall. Minutes felt like hours, and the hour she spent on the floor felt like years. She guessed they were being questioned in another room. The muffled gunshots were executions for those whose answers were unsatisfactory.

Charlotte laid her head on Lilith's hip. She felt Charlotte shaking. If she stretched out her hand to comfort Charlotte, she would risk both of their lives.

The blood of the woman killed beside Charlotte continued to flow from the massive opening in her head. Lilith's leg lay in the path of the blood flow. It sickened her to feel the blood's warmth as it crept along her leg. Before long, she could tell that she and Charlotte were lying in a pool of a dead woman's blood.

All the while, a pattern of the flow of people became evident to her. Gunmen barked orders. The guests rose and walk into the hallway. Minutes later, they came back and returned to the floor.

One gunman kicked Charlotte in the leg and told her to stand. She did as ordered and disappeared down the hall.

Lilith waited for her roommate's return, but the rhythm of exits and returns had been interrupted. Charlotte's return was outside the normal routine. Before she could wait a second longer, a gunman ordered her to stand.

She walked down the hallway and tried to look past

the carnage of blood-splattered walls and dead bodies. The surreal scene contrasted with the beautiful marble floors, ornate floor, ceiling molding, and pristine eggshell-colored walls. She locked her eyes at the end of the hallway and walked to an office door. Charlotte stepped out of the office as Lilith approached. Neither spoke as they passed the other.

The door opened to an expansive circular office. Paintings of nature and towering windows accentuated the tropical theme. Two chairs sat across from a white marble-topped-desk. The wicker cane chair had infinite more appeal than the bloodied Gothic chair.

A gunman pushed Lilith into the wicker cane chair. Ernesto Cottrell sat behind the desk in a soft leather-seated chair. He combed his thinning silver hair over his bald head. Years of sunlight had tanned his skin to an unhealthy, leathery brown. Under his bushy eyebrows peered ice-blue eyes.

Ernesto leaned forward to see Lilith. "Beautiful. You would be the most beautiful woman tonight if you weren't covered in blood. Why are you here, baby doll?"

She didn't answer.

"Come now, Lilith. We haven't seen each other in six months."

The door opened, and a man stumbled in, catching Lilith off guard. One of Ernesto's men shoved the man toward the Gothic chair. He sat, and Ernesto's man strapped down his arms and legs. He also used thick straps around the man's waist and chest to pull him tight against the back of the chair. A leather strap went over his forehead, pinning his head back.

Lilith watched in horror as the man was strapped in place.

"Greg, are you ready to talk?"

"I'm ready to talk about whatever you want. The weather, sports, this fabulous party—"

"Shut up, Greg," Ernesto ordered. "You see, Lilith, Demon's Breath reduces your inhibitions. Aftereffects of the drug include chattiness, heightened suggestibility, a raise in body temperature, and an increase in one's libido. Suggestibility is wonderful for hypnosis and for amorous encounters. Aftereffects you aren't displaying."

"I'm not chatty today," Lilith sneered.

"See there, Nico. An answer we can believe. Lilith, I'd like you to meet my nephew, Nico."

Nico stepped forward and leered at Lilith. The evil intent in his gray eyes terrified her.

"Nico, she didn't come alone. Send someone to find AJ de Faria. He is likely in whatever room you took her from."

Nico pulled out his phone and texted.

"While we wait for AJ to join us, my dear, dearest Lilith, I want to prove to you that you have a choice."

Ernesto pointed to the man next to her. "Greg is on my shit list. He has done nothing wrong, but his incompetence has slowed my return on investments. He designs containers to bypass your country's intrusion into my business. Recently, he constructed a fantastic container, which, a week later, on the container's first run, your Drug Enforcement Agency confiscated. They knew what to look for."

Lilith looked at the man and feared for his safety.

"Greg didn't betray us by turning informant. He unknowingly hired someone who did. Tonight, we send Greg back to his town as a message: betray me and suffer the consequences. Machiavelli asked if it is more important to be feared … or loved. Money can buy you love, or something close to it. But fear—*there's* the real power."

Nico stepped behind the Gothic chair and unstrapped a long double-bladed knife.

Lilith cringed at the sight.

Ernesto continued with his joyous description. "Nico designed a razor-sharp knife which slides into the slots in the back of the chair. Those slots align between the vertebrae of the spinal column. We start with the T12 vertebrae—"

Lilith jumped up. "You don't have to impress me. Let Greg go and we can talk."

"Sit down, Lilith. Or when … " Ernesto snapped his fingers. "We've got another one to bring here, Nico. The smoking hot Latina with the platinum hair, the one we just talked to, retrieve her."

"Ernesto, stop it. This is senseless—"

"Sit down, Lilith, or we'll force you to watch everything we do to Charlotte. I guarantee you, it will last longer for her than it will for old Greg here. Nico, proceed."

Lilith turned her head away.

Greg screamed. She refused to look in his direction and stood with clenched fists. The urge to attack Ernesto succumbed to the reality she couldn't handle him and Nico together.

Ernesto spoke without an ounce of emotion. "The bottom slot positions that knife for a surgically precise cut. It paralyzes Greg from the waist down, and we send him home as a message to any who think about betraying us. I don't want him dead; I want him as a constant reminder."

Nico released the straps, and men entered to attend to Greg.

"What do the other slots do, you may ask."

Lilith held up her hand, stopping Ernesto from talking further.

The door opened and in walked AJ and Charlotte.

Charlotte ran over and climbed into the chair with Lilith.

AJ studied the Gothic chair as Greg was placed in a wheelchair.

"AJ, how are you?" Ernesto asked.

"Hey Ernie. What happened to this guy?"

Lilith noticed AJ's behavior had become more cavalier.

"Ignore him and take a seat."

A glance at the bloodied chair stopped AJ from sitting. "That's okay. I prefer to stand."

"Whatever you want."

The men rolled Greg out the door.

AJ twisted around to see the office. "Nice place you've got here. Who is your interior decorator? Magnificent decor, and what a location. Is the wood molding Jatobá?"

"Learn from your boss, Lilith. Life is short. Enjoy it before you die," Ernesto said.

"Enjoy life, that's right. God, this is great. Does this mean a little of the Demon's Breath got into me? I fake sneezed, but I feel really … chatty. Yeah, that's the word, chatty."

"AJ, shut up," Ernesto ordered.

"Why? Don't you wanna talk? I wanna talk. What do you wanna talk about?"

"Dear Lord, you're going to be annoying. Would you like us to top off the dusting?"

"And kill this buzz? No thanks. Hey, while I'm

talking, let me ask: why did you kill your guests? Granted, it allows you to say this 'was a killer party,' but it doesn't do anything for the 'I'll die if I miss that party' vibe. Ya-know-what-I-mean-Ern?"

Ernesto pointed at Nico. "Pull out a chair for him. This could be fun."

"Thanks, Ernie."

"Don't mention it. With the chit-chat done, tell me, AJ, why did you come here and blow up the old wing of the mansion?"

"Blow up the wing? I didn't hear an explosion, did you, Lilith? Hey, Ernie, do you have a dog, like a beagle? I love beagles."

Nico scooted a chair in place for AJ.

"Thanks, buddy. Now, back to the blowing up thing. Are you referring to the hospital explosion in the *Dark Knight*? I'm hearing 'wing' and 'blown up,' so guess what's hitting my frontal cortex?"

"The old wing has crumbled wall on the ground. You're here; it's down; I'm guessing you caused it," Ernesto said.

"Nope, not me. Hey, the old broad in the picture on your shelf … That's Gabby." Turning to Lilith, he said, "Oh boy. The old lady in the wheelchair, Gabby. She's his mom, and I'm her nurse for the evening. Can you say *awkward*?"

"AJ, start explaining the destroyed wall in the old wing or I'm going to hurt these ladies."

"Touch them and you'll never touch the twenty-billion-dollar treasure."

Ernesto recoiled at AJ's lucid threat.

AJ placed his hands on his hips. Looking down at Ernesto, he said, "Demon's Breath may have me giddy, but rest assured, I'm in full control of my faculties. Harm my people and you'll lose the treasure of the ages. Let us go, and you can have the treasure."

Ernesto sat on the edge of his chair. "You accessed the map room. That priest, Father Amare, he blocked your memories with Demon's Breath so we couldn't retrieve your info off the map."

AJ shook his head. "Damn, this fogginess is stronger than a six pack of beer."

Ernesto waited for him.

"What you're saying about Father Amare sounds true. We've been hypnotized so many times, it is hard to keep things straight. But out of curiosity, did you find a skeleton in the rubble of your destroyed wall?"

"You were back there. We found a skeleton," Nico said.

"I wandered down the hall and saw your game table with the ivory chess pieces. Above the table is an antique-framed map. I'm sure you never looked at it closely," AJ said.

Nico stepped toward AJ, intent on silencing him for his disrespectful tone.

"Nico, stop," Ernesto ordered. "I'll hold my nephew back once, but watch what you say to me, AJ."

"The guy who drew the map and built the old mansion was Bill Bennington, the namesake of your criminal organization. The skeleton is his," AJ said.

"Nico, have Patty investigate the rubble. AJ, why do you say a twenty-billion-dollar treasure?"

"What do you know of the map room?"

"I'll ask the questions."

"You can have the treasure, Ernie. Since you dragged us into this, all we've longed for is to drop-kick this mess out of our lives. I'm not joking. You get the treasure, minus a small finder's fee, and we part company forever."

Ernesto leaned back in his chair. "Clues are hidden on a wall, and those clues lead to the treasure."

"Five clues. One of which I broke earlier this evening with your daughter's assistance. And it's not a treasure, it's *the* treasure."

Lilith and Charlotte's focus switched to AJ. They sat motionless and open mouthed.

AJ swung his arm and pointed at the door he came through. "The picture below the Bennington map, the one of Melody's dance recital. The caption under her picture you titled, *Your Flower of the Sea.* Inspirational, truly. You love your daughter. But her dance recital picture and your caption unlocked a clue on the map wall: DARE FROM ALL. It is a word scramble. Unscrambled, it is the ill-fated ship which sunk five centuries ago, taking with her the greatest treasure ever lost at sea: the *Flor de la Mar.*"

20 - Adela Frontera

Lilith couldn't process any more. AJ's solving of the DARE FROM ALL clue left her stunned. A Portuguese ship sinking in a storm off the Indonesian coast five centuries earlier meant nothing to her. But the alertness in Ernesto's eyes betrayed his intentions about the ship.

"What else did the wall say?" Ernesto asked.

AJ's confidence had soared to manic heights thanks to the modest dust ingestion. "Walls don't say things unless you're schizophrenic. Besides, the writing on the wall wasn't designed for your eyes. It was designed for hers."

AJ had turned his head toward Lilith. His sympathy and compassion poured through his eyes. She glanced at Ernesto, whose eyes no longer projected hostility. Their eyes locked. Even though he looked at Lilith, his question was for AJ.

"Lilith is the Voodoo Priestess descendant?"

"Yep, and her team can find the treasure. If you don't interfere."

"You led her into my home."

"Sorry, Ernie, we weren't aware this was your home. I offer you my sincere apologies." AJ headed toward the door. "Lovely party. We must do it again sometime—"

"Sit down. You aren't leaving before I have my answers."

AJ turned around and looked at his seat choices. "I'll skip the bloodied one. Am I seeing slots in the chair's back?"

Charlotte leaned forward to see the chair.

"Oh, you sick mother," AJ shrieked. "A paralysis chair?"

"Would you like a demonstration?"

"Ernie—" AJ stopped when Lilith clamped onto Charlotte's arm. Ernesto's sadistic glance at the girls shot a jolt of terror through her. AJ spoke boldly to assert some semblance of authority over the drug lord.

"This team must be mobile and intact. Time is of the essence and severing a spine to instill fear and dominance over us won't work to your advantage. If you want the treasure before others reach it, my team must remain untouched."

"Shame on you AJ. Using the high-pressure sales technique of *immediacy* on me? That's an act of desperation on your behalf when I hold all the cards."

"Tell me, you have bugs throughout my house, right?"

Ernesto pulled a keyboard onto the desk. After typing, he swiveled the monitor around. "Round-the-clock surveillance, both audio and video."

AJ squinted at the monitor. "Why are you showing me

the governor of Georgia's office?"

Frustrated, Ernesto swiveled the monitor back.

"Can't blame you for monitoring that *son-of-a-bitch*."

Ernesto swiveled the screen again.

"One video monitor in my living room table lamp. Where's the audio button on your screen?" AJ tilted his head to one side. A smile grew across his face.

Lilith and Charlotte leaned toward AJ to see the cause of his smiling. Ernesto swiveled the monitor back before they saw it.

Ernesto screamed, "That damn cat, Shazoo!"

Lilith and Charlotte fist bumped. AJ's enthusiastic Himalayan cat was dislodging the hidden micro-camera. If history repeated itself, they knew a final scratch from Shazoo's claw would send the bug twirling to the floor, where a dog's tongue—Sonny's, most likely—would be the last image before the transmission stopped.

"Shazoo has cost me a small fortune in surveillance," Ernesto said.

"I'll ship it back after Sonny shits it out."

AJ continued before Ernesto exploded. "The point is, you're not the only one with monitoring systems in my home. Some might be your competitors. The Indonesian devices sent out two signals. The governmental device had a piggy-back on it. If not for a superb IT guy, the piggy-back device would have escaped us. Tech that advanced requires expertise and cash. You are aware of a private Indonesian citizen who has the expertise to hack a governmental spy device?"

"I may be."

Not hearing Ernesto elaborate, AJ said, "The Chinese devices had separate transmission frequencies. We think one belongs to their government. Another belongs to a bank ... or somebody at the bank? But the first one we traced came out of Nanjing."

Ernesto swung his head down and to the side.

"Well, my god. How terrifying for you? Not that it eases my mind, but you just confirmed my fears. The Nanjing Twins are involved."

Ernesto raised his head. "How does a golf course owner know about the Nanjing Twins?"

AJ ignored the question. "Listen, my team has to be ready, available, and at the top of their games. If you stick one in the back and our hunt slows to a crawl, your competitors gain the advantage. Let us go, we'll find the treasure, you take it, and we split up. Needless to say, we don't find the treasure. You kill us, and we still split up. We're heavily incentivized to find. My god, this stuff really makes you talk."

Ernesto pulled open a desk drawer. "Why are you here, and why destroy my wall in the old mansion?"

"The Bennington map, above your daughter's recital picture, we need it. As to why your wall collapsed, I honestly couldn't tell you what hap—"

AJ's train of thought broke when Ernesto placed a bottle of Scotch on the desk. "Holy mother of god, a twenty-five-year-old Scotch. Girls and boys in Scotland reach that age, but no Scotch in my house ever turned twenty-five."

Charlotte and Lilith strained to understand what was happening to AJ.

Ernesto shifted his gaze from AJ to the girls and back. "Sorry. Alcohol and Demon's Breath are a dangerous—and deadly—combination."

"Girls, the Ern and I have an agreement. He won't kill me with alcohol, and we'll find his treasure minus the finder's fee. We should leave. He's got cleaning to do, and I have bugs to retrieve from the dog shit."

Lilith held Charlotte back with her arm.

"Sit down," Ernesto ordered. "Tell me everything, then you can leave if I like what I hear."

"My first inclination is to question what you mean by 'everything.' I'm going with my second impulse and guessing you mean everything pertaining to this treasure hunt. Man, am I talking way too fast or what?"

"Reinstall my monitoring devices. I want to know what you learn the moment you learn it."

"It won't work. You saw—Hey."

Lilith held her breath. Demon's Breath had kicked AJ's ass into the loony bin. Charlotte's frantic taps on her hip meant both of them were watching AJ's break with reality.

"It took a while, but your previous comment about my cat just sank in," AJ said. "You've spied on us long enough to know Shazoo's name?"

Ernesto slammed his fist on the table. "Focus. You've convinced me to let you go."

"I hear you Ernie. But face it, hearing that the Nanjing Twins have bugs in my house swayed you more than my musings."

"Reinstall the monitoring devices and keep the goddamn cat away."

"Really? I'm here, he's there, and he dug it out. I can't control him. This is his world, and I'm simply passing through. Can we leave now?" AJ began wiggling his leg.

Ernesto turned to Lilith. "Tell your IT guy to activate the programs we installed on your electronics. If we don't hear your conversations when you return to Portland, I'm sending Nico up for a visit. Do you understand?"

Lilith nodded.

"Nico, take them to the chess table, but don't release them until I say." Ernesto waved his hand, expecting his orders to be carried out.

AJ walked next to Nico down the bloodied hallway with the girls close behind. Once at the chess table, Nico pulled down the framed Bennington map. "You said you needed this, so you've got it. If my uncle finds you're lying, I will take great delight in killing you. Your girls will have a different fate. A fate I will enjoy, even if they don't. Do you understand?"

"Then I consider this farewell. Shall we never meet again," AJ said.

"Wait here until I come back." Nico thumped into AJ's shoulder as he left.

Charlotte and Lilith slumped together in a chair, leaning against each other for support. Charlotte clutched her chest and struggled to catch her breath. Lilith couldn't blink. She stared mindlessly out the window. Spent gunpowder filled the air, which made her queasy. Gun shots hadn't stopped ringing in her ears. And the woman's blood, which covered her, had lost its warmth.

A gunman approached them and led them down the hall. Through the front doors and down the avenue, they turned onto a narrow path to a landing pad. A helicopter's whirling blades blew dust in their faces. The gunman aimed his gun at them and told them to board.

AJ helped the girls into the back seat, climbed in himself, and shut the door. But their terror was renewed when they found the pilot slumped in his seat. He was dead with a knife dangling in the side of his throat.

The second pilot yelled, "I hope you can point me to a

place where you will be safe. Whatever you said to Dad, it pissed him off."

Lilith scrambled to put the headphones on. "Melody? Why are you flying this?"

The helicopter powered up and lifted off.

"Something was taken out of the crumbled wall," Melody said. "Dad ordered this flight to the warehouse, where they would've held Charlotte hostage while you did what he wanted. He lied to me about why we interrogated you in New Orleans, and I can't let innocent people die because of my inaction. So, where am I taking you?"

"I can't tell you where to fly us," Lilith said.

AJ lowered the headset micro so he could speak. "Is your dad aware you're flying us?"

"No." Melody turned to the dead pilot. "No one does."

"Then how about Adela Frontera? Can you take us there?"

"I don't remember exactly where Adela Frontera is. I know the road and the bend it sits on."

Charlotte's voice came through the headphones. "This is my fault. People died because of me."

"Some of our downhill oasis fellows joined the caterers late this afternoon when we left for the mansion. They saw me sneaking over to the old wing and followed me."

"Downhill oasis; the refurbished barn. You have a knack for naming things," AJ said.

"I found the wedge wall, but we didn't see how to open it. There was a ring on the bottom of a beam, just like those in the map room in New Orleans. I shoved a fireiron into the ring and pushed. A loud crackling came from inside the wall, and seconds later, dozens of cracks formed. In a second, the whole wall crashed to the ground."

Lilith put her arm around Charlotte's shoulders.

"The wedge wall didn't hide a six-foot-wide room . It hid a three-foot wide wall. The maid messed up her measurements. It is why it remained undetected all these years. It was a design quirk, not a secret compartment."

Melody said, "Yep. The exact comments about that wall."

Charlotte raised her fist in the air. "The guys took the two chests and loaded them in the caterer's van. While they drove away, I searched for anything else. Bennington's skeletal remains were there, and one other item. I returned a few minutes later to the kitchen, and that's when the shootings started. I started this."

Lilith wasn't having it. "Nope. No. You are not responsible. A psychopath ordered those killings. Normal people file an insurance claim when something breaks in their home."

"What was the last item?" AJ asked.

Charlotte unclenched her fist, causing Lilith to gasp.

AJ leaned forward for a better look.

Melody twisted around to see what Charlotte had. But flying the helicopter kept her from getting a good look. "Is that a gold hockey puck?"

"If it is, I'm taking up hockey," AJ said.

Charlotte said, "It is a large gold coin with the face of a princess. Two oval-shaped sapphires make up her eyes. This can't be real. This is beyond me."

Lilith took the coin from Charlotte and held it up for Melody.

"It's you on the coin. Jesus. That's troubling."

"I was raised to be good trouble. This is OG trouble."

AJ took the coin and held it up next to Lilith's face. "It doesn't take a genius to see the resemblance between the princess on the coin and you."

Numb to the world, Lilith said, "Land this thing. I gotta … I can't deal with anymore of this tonight. My head hurts and I want to throw up."

"I can't say how close we'll land to the exact spot you need." Melody flipped a switch on the console. "Oh, dear. That might complicate things. I forgot to switch off the transponder code, doohickey thing."

"What does that mean?" Lilith asked.

AJ planted his palm on his forehead. "It means Ernesto knows where this helicopter flew to. He knows where we are."

Melody landed the helicopter and let them out. When they cleared the rotors, she shut them down. She opened the door and jumped from the pilot's seat. "So much for flying back to the mountaintop. I forgot to check the fuel level."

Minutes later, they crested a small ridge, and Adela Frontera faded into view. Ethereally lit by antique gas lamps, a light blue haze hovered over and enveloped the patio. Adela was an enchanting sight for the four weary travelers.

"What happens now?" Lilith asked.

AJ stepped onto the patio first. "Perhaps a local of these parts can help us."

Melody looked around the patio. "Adela Frontera is a fair market, a local trading post. Mom brought me here several times, but I'm no expert on this place."

"I wasn't referring to you, but to the guy who owns this place," AJ said.

"No one owns Adela Frontera."

"I beg to disagree. The caretaker who served us lunch

the other day. His barbecue pit … ” AJ pointed behind the small one-room building. “Where's the barbecue pit?”

Lilith entered the gallery side of the small building. “The shelves are empty.”

“Strange,” Melody entered behind Lilith, “this place hasn't changed since I was a kid.”

“I figured the guy lived here, and he'd contact the Péchettes for us,” AJ said.

“Oh, thank God,” Lilith said, “a bucket of water. Charlotte, come here. We can wash the blood off.”

AJ and Melody sat on the stone wall as the girls washed the blood from their arms, legs, and faces.

“How long before your dad arrives?” AJ asked.

“It's about a half-hour drive from the mountaintop. Will your friends get here before Dad does?”

“Not a clue. We drove to the town down the road, got abducted, and were taken to a barn.”

“Abducted? You were abducted? Biscuits. You were the ones who were kidnapped in front of the church. It made the news for the last two days.”

“Great, we made the news, again.”

“What do you mean by *again*?”

“Did you hear about Beagle's Bluff last summer?” AJ asked. “Or the emblem covering the streets the night after you danced with Lilith? Or the museum we torched in Tampa?”

Melody dipped her head. “I thought you folks were innocent of wrongdoing?”

AJ dismissed her question. “You said this place hasn't changed?”

“Not since I was here last. I don't remember these gas lamps, but, then again, it was during the day.” Looking down at the stone flooring and lifting her leg, she asked, “Is it me, or does this lighting eliminate shadows?"

Melody moved her leg around so AJ could see.

He pointed at Melody's nose. "No shadows on your face; no shadows from our bodies; no shadows, period. I know my people well enough—"

"Holy hell, there aren't any shadows out here," came Lilith's startled realization.

"Yep, you know your people," Melody said.

Charlotte fell to her knees. "I can't take anymore. Stop it! Just fucking stop it! I can't take one more goddamn fucking thing!"

Lilith raced to her side. She cradled Charlotte in her arms and stroked her hair.

AJ spoke. "We've been through hell tonight. Pick a pleasant memory and focus on it. Lilith's touch, my voice, whatever you can find, focus on it."

Charlotte rolled over, dropping her head and shoulders in Lilith's lap. Lilith stroked Charlotte's forehead like a mother comforting a sick child. AJ inched toward the stone wall with his back to them. Charlotte's pain was breaking him.

Melody turned and faced the same direction. Her feeble attempt to not cry resulted in a botched question to AJ. "Are you staying here to die?"

"We are an hour's walk from any town. If we ran through unfamiliar terrain, in this darkness … One step in an unseen hole breaks a leg, and then we'll be in worse shape. We'll have to take the chance that our downhill oasis folks reach us before your dad."

Half an hour later, six black SUVs sped down the road, slowing as they neared. They stopped yards past the sidewalk leading to Adela Frontera. The doors flew open and armed men ran across the field and up the small ridge. Ernesto walked behind them. But before he reached the ridge, his men rushed back.

AJ and Melody exchanged confused looks. Ernesto cursed as he kicked the ground. "Find out who helped them escape. I want them and the pilot dead. I don't care how many you kill." Ernesto continued to kick and curse his way back to the road. Before long, they were all back in their vehicles and sped back toward the mansion.

Melody pushed her finger into AJ's shoulder. "I'm here, you're here, and they were here. What the hell is happening?"

Charlotte lifted her head. "I'll go down on the one who can explain what just happened?"

"Not my lucky night," Melody said.

AJ cleared his throat. "They didn't see us, found the helicopter, walked in front of us, and left."

Charlotte gave him a dirty look.

"I explained *what* happened."

"You have to explain the *why* of what happened for me to go down on you, you idiot."

"Technicalities," AJ growled.

"Can we focus, please?" Lilith asked.

Melody nudged AJ's arm. "The guy who fed you lunch. Can you describe him?"

Lilith answered before AJ could. "He wasn't black, but he didn't quite look Hispanic either."

"Native American," Charlotte said. "His bloodline hadn't crossed with European or African bloodlines."

"Yeah, that's a good way of putting it. He had a full head of hair, and was nimble for an old guy. He had a cane, but I can't imagine why he would need it."

Melody cocked her head. "And his huge white dog?"

"The breed is called Great Pyrenees, and yes, that was the dog. Do you know him?" AJ asked.

Melody stared past the one-room shack. "Mom introduced me to him. The dog scared me because he was so big. Don't ask me who the old guy is. And don't freak out when I tell you he is walking toward us."

Behind the small one-room gift shop, the caretaker emerged from the darkness, holding a cane and with the colossal white dog at his heels. He stepped on the patio, wearing a red dress shirt and black dress pants.

"No, Melody, daughter of Bristol, you wouldn't remember me."

Charlotte raised from Lilith's lap and rolled over to sit on her ankles. "*Amigo*, would you call us a cab?"

"Already done." The caretaker bent over and kissed her on the forehead. "Healing to you. You'll be better after a good night's sleep."

Charlotte rose.

Lilith continued to sit on the stone patio floor. The dog towered over her and tilted his head to the side. She offered her hand for the dog to sniff. Her hand didn't interrupt his deep, distrusting gaze at her face.

AJ watched the caretaker with suspicion. "Tonight you can speak English. Why not when we were here two days ago?"

"I needed to hear what you told Lilith in translation." The caretaker patted the top of his dog's head. "If what you told her differed from our conversation in Spanish, the malevolence in your heart would have been exposed. Adela Frontera cannot extend its protection if your intentions are deceitful. However, you faithfully translated our discussion, so Adela Frontera's protection was extended to you in your time of need."

AJ looked around at the haze covering the patio. "Ernesto and his men failed to see us, because of this?"

"Adela Frontera found favor with you. Divine protection extended and surrounded you on this holy ground, my son. No harm may come to any spirit whose intentions are pure. A dark soul sought to inflict suffering on you, but he was thwarted."

The caretaker raised his hand and waved at the gas lamps. "A soft yellow light emits from these lamps when purity of intention presides. Some call it a fog, others an enchantment. In daylight, it is imperceptible. At night, it appears as a cloud of warm candlelight. The fog protected you by obscuring your presence from those who wished to do you harm."

Lilith stared at the gas lamps. "The glow is a light blue."

The caretaker swirled his hand in the haze. "Priestess LaTonya spoke of this. Certainly, she told you?"

"Oh boy." AJ sat on the patio border wall.

Charlotte scrunched her nose. "Not her again."

Lilith growled, which made the dog growl back. "Down, Cujo," she said.

"Kongo, behave," the caretaker ordered.

Kongo obeyed. He sat and fixated on Lilith's eyes. She returned his stare. "Cujo, Kongo. Whatever."

"*Amigo*, I don't have memories of LaTonya. If she shared with me, I don't know what it was," AJ said.

The caretaker said, "A horrible battle occurred here. Innocent lives paid the ultimate price while the guilty escaped justice. The Voodoo Priestess consecrated this spot to protect future innocents. Her mark is the blue light. It belongs to her and her daughters alone, and only once before has it shone.

"The legend of Adela Frontera lives here among the people. Accepting and abiding by the fair trade protects the innocent. Those who disregard Adela Frontera will find the will of Vilokan opposing them."

The caretaker pulled a small pouch from his pocket and walked to a gas lamp. He poured a palmful of powder in his hand, then blew it into the flame. The powder diffused in every direction, leaving tiny sparkling flecks floating in the air. It took a few moments to spread high and low through the blue haze.

Lilith held out her hand to catch them, but they were too small to see on her hand. Only the sparkling showed something was there.

AJ had his hand out, mirroring Lilith's gesture. He raised his head to look at the fog-dome over the patio. "This looks like a three-dimensional planetarium."

The caretaker walked across the patio, took Lilith's hand, and said, "These eyes, protected still, bound to blessing and curse, as promised at the river's confluence. The centuries have passed, and her eyes have returned. But which does Jade's daughter bring: eternal blessing, or wretched curse?"

Melody leaned forward. "Jesus. What is happening to Lilith's eyes?"

21 - Faraday and Marie Daly

Tayen waited in the van at the airport. A text from a blocked number confirmed AJ and the girls' arrival time. It carried an authentication code which identified Charlotte as the sender, but it did nothing to ease Tayen's frayed nerves.

A man wearing a wide-brimmed leather safari hat exited the oversized revolving door. Her hands froze on the steering wheel when he turned, revealing a large wound dressing above his eye. She stared at him as he opened the door and took the passenger front seat.

AJ cinched down the seatbelt and pointed. "Drive to the next exit door, now."

Tayen didn't question him and drove to the next exit door. A short woman dressed in a tan hijab rocketed from the exit and hurried toward the van.

A tall, bald woman scampered closely behind the Muslim woman. Comically huge sunglasses concealed her face, leaving nothing to see but brilliant red lips, a blanched chin, and a shaven bald head.

"Who is that?" Tayen asked.

The short woman launched herself through the door and thudded into the seat. The bald woman scurried in and slammed the door shut.

Tayen swung her head toward AJ. "You left here with two women. One is under the hijab, but what about the other? Did you trade her in for a taller model?"

"Trade-in and model? I see you're in the market for a new car."

Tayen punched the gas pedal and drove them away from the airport terminal.

"My turn for storytelling. I ask that you don't launch us through the windshield when you slam on the brakes," AJ said.

"Where is Lilith?"

"We will pick her up at the port in a week, along with the chests we found."

"She's on a cruise?"

"If only," Charlotte interjected.

"I put her on a cargo ship, economy class," AJ said.

"Lilith wasn't dumb enough to fall for the economy class lie."

"At least I was trying to put her mind at ease."

"AJ, Charlotte. Stop it!" Tayen ordered. "Enough of the bickering and explain why Charlotte is disguised as a Muslim."

"I'm taking advantage of the trial membership and thirty-day money-back guarantee," Charlotte retorted.

Tayen sighed. "I figured it was bad when I received the text that you were going dark for a couple of days. How bad was it, and who is our guest?"

"We found a lost puppy," AJ said.

"I'll run her to the vet for her shots, but you didn't answer who she is."

"I don't want to answer while you're driving."

"You're scared of her slamming on the brakes after what happened at our killer party?" Charlotte asked.

AJ faced Tayen. "Her state of agitation is a defensive mechanism."

"And yours is to dip into a state of analysis. Answer the question. Who's in my van?"

"Melody Sharpe," Charlotte blurted out.

Tayen looked in the rear-view mirror and saw Melody twirling her fingers to say hello.

The van veered wildly to the right when Tayen released her hands from the steering wheel. AJ took the wheel despite the frantic calls for Jesus.

"You brought Ernesto's daughter here?" Tayen asked as she took control of the van from AJ.

"She's a good kid, nothing like Ernesto. She saved us when she didn't have—"

"Does Ernesto know she is here?"

"God, I hope not. We need a little down time before we see him again." AJ raised his hand to draw her attention to the road sign. "This is our exit."

Tayen's preoccupation with Melody distracted her from taking the exit. She jerked the steering wheel and lurched the van into the exit lane.

"Smooth. Let AJ drive so you don't kill us."

"Watch it, young lady." Tayen had had enough of Charlotte's attitude. "Just lay out the basics."

"We have exceptional allies in the Dominican Republic. They're helping organize other friendly Caribbean cells. We're the spearhead," AJ said. "Father Amare said people would watch us from the shadows. He was right. They came to our aid and we'll find them spread throughout the Caribbean."

"Strong enough to protect us from a drug cartel?"

"Not at all. We need to create defenses Ernesto wouldn't expect. Stopping him isn't possible, but slowing him down could save us. Give me your phone, so I can have Scott activate our first Code Purple. Melody is in imminent danger."

"She needs a new name. We miss a bug and say her name, and he learns her location," Charlotte said.

"Why did we leave the airport without your bags?" Tayen asked.

AJ dropped his hand into his lap and stared out the window.

"The trip went badly."

AJ thumbed toward the back seat. "If Melody hadn't flown us off the mountaintop, we wouldn't be here."

Melody lowered her sunglasses. "I'm not taking credit for what happened at Adela Frontera. Jeez. That was a hell of an introduction to the world of Vodou."

Tayen kept glimpsing in the rear-view mirror. Even though she kept staring at Melody, the question went to AJ. "Did you find Adela Frontera?"

"Yep." AJ's weakened voice reflected his exhaustion. "We found it. But we weren't prepared for Vodou's two-day-long bitch-slapping once we got there."

***

AJ and Charlotte camped out in AJ's house for the following week. Liberal amounts of marijuana and Scotch were their therapy for decompressing. Scott, Talia, and Kimiko ran the golf resort at Tayen's direction. The grand opening was fast approaching and finalizing last-minute details required extra work.

Melody liked Charlotte's suggestion for her new name: Aniah Clemons. Talia and Scott guided her through The Village complex and explained the security measures for her, Aniah Clemons, the first Code Purple client.

Before leaving the Dominican Republic a week earlier, Lilith shaved off Aniah's hair. Little did they know it would prove a valuable decision. An assortment of wigs kept her identity a mystery, except in Kimiko's sewing room. Aniah proved to be skilled with a needle and thread, so she helped with Kimiko's clothing orders.

A week after Aniah's arrival in Portland, AJ and Charlotte were chilling with the dogs in AJ's atrium when they received a text from Lilith. AJ dragged Charlotte off the couch and into the garage, where he opened the garage door. Moments later, an SUV sped into the driveway and backed into the garage. Scott, Tayen, Elliott, and Aniah ran in the side door before it closed.

Lilith opened the SUV door and jumped out. Charlotte wrapped around her, hugging her roommate, whom she hadn't seen in over a week.

"Good to see you too." Lilith tossed the keys to AJ.

AJ opened the back hatch. "Tayen, can you help me with this chest? Scott and Elliott get the second."

Tayen and AJ moved the chest into the atrium and lifted it on top of the dining room table. Scott and Elliott lifted theirs onto the far end. Tayen took a whiff of the air and confronted AJ. "Weed and alcohol aren't healthy coping tools."

"Agreed. However, for now, we push forward. Charlotte and I have talked, *blunting* the impact of our darkest horrors." AJ smiled at Charlotte for his clever play on words.

Elliott caught their exchange and smiled. "Okay, you two. Do me a favor and explain what happened with Lilith's eyes. They turned bluer under the gas lamps? And Ernesto walked right by you and didn't see you?"

"What part of Haitian Vodou don't you understand?"

"Dad."

"If you want further insight, you're asking the wrong person. We were out of our minds when we reached Adela."

"And yet," Elliott brushed his hands, "the Péchette faction arrived within a moment's notice?"

AJ shrugged. "Ernesto left, and the caretaker blew powder into a gas lamp. The flame ignited the powder, which streamed out like you would see from a fire extinguisher. A faint bluish light enveloped the patio. Our friends arrived moments later. Brilliant blue flames shone from Lilith's eyes. One look at her and down they went, to one knee. The caretaker had disappeared somewhere in the confusion."

"Why didn't they open the chests at the downhill oasis?" Elliott asked.

"Are you kidding? After her eyes lit up, the thought of messing with a childhood folktale coming to life didn't enter their minds. They held a deep admiration for Lilith. While we debated what to do at the downhill oasis—"

"Why do you call it the downhill oasis?" Tayen asked.

"Because that's what Charlotte called it, and god pity the fool who tries to change what she has named," Lilith said. "Has anybody challenged what we call our resident moose?"

"We've never called her anything but Gertie since

Charlotte named it," Tayen said.

"At the Péchette barn,"—AJ stared down Charlotte, daring her to challenge his renaming—"Lilith and I agreed the chests needed to be opened in a safe place. So, she impressed on them the need to transport the chests back to Portland."

"Why not pick you up at the Port of Portland? Why rent an SUV?" Tayen asked.

"I never got to Portland. The Coast Guard boarded my ship down the coast." Lilith pointed toward the ocean. "The ship's captain, a Péchette, didn't want to chance the Coast Guard taking them. He cast me off in a dinghy with the chests and maneuvered his ship in front of the Coast Guard to hide my escape. I rowed ashore and dragged the chests behind a small dune.

"I waited a long time for the Coast Guard to leave. April on the Oregon coast ain't exactly warm weather. I was miserable, but I couldn't leave the chests and go to a store to call for help. Then four delightful teenagers wandered by. They helped me with the chests and drove me to the car rental. When I get rich, I'm paying for their college."

Tayen nodded. "Give me their names. I'll take care of them."

"Time for AJ to open the chests," Lilith said.

"Why me?"

"In the movies, the curse goes to the one who opens the chest."

AJ thought about it for a moment. "Elliott, get me the rubber gloves from under the kitchen sink. At least my hands will be protected."

While Elliott retrieved the gloves, AJ asked Lilith, "Are you alright?"

Lilith waved him off. "Open the chests, please."

AJ didn't respond. The silence forced her to repeat herself. "Open the chests, please." She stared at the chest in front of him. It was all she could handle at the moment.

AJ lowered his head and examined the chest. "There's a waxy seal here. Just like the Tampa chest."

He held out his hand, palm up, without saying a word.

"Are you doing the Macarena for us?" Tayen asked.

Elliott slapped a knife into his father's palm.

"That's the universal sign a father uses to ask his son for a knife," Charlotte said.

"Men." Tayen rolled her eyes and huffed. "Women ask politely."

Charlotte huffed back. "Dad and I don't. How do you think I knew the hand gesture?"

AJ sliced into the crevice and cut around the chest's full circumference. He handed the knife back and popped open the lid.

"Cute … tiny … boxes?" Lilith's sarcasm was palpable.

AJ lifted a three-inch wood box from the chest. He cut the box open and pulled out a dark object. "This is a piece of iron."

"Iron, sealed in a teeny-tiny box?" Lilith asked.

"Not a simple piece of iron … but pure iron."

"Oh-well-now that changes everything."

Charlotte took the iron piece from AJ. "Pure iron corrodes very fast. Yet it has sat intact in this teeny-tiny box for three centuries, showing no signs of corrosion. That isn't possible."

AJ opened a second box. "Tin, pure tin."

Charlotte stood by AJ. "Two pure metals from the

periodic table sealed in boxes and placed in a chest. Why?"

Scott picked a box out of the chest and examined it. "Looky here. There are letters and numbers carved on the tops. This one is E-12."

AJ added, "And it looks like they're color-coded."

Charlotte examined a box. "C-4." She flashed it at Elliott after seeing his panicked face. "The box is lettered C-4. Dear God, if this is the explosive C4, I'm moving to New Zealand."

Elliott sighed. "If that is an explosive compound, you're getting the engagement ring you've been threatening Dad with."

Charlotte dangled her hand and wiggled her ring finger at AJ.

He didn't see her. He was too busy rummaging through the chest. "*E* is on some of these, and the others have a *C*."

Charlotte stopped her hand taunting. "What did you find, Professor?"

AJ held up the tin and iron boxes and tilted them for her to see. "The two boxes with elements. Their box top has an *E*. Maybe I'm stretching this too far—"

"*C* is for compounds. *E* is for elements. No, you're not stretching it too far."

Tayen held a box up. "A woman discovered and mastered chemistry during the Golden Age of Piracy. People didn't understand her craft, so they called her work Voodoo and gave her the title Voodoo Priestess."

"We need a professor in chemistry to analyze them. If we open a box, which has an unknown compound, we could kill ourselves. Precautions have to be taken," Charlotte said.

"Then let's open the other chest," AJ said.

He stepped to the next chest and sliced open the waxy seal. He pushed the lid up while Charlotte squeezed beside him and peeked inside. Scott and Lilith stood side by side and peered into the chest.

"Son of a bitch." Charlotte took out her phone and tapped quickly.

"What's wrong?" Tayen asked.

AJ held up his hand.

"Is this another father-son sign?"

He shot Tayen a dirty look. "For your birthday, I'll send you a picture book of father-son signs."

Charlotte lowered her phone. "According to the pictures and this article, this is a Faraday generator. More precisely," she leaned over the chest and poked at the object, "this is a third-generation homopolar generator."

Lilith rested her hands on her hips. "Damn, girl. Why didn't you apply to MIT?"

"I did. That's how I learned they had woodshop."

AJ chuckled. "This is fringe. A century and a half before Faraday invented a generator, Jade Péchette invented a third-generation advancement of his landmark invention."

Charlotte clanked through the spools. "Electrical wiring of different gauges, and I'm guessing it's all the same material. I bet these are samples for testing load capacity."

Incredulous, Elliott said, "Before Benjamin Franklin's work with electricity, before Faraday's invention of a generator, an unknown woman mastered the science of electricity. Move over Emmett Brown."

Lilith parsed Elliott's statement. "Franklin is on the hundred-dollar bill. Faraday invented a generator, but who's Emmett Brown?"

"Another person from the Roanoke Colony."

"Charlotte," Tayen rebuked, "not funny."

Lilith waved her hand dismissively. "So, what's the big deal about discovering electricity before everybody else?"

AJ put a box on the table. "A pirate's success at sea would last three years, tops. This pirate held court for over a decade. You don't outrun colonial navies—armadas, really—without an advantage. Advances in chemistry and electrical engineering also mean advances in medicine and weaponry."

"Electricity powers lights and machines. So what did she invent?" Elliot asked.

"Foreign powers swarmed the Caribbean in the early eighteenth century. They had superior firepower. To offset the power imbalance, she created something to protect her pirate base."

"Demon's Breath was her creation," Lilith said. "She evaded capture and pirated a fortune for the ages. They never caught her infiltration. A network of spies and saboteurs operated right under their noses. She had a perfect espionage ring."

"Maybe we made a false assumption in New Orleans," Tayen said. "We assumed the courses mapped on the wall were single ships. Why couldn't they have been small flotillas or major sailing armadas?"

"We can't exclude flotillas, but Captain James Andrews' journal describes a stationary pirate base. Which is confusing," AJ said.

Lilith and Charlotte whirled their hands, prompting him to not leave them in suspense.

"Pirates' success depended on launching surprise attacks and then evading capture. Open runs are the pirate way. They would avoid confining themselves to ports, except for the Brethren of the Coast, who controlled Nassau. Life as a pirate is running on the open sea. It is harder to hit a small, moving target, like a single ship. Whereas a flotilla is larger and easier to find."

Tayen shielded her eyes. "I'm going to regret asking, but here it goes: when did you become an expert on naval strategy?"

"That isn't general knowledge?"

"Naval strategy, a favorite pastime of landlocked country club members."

Tayen's sardonic reply made Lilith laugh. Charlotte typically had the rights to those verbal jabs.

"So much for Captain AJ. Any ideas on a professional box investigator?" Lilith asked.

Tayen poked her on the shoulder. "Look who's learning leadership."

Charlotte said, "I'll call Dr. Tolbert at the University downtown. But what cover story do I give him?"

"Tell the truth. If one box is linked to a sunken treasure, where a country has a verified claim, we would find ourselves buried in litigation," Tayen said.

"Someone researched maritime law," Elliott said. "In the meantime, where do we hide the chests?"

"In a safe room," AJ said.

"Dad, unless you built one in the past week, this house doesn't have a safe room."

"It does now."

Tayen smacked her forehead. "God almighty, I suspected you had Manny doing working behind my back."

"Chill, this is my house. Grab the chests and head to the turret stairwell."

Lilith looked up at the second-floor walkway. There were only bedrooms on the second floor, and nothing was on the third, except AJ's bedroom.

The entourage approached the turret with the chests, along with two hyper dogs and one relaxed but curious cat. AJ flipped a light switch inside the turret. Broken Cove Industries' voice assistant came over the house speakers. *"How may I assist, AJ?"*

"Athena, initiate house protocol Norman Bates 1960."

"Please give the password for Norman Bates 1960 protocol."

"Oh, Mother, what have you done now?"

"Password accepted."

All heads drifted Elliott's way. "Hey, I am only related to him biologically."

Across the landing from the stair's bottom step, the floor slid back, revealing a stairwell which descended into the darkness. Lights flickered on. With the chests in hand, they descended into the stairwell.

Lilith complained. "How far down do we go?"

"Sixty feet, give or take a foot. I can't guess at our adversaries' technological advancement, but the deeper, the better, seemed wise. Unfortunately, it becomes worthless if anyone blabs about it."

"Somehow, I think that was directed at me," Charlotte said.

They reached the bottom and followed AJ through a short, narrow hallway. At the end, they entered a garage-sized concrete room.

Tayen lowered her end of the chest to the floor. "When did Manny finish this?"

"A week ago."

Charlotte punched Scott in the arm. "This is where you kept disappearing to this week? Every time I looked for you in your IT office, you were gone."

Scott placed his hand over the spot where Charlotte had punched him. "I was busy running the wiring and installing a couple of lights."

Lilith pointed to the second exit across the room. "Where does that go?"

Scott said, "It will connect to the other turret stairwell leading to the third-floor office. Two entrances—"

Tayen's interruption echoed off of the concrete walls. "Two entrances which mimic the map room in New Orleans. Is there something you aren't telling us?"

AJ glared at her. "A single corridor is dangerous. Crap happens to one, and we escape through the second."

"She has a point. The parallels between here and New Orleans are becoming more curious. Why are you doing this?" Lilith asked.

AJ heard her accusatory tone. "You think I'm going to build a replica of the map room here? This is a coincidence. This safe room's function is to hide below ground. I didn't design it as my fantasy playroom."

"Replica?" The tone in Charlotte's question paused their discussion. She looked around the room. "This looks bigger than the map room. If we return there and record it, then build a replica here. We could do research without fear of being exposed in New Orleans."

"Don't be silly. We don't know how the lighting worked. We'd have to take the room apart and transport it," Lilith said.

Aroused by the idea, AJ turned to Tayen. "Tweedledee and Tweedledum have stumbled onto something. Disassembled, it could fit in a single semi-trailer."

"Disassemble a room we don't have access to and

don't understand?" Tayen folded her arms. "Evade Ernesto's monitoring and trudge a room's worth of building materials through your house? A day afterwards, he would come and establish permanent residency in your bedroom. Imagine your trauma levels then."

"Leave the map room where it is," Lilith said. "The first goal is to understand the chest's contents. Is everybody up to speed with the DARE FROM ALL wall clue?"

"It is a word scramble," Elliott said. "Unscrambled, it is the *Flor de la Mar*, a Portuguese ship hauling twenty billion in gold and gems. It was lost in the Strait of Malacca at the command of Captain Albuquerque five hundred years ago."

"Okay." Lilith expected she knew more than the others, but Elliott's thorough answer disabused her of that notion. "I see everyone has researched a bit. Who is Captain Albuquerque?"

AJ raised his voice to cut Charlotte off. "He was a famous Dutch military genius who conquered the Indian Ocean way back when."

"I opened myself up for a Roanoke joke, didn't I?"

"Why do you think I was so loud?"

Lilith walked toward the turret stairwell. "I'm going home and to bed. Call me when you know something. AJ, can you add us to your psycho-house protocol thing?"

"Athena," AJ called out, "add to the—"

After everybody left the house, Elliott and AJ sat in the living room to relax. "Grand Opening is about here, Dad. Two weeks and we're ready to go. But I'm concerned about two of our employees and the owner. If you three aren't suffering from PTSD, you should be."

"How does anyone cope after the entire episode on the

mountaintop? Charlotte and I have had deep discussions since we returned. It has reduced our anxiety. I have no doubt Charlotte and Lilith will talk, so I'm not too worried about their future."

"Still, get counseling. You've been through hell."

Shazoo jumped in AJ's lap and nestled in place. "A band of pirates operated in the shadows of colonial armadas. I don't think they understood what I meant by armadas. If I used a shopping analogy, I may have expressed it more meaningfully."

"Perhaps I didn't understand either."

AJ scratched behind Shazoo's ear. "Imagine armadas like crowds on a Black Friday. Except Black Friday is every day on every Caribbean Island for sixty years. And the shoppers are nothing but armed, belligerent naval ships."

22 - Grand Opening

Tayen waited for the right time before she initiated a conversation about the Dominican Republic tragedy. But her desire to understand pushed her into action before the grand opening.

She commandeered *The Mini Black Pearl* from AJ's driveway and took Lilith on an impromptu golf course inspection. Lilith understood her intentions once the golf cart veered off the path behind the fourth tee. A grove of trees secluded a tiny spot from passing golfers and unwanted intrusions. Tayen drove the cart to the top edge of the basin, which formed the pond for the picturesque sixth green island hole.

"This area reminds me of the mountaintop. The view over Lake Enriquillo, with the mountains in the background, was so beautiful and serene. A paradise … constructed by evil men." Lilith shuddered as intruding images of the murderous gunmen's shots echoed in her mind.

Tayen placed her hand on Lilith's.

"Things happened so fast. Ernesto left, the caretaker spoke to us, and the Péchettes arrived to drive us back to the downhill oasis. Charlotte and I shared a room. Melody—Aniah—and AJ had rooms to themselves. I showered and laid down, but when I tried to fall asleep, sensory overload kept me awake. The smell of burnt gunpowder, gunshots ringing in my ears, the concussions from the gunshots on my chest … The sight of Charlotte's face covered in blood. It's as real now as it was then.

"The woman next to me … " Lilith slumped her shoulders forward and lowered her head. "Her blood poured … from her head. It flowed over the floor and up my leg like I was a magnet. I pretended to sleep through the gunshots and the screams. But her blood kept crawling up my leg."

Tayen didn't move or blink.

"AJ hasn't rebounded since we've returned. His spontaneity died that night. If he acted normal, Charlotte and I could bounce back, but his trademark of carrying forward is gone. He played the fool with Ernesto. The small dose of Demon's Breath unlocked AJ's manic blabber-fest. Ernesto was not—and let me repeat, not—in control of their exchange."

Lilith paused for a moment. "Hey, that reminds me. Who are the Nanjing Twins?"

Tayen shook her head. "Ah, let's stick with one nightmare at a time."

"I'd press you on them, but you look as nervous as a cat shitting razor blades."

"Let's keep the discussion on this hemisphere, please."

Lilith faced toward the sixth green. "Aniah cried in the room next door. Charlotte rose halfway off her bed when she heard the sobbing, as did I. We were helpless to comfort her. Five hours earlier at Adela Frontera, her father gave the order to kill the pilot who helped us escape. He passed so close she could have spit in his face.

"We spent the morning wandering through the downhill oasis in a daze. Our hosts had us ready to flee should Ernesto's men come-a-calling. In the afternoon, we discussed opening the chests, but AJ politely objected, saying we should wait until they were back in Portland. People at the downhill oasis were disappointed, but after I lied to them—"

"—Scott is thrilled. And I'm not saying it sarcastically. AJ handed over their thumb drive to him and he is following through on your lie." Tayen said.

"It seemed appropriate to establish a secure line of communication."

"It was. Whether it was foresight, intuition, or a dumb lie on your behalf, it worked out to our favor.

Lilith nodded. "Our friends took care of disguising and transporting us. The others to the airport, and me to the docks for a week-long boat ride home. Economy class, my ass."

Tayen chuckled. "Why does AJ say things like that?"

"Who knows? In accompanying the chests, I got the better deal. The captain, a Péchette, came from Africa and survived the Rwandan Genocide. He experienced terror like we did. He knew what to say, when to say it, how much alone-time I needed, and when to nudge me forward. I can never repay his kindness and support."

"But are you stable?"

Lilith threw her head back. "If you'd asked if I'll be okay, the answer might disappoint you. But stable? I think so. At least I can function."

"Does it help to talk? Or would you rather I avoid this altogether?"

"I can share now, but in little chunks."

Tayen placed her hand on Lilith's shoulder. "What you told me was a tectonic plate, not a little chunk."

Lilith cupped Tayen's hand. "Aniah has been my talk partner. Did you know she was enrolled in a master's program in psychology? She's in grad school in New Orleans."

"I was not aware. Master's level? I bet she has a set of tools to help herself, and others, in working through trauma."

"She does. The cargo ship captain wasn't as eloquent, but I can see they draw from the same techniques. My progress wouldn't be as far along without her."

Lilith twisted in her seat. "Between the sewing room and the flat above AJ's detached garage, she doesn't get outside much. If not for her dance-therapy studio in Kimi's sewing room, I believe she would fall apart."

"I ordered Kimiko to find her a dance place. It seemed to be her forum for coping and we needed to monitor her." Tayen asked.

Lilith snapped her head around and confronted Tayen. "Why are you having Kimi monitor her?"

"I'm not allowing a drug lord's daughter on the premises without any monitoring. Back to her dancing. Does she dance alone, or does somebody join her?"

"Lydia dances with her about every day. I ... watch."

"What do you mean, you ... watch?"

Lilith folded her arms and rested them on her chest. "What do you mean by, what do I mean?"

"Your relationship with Charlotte is done—"

"Lydia's straight, Aniah's lesbian. You'd be blind if the desire to fu—find them beautiful—I mean find them to be attractive."

Tayen half grinned, half grimaced. "Everybody's emotions are raw. Don't confuse them for passion."

"Thanks, mom? But why are you warning me?"

"Because you need a clear head. Your pounding heart is from an adrenaline rush which came from fear. Residual fear from your mountaintop experience won't disappear overnight. Adrenaline increases the blood flow to *all* parts of your body. If a feeling of unbridled passion surfaces, be assured, it may not be a clean attraction, but a hormone induced infatuation."

Lilith frowned. "Where d'you get that bitch of a fact?"

"A course in social psychology."

Lilith's irritated demeanor didn't fade.

Tayen relented. "AJ copes by going analytical."

"Figures. He talked with you, to talk with me, so I didn't end up sleeping with the enemy. Have you had this discussion with Charlotte?"

Tayen skipped the question. "Watch both new girls. Aniah earned leeway by helping you off the mountaintop. But she is a drug lord's daughter. On the flip side, Ms. Calveiro's work is exceptional. Her baristas and kitchen help—"

"—Chocolatiers. How 'bout Charlotte?" Lilith asked.

"Oh, yes. That's what we call them, chocolatiers. They are impressed by her kindness. Lydia helped frame an old family portrait for one of her chocolatiers. She did the frame in short order."

"Great pastry chef, proficient frame-maker, and great dancer. What about Charlotte?"

"I believe AJ's suspicion is warranted." Tayen wasn't yielding to Lilith's question. "The chest documents gave us Captain Morena Calveiro, and weeks later, Staff-a-Job gave us Lydia Morena Calveiro."

"Should I spy on them?" Lilith decided Tayen wasn't going to address if she warned Charlotte about the dangers of unchecked passion.

"Yes. Kimiko is. However," Tayen pulled out her phone, "I need to spy on Kimiko. Even after my harshest verbal threat, I sense she is prepping Aniah for one of the *Mediterranean Mischief* outfits. That damn Broken Cove Accessories catalog will be the end of me."

"Charlotte says it's sensational."

"Provocative, tasteful, and sophisticated. No doubt. After lunch, Scott is taking the photos for the grand opening banners. Five models displaying the five versions of *Mediterranean Mischief*. I'll kill her if Aniah is in the *Moroccan*."

"Well," Lilith couldn't leave a fashion comment unaddressed, "Aniah in the *Moroccan*, Talia in the *Italian*, me in the *Egyptian*, Charlotte in the *Greek*, and you in the *French*—"

"You SPOKE to AJ about the *Mediterranean Mischief* line," Tayen roared.

Lilith dipped her head. Her hand had done been caught in the cookie jar.

"Ever since Tampa, he's been hinting I should lead by example and wear Kimi's pirate outfits. He won't shut up about the *Mediterranean Mischief - French*."

"Would you be as angry if you learned I was the one

who suggested you model the *French*?"

Tayen glared at Lilith. "We're two days away from opening. My only concern is The Village gift shop and reception area."

Astonished, Lilith pointed to herself. "Me?"

"I said the area, not the gift shop/reception desk lead. If I've marketed this right, shoppers will flood your space. You're in the dead center of our business. After grand opening week passes, we'll fall into a regular pattern, and staffing won't be a nightmare. But the projections for grand opening week mean we must add a few personnel from the clubhouse."

"Oh," Lilith clapped her hands, "that's why Charlotte has been snippy with me. She can't stand me being her boss for a week."

***

Grand opening.

Golfers drove golf carts along the winding paths, marveling at the beauty of the golf course. Manny, the head groundskeeper, had the course in immaculate condition. Uniformly cut fairways and greens, blooming spring flowers, and pristine tee boxes waited for the army of photographers, who raced to capture images of Portland's new golf resort.

An armada of fashionistas invaded Broken Cove Accessories. Tayen's marketing had struck the center of a fashion desert, and women across the region flocked to the store. Catalogs were placed around The Village complex and were swept up by the curious shoppers. Kimiko's crew didn't have a chance to breathe between customers.

Special invites to the rooftop restaurant had been sent

out a month in advance. Talia and the servers dazzled customers with their pirate regalia. While not as risqué as the *Bella Donna Short*, the standard *Queen Anne's Revenge*, chosen by the women staff, was sexy enough to make AJ uncomfortable. He stood at the railing and watched customers. Ear to ear smiles, enthusiastic nods, and checking out the servers from head to toe, from men and women alike; it all helped alleviate his anxiousness.

The view over the golf course from the restaurant garnered rave reviews. Chef Dean and Chef Ladonna's dishes consumed most of the attention. Customers switch plates to try as many tastes as were at their table. The servers' snarly attitude, playful banter, and timely service generated endless smiles and laughter. Pasta-de-faria's rude, crude, and almost lascivious customer service turned out to be a winner.

The Pirate Rum House poured rum concoctions and dispensed the best of the local microbreweries. Gentlemen behaved due to the overwhelming influx of women. BCA bags were commonplace in the bar, which confused the typical male patron. Their man cave had turned into a ladies' apparel bar.

Lilith's reception desk crew kept pace with customers, thanks to Charlotte's caffeine-induced mania. Her energetic work came from across the causeway at Coffee Cov*fefe*.

Lydia had the coffee shop and bakery churning out orders. Charlotte bought the Man-O-War sized Widow Maker blend twice. It was enough caffeine for a small country, let alone a petite Latina.

The crowd for Pirate's Chocolate had grown through the day. AJ heard the praises of satisfied customers. Everybody texted their friends, and the lines grew. By the dinner hour, swollen lines forced Tayen and AJ to the bakery for crowd flow control. The transport buses couldn't pass through because of people standing in line for the bakery.

Orders overwhelmed the bakery. Tayen prohibited staff orders until the wave of orders had subsided.

Charlotte led a mutiny against Tayen until Lydia passed a bag to her and whispered in her ear. The mutiny was over. Charlotte backed the employee-order-ban and vehemently denied the existence of any bag in her possession, even though everybody saw her hiding it behind her back. She dragged Lilith into Scott's IT office, where they pulled out the individual containers and sampled the chocolate candy bar cake, the chocolate-peanut-butter cookie cake, and the chocolate-pretzel cereal treats.

Night came, and the center attraction of The Village complex came to life. Pasta-de-faria's lunch was a success, but it was lunch, not the highly anticipated dinner. Dinners received five-star ratings, with an occasional four-star rating sneaking in. Servers switched their outfits to the *Evening Captain*, which featured large tricorne hats with long feathers and captain's jackets.

Tired from the long day, and despite the stunning success, Lilith couldn't stop watching AJ. He kept stealing glances at a group who were preoccupied with their tablets and phones. She strained to see the knapsack a woman had over her shoulder. After a minute, she understood who they were: the professional golf assessors.

The dozen assessors led the morning golf rounds. They pored over charts and graphs. Lilith's heart went out to AJ. *He must be nervous. Are they impressed? Please be impressed and offer him a tour event.*

Lilith crept up next to him. "Relax. Today was a colossal success. If the professionals don't post a good score here, you can take comfort in Pirate's Chocolate. Its sales pace will cut your mortgage in half by itself."

"Thank you. I appreciate it."

Unconvinced her encouragement had any effect on him, she was about to speak when AJ cut her off. "Other than where the first tee is, you know nothing about golf, do you?"

"I may not understand some aspects of the game."

"Yeah, I guessed that. 'Post a score' doesn't sound natural to you."

"I'm learning."

"You've run a register at a country club for half a year, and you are still learning? What goes through your mind when someone tells you they shot a birdie?"

"I never hear a gunshot. So it must be photography."

AJ peered down at her. "What about shooting an eagle?"

"Oh, crap. You talked with Mr. Douglass."

"He was puzzled by your request to see the picture of the eagle he shot."

Lilith folded her arms. "Shit. So, the golfer's handicap comment got back to you too?"

"Yes. Mrs. Douglass's husband is a scratch golfer. He doesn't suffer from a long-term rash."

"Why does everyone play golf angry?"

AJ closed his eyes. "Ah, the discussion with Mr. Kline."

"People are always teeing off on a hole!"

"It means they're hitting the ball from the tee box." AJ turned and walked away. "Tomorrow, 5 a.m., you and I will go over golf terms and the history of golf."

Lilith stuck out her tongue, only to be reprimanded by Tayen, who'd arrived in time to see AJ leave. She poked

Lilith's tongue back into her mouth with her finger. "I expect that from Charlotte, not you."

"I don't want a three-hour lecture on golf in the morning."

Tayen wiped her finger on her hip. "If we land the US Open, AJ can pay off his debt faster. It doesn't help when the face of the country club thinks being 'under par' means the person isn't feeling well."

"Shit. Mr. Calhoun."

"He adores you, but you must learn golf terms."

"Okay, I'll learn how to fake golf. Are you done directing Pirate's Chocolate traffic?"

Deputy Castillo was standing in line for the bakery a few yards away. Tayen waved hello to her. "It looks like we have it under control."

"Can I go home? I'm exhausted."

Tayen placed her hand on Lilith's forearm. "I'll share this with AJ tomorrow, but I want to tell someone before I burst. I overheard an association member say the course met his standard for US Open quality. But they want data before rating us."

"That sounds good?"

"Yes, my dear, that is a major shift in AJ's favor."

Charlotte zoomed up beside them in a golf cart. "I'm taking Lilith. Cover for me."

"Excuse me. I'm the general manager, and you're my assistant. Why are you giving me orders?"

"Because I need to. Where's the keys to AJ's SUV?"

"I'm not saying until you explain why you need his SUV."

Charlotte gritted her teeth. "Because I'm taking blue eyes to the university downtown. I'd explain more, but you and I have a chemistry between us, which allows you to trust me."

Lilith and Tayen exchanged glances.

"I'm not saying this out loud unless we are in the turret stairwell."

Tayen held up her keys and slid off a key. "Alright. I'll ask Olivia—Deputy Castillo—to assist me with crowd flow. Her uniform may give her directions a bit of gravitas."

"Thanks, Mommy Dearest." Charlotte snatched the key while Lilith got into the cart. She held on for life as Charlotte sped away. "Why are we headed to the university downtown?"

"First, to flee from Tayen after my last comment. Second, I have a friend who is finishing their doctorate in biochemistry, and they can help with our chests—pirate chests, that is. It will be dark soon, which will help keep them out of sight while we load them in and out of the SUV."

"Awesome. But we have to carry the chests?"

"Aw, princess, don't worry about messing up your hair. Scott is using a handcart to put them in AJ's garage, and Dale will help us downtown."

"It's my shirt, not my hair, that I don't want soiled." Lilith poked her finger in Charlotte's side. "Who is Dale, and how do you know him?"

"They, not him. Dale and I are old acquaintances from the Mensa meetings I attended when I was little. Dale was the only one within five years of my age, so we bonded."

"Great. Another brainiac in my world."

"IQ scores measure one's capacity to learn, not how smart one is," Charlotte said. "So what if you take longer to multiply and divide? When it comes to social intelligence, I challenge anyone to meet or exceed you."

"Thank you." Lilith leaned over and kissed Charlotte on the cheek. "You are my bestie for life. But don't think for a moment that I'm not jealous at times. You are gifted in academic and social intelligences."

"Don't forget my body and face."

"God. You're a complete narcissist."

An hour later, Charlotte backed AJ's SUV into the loading dock bay to the university's downtown chemistry building. The bay door zoomed up, and a short-haired person walked out.

Charlotte scurried out of the driver's side door and ran to the back of the vehicle. "Dr. Dale Scroggins, this is my roommate, Lilith."

"Hello, Lilith."

Lilith rushed around the vehicle and extended her hand. "Dr. Dale. Thank you for helping us at this late hour."

"No worries. And Dale, please." Dale turned to Charlotte. "What am I going to get in trouble for this time?"

"Let's get these upstairs before I answer." Charlotte pressed the remote to open the SUV's back hatch.

The three lifted the two master chests out of the SUV and on to the loading dock, where Dale had a pallet and pallet jack ready. "We'll use the freight elevator, but from the hall back to my laboratory, it's manual labor."

"You got a laboratory already?" Charlotte asked.

"Of course. They'll confer my Ph.D. later this month, and they have already offered me the teaching position."

Up the elevator, and into the hall, the three moved the chests into Dale's combo lab/office. With the second chest on a low-rise bench, Charlotte said, "These chests are *rumored* to be ancient pirate chests."

"To what degree do you emphasize *rumored*?"

"If I said *confirmed,* would ya kick us out?"

Dale paused. "Is this another jewelry heist?"

"How was I supposed to know the open door to the jewelry store in the alley was the robbers' getaway plan? Jeez. Let my mistake die in peace, please."

"What is it you want me to do?"

Lilith stood next to the chest, whose lid she had lifted open. "I'll ask about that open door incident later. For now, this chest has boxes we need help with. Our resident expert put them in two categories: elements and compounds. We're hoping to confirm his idea."

Dale stroked their chin. "Elements and compounds? In a rumored ancient pirate chest?"

Lilith opened the box AJ had opened first and held it up to Dale. "Pure iron?"

Dale rolled it in their fingers. "I'll need to test it."

Lilith opened the box containing the tin sample.

"Tin?" Dale looked inside the chest. "Am I going to find elements in each one of these?"

"You're asking what we are trying to answer, Doc." Charlotte lifted a box and used a scalpel to open it. "There is a waxy substance sealing everything."

Dale took the box from Charlotte and finished opening it. "Well, well. What is this?"

Lilith strained to look over Dale's shoulder. "Lead?"

"Nope. This isn't lead." Dale walked across the room and turned on a device. "The spectrometer will tell us."

Lilith and Charlotte mouthed their conversation in silence while Dale worked on the samples. After a minute, Dale conveyed their disbelief in a single word: "Cobalt."

Lilith gritted her teeth. "Cobalt is a pretty shade of blue."

"What did you two bring into my lab?"

"Dr. Dale," Lilith held her hands up, "I inherited these, and we are seeing them for the first time, just as you are. We suspect the chests come from around three hundred years ago."

"Technology wasn't advanced enough to extract a sample of cobalt like this three hundred years ago."

Charlotte pointed to the other chest. "Yeah, actually it was. Chest number two, the Faraday Chest, as we call it, stores a third-generation homopolar generator. We think we stumbled across a historical anomaly. A genius scientist who lived well before her time."

Dale opened the Faraday Chest. "Extraordinary. You're not expecting me to do this tonight, are you?"

"Take your time," Charlotte said. "However, we hoped you might be able to fast-track your analysis."

"What do you want? Analysis or identification?" Realizing their question, Dale said, "What am I asking? Identification of the elements and analysis of the compounds."

"Are these chests secure here?" Lilith looked around the lab, unconvinced of the building's security.

"I'll put these in the room behind this lab and lock it off. Only I'll have access to it. Should I be worried about someone in particular?"

Lilith dipped her head and spun around to avoid looking at Dale. "If you're not comfortable, we can take the chests away."

Dale turned around to find Charlotte clenching her fists. "What did you bring into my lab, ladies?"

"Inheriting these chests isn't quite exactly how we got them," Lilith said.

"Goddamn it, Charlotte. You got into another jewelry heist?"

"Well, I wouldn't oversimplify it as *another* ... Perhaps *the* is the best determiner."

Lilith couldn't tolerate their skirting around Dale's question. She ended it, bluntly. "We stole these from Ernesto Cottrell."

Dale didn't respond.

"I apologize for barging in with our problem. Involving you was a dumb decision, and I am sorry. We should take these and leave you in peace." Lilith's voice cracked. The lines on her forehead showed her frustration.

"Don't move them." Dale leaned back against the lab table. Their eyes surveyed the contents inside the Faraday Chest. "I'll help if you can guarantee the son of a bitch doesn't know the chests are here. Will the analysis help take that idiot down?"

Lilith shrugged. "I couldn't say. We don't know what we have."

Charlotte jumped up. "Leave everything as is for tonight. No one followed us here, I can guarantee you that."

Surprised, Lilith asked, "How can you guarantee that?"

Charlotte held up her phone. "I had a couple of the groundskeepers follow us, checking to see if we were followed. They texted we weren't. Julio is standing on the corner, waiting for us to leave, so he and Maribel can go home."

"Where is Maribel?"

"On a food run."

"Then let's get Maribel home. Dr. Dale, are you okay with this arrangement?" Lilith asked.

"I agree under one condition. Every time we meet, I want a piece of the chocolate-peanut-butter cookie cake."

Lilith pivoted on her heels to leave. "Our pastry chef created a monster. Word of mouth reached downtown in less than a day, and we are forty miles out."

Dr. Dale led them out to the dock. Charlotte started the SUV, but before she drove halfway to the street, a man walked in front of the exit. He knelt and tied his shoe. Charlotte stopped and turned off the headlights. Her eyes bulged as she clung to the steering wheel.

Lilith yelled. "Why slam on the brakes?"

"My dad is in front of us." Charlotte scanned the vicinity.

Lilith didn't understand her roommate's behavior. "Why are you worried about your father seeing us?"

"We're far enough back. Nobody can see us from the street."

"Charlotte, it's your dad."

"He's tying his shoe and smoking a cigarette."

Charlotte's phone vibrated in the center console pocket, but she ignored it.

Lilith reached inside the console. "Answer your phone and stop being paranoid about your dad."

Charlotte slapped Lilith's hand. "No light from the inside, or he'll be able to see us. Son of a bitch. That's why he is here." Charlotte pointed at the street.

Lilith looked past Charlotte's father to see a dark SUV creeping past the entrance. "The greenskeepers said we weren't followed."

"Sit still and be quiet. I need to see what Dad is doing."

Charlotte's father puffed on the cigarette and acted

like he had nothing to do. His head turned toward the dark SUV as it moved down the street. He dropped the cigarette, crushed it with his foot, and picked it up. As he stood, Julio ran up beside him. Together, they approached Charlotte and Lilith.

Charlotte unlocked the doors. "God, this ain't going to be fun."

The two men entered AJ's SUV.

Charlotte refused to look in the backseat.

Lilith spun around and gleefully greeted Charlotte's dad. "Hi, Mr. Tavares. What are you doing here?"

"Hello, Lilith. I had a late-night meeting and was headed to my car when I saw Julio standing on the corner. By himself."

Charlotte leaned forward and pressed her forehead to the steering wheel.

Lilith didn't have to guess. Mr. Tavares's tone was of a father who was about to unleash his anger.

Julio said, "Maribel dropped me off to watch the loading dock before running to the Burger Barn. While I was standing on the corner, I saw that SUV circling the block over and over. Mr. Tavares came up behind me, so I told him what was happening."

Lilith bit her lip. She wasn't about to say what they were doing should Charlotte's dad ask.

"Why was a federal surveillance vehicle circling the building? A building which had you two in it?" Mr. Tavares asked.

Charlotte whipped around. "It was federal."

"Excuse me. How did Charlotte know you were warning us? I thought you hated smoking?" Lilith asked.

"Old school messaging," Charlotte said. "Blocking an

entrance while tying your shoe means don't come this way. Smoking means this may take a while. Stay put and don't draw attention to yourself."

Mr. Tavares leaned forward and kissed his daughter on the back of her head. "You remembered."

Lilith wagged her finger from side to side, not wanting to speak, but wishing to understand.

Mr. Tavares addressed her. "Street signals aren't widespread in urban areas, but once in a while, you can find a neighborhood which has developed a full lexicon to guard against undesired entrants. Years ago, Charlotte overheard a discussion of mine with a client. I hoped she remembered that day and our discussion afterwards. Now, your turn to answer me. Why was a federal vehicle following you? If this is about that jewelry heist on Burnside—"

"Oh sister! You're telling me about that incident someday," Lilith demanded.

Charlotte turned her head away looked out the driver's side window. "Julio said nobody followed us. Dad said the dark SUV was the feds. Why were the feds circling a university's chemistry building?"

Mr. Tavares said, "Don't try misdirection, *mi reinita.* The question is not about the chemistry building, it's about why the feds were following you,?"

"Are the feds part of Ernesto's organization?" Lilith asked.

Charlotte turned her head and faced Lilith. "Not as an organization, but individuals inside the FBI is a fair bet. You don't need to tail a suspect if you know their destination."

Lilith turned around to Mr. Tavares. "Sorry. I'm sure you don't want to know what this is about. And for your safety, we shouldn't tell you."

"You said Ernesto. As in Ernesto Cottrell?"

Lilith bit her upper lip. "I have to insist you recall my last statement. We haven't done anything illegal—" Images of a museum burning in Tampa flashed into her mind. "—We aren't doing anything illegal."

"Smooth, Lilith, real smooth." Mr. Tavares opened the door. "Julio, let's leave the ladies. They need to get their story straight before I tear them apart."

Julio left the SUV with Mr. Tavares.

Lilith straight-armed Charlotte as the men walked away. "Your dad called you *mi reinita*. Is that his nickname for you?"

"When he's not pissed off, I'm his little queen. However, right now he is calling me *su pequeña reina malvada*."

"His little evil queen, I'm guessing." Lilith waved her hand in front of Charlotte's face. "Snap out of it. Did you mention our destination to Scott?"

Charlotte started the SUV. "Not to Scott, but I did to Tayen. I said university and downtown—"

Lilith rushed her hands to her mouth. "And chemistry."

"Words spoken outside the bakery and coffee shop. The businesses ran by our *pequeña reina malvada*, Lydia Morena Calveiro."

23 - The Drone Wars

A month after the grand opening, a steady routine had taken root for the staff of Broken Cove Industries. Mondays were the worst day of the week for restaurant sales and golfing, so Tayen closed all business operations, which allowed the greenskeepers to work on the golf course without disturbing the golfers.

Thom and AJ led a group of employees for a round of morning golf on Mondays. They were too busy for each other after the grand opening. The round of golf allowed them time to talk about the course and improvements.

Food and beverage personnel loved walking the course. They listened to the club members' stories, but without walking the course, they had no frame of reference to understand and enjoy the members' stories.

The only normal nine-to-five Monday through Friday jobs within BCI belonged to Broken Cove Charities,

Education, and Publishing. These intangible jobs, as AJ called them, tended to be isolated from the rest of the BCI staff.

The pool area rose above the ground, far behind the clubhouse. Three kiddie pools preceded the enormous main pool. A wall designed like the broadside of a pirate's ship stood tall at the deep end of the pool. Every fifteen minutes, cannons protruded from the ship-wall and shot jets of water into the pool. Above the ship-wall was the tanning ledge, a shallow pool for sunbathers to tan in. Tayen's reworking of AJ's design put it high enough to keep it out of sight from the main pool.

In the center of the tanning ledge stood the statue of the Goddess Athena. The water fountain gently flowed water into the tanning pool. The excess water spilled over the vanishing point edge and cascaded into the main pool below.

A parade of sunbathers climbed the steps to the tanning ledge at noon. First to take a teak-finished chaise lounge, Charlotte asked, "Do we need a lifeguard up here?"

Lydia spread her blanket over a chaise lounge. "You're asking me? You'd think management would have addressed that before opening. Besides, you're the general manager's first assistant."

"But you're on the admin team. Had it not been for your boyfriend, I would have been the assistant general manager."

"I had nothing to do with that. Stop being mad at me for him getting the job."

Lilith took the chaise lounge next to Lydia. "She's mad she didn't get the position, and because you stole her sugar daddy."

"I what?"

"Don't take her seriously," Lilith said. "This gold digger was making a move on the owner's son when you arrived. Her plans to be a trophy wife by her twenty-second birthday were scuttled when you came."

Talia laid on her stomach in the pool. She supported her chin above the waterline with a small pool pillow. "Retirement that early in life? That would kill me. Idle hands are the gateway to the devil's playground."

"Who cares whose playground it is?" Charlotte laid back on her towel. "A playground is a playground."

Lydia turned to Lilith. "How do you deal with a wild roommate?"

"Patience and a constant supply of your chocolate desserts."

"We need a chocolate bank," Talia said. "Any item you eat from Pirate's Chocolate deducts from your account, and we all start out with next to nothing in the bank. Otherwise," she pointed to everyone in their bikinis, "this group won't be as sensational as we do today."

Lydia scanned over the four dozen women sunbathers. "Where are the guys?"

"I reserved this for ladies only from noon until three," Charlotte said.

Aniah rushed up the steps and took the lounge next to Lilith. "Don't we need a lifeguard?"

"Lydia's on it." Lilith lifted her head to see why Aniah sounded rushed. "Where have you been?"

Aniah lifted her beach shawl to show them her new bikini.

Lilith rolled her eyes. "Jeez. Never mind. I see who made you late for the pool."

"Don't blame me for Kimiko's obsession in dressing

me in every damn thing she creates. Besides, who let her up here last Monday?"

Charlotte lowered her sunglasses to give Aniah the once over. "Kimi heard about lady's hour on the ledge from the groundskeepers. Naturally, she was inspired to try her hand at designing swimwear. Damn, you're on fire."

Lilith pointed at Aniah's top. "Boy, get a load of Kimi's first bikini. A marbled silver top and solid white bottom. Too much for Rio, but perfect for Portland."

Aniah buried her chin on her chest for a close examination of her top. "You mean to tell me I am wearing the first Kimiko?"

Lilith spun off her chaise lounge when a screeching buzz zipped past the pool area. "What the hell was that?"

Charlotte leapt from the chaise lounge and faced toward the parking lot. "A drone? Sounded like it dove over the clubhouse parking lot."

"Why is there a drone diving over there?"

Talia pushed herself up from the water as she looked to the sky. "I guess the word is out about lady's hour on the ledge. Wanna bet a guy put a high-res camera on a drone to take videos of us?"

Scott rushed up the steps and raised his hand to shield his eyes from the sun. A slingshot was in his left hand. He turned in a complete circle while scanning the sky.

Lilith was about to ask Scott what he was doing. But with four dozen women in the tanning pool unable to draw his attention, she decided not to call out his name.

Scott circled around a second time before he hurried down the steps, leaving the sunbathers confused.

Charlotte clapped her hands. "Good boy, Scottie. He used a slingshot to down the drone."

Lilith led the light applause. "Our boy Scottie. Speaking of a good boy, how's it coming along with Elliott, Ms. Calveiro?"

Lydia banged her head with her palm. "Why do I feel everybody is listening to me?"

"Oh, come on." Lilith had learned from Charlotte how to worm information from somebody. "You two are the hottest topic on campus. If you weren't such a damn cute couple, no one would care."

"How much can I share without betraying his trust?"

"No one will gossip."

"You just said he and I are the hottest topic on campus."

Lilith didn't have a comeback.

Lydia shook her head. "All right. Seven, maybe eight."

"Seven or eight?"

"On a scale of one to ten. Everything nowadays is judged on that scale, so I'll simplify it to that."

Charlotte had raised her head. "Oh, okay. I thought she was spilling the tea on how long Elliott's—"

"Shut up, Charlotte," Lilith barked.

Lydia ignored Charlotte. "We're still in the early stages of a relationship, so I give it a solid seven with steady progress toward an eight."

Lilith nodded her agreement with Aniah. "Solid and steady."

Lydia didn't need to see the exchange. She asked, "Why did you check with the psych major?"

"Because she's the psych major. And from her reaction, you gave a pretty solid answer."

Lydia opened her eyes to find Aniah nodding in

agreement. Satisfied, Lydia asked, "How's your relationship with Aniah coming?"

Lilith squirmed. "We're not in a relationship."

Aniah restrained herself, hiding her reaction from Lydia.

"Faithful, solid friends. Those relationships are like being on a mountaintop above the forest, with awe-inspiring vistas. God, if only there was such a place."

Lydia reclined with her eyes closed. She didn't see the murderous rage brewing inside Lilith.

***

Lady's hour on the ledge resumed the following Monday.

Lydia bellowed her announcement to the fifty-plus women. "We are working on the lifeguard situation. It never crossed the admin's minds to have a lifeguard on our day off. More to come next week. Until then, watch those next to you. I don't want to give out any Darwin Awards for somebody falling asleep and drowning in ankle deep water."

"Fantastic words to start the trial for an accidental death lawsuit," Charlotte said.

Lilith stared at the steps. Aniah worked for Kimiko, so her tardiness to the ledge had to be her fault.

Aniah rushed up and took to her lounge. She suspected Lilith was waiting for the unveiling of the newest Kimiko. Lifting her beach shawl, she twirled for Lilith's inspection.

"Lime green with dark green pinstripes," Lilith said. "I could never pull it off. Everything Kimi puts you in is sensational."

Talia pushed herself up from the water, showing the same bikini top as Aniah's.

"Wow, Kimi dressed you too."

"I better be next on the design-testing carousel," Charlotte said.

"If you weren't so busy traveling to the university, perhaps Kimi could fit you," Lilith said.

Aniah fumbled with her water bottle and sent it sailing into the pool. Charlotte clenched her fists, angry with Lilith for exposing her visits to Dale.

"The university downtown? Are you pursuing a degree?" Lydia asked.

"I am considering it."

"Why?"

Lydia's questioning made Lilith uneasy. *Damn it. She's probing for information about the chests.*

"My parents always told me to have options ready at a moment's notice," Charlotte said.

Lydia asked, "You're not happy here?"

"I'm ecstatic about my job. I just—"

The sound of screaming drone engines revving up to full speed in the parking lot saved Charlotte from having to answer.

The motors roared as they ascended from the ground.

Lilith seized the opportunity to steer the conversation away from Charlotte. "That sounds like more than one drone. What do you think, Aniah?"

"Yeah, it does."

Lilith spun toward Aniah and gave her a dirty look.

"More than one for sure?" Aniah wasn't following Lilith's lead.

Charlotte had stood and rolled her towel up. She

whipped her arm at Aniah, snapping the towel in front of her face.

Aniah held her arms out, not knowing what to say.

The roar of drone engines crescendoed. Screeching dives ended in crackling explosions on the parking lot pavement. Engines choked off while others zoomed behind the hedges.

A drone zipped from the parking lot and soared above the tanning ledge. Another drone streaked behind it. The pursuing drone had a fantail of six wires lowered behind it. It overtook the first drone, tangling the wires in the first drone's blades. The drone's engine cut off, and the immobilized drone plummeted to the ground.

Scott sprinted up the stairs and scanned the sky. After a minute, he ran down the steps.

Everyone turned to Lydia. "I may be a part of the admin team, but I don't know what this is about." She turned to Charlotte, who was busy texting. "Charlotte's working on it, ladies. Relax."

"I bet other drone operators want to crash our tanning party," Talia said.

"If that is the case," Lilith pointed up, "who's attacking the spy drones?"

Charlotte read her texts. "Our groundskeepers are calling it The Drone Wars. Idiots around the neighborhood are trying to video our tanning ledge. Scott and the greenskeepers are defending our airspace."

Lilith fell back on her chaise lounge. "This place gets weirder by the day."

Charlotte continued reading the texts. "Maribel reports four downed drones. Two escaped. Scott's six screaming feathers worked to perfection. Pooping Toms …

Shit. I'm texting her back. Peeping Toms, Maribel, not pooping toms."

"What's the six screaming feathers?" Lydia asked.

"The drag lines tailing the drones. They wrap around a drone's propeller blades and shut it down."

Talia returned to laying face up in the water. "Wonderful. Perverts' flying toys to get videos of us."

Lilith played with her amulet. "Six screaming feathers of the sun," she said out loud without realizing it.

"You're a Screaming Feather cultist?" Lydia asked.

Lilith slipped out of her daydream. "I'm sorry. Did you say a Screaming Feather cult?"

Lydia flipped on her side and faced at Lilith. "*Six Screaming Feathers of the Sun* was painted by an unknown artist in the mid-eighteenth century. It was displayed inside the St. Louis Cathedral in New Orleans but was stolen the night after its debut. The few who saw it said it was beautiful.

"It portrayed the Great Comet of 1744. Supposedly Realism's first star map where the stars were featured. The only earthly landmark in the painting was at the bottom."

"What landmark?"

"Considering the work originated in New Orleans, it would be fair to say it was the Mississippi River. So, how did you run across this obscure piece of art history?"

Lilith regained her composure and rested her head. "We heard about it in the farmer's market when we attended the convention."

Lilith's intuition informed her Lydia was watching. She raised her hand and thumbed her amulet. *Six Screaming Feathers of the Sun and a comet in 1744. Why didn't Grandma and Mom tell me?*

***

The following Monday, Tayen joined the ladies on the tanning ledge. Her white sun hat matched the white shawl and matching shirt and bikini top.

Charlotte reached the top of the steps and saw Tayen. "Outclassed again. We're nothing but cheap imitations compared to you."

Tayen smiled. "Until I hire a lifeguard for these Monday tanning sessions, I'm your lifeguard."

Light applause rose from her announcement.

"Wow. Look at this group. It explains the drone problem. Don't worry, ladies. Scott and the groundskeepers are ready."

"Is that why they're decked out with binoculars and slingshots?" Lilith asked.

"Precisely."

"Hey, Talia." Charlotte dropped her shawl to show her bikini. "We match."

Talia rose from the water. "If you were a foot taller, I'd say we were twins. Dark teal is better on you than me."

Lilith looked around the ledge. "Where's Lydia?"

"And Aniah?" Talia added.

"Kimi got them both?" Lilith sipped from her water bottle, unsure of where Aniah was.

In the background, the low hum of drones approached. Closer to them, a fleet of drones roared to life.

"That's the sound of our drone fleet lifting off to intercept the invader drones," Tayen said.

Lilith raised her face to the sky. "Is this going to happen all summer?"

"We have deeper pockets than the invaders. Plus,

several greenskeepers have family members up here. They're taking these intrusions personally."

Charlotte covered her ears. "It sounds like a thousand angry weed whackers."

All fifty-plus women stepped out of the tanning pool and wrapped towels around themselves. They flinched at the sound of a whizzing bottle rocket from the parking lot. A split-second later, the bottle rocket exploded, and a drone screamed down from the sky.

"What the hell was that?" Charlotte asked.

"Scott's newest contribution. Miniature heat-seeking bottle rockets," Tayen said.

"Sorry, boss. Bottle rockets pop; they don't reverberate when they explode."

Tayen's attention fell from the sky and landed on Charlotte. "They carry quite a punch … Don't they?"

"Is anyone videoing this?" Lilith asked.

"Video evidence for the police wouldn't be in our best interest," Tayen said.

Drone engines screamed, bottle rockets screeched, and the ladies waited for more. Two drones passed the tree line and zoomed toward the pool area. Four drones streaked after them in hot pursuit. One after another, rockets streaked out from the chasing drones. One hit a fleeing drone, which crashed on the eighteenth fairway. The other raced over the lake and out of their sight.

No sooner had this battle ended than a surge of streaks came from over the parking lot. Seconds later, repeated and consecutive explosions echoed eerily from far away. The sharp ringing of metal indicated that a target larger than a drone had been struck.

All eyes watched Tayen as she read her texts.

Lilith refused to ask about the faint sound of a dog yelping in the far distance.

Tayen hurried off the tanning ledge, which prompted Charlotte to ask, "Where ya headed, boss?"

"To the Kennedys," Tayen shouted as she ran away.

Talia scooched next to Charlotte, who had her phone in hand. "Get us some recon. What did they hit?"

"Maribel hasn't texted back. But Tayen said the Kennedys, didn't she?"

Talia angled herself toward the parking lot. "Their house is closest to the driving range."

Lilith eased next to Talia.

Charlotte said, "Scott designed heat-seeking bottle rockets for the drones. Is it possible his heat-seekers found something else?"

"Oh, holy shit." Talia closed her eyes. "Mr. Kennedy barbecues for lunch, and he has that big-ass-I-can-feed-a-hundred-people-dual-barrel barbecue on his back deck."

"Oh, no," Charlotte slapped her leg.

Lilith gasped. "Their cute little dog, Tuffy. He burnt his little nose on that monster sized grill a ways back. He hates that grill so much that he sits at the far end of the deck."

"Thank God we didn't hit the dog," Charlotte said.

"Oh, poor Tuffy," Lilith lamented. "I can imagine him sitting on the deck with his pretty pug eyes watching Mr. Kennedy when—out of nowhere—a dozen streaks explode on the grill. Poor little guy wouldn't understand. That's why he's yelping."

Charlotte bit her lip, and Talia turned her head.

"It's not funny," Lilith erupted.

***

A week later—after the Monday ladies' hour on the ledge—Tayen called an emergency meeting of the greenskeepers and any BCI employee present in the facility that afternoon. She made no apologies for meeting during the dinner hour, nor did she wait to reach the podium in the mini amphitheater before unleashing her tirade.

"The Drone Wars are finished. When authorities question you about today's re-enactment of the Battle of Britain, decline to answer without the presence of an attorney. Don't worry about paying for them; they're on the house."

She slammed a folder down on the podium. "Scott, explain what happened today."

Scott stood. "To protect the tanning ledge from drone voyeurism, we launched three dozen attack drones, but no heat-seekers. Not after the check you wrote to Mr. Kennedy."

Lilith closed her eyes. Last week's dozen bottle rocket ambush of Mr. Kennedy's dual-barrel barbecue had scared poor Tuffy out of the yard and down the street. Tayen and AJ wrote Mr. Kennedy a check to compensate him for the surprise attack. AJ said it was the longest afternoon he ever lived.

Tayen plowed into Scott with damning questions. "But you created something more sinister, didn't you?"

"Sinister is a bit strong."

Not amused, Tayen mad-dogged Scott.

"Our drones now carry disruptors, which interfere with other drones' input-output signals."

"Fuck me running."

Scott didn't stop after Tayen's cursing. "After today, the other drone operators in the neighborhood can't have the stomach or cash reserves to keep this up."

"Whose idea was it to blare the Ride of the Valkyries from The Village speakers?"

Scott fixed his glasses with one hand, hoping Charlotte didn't see him pointing at her with his free hand.

Tayen glared at her assistant.

"Narc." Charlotte murmured.

"Scott, keep going."

"The disruptors downed twelve enemy drones. Friendly fire took out eight of our own. Six screaming feathers, three guided collisions, and a couple of accidental collisions helped finish the battle."

"Did you calculate how far the disruptors would reach?" Tayen asked.

"I let Charlotte run the numbers."

Tayen faced her assistant.

"Hey, I ran the numbers twice, and those distances were within a five percent margin of error," Charlotte said.

"What unit of measurement did you use?"

"Feet."

Scott's head dropped to his chest. "I gave the numbers in meters."

"Oh, fudge. That would extend the range—"

Tayen's voice rose to just short of yelling. "I was at the shopping square ten miles away. I assumed after last week's heat-seeking bottle rocket massacre of Mr. Kennedy's grill that The Drone Wars were over. Boy, was I wrong?

"A hundred-plus stores lost their internet and satellite connections thanks to your disruptors. Credit and debit card purchases ground to a halt. Merchants are so reliant on those systems that when a disruption occurs, there aren't any backups. Word spread throughout the stores that today's record-high heat was the reason for the … disruption.

"Forgive me for overusing the word disruption, but at this very moment I'm having difficulty coming up with a synonym."

"Interference."

"Charlotte. Knock it off," Tayen yelled.

Charlotte shrugged and kept her shoulders up in fear more wrath was coming her way.

"So, if shoppers can't shop, they go to their cars and head home. Which I was going to do, but there's a little security measure car companies have installed … "

Tayen took a breath before proceeding. "I'm guessing over ninety percent of the cars there had keyless entry systems. How do I know? Because that is my estimate of what proportion of the customers, including me, stood next to their cars, which they couldn't enter on the hottest day in Portland's recorded history."

Scott raised his hand, but Tayen ignored him.

"The last thing the keyless entry systems did before shutting down was to override the manual locks, so the keys didn't work either.

"As bad as that was, one other crisis was erupting: everyone's cell phones were dead. Your disruptors took out all the cell towers, satellites, and cable systems throughout Portland's western suburbs. Hundreds of thousands lost phone and internet service this afternoon. Thank God they didn't kill the power lines.

"Mrs. Kennedy saw me and drove me back here, where, by damn luck, we hadn't been disrupted. I turned on the news and learned the airport had lost communications."

A loud gasp resounded through the amphitheater.

"The regional airport, not Portland International."

Relieved, aws filled the space.

"However, it doesn't take a genius to triangulate the regional airport and the shopping square to the source of today's disruption. Hopefully, investigators won't connect the burning delivery truck on the Sunset Highway to the satellite outage."

Lilith asked on behalf of all attendees: "There was a burning delivery truck on the highway?"

Tayen placed her hands behind her back. "One drone was impaired by a disruptor, but not taken down. It must have flown to the highway, crashed through a delivery truck's windshield, and exploded in the package compartment. The dive-bombing drone sparked a fire and burnt the truck to a crisp."

AJ rushed into the amphitheater and down the steps to the podium. "Thanks, Tayen. I'll handle it from here."

Stunned, everyone fixated on AJ. He never took charge from Tayen.

"Thank you to everyone for attending. I'll make this short. Go home, and if approached for questioning, refer the authorities to the attorney on the card we have for you at the reception window. Go home and enjoy the rest of your day."

AJ rushed up the steps and waved for Lilith to join him. Together, they entered Tayen's office, where Elliot sat with Dr. Dale at the conference table.

Lilith ran to take a seat. Scott, Tayen, and Charlotte entered moments later.

AJ shut the door. "I paid Dr. Dale a visit this afternoon. Little did I know western Portland was under attack. Dale contacted me rather than Charlotte once they'd finished studying the chest's contents. Dale will correct anything I don't adequately outline for you."

He took the seat reserved for him during the admin

team meetings. "The *E* boxes numbered sixty-seven in total. All were elements. It didn't take long for Dale to identify them, but the *C* boxes presented some problems. They are indeed compounds, and they range from medicines and explosives to paint mixtures. Many defy designation.

"The waxy substance, C-3, is a non-biodegradable latex, which protected the boxes for the last three centuries. Latex lasts around ten years. This stuff will last an eternity.

"Other compounds included laughing gas, penicillin, minor and severe burn medicines, advanced accelerants, sunblock, morphine, a black-light kit, and paint mixtures. We may have the paints which covered the wall in the map room. Some compounds have warning inscriptions. But here again, we need to find Jade's notes to unlock the paints and the compounds.

"However, Dale made significant progress on compound #26. Apparently, it is a medicinal substance with psychotropic features which use beta-blockers. In sufficient quantity and with diligent application, these beta-blockers block memory formation."

Lilith gasped.

"I take it this is what screwed with you in New Orleans?" Elliott asked.

"Most definitely. Thanks to Dale's work, we can figure out the chemical composition to Demon's Breath and learn how to counteract it," AJ said.

"Can you replicate it?" Tayen asked.

"Possible." Dale said. "If I were devoted to full-time research, I could. But having the owner's manual sure would help, especially if we are going to access the last nine boxes."

Tayen's eyes widened. "Why haven't you opened the last nine boxes?"

AJ answered for Dale: "Those nine boxes are grouped together and sealed in a glassy material which we can't break through. The only box number we can read is the top one: C-106. Dale and I figure we don't open those without the owner's manual."

"They weren't covered in latex?" Lilith asked.

AJ shook his head. "Tayen, BCI needs a chemist. Write the job description as a dietitian for our records. Ask Manny to construct a storage room in the tunnel between The Village complex and my house. Make it to Dale's specifications. I want our chemistry lab running by tomorrow night."

Tayen's eyes sprung open. "Wait, whoa. Why the immediacy?"

AJ slammed his fist on the table. "Because last night, someone broke into the university chemistry building and stole the Faraday Chest."

24 - E.L.F.

Lilith relished the calm before each day's opening of The Village complex. Her routine started before the birds awoke at dawn. She took the corner seat in Coffee Cov*fefe* with her coffee and watched the baristas carry out their proficient and precisely choreographed openings.

The baristas enjoyed having Lilith as company. They brought coffee out to her and threw in a treat or two from the day-old bakery leftovers. She understood their routine, and they enjoyed her company. However, this morning, the atmosphere was guarded and tense.

The vigilant barista crew of three scowled at the gallery door, honing their shaming skills for he who was to come. On cue, Elliott eased from the darkness and slipped into the coffee shop. The baristas closed ranks. The double whammy of glares and guilt-inducing silence kept him from approaching the counter. Seeing Lilith at her table, he avoided the counter and took a seat next to her.

"Good morning, Lilith."

"Boy, are you in trouble? What d'you say to Lydia?"

"She told you?"

Lilith pointed at the hostile pack of baristas.

"She told them?"

"Nah. I'm sure they picked up on her negative vibe this morning . . . And guessed you were at fault."

"How do you figure?"

"The baristas and chocolatiers are in phase with the alpha female. They take their cues from her. If she's pissed at someone, they pick up on it and project her anger on … you."

"Great, an angry wolf pack," Elliott huffed. "When will they stop glaring at me?"

Lydia popped out from the back hall and spotted Elliott. Not saying a word, she approached the barista wolf pack. "Get him a coffee and a muffin. But do so coldly."

Elliott stood. "Lydia, can we talk? Please?"

"I'm not stopping you."

"Without the wolf pack."

Lydia squinted. "Wolf pack?"

Elliott pointed at the baristas.

Lydia dropped her head to the side, laughing without making a sound.

"Lyd, please."

"In my office." Done with her orders to the boyfriend, she ordered her barista team, "Down, girls. You can shred him afterward."

"Not funny." Elliott twisted toward Lilith. "Dad needs you up at the house before you start."

"Why didn't he … Oh, my phone isn't on."

Elliott gathered himself and followed his girlfriend into her office. The pack of baristas never blinked, but the growl of a wolf didn't escape her.

Lilith grabbed her coffee and headed for AJ's house. "Girls, text me the details."

"You mean the pictures of us shredding him, if he doesn't admit he was wrong?"

"How do you know he was wrong?"

"He wouldn't let her shoot the .308 Winchester Tikka A1 at the gun range. He said it was too much firepower for a girl."

"Shame on him. Girls can shoot the Tikka as well as any guy."

"You have no idea what we're talking about, do you?"

Lilith winked. "Not a clue, but before you met Lydia, you didn't weren't firearms literate either."

The baristas turned their backs to Lilith, refusing to give her the victory on this occasion.

She stepped out of the coffee shop and was nearly run over by a golf cart.

"Whoa, too close," Charlotte said.

Lilith took a seat. "Your golf cart restrictions have been lifted?"

Charlotte slammed on the accelerator. "For today, yes. Tayen left it at the clubhouse last night, much to AJ's irritation, so she ordered me to return it. I miss driving the *Mini Black Pearl*."

"What's this impromptu meeting about?"

Charlotte had them zooming down the ramp to the underground garage. "Nope, but the whole gang is waiting. This feels like a turret conversation."

As they zipped through the tunnel, Lilith asked, "Any more newspapers from Adela Frontera?"

"A couple which identify more Benningtons, but nothing else."

Charlotte launched the golf cart into the air at the top of the ramp leading to AJ's house. It bounced and skidded on the pickleball court. She had to stomp on the brakes before they careened into the garage door.

Lilith managed to stay in her seat through the wild ride. "I'm recommending they revoke your driving privileges, permanently."

"Hey, the *Mini* is the only four-seated cart in the fleet with enough power for hilltopping."

"You tested them all?"

"You know I did."

They entered the house and joined AJ, Scott, Tayen, and Aniah in the turret.

"Turret talk it is," Lilith said.

"How does a trip to Barbados sound?" AJ asked.

Charlotte spun around and headed out.

"Back here, young lady. You will not be going."

"Praise ye the Lord. I'm not ready for another trip."

"Tayen, Aniah, Lilith, and I will take this trip."

"What's in Barbados?" Lilith asked.

Tayen held up a letter. "This is an invitation from the Péchettes in Barbados. Your friends from the Dominican Republic confirmed the authenticity of the invite and assured us our travels will be safe. An acquaintance of ours may be there too. Father Amare."

"But why Barbados?"

AJ answered: "If you don't remember, the map had Barbados as a point of landfall twice. It was the beginning of one ship's course and the last point of contact before sailing across the Atlantic. The Barbados cell says the heritage of the Péchettes refers to a captain who worked with Jade Péchette. A tall woman who spoke French."

"Calveiro." Lilith couldn't contain her excitement. "Now we find out about the third person."

Aniah cleared her throat. "I'm sorry, did you say Calveiro? As in the doe-eyed pastry chef, Lydia?"

"As in Lydia Morena Calveiro. Since your arrival, we've kept tabs on her. And you, to be honest," Tayen said.

"You thought we had a connection?" Aniah leaned back. "You suspected me and legs?"

"In a short span—" Aniah's nickname for Lydia caught Lilith by surprise. "You call her legs?"

"She is a phenomenal dancer. Yeah, legs."

Lilith shook off the distraction. "In a short span, we've housed a drug lord's daughter and hired a woman whose name is involved with our treasure hunt. Yeah, we were suspicious."

"And now?"

"You passed, and Lydia raises no suspicion. Unless she's skilled at hiding her intentions. In that case, she's extremely dangerous."

"You are a trusted insider, Aniah. Don't be offended. We're new to this world of espionage and secrecy. We had to be sure," Tayen said.

Aniah waved her hand. "I don't blame you, but what about leggy Calveiro?"

Lilith laughed. "The pirate leaders who started this are named Bennington, Calveiro, and Péchette. When you and I first danced in New Orleans, I wore a top with the logo for Broken Cove Publishing, BCP. It was supposed to be Broken Cove Industries, BCI, but due to a processing error, the sleeve on the shirts said BCP."

She stopped and turned to AJ. "When did you finalize the business's name?"

"Well before we traveled to New Orleans. It is still a mystery how the BCP logo ended up on our sleeves."

Lilith turned back to Aniah. "Calveiro is a mystery. Did she side with the Benningtons or the Péchettes? Is Lydia a lucky coincidence, or a spy?"

"She's a pastry chef, nothing more," Aniah said. "My whole I've been surrounded by deceitful people and I'm telling you, she's harmless."

"But if she can deceive you, admit it: she is dangerous."

Aniah waved Lilith off. "The one thing I find peculiar is her glances at me. She has seen me somewhere, or we've met, but she can't place me. I confronted her about it."

"Was that the day of the bottle rocket assault on Mr. Kennedy's barbecue?" Lilith asked.

"We haven't met, but she is fascinated with my dancing. If I were honest with myself, I'd say she might be the better dancer between us two."

"Okay then." Tayen took a deep breath. "Security threat assessment on Lydia: nil."

Late to the meeting, Shazoo kitty-jogged up the steps to Lilith and leapt into her lap. He flipped over, exposing his tummy for a rub. Lilith obliged. "Has Shazoo dug out any further bugs?"

AJ sighed. "Not for a while, but that could mean we aren't finding them. I am confident there aren't any more. Scott has four live feeds running to appease the interested parties."

Aniah lowered her head. "I shouldn't be out here then. Dad could see me."

"Relax," Scott said as he turned his laptop around for Aniah to see. "I have tapped into the bugs and am playing prerecorded footage into the feed. All anybody sees is what I want them to see. Right now, I'm playing last night's footage … when nobody was here."

"And you believe they're none the wiser to the recordings?" Aniah asked.

Lilith interrupted before Scott could answer. "Have you seen any signs of your dad or his men on the grounds?"

"I haven't."

Tayen winked at AJ.

Lilith caught it. They were happy to see her asserting a leadership role. She ignored them and said, "Then we can assume Ernesto is content with the info from his feeds and isn't aware you are here. But what do you think? What is going through his mind concerning his daughter's whereabouts?"

"Aunt Patty has him convinced I'm in school. If I could somehow shoot her a text to confirm I am studying—"

"Give me a day to disguise the origination point, and we can do a video chat. That would be more convincing than a text," Scott said.

"Excellent." Tayen said. "Video chat with Aunt Patty. The travel team leaves for Barbados in three weeks to search for information on the *Flor de la Mar* treasure. I'll leave for vacation a week earlier, while Lilith and Aniah leave a week later. AJ, you find a funeral to attend so you can use that as your cover when you fly out."

"Um. Are you talking about the time around June nineteenth?" Lilith asked.

"Yes. Is there a scheduling … Oh, yeah. There is a scheduling problem for you. I'm sorry to impose our travels on you over a national holiday."

"Well. It is just a onetime miss for me. I'll survive."

Charlotte stared at AJ, and he stared back. "If that's the concern, I think we are okay," she said.

"I don't want our trip to interfere with the week-long prelude to the fourth of July," Tayen said before AJ could respond to Charlotte.

Flustered, AJ strained to ask, "How about earlier?"

"Not possible. Flights are booked solid. Barbados is a very popular destination in June. I understand Lilith's concern, but what's the problem with you two on traveling around June nineteenth?"

Charlotte deferred to AJ by bowing her head.

"Thanks, chickenshit. I'm not happy that I'm the one who gets to tell her we're going to Barbados on the summer solstice."

***

Three weeks later, Lilith and Aniah exited Barbados's International Airport. Tayen stood next to an SUV in her white shorts and perspiration-saturated T-shirt. She pulled the clingy shirt from her chest. "I hate humidity."

Lilith gathered her locks behind her head and fanned herself with her free hand. "Girl, heard."

Beside Tayen stood a tall, muscular man. His towering physique gave him an imposing presence. He took a small step forward. Lilith was forced to look up at him. His smile and kind eyes reassured her this hulk of a man was a teddy bear.

"Lilith Peters, meet our host and the head of the Péchette cell in Barbados, Tony," Tayen said.

Tony stretched out his hand. "Glad to meet you, Madam Priestess. It's an honor to welcome the heir of the reawakened Péchette Network. I look forward to assisting you in fulfilling the mission of the Voodoo Priestess."

"Nice to meet you Gony, torgeous." Lilith tilted her head further back. "Tony, gorgeous you are. Oh, hell. Now I sound like Yoda."

Tony turned to Aniah. "Aniah M. Clemons, you've had an arduous journey. We don't hold you responsible for your father's actions. At the Hovel, you will find we are your friends, and we welcome you with open hearts."

Aniah shook Tony's hand. "Who told you about me?"

"AJ's description helped, but it would be hard to forget your dance troupe's appearance at The Grand Kadooment festival."

"I remember it. But you remember me?"

"It got around as to which one of the dancers was Ernesto Cottrell's daughter. Plus, footage of you dancing ran nonstop for a year on social media," Tony said.

"Wonderful." Aniah stepped into the SUV. "I was a hit before TikTok was."

Lilith pushed Aniah into the back seat. Unsure if she could speak freely, she asked Tayen, "Other than the humidity, nothing else is sticky, is there?"

Tayen slipped beside her. "Stop trying to talk in code. There isn't anything sticky down here except the humidity. You're gonna love the Hovel when you see it. This has been a vacation for me since I arrived, not work."

"Hovel? Doesn't 'rat-infested' usually come before that?"

"It's a *suppressio veri:* a suppression of a thing's truthful essence with an imposter equivalent."

"Strong words, Eastwood."

"It's Latin, McFly."

Lilith whirled her finger. "Stop listening to AJ's history lessons."

Tony sat in the driver's seat. "We call it the Hovel to keep from drawing attention. People stop to look at mansions, but hurry past rat-infested hovels."

Tayen cinched down her seatbelt. "The Hovel originally was an elongated ranch-styled home, with a second floor added decades later. Through the years, the building was divided into individual mom-and-pop shops. Tony brought the shops back under single ownership and is restoring the combined units into an education and public assistance center. Ground floor for business, second floor for living quarters, and then there is the underground."

The SUV lurched forward.

"Did you say underground?" Lilith asked.

"Something straight out of a James Bond novel. Not as grandiose, but potentially a three-story underground spy center."

"Three-story underground spy center?"

"You're parroting everything I say," Tayen said.

Lilith threw her hands up. "I'm tired. Plus, we haven't had an advantage in this whole adventure. A hidden underground spy center is a bit of a shocker. Am I to understand we have spies? Or are they wannabe spies?"

"We have nurses, accountants, hotel managers, a few with MBA degrees, three tech nerds with exceptional computer skills, and pilots."

"So, wannabe spies?"

"Rule number one in spying: find the bank accounts and watch what happens," Tayen said.

"Nurses and pilots … bank accounts … How do nurses and pilots fit under rule number one?"

"They help with access into hospitals and the island-to-island transport system in the Caribbean. Criminals use hospitals, planes, and helicopters too."

"The Péchette Network is resurrected, at the behest of the Voodoo Priestess's descendant." Tony's joy couldn't be contained.

Lilith closed her eyes. "I can do without the title."

"A little overwhelmed with the attention and celebrity treatment?" Tayen asked.

"Four years out of high school and I'm handed the keys to an international spy network, hunting for a lost treasure with a drug cartel in close pursuit. At my age, I'm supposed to be drunk off my ass on a beach."

"Drinks and the beach tonight," Aniah said. "Hell yeah. Count me in."

Minutes later, the minivan pulled into a private underground parking garage. Lilith looked around in a constant state of disbelief. Tony took their bags to their rooms while Tayen gave Lilith and Aniah the tour of the Hovel.

A large office space consumed the ground floor. Plans were to make it a community outreach center. The first sublevel consisted of guest bedrooms. They were clean and simple, and didn't boast of many creaturely comforts.

Sublevel two was far more spartan than the first sublevel. Two young men and a young woman worked at makeshift desks in the middle of a gargantuan sized room. Dozens of boxes filled with new computer equipment and electronic gadgets lined the walls in the dim light. Upon seeing Lilith, they stashed their snacks and Goliath-sized soft drinks behind boxes.

"Lilith, I'd like to introduce you to ELF: Eboni, Leonard, and Fred," Tayen said.

Fred nearly knocked his unstable desk over when he stood to greet Lilith. "Holy Toledo. You are pretty." He saw Aniah and leaned to his side. "Damn. Her too."

"Fred, shut up and sit your ass down."

Eboni's harsh rebuke informed Lilith who the leader of this group was. She extended her hand to Fred. "Thank you for the sincere compliment. Please, don't let me disturb what you were working on."

Eboni stood and wiped her hands on her shorts before offering her hand to Lilith. "Cheese-flavored corn chips should never be in a computer room, but I like them."

Lilith held her hand back. "How about an elbow bump?"

Eboni didn't have to raise her arm much, whereas Lilith had to elevate her elbow to her ear in order to reach Eboni's elbow. Lilith turned to Tayen. "Do you hire anybody who isn't six-feet tall?"

"Hey, I don't hire outside wacky weeds country club. Tony manages this small forward."

"Oh, dear. How long has AJ been on your nerves?" Lilith asked.

Tayen frowned. "Why ask?"

"You called his golf course wacky weeds, and you're using sports metaphors to describe personnel. Are you two fighting again?"

"We don't fight—"

"Yeah-yeah, I know. Lively, spirited debates."

Lilith turned away and saw Eboni mouthing 'fighting' behind her hand.

Tayen pretended not to see Eboni's mouthing. "I've been here four days, and AJ arrived the day before last. We spent yesterday on the northern coast, researching for a rum supplier. He insists if we run a pirate rum house, we better have at least one rum from the birthplace of rum."

"Oh, wow. I didn't know rum originated in Barbados. Did you find one?"

"Yes, and no. The fifteen- and twenty-two-year-old rums were fantastic, but the waiting list is three years out. But the five- and eight-year-old rums are within a year."

Before Lilith could ask her question, a familiar voice came from the spiral staircase. "Thank you for showing me the layout."

AJ had finished shaking hands with a plumber and was walking toward the ladies. His enthusiasm was evident. "They're installing a geothermal vent to power this building. It won't have to rely on external power sources, making this place self-sufficient and self-contained."

Lilith held out her fist. "Tony said the Péchette Network was resurrected. But what is that?"

AJ fist bumped Lilith upon reaching her. "Our arrival in New Orleans set things in motion. People across the Caribbean are coming together and creating a shared network. New Orleans, the Dominican Republic, Barbados, Jamaica, the Caymans, Grand Bahamas, and others—all stirred awake and opening offices in homes and the back rooms of office buildings. ELF is establishing secured communications and electronic surveillance. Scott would love it here."

"So," Lilith whirled her finger, pointing to the computer boxes, "what can this do … exactly?"

"Too much for you?"

"Yes." She hoped AJ would hear her plea for help. Everything was beginning to overwhelm her.

AJ took her hand. "Hey. If you agree to head this organization, Tayen will help you with management, Tony can handle the day-to-day operations, and ELF will break things down into manageable chunks. Learn to trust and rely on the people around you."

Lilith nodded. She got his help. "The computers? What can they do for us?"

"With ELF and Scott sharing the same workspace, the sky is the limit," AJ said.

"Wonderful." Aniah was ready to move on. "Arrange for dinner and drinks on the beach for tonight."

"What time?" Eboni asked.

Lilith bumped Eboni's shoulder. "These people joke around all the time, so never take them seriously."

"Are you sure? There's nothing to set up. Except who to bill it to."

Lilith glanced at Tayen, who was absorbed with Leonard's screen. "When the finance person is less busy, I'll ask if she'll spring for it. Until then, tell me what you do."

"Leonard is the encryption genius. When we whittle into a system, he breaks the—" Eboni stopped when AJ gritted his teeth. "Let me put it another way. We are gifted in accessing computer networks, in particular, banks."

Lilith turned to AJ. "Why are we hacking into banks?"

"ELF's first responsibility is setting up secured communications. After that, Tayen suggested we go on the offense and see if we can cripple Ernesto's finances. If we run across the Benningtons along the way, maybe we can hinder their syndicate. Either way, follow the money, and in today's world, that means a robust electronic division."

"But Tayen said on the ride here that we're recruiting hotel managers, nurses, and pilots. How do they fit into the electronic division?"

Eboni pointed at her friends. "Leonard, Fred, and I

can break through Wi-Fi and microwave connections. But at times, hard contacts are needed, and those require on-the-ground assistance. A sophisticated network of accountants, hotel personnel, and bankers can help us access anybody with a digital fingerprint in the Caribbean. Even if the fingerprint is simply their cell phone."

Lilith stared at Eboni's laptop. "Money is moved via the internet, not by wheelbarrows or stagecoaches."

Tony had snuck into the room unnoticed. "Excellent analogy, Madam Priestess. ELF has made headway on several banks. Banks have the best security, and it takes all of them to bypass the firewalls. Regretfully, we haven't had access to the Bennington Mansion ... until today?"

Aniah caught the insinuation. "I'm not able to assist. Dad's computers are beyond my reach."

"The mansion has access points. We can work with you to crack those," Eboni said.

Lilith twisted around to ask Tayen what she thought. But Tayen wasn't listening to their conversation. She assumed a near permanent position bent over Leonard's shoulder, directing him on his monitor.

Lilith walked beside her. "Something of interest?"

"I know this guy," Tayen said.

Leonard clicked where Tayen pointed. "His bank account in Switzerland transferred ... " She waited on Leonard to click on an account.

"To an account in the Caymans, which is linked to this account in New Jersey. Son of a bitch. I broke his financial puzzle. Proof of his embezzlement from charities. I never knew how much or how, but there it is."

Tayen pulled two phones from her pocket. Lilith recognized the second as the phone she always denied having.

"Leonard," Tayen's hands shook as she held the phone out, "connect this to your computer."

Lilith held her arm out, keeping AJ and Aniah behind her. She listened to Tayen give the first pass code to Leonard. A moment later, she gave a second code.

"Care to tell us what you are doing?" AJ asked.

Lilith answered for her: "It's the Marauder's Map of the financial underworld."

A chorus of *ohs* filled the room. The one who didn't *oh* was AJ. "What is the Marauder's Map?"

Lilith swung her arm into his stomach. "Watch a movie instead of reading a book for once."

"Dear, it was a book before it was a movie," Aniah said.

Lilith swung her other arm into Aniah's stomach.

"Fred, I'm sending you an encrypted file," Leonard said.

Tayen held her hands to her face. "The file contains coding which can break other encryptions on information on a secured server. Lilith is one hundred percent correct in calling it the Marauder's Map of the world of dark finance."

"Where's the server?" Leonard asked.

"I couldn't tell you. Not because I'm not willing to, but because I don't know. My cohorts from years ago might, but I haven't heard from them in over a year."

"How many others?" AJ asked.

"Three. Two of them hold phones like mine, while the fourth has a transmitter to access the server. He is the one we haven't heard from, but we know the transmitter is working."

AJ rolled his hands over each other, asking for her to continue.

"The server sends out confirmation codes every day.

We have to reply in order to keep our links. If forty-eight hours pass without our reply, our link to the server is severed. We have waited a long time to break open these files. This seems to be it."

"Not to kill the analogy, but will your phone unlock the Marauder's Map?" Fred asked.

"No. The code I gave you will open the server temporarily. Notification codes will be sent to the other two, and they will—or should—send their codes. Mine alone gives partial access. If they don't respond, their section on the server freezes, and the fourth member has to access the server by hand."

"This guy is rotating origination signals, rerouting and/or recoding digital encryptions, and a host of other high-level programming techniques. Your fourth is a tech genius," Eboni said.

Tayen closed her eyes. "And we haven't heard from him."

Lilith felt Tayen's pain. Taking a page from her, Lilith tried to divert the conversation. "Well, print it up and send it to the appropriate prosecutors in New Jersey."

"We can't." Tayen made a fist. "Leonard and I accessed his bank accounts illegally. Therefore, no district attorney can present it in a court of law. Worse ... if we attempted to run this through the courts, this jerk-off lives in a district where the federal judge is on our Bennington list."

"So, he walks away."

"Yep, he walks away, scot-free. I'd kill to empty his account."

"How much?" Eboni asked.

"All of it,"—Lilith paused before finishing her scream—"pisses me off. Loopholes and jury-rigged laws protect the rich, and there's not a damn thing we can do. Someday, I want to reverse the tables and redistribute the fortunes of the wealthy to those who are less fortunate. They have more money than they could spend in ten lifetimes."

"Done," Eboni said.

Surprised, Lilith asked, "What's done?"

"We emptied his account."

"Whose account?"

"Tayen's sugar daddy's account."

Lilith looked at Eboni's screen. "The one she just said she knew in New Jersey? You emptied the embezzler's account?"

"You said all of it. Thirty-three million dollars."

"Where did you put it?" Tayen asked.

Leonard switched screens to show her. "It is in the Caymans until tomorrow morning. But at 12:01 am, it'll be here in Barbados."

Lilith covered her eyes. "I paused in the middle of my tirade, which you thought … Crap. Can you put it back?"

"We play for keeps; putting this back ain't happening," Eboni said.

Lilith put her hands on her hips. Before she could process what had happened, AJ asked, "Eboni, can you divert a couple million to pay off my loans?"

She didn't hold back on her punch into AJ's stomach. "Stop joking around. I haven't been here an hour and a bank robbery has my name on it."

"We can't keep this. Give it to a homeless shelter," Aniah said.

AJ added, "Stealing from those who stole from others is not against the law, but it is a gray area."

"How about ill-gotten gain?" Tayen asked.

AJ objected. "Are you suggesting we become judge, jury, and executioner? What right do we have to take that responsibility? We submit to the rule of law to maintain civility and to keep from falling into anarchy."

Tayen shot back. "You know as well as I do that many fortunes were acquired through morally wrong, yet legal, means. Criminals and the wealthy hide behind laws which protect them from prosecution. I fled from international finance because I saw it all. I know where these bastards get their money."

"Steal from the rich, and give to the poor," Aniah said.

"Fire," AJ said. "I'm not opposed to taking down the untouchable. But if by mistake we drain somebody's legitimate life savings, we could destroy their and their loved ones' lives."

"Did AJ just say fire?" Aniah asked.

"What? Am I being cheugy?"

Lilith cut Aniah off. "To the best of my knowledge, there isn't a language he hasn't mastered. Although, how he picked up Generation Z is weird AF."

AJ redirected. "As I was saying, if we steal, when do we join the ranks of the untouchables? When does hubris take over, and we evolve into the people we despise? When do the Péchettes start competing for the same turf as the Benningtons?"

"Good questions for the future," Tayen said. "Until we are out of this mess, we play their game. The guy we stole from is a suspected Bennington. He was the third person identified from the Adela Frontera newspapers."

"Oh, never mind," AJ recanted.

"Bravo, AJ." Aniah said. "You showed moral

certainty until a Bennington was mentioned, then you jettisoned your ethics."

"Thpppt."

"Aw, he's learned to respond like Lilith."

"I can work with ELF. We set up the dominoes so when, and if, we decide to steal, they fall in quick succession," Tayen said.

Lilith stood beside Tayen. "You know, or suspect, where the bodies are buried. This is your chance to exact revenge."

"Yeah, I can." Nodding at AJ, Tayen said, "I say we aim for legal exposure first. If they fail, we get justice the old fashion way—through piracy."

Lilith bumped Eboni's shoulder. "Can you order food for us and bill it to my new account? I think I can afford this treat."

Eboni lifted her hand from the keyboard and said, "Done."

25 - Manicato I'naru'

New custom-made bookcases lined the walls of the Hovel's upper floor. The fumes from the dark English chestnut stain filled the air. Under Tony's plans, construction crews had removed the interior walls before BCI's treasure hunters arrived. He wanted to make the upper floor an elegant reading parlor.

Lilith was enamored with the high-pitched vaulted ceiling with cream-colored fans. The open concept of the upper floor had ensnared her. Other than AJ's atrium, no room had ever struck her more profoundly.

A dozen side-by-side French doors led to as many balconies. Tony opened the doors, allowing the ocean breezes to sail through unencumbered. Aniah commented when the furniture, books, and decorations were brought in, the room would be perfect as a stress-free decompression loft. AJ and Tayen laughed. They told her to take a break from her psychology studies.

Lilith stood on the balcony, admiring the sea in the distance. Off to the side, a group of children played football on a dusty field. Across the road sat an open market, which bustled with people. She raised her shoulders and rolled them back. She closed her eyes and took a deep breath.

It seeped into her body bit by bit. The one thing that had eluded her all her life finally came to her: absolute peace. It centered her and fortified her assuredness.

She turned around. AJ and Tayen immediately saw the change in her face. Her characteristic look of searching was replaced by certainty and the sublime. Their gift shop clerk had changed.

The next day, Aniah and Tayen worked with ELF on sublevel two, three stories below. Aniah outlined the details of the mountaintop mansion's computer system as best she could to Fred. Tayen and Eboni worked on the partial codes received from Tayen's financial partners in crime.

AJ left for the marina where an acquaintance of Tony's had agreed to teach him the ins and outs of sailing. Tony was right. Since they were chasing a pirate's treasure, knowing a bit about sailing seemed prudent.

Tony had carried a small crate up to the Hovel's top floor. Lilith turned at the sound of his flip-flop sandals reaching the last step. "This is beautiful, Tony. You have wonderful taste."

"Thank you. Interior design is a hobby, but my husband has the eye for color coordination. I'm eager for you to meet him after he returns from Chicago."

"I can't wait to meet him. Whatcha got in the crate?"

"Old relics and whatnots from decades of previous tenants. I figured you and I could start sorting through the storage room on sublevel three. The room is packed solid, and you never know what we might find."

"You carried that up five stories?"

"We don't have an elevator."

"Well, don't do that again. I'll go down to save you the trip up."

Tony smiled. "Wouldn't it be exciting to find something for the antique roadshow?"

Lilith sat on the floor next to the box. "You're aware of what we are looking for, right?"

"Yes, I am aware we are searching for a twenty-billion-dollar pirate treasure. You can't deny it would set the antique roadshow record." Tony sat on the floor with the box to his side.

Lilith reached into the crate and pulled out a book. She flipped it around to show Tony. "*The Adventures of Huckleberry Finn.*"

Tony flipped his book around. "Voltaire."

"Alright. We have a grab-bag of books. You go again."

He pulled out another book. "*Treatise on Light*, by Christiaan Huygens."

Lilith snatched it from him.

"You're interested in the history of science."

"Say," Lilith thumbed through the pages, "what can you tell me about the Roanoke Colony?"

"Aren't you the intellectual eclectic? From a pioneer in science to one of history's greatest mysteries."

"This is in Latin ... or Italian. I'll let AJ tell us which."

Tony held another book open. "This has lettering on the cover, and on the inside ... Whew! Atrocious handwriting in Spanish." He handed it to Lilith.

She thumbed all the way through it to the back. "These sketches in the back are unbelievable." She whirled it around for Tony and pulled out her phone.

Tony looked at the sketch, then at Lilith's phone. "She can't be. That can't be the same person, can it?"

"The picture on my screen is our pastry chef, and that sketch in the old journal has to be her ancestor."

Tony stood. "I'll call for help to get those boxes up here while you sort through this one."

Lilith compared the images as Tony left. She murmured to herself, "Horrible handwriting, and a skilled artist. How can that be?"

***

After a full day of learning about sailing at the marina, AJ returned to the Hovel. Nobody was in the kitchen or common room. A light shone down the stairs from the upper floor. He followed the light up the stairs and stopped. Lilith and company were tiptoeing around like they were in a cemetery. They wore rubber gloves and exercised extreme caution as they handled books and loose papers.

Lilith had a small stack of papers at her side on the floor. All the French doors were shut. Tony positioned two floor lamps as best he could to light the room. It was quieter than a library at midnight, and nobody noticed AJ.

He broke the quiet. "Is there a contagion in here, or is

it something more exotic?"

"About damn time." Lilith pointed at the floor, where she'd laid the book open with the sketch showing.

He walked over and peered down. "Stupendous. A portrait of Captain Morena, and a dead ringer for Lydia. Absolutely no way of disproving she's connected to this whole mess in some capacity."

"You've got reading to do. Start with this journal. We're guessing a multigenerational grandmother," Lilith said.

AJ looked around the room. "Slow, gentle, and using gloves. Excellent job."

Lilith stood. "The storage room in the basement has old collections from the previous tenants. Tony pulled the portrait book on his second draw. His first pull was a book by Christiaan Huygens."

"Tony, is it possible to bring a chair and table up here?" AJ asked.

"I'll go get them."

As Tony descended the stairs, Lilith handed a book to AJ. "I found this: Christiaan Huygens, *Treatise on Light*."

AJ stared at her. "Wonderful. We find Huygens nine months after the joke."

Lilith scrunched her nose. She didn't have to look to know what Tayen's reaction was.

AJ opened the book. "The map wall was designed by somebody with scientific knowledge about light, and Huygens preceded her time period. But you pulled a major find on the third book in the crate?"

"So what if it was the third one?" Tayen asked.

"First crate, third book. What are the chances someone else had this before us? Researchers don't have major finds in the first place they look. And yet, Lilith has a major find with the third book?"

"You're paranoid." Tayen said. "When past residents consolidated these relics, the last ones put in the storage room where the last ones found in other parts of the building."

AJ nodded. "Reasonable. First pulled, last in."

Tony ran up the stairs with a folding chair and a cardboard table. He set up the workspace for AJ.

"Thank you, Tony. Give me a chance to review the journal. Could you open a door? The fumes from the stain are making me high."

"No," came a chorus of objections.

"Loose pages like the breeze. We shut the doors to keep them from flying away," Aniah said.

"Dinner," Lilith ordered. She held her arms over her head and pointed to the stairs. "Leave him to his reading."

Descending the stairs, they entered the redesigned modern-country-rustic kitchen. The women climbed on the bar stools around the spacious kitchen island.

"Tony, can we help you?" Tayen asked.

"Can you use a fungi stick on the okra and cornmeal?"

Aniah's face lit up. "Ah, we're having cou-cou and flying fish. Conkies come after dinner."

Tony handed the fungi stick to Aniah. "Tayen pours the wine. The wine cooler is under the island counter, front left."

Tayen opened the wine cooler cabinet door.

Lilith stretched and yawned. "How nice. A taste of the local cuisine."

Aniah held a fungi stick above a bowl. "Tonight's dinner is the national dish of Barbados. It's very simple, but I like it. I have fond memories of Mom having me mix the cou-cou."

Lilith hadn't heard this level of enthusiasm from Aniah in Portland. "You seem at ease here."

Aniah waved the fungi stick as she spoke. "Nothing against the Northwest, but being coerced to flee from home didn't make for the best mindset in saying hello to Oregon."

Tayen opened a cabinet looking for glasses. "Hiding in Kimi's sewing room and in AJ's flat doesn't help. You're not free to roam and constantly worrying about your dad's men converging on you. You need a relocation, somewhere where you are free again."

"Somewhere that can offer you protection, a Péchette-friendly home," Lilith said.

Tony used a long, sharp knife to cut behind the flying fish's wing. "We're open to newcomers, even ex-Benningtons."

Aniah hit the fungi stick on the mixing bowl. "I'm not part of the Bennington Syndicate."

"So, what is the difference between your dad's cartel and the Bennington Syndicate?" Lilith asked.

"The Benningtons are elusive and hidden from the public limelight. They are scattered around the globe, and their influence is undetectable until, as Aunt Patty says, you examine who was on the plane before it crashed or whose home exploded from a natural gas leak. The Benningtons use organizations like Dad's to do their work."

"The Bennington Syndicate has a network of criminal organizations—"

"Who say criminal organizations? I said organizations."

Lilith knocked over her wine glass.

Tayen reset the glass. "Don't worry, honey. I about dropped this bottle of wine after that ass-pucker of a detail."

"Wait just one freaking minute." Lilith put her elbows on the countertop and leaned forward, lifting herself from her seat. "Legit organizations and criminals?"

Aniah stopped stirring the okra. "Courts, legislatures, bankers, drug cartels, the teen-Soprano wannabe who delivers an explosive package, the anesthesiologist who wants the newest Mercedes-Benz and agrees to give a lethal dose of ketamine—"

"Yeah, okay. Whoever has a heartbeat. So, the Benningtons have a system of corrupting people to get what they want. And very little stands in their way. If only somebody could wreck their system."

Tony stopped preparing the fish and looked at Lilith.

Oblivious to Tony, Lilith said, "Some group that would be. Computer nerds, business insiders, government officials and civil servants—"

Tayen lowered her wine glass.

"—all sharing information about corrupt leaders. They would stay out of sight—"

A piece of frozen okra hit Lilith in the face, cutting off her daydreaming. Seeing it was a piece of okra, Lilith stared at Aniah. "What was that for?"

"Did you hear what I said this morning?"

"Please, repeat it."

"Take from the rich and give to the poor. You have the core of a computer tech center with Scott and ELF. This place is off the radar, and Tayen's map to the financial underworld can help target your covert activity."

"When did you say that?" Lilith asked.

Aniah armed herself with another piece of okra.

"Stop." Lilith raised her hand. "I heard 'take from the rich and give to the poor,' but the rest of it you just made up."

"Given time, I can organize my thoughts and better state my idea. But getting back to what you just said. You have an outline for what is needed to counter the activity of the rich and powerful."

"The Benningtons. I didn't say the rich and powerful." Lilith thought for a moment. "There is an overlap between the two, though, isn't there?"

Tayen sipped her wine and lowered the glass. "A covert, modern-day Robin Hood organization. Helluva mission, if you ask me."

Tony turned on the faucet to wash his hands. "This morning, you said we could help you with the Voodoo Priestess's mission, but you don't know what the mission is?"

"I don't. The folks in the Dominican Republic said the same thing. They were there to help me complete her mission."

"What do you know about her?"

Lilith planted her elbow on the counter. "Her name was Jade Péchette. She was born in the New Orleans area, ran a pirate organization, and controlled a large section of the South American—"

Tony held up his hand to stop her. "She ran a refugee camp on the South American coast. If it practiced piracy, it was to secure what was needed for the refugees."

Lilith and Tayen's jaws dropped open. Tayen beat Lilith to the question: "A refugee camp?"

"I suppose some cells had better success in handing down oral traditions. Jade Péchette rescued a town from annihilation at the hands of the colonizers and hid them in a city on the South American coast. She had a daughter, Tempest."

Lilith hopped off her seat. "Tempest, daughter of

Tristao. Bound in the fog and eternity. The caretaker told us. The Voodoo Priestess's daughter was named Tempest."

"Ah, no. Tempest was Jade's daughter, but together, they were the Voodoo Priestess."

"Damn it, Tony." Lilith squared her hands on her hips. "Spill it."

"The daughter lived in New Orleans until her death in 1796. She assumed her mother's mantle to extend the legend of the Voodoo Priestess and the protections afforded to her faithful followers. Jade never called herself the Voodoo Priestess, but Tempest became the defender of New Orleans."

"Arrrg!" Lilith screamed. "Finally, we know something."

Tayen gulped her wine.

"What else, Tony?"

"Not much, I'm afraid. The refugee camp grew by accepting other refugees. Tradition says the camp included many groups that weren't Chitimachan … That is, those not from the New Orleans area."

"My ancestry extends back to a refugee camp director?" Lilith asked.

Aniah added, "And a pirate who stole from the powerful to protect the powerless. Nice mission statement if you ask me."

Lilith turned her back to them and walked to the window.

A steep hill sloped down to the backside of the Hovel, where the kitchen window faced. Not a person was in sight in the wide-open space. Its vacancy matched Lilith's lonely mood. A decision had to be made, and she had to choose.

"My work as a gift shop clerk has been a thrill ride. The wonderful and gifted people I've had the honor of working with have been a gift. From sweeping the floors in Mama-Titi's salon to the country club, and now here. My horizon has expanded beyond my wildest dreams.

"But now, the mission is … carrying forward. That's how AJ says it."

She spun around and faced them. "The mission of the Voodoo Priestess and her descendants was to help refugees. While I'm not sure what refugees we could assist, I believe the downtrodden could use our help. So we expose corruption first, and if the scales of justice fail, then we … do what we can to exact justice."

"Why did you pause?" Tayen asked.

"I don't know what we call ourselves. The Péchettes?"

"Péchette is a French surname. This group's origins are from the Caribbean and Gulf Coast. I think we can find a more appropriate name," Tayen said.

"What was that you called me when we were approaching the sheltered gate?"

"Manicato, from the Taíno people. It means the bold and valiant of heart. Manicato Lilith is what I said to AJ."

"Manicato Lilith?" Lilith frowned. "How about a substitute for my name? Something which captures my ancestry?"

Tayen thought for a moment. "Something that reflects the spirit of the women in your bloodline, whose origins are tied to the Caribbean and Gulf Coast? What would work?"

Lilith waited for her boss, which didn't take long. A spark in Tayen's eyes excited her and forced an involuntary hand clap.

"Settle down. This captures your and my Native American heritages. I'naru'. It means the spirit of women.

Personally, I think The Manicato I'naru' Network would be a terrific name."

Tony spoke reverently. "Manicato I'naru'. It is lovely."

"Cool. One person likes it," Lilith said.

"Make that two," Aniah added.

Lilith grinned. "It is dope, isn't it?"

"It is settled. Today the Manicato I'naru' Network is born," Tayen proclaimed. "The Hovel will be the base of operations under the direction of the new CEO, Lilith Daisy Peters."

Tony raised a glass of wine for a toast. "To the Manicato I'naru' Network and Madam Priestess Lilith."

Lilith lifted her glass.

"So, it is official. You've accepted the mission of your ancestors and will relocate here to Barbados," Tayen said.

"Move? What do you mean, move?"

"You're not running operations from the gift shop, nor from Scott's underground IT office. The Hovel is on its way to becoming our central hub of intelligence. Portland is now a subsidiary cell, just like the cells which are forming across the Caribbean. The millions sitting in your new bank account can fund development and improvements to this facility and other cells as they come into existence."

Lilith sat, incapable of speaking or blinking.

Tayen continued: "Keep Aniah here. She and Tony will work as your senior administrative team while you transition down here."

"Hey, hey, hey. I didn't commit to joining a pirate organization," Aniah said.

"When you flew them off the mountaintop, you sided with the Péchettes. The Benningtons won't be kind to you when they find out. And if you don't join us, you put these people at risk of death. You know as well as I do you will be dusted and interrogated, which will lead your dad or the Benningtons straight here."

Aniah aimed her fungi stick at Tayen, but didn't release it as dangling pieces of okra fell on the counter.

"Tony, forgive me for overstepping my authority," Tayen said. "You are the administrator of the Hovel and you have the final say on the matter."

Unfazed by the developments, Tony said, "You laid out what must be done. If Madam Priestess doesn't object, neither do I."

Lilith and Aniah stared at one another, shocked by the new developments in their lives.

***

Lilith enjoyed Tony's dinner of cou-cou and flying fish, but she didn't understand why she'd prepped sweet potatoes when they weren't served during dinner. Tony placed a conkie on her plate. Then she understood where the sweet potatoes went.

Tony carried a dinner tray up the stairs for AJ. Tayen followed with two bottles of wine while Lilith and Aniah brought the glasses.

AJ rolled his neck as he sat in the folding chair. He hadn't left the second-floor room while they ate dinner.

Lilith put the glasses down on the cardboard table and began rubbing his neck. "What mind-blowing facts did you find, Professor?"

AJ took his glasses off, closed his eyes, and accepted Lilith's neck rub. "The writings of Captain Morena Calveiro are authenticated. Single-minded, purpose driven, and goal oriented. She was a tactician. A no-nonsense mayor with atrocious handwriting."

Surprised, Tony asked, "She was mayor in Bridgetown?"

"De facto mayor of an advanced city facing the Caribbean Sea, but not in Barbados. This secret pirate base we search for sat next to a legitimate city at the edge of a," AJ air-quoted, "'Fog Bank.'"

"Where's the city of the fog?" Tayen asked.

"She didn't leave us another frigging map to solve, if that's your question. She journaled to capture her state of mind as a proficient administrator—captain. Seldom does she expose her feelings. And she is well acquainted with the artist who did the map wall. The question is: did the mother or the daughter paint the map wall?"

Lilith couldn't help herself and blurted out, "Tony told us the daughter's name was Tempest."

"Awww. He spoiled my big reveal. Aniah, stretch your psychology skills and review this journal. See if you and I agree on her state of mind."

Aniah spun the journal around as she bent over the table. "Written in Spanish. No problem. But don't tell me any more and we'll compare notes later."

"What smells so good?" AJ opened his eyes and found dinner in front of him.

Lilith bumped the back of his head. "Eat. You can tell us what you found afterwards. It's our turn to share with you."

"Why am I getting two servings of cou-cou?"

"A-ha, my first lesson of Bajan cuisine. The side dish is a conkie, not a second serving of cou-cou."

The clanging of metal chairs marched up the stairs, and all heads turned to see what was approaching. Eboni appeared carrying a tray of conkies. Behind her, Leonard and Fred were hauling up folding chairs for everyone.

Eboni laid the tray on the floor. "I brought my mother's dessert, thinking I'd introduce conkies to our new arrivals. But from the smell in the kitchen, I'm too late."

Tayen sat in the chair Fred unfolded for her. "We don't mind having another dessert. Give me a piece."

Tony took the seat Leonard gave him. "With your permission, Madam Priestess, I would like to call to order our first meeting."

"Oh," Lilith sat with her hands in her lap, "please do."

Tony looked at Tayen. "Should I have a gavel to bang in the meeting?"

"My god, with your body, clearing your throat will do it," Tayen said.

"Ahem."

"It works. I about crapped my pants," Leonard said.

"This is the first meeting of what was the Péchette Network. Madam Priestess—"

"Lilith, please. Save Madam Priestess for when I need an intimidating introduction."

"Lilith—with the aid of the highly esteemed Tayen from the Confederated Tribes of the Grand Ronde—renamed our organization this afternoon. We are the Manicato I'naru' Network."

AJ licked the residual conkie from his fingers. "The valiant spirit of women. Totally dope."

Tony grinned. "It reflects the heritage of passed down to Tempest from her mother, Jade Péchette, and her father, Tristao. Sadly, we don't have a record of his surname."

AJ fell back in his seat. "Did you say Tristao?"

Lilith saw the shock on AJ's face. "Did you run across a Tristao?"

"No. The caretaker at Adela Frontera mentioned him." AJ shuddered to shake himself free from the distraction. "Sorry, carry on."

Tony smiled. "The Hovel will become the center of operations. Our computers need to be state-of-the art, and communication security will have to match up to the best in the world."

"Money—Oh wait, never mind. For a moment, I forgot we had thirty million plus in the bank," Eboni said.

"Isn't that my bank account?" Lilith asked.

"Ahem." Tony cleared his throat. Lilith and Eboni fell silent.

"We'll put together a finance subcommittee in the morning. For now, we are a Robin-Hood-esque network. We expose corrupt money for prosecution, and exact revenge if the courts fail. We are a continuation of the refugee savior, the Voodoo Priestess, whose pirate base resided in this area."

"The Fog Bank," AJ said. "Jade and her pirates resided in the Fog Bank, a sixty-mile stretch on the South American coast. A massive Portuguese port marked the eastern boundary, and a city named Maman Brigitte marked the western edge."

Tony and ELF gasped.

AJ tilted his head at Lilith. "Oh goodie. I'm not the only one who has heard of her."

"Heard of who?" Lilith asked.

AJ turned to ELF. "Could you search for mysterious deaths in New Orleans on September seventeenth of last year?"

"Brayton, our doorman at the hotel?"

AJ held up his hand to hold Lilith off. "Sorry for commandeering your meeting, Tony, but what can you tell me about Zaiaqui?"

Tony leaned forward to the edge of his chair, making it creak. "Zaiaqui and Maman Brigitte? There is no way."

"How about Damballa's legions and Mambo LaTonya?"

Tony jumped from his seat and walked behind his chair, turning his back to the room.

"What did you find in the journal?" Lilith asked.

"Oh, holy hell," Eboni exclaimed. "Five unexplained deaths of five men."

"Did the deceased have French surnames?"

Leonard read from his phone. "Colliot, Boudet, Gravier, Morin, and Trichet. Are those French?"

AJ pinched the bridge of his nose. "I'd say so."

"Another five on December eighteenth, and again on March sixteenth," Fred added.

"Search June fifteenth," Tony ordered.

Leonard lowered his phone. "Five men didn't die on March twenty-first. It was three men and two women. Both women's surname are Devereux."

"I bet their ancestry extends back to military personnel from the early eighteenth-century France."

"Oh, shit. Five more on June fifteenth," Eboni said.

"AJ?" Lilith grew more uncomfortable with each death of five.

He held her off with a hand wave. "Tony, did I understand you correctly when you said the Voodoo Priestess was a refugee savior?"

"Yes."

"What about Mambo LaTonya?"

"She died after last summer's solstice. New Orleans no longer has a Mambo's protection."

Lilith growled, "Arrrg. AJ, spill it before I lose it."

He pressed his hands together under his chin. "Jade Péchette rescued the remnants of a Native American tribe, the Chitimacha, from the area we now call New Orleans. The French started a war with them and incited the surrounding tribes against the Chitimacha. Legend has it, a woman who died during the conflict became a ghost and set out to exact revenge on the French invaders. But she was kept in check by a New Orleans Voodoo Priestess, who guarded the city against retribution from the ghost, Zaiaqui."

Lilith interrupted. "Tempest, the great protector of New Orleans—"

"And her descendants."

"So, I'm related to Priestess LaTonya, your friend."

"You've got to research your ancestry. I couldn't say you are, but until we have confirmation, you very well may be related to her," AJ said.

Tony looked at Lilith. "With Mambo LaTonya's death, or Priestess LaTonya, as you called her, New Orleans no longer has a protector."

"Which explains five deaths on each solstice and equinox," Tayen said.

"AJ," Tony said. "You mentioned Damballa legions. What did you find?"

"Oh, joy. Nobody tells Charlotte unless she's sitting on a toilet."

Lilith stomped her foot on the floor.

"Chill, girl. Damballa's legions represent the seven thousand coils which created the cosmos. Since you're not the outdoors type, coils refer to snakes—"

"Goddamn Beagle's Bluff," Lilith yelled. "Seven thousand snakes crawled through that town?"

"Damballa's legions signal a change," Tony said.

Aniah hadn't spoken, but her impatience got the best of her. "AJ, finish this off before it finishes us."

"Vodun has entered our lives. Events occurring on the equinoxes and solstices, LaTonya's death, Damballa's legions at Beagle's Bluff, Adela Frontera, and Zaiaqui whom we encountered in New Orleans—"

Lilith raised her voice. "I don't remember meeting Zaiaqui outside the hotel."

AJ turned in his seat. "The fog which hugged the ground outside the hotel, and the sickly-sweet scent which we rushed inside to escape: those were signs of Zaiaqui. We sniffed her scent."

"We had a descendant of the Voodoo Priestess present to stop Zaiaqui." Tayen rested her elbows on her knees. "But Lilith wasn't trained to stop her."

AJ stood and joined Tony at the open French door. "Yeah, well, it gets worse. Father Amare—unwittingly—unleashed something worse. Zaiaqui is a problem, but Maman Brigitte is the real threat."

Tony swung around to AJ. "How did Father Amare summon her?"

"Summon?" Lilith and Aniah asked in terrified unison.

"He didn't mean too," AJ said.

Lilith waved her hand. "Wait, wait. Who did Father Amare summon: Zaiaqui or the other person?"

AJ's answer was directed at Tony, not Lilith. "To hypnotize us, he must have copied the rituals Priestess

LaTonya performed. But he didn't understand the implications of doing it inside the turret stairwell."

"No!" Lilith screeched. "You talked with Kimiko and learned about Voodoo?"

AJ said, "Father Amare unleashed Maman Brigitte, the Goddess of Death and the Grave, and the most provocative dancer in the universe. Entire villages succumbed to her will, whenever and wherever she danced."

He turned around and faced Lilith. "I wouldn't believe it if it hadn't happened in front of my eyes. Maman Brigitte took possession of a small girl at the convent museum. You walked like a queen to the dance club. And you danced … a rhythmically erotic dance which enchanted every soul in the nightclub. She bent their wills to hers. You didn't miss a step because she made sure you wouldn't. Then you spit alcohol over a burning candle where she danced in the flames."

Lilith fell to her knees.

"Sorry, kiddo. Maman Brigitte, the Goddess of Death and the Grave, took control over you for one hellacious dance.

26 - Transference

Lilith dangled her bare feet above the floor and reclined in the oversized papasan wicker chair. She had a water bottle full of chilled strawberry-infused tea, and the open French doors allowed a gentle ocean breeze to bathe her in luxury. The vivid mauve, tangerine, and peach sunset pulled the toxins from her day, replacing it with a soothing calm. Heaven had arrived for her.

AJ and Tayen had left for Portland a week earlier, leaving Lilith and Aniah in Barbados. The ladies had helped transform the second floor into a spacious living area, replete with bookshelves full of books and decorations pulled from old crates. They'd taken plenty of little shopping jaunts into Bridgetown to find complimentary knickknacks for the warm, homey vibe Lilith wanted.

The sole disruption of her serene Bajan loft came from her Bluetooth earpiece. Charlotte had called from Portland.

"Oh, Charlotte. Your tiny bladder would have exploded after AJ spoke," Lilith said. "I'm not a vodouisant, but the oddities that happened at Adela Frontera, and what we've learned here have got me rethinking Vodun."

"How about your possession by the Goddess of Death?"

"One night, my inhibitions vanish and I dance lights out. I can dance wickedly without having to be possessed."

"I don't know, Regan. You did turn heads."

"I'm not asking who Regan is," Lilith said.

Charlotte's voice crackled from holding her laughter back. "Tayen said she was freaked out after AJ showed the connections. People dying on the solar events, your possible relation to Priestess LaTonya, and the shocker … Damballa's legions pouring into Beagle's Bluff. Way too much for the boss lady. What did Aniah do?"

"Beats me. My head felt like the lone sock in the tumble cycle before I collapsed on the floor."

"You fainted?"

"Dropped off the chair and laid on the floor like the next clothes pile waiting for the washer."

"You're doing laundry, aren't cha?"

"How did you guess?"

"You're using laundry similes to describe your feelings."

"Sue me," Lilith said. "Aniah turned into a wallflower. This goddess stuff was nothing but a folktale to her. She dug into the journal that night as AJ had asked."

"Did the psych major agree with our psycho owner?"

"Yep. Captain Morena didn't write her emotions down. She had an extreme focus—obsession—on her mission to Europe in 1724. But she didn't journal what her mission was about."

Charlotte yawned. "So, shit hit the fan, and you spend another restless night tossing about until the sun rose, when Tony fixed you breakfast."

"Morning coffee was the only thing my stomach could handle. On my third sip, AJ decoded the next clue, and holy hell broke loose."

"He never ceases to amaze me. He plucks obscure facts out of midair, and boom, we have a puzzle piece."

"This wasn't an obscure detail. Tell me your version of events. Tayen and AJ weren't chatty with the details. So, who is ELF? With Scott, it sounds like three people, but with Tayen, it's one?"

"Eboni, Leonard, and Fred were hanging around the kitchen, hoping to snag Tony's frittata."

"Okay. Three people."

"Tony and AJ were in a serious discussion at the kitchen table. They used big six-syllable word lists with funky pronunciations. Church councils reared its ugly little head and AJ drifted into another universe."

"Ugly little head? What do you know about church councils?" Charlotte asked.

"A rat presided over one."

Charlotte didn't respond, and Lilith wasn't waiting for a sarcastic comment. "Tony drew a diagram for AJ, and that's when—"

"Isn't it weird that theologians, who work with the abstract, have to concretize their ideas in diagrams?"

After a long silence, Charlotte asked, "You're

whirling your hand in the air, in effect to say *whatever*, aren't you?"

"I am not," Lilith said as she whirled her hand around.

"Forget it. What was the diagram about?"

"Tony drew a timeline with Vatican II as the last event. AJ sat like a statue; unresponsive and oblivious to the comment. Tayen noticed and shooed Tony away from other comments. She has learned how to read him. I hope someday—"

"Dear," Charlotte interrupted, "you're trending elsewhere. Back to the timeline."

"Tony stopped after seeing Tayen wave at him. AJ rapped the table with his fingers before he … Forget it. I can't say that guy's name."

"Schillebeeckx ain't an easy name when you look at it."

"How do you say it?" Lilith asked.

"Father Eddie Schillebeeckx."

"I don't think they called him Eddie."

"Perhaps not, but for us Catholics who know what Schillebeeckx did for Catholicism, it's Eddie," Charlotte said.

"So, explain to me, in simple non-hyperbolic terms, how AJ solved the *Victor Visibly Vanquished* clue?"

"General church councils are the big ass events in the Roman Catholic Church."

"You don't have to go overboard on simplifying."

"They set doctrine, establish orthodoxy, and prescribe what is heresy. In two millennia, they've held twenty-one of them in the Western church. Vatican II was the last one. Schillebeeckx worked behind the scenes to transform the theological outlook of Vatican II. He helped decentralize the hierarchical power of papal authority."

"Vatican II was on Tony's timeline," Lilith said.

"Hardliners didn't like Schillebeeckx and charged him with heresy. The ideas he advanced at Vatican II were rejected. To be heard, he submitted his proposals under a pseudonym. With his name not connected to the topic under debate, his ideas gained traction and were adopted. Eddie proved the most influential person at Vatican II, albeit anonymously.

"Joseph Ratzinger—"

"That's the rat AJ referred to."

Charlotte chuckled. "Ratzinger was a hardliner who wanted to preserve the assertion of unquestionable papal authority. He squeezed into a powerful—and highly a visible—position, overshadowing Schillebeeckx in the public eye. Schillebeeckx received dubious investigations of heresy; Ratzinger received the papacy.

"Preserving a harmonious public image was paramount for the church. The victor, Schillebeeckx, became less visible. The vanquished, Ratzinger, became more visible. A theologian writing about the history of General Church Councils referred to this role reversal as the *Victor Visibly Vanquished.*"

"Who was the theologian?" Lilith asked.

"The article was written under a pseudonym, but it wasn't Eddie. "

"Well then, okay, what," Lilith gathered herself, "what does it mean?"

"The anonymous theologian referred to the *Lumen gentium* and a phrase: *Nevertheless, many elements of sanctification and of truth are found outside its visible confines.* From a theological perspective, it doesn't mean a thing to you and me. But for AJ, it was a revelation.

"To unlock the map room wall, we must find the truth of the elements found *outside the visible confines. Victor Visibly Vanquished* is a cunning play on words, as is the truth of the elements, the elemental candles left by your ancestor."

"But Vatican II occurred in the 1960s. Jade Péchette lived two and a half centuries earlier. The clue on the map wall isn't hers?"

Charlotte sighed. "The original clue was changed after the 1960s. Father Amare said Priestess LaTonya was the last one in the map room. Worse yet, the article by the anonymous theologian came from a New Orleans seminary. It was posted a year before AJ started his graduate work in New England."

"What does that mean?"

"Tayen and I aren't literary analysts. But we aren't stupid either. I dug up the copy of the article AJ spoke about in Catholic Biblical Quarterly. Tayen and I studied the article word for word. We then compared it to AJ's book, *Historical Preludes to General Church Councils*. The word choices, the style of voice, the continuity of thought … It all lines up. The article from an unknown author matches AJ's book."

"*Victor Visibly Vanquished* was for AJ," Lilith said.

"Scott told us when Father Amare greeted him, he said 'welcome, my old friend.' When AJ didn't respond, Amare added, 'I see. Not yet.' Tayen thinks AJ was dusted before leaving for grad school. He was hypnotized to forget his time in New Orleans."

"Do you think he visited the map room as a young man?"

Charlotte shot back. "Do you believe the Goddess of Death possessed you for a quick dance in a nightclub? Do we believe AJ stumbled in the river after Priestess LaTonya died? When she did, he mystically poked his walking stick through a rusted platform, and sent seven thousand snakes slithering through Beagle's Bluff?"

"Nobody took a snake census to confirm it was seven thousand," Lilith said. "Has Kimiko explained Vodun to you folks?"

"She told us the basics. Spirits are called loa, and they reside in Vilokan. You summon them through the graces of Papa Legba. The loa are too many to list for you, but there are some important ones to know. Bondye, Damballa, Papa Legba, Erzulie Fréda, Erzulie Dantòr, Ayida-Weddo, and, of course, Maman Brigitte."

"Send me a link to read about them," Lilith said.

"Will do."

"Charlotte … " Lilith felt comfortable enough to ask, "do you believe I was possessed?"

"A lovely question. Frankly, I don't know. While Kimiko was outlining the basics of Vodun, I wondered if the rest of us were possessed by lesser-known loa."

"Are loa demons?"

"Not at all," Charlotte's answer resounded with conviction. "Loa are people who have passed on from this life to the next, except for a few who assist with the administration of creation from Bondye. Bondye equates to God the Father in Christianity."

"Thanks. I was about to ask who Bondye was. So, why do the loa possess people?" Lilith asked.

"Not in the evil way which Hollywood and Evangelical Christianity present it. Think about it as your grandmother's spirit returning to you to provide guidance and insight, not to go on a murderous rampage."

"What got in me wasn't grandma. This Maman

Brigitte rocked my world. You're a spectacular sex partner, but this loa had my crotch dialed up to thirty."

"Okay. Enough about your dance with the Goddess of Death. Tell me, what is life like in Barbados?"

"Well, it's different," Lilith said. "This version of a Robin Hood avenger group comes with a 007 underground spy center. I can't say it ever came to me in a daydream during third-period algebra, or chemistry."

"Don't let it go to your head, princess. The murderous drug lord front hasn't changed. Those countries and other spy agencies who have bugged BCI have reached the count of eighteen. Scott wants to designate a hole for each country."

"Should you and I be talking?" Lilith asked.

"Scott secured our phones and computers with the help of your elves division."

"ELF, not elves. How are your night terrors?"

"Ouch. Way to cut to the chase without warning."

"How are your night terrors, Charlotte?" Lilith's concern was that her roommate had self imposed a burden on herself that wasn't hers.

"Less severe and less frequent." Charlotte took her time to word her answer. "My triggers. I can't identify them for the daytime intrusions."

Hearing the uncertainty in Charlotte's voice, Lilith said, "I don't get daytime intrusions, either. My night terrors are less frequent, but they're still there. I'm sick of them."

"Hey, hope is around the corner. Dale thinks Jade synthesized a compound like psilocybin mushrooms. With a skilled hypnotist's guidance, like Kimiko, they may have therapeutic uses for PTSD."

"Kimiko and Dale?"

"An unlikely pairing, I grant you. I catch Kimi staring

at them. She must be trying to figure out their gender, but can't," Charlotte said.

"Kimiko is a binary thinker. She sees someone and clothes them according to the gender she perceives. Dale's androgenous appearance confuses her. Her mind can't decide on which direction to clothe Dale, female or male. That's why she stares. Tell Dale to ask Kimi to design specific clothing for them. It will break Kimiko's fashion block and help her move on."

"Oh, that makes sense. How did you figure that out?"

"Know the people around you and what's important to them. Their minds answer to their desires, dreams, or wishes. Kimiko's mind can't stop picturing how everyone she meets should be dressed."

"Astute observation. I'm afraid to ask what you've observed about me."

"Balls to the wall and screw subtlety." Lilith had prepared for this opportunity. "You love your parents, but walking in their shoes would kill you. You charted your own path in life; accepted Tayen and AJ as another set of parental figures and molded yourself after them. You take your business savvy and professionalism from Tayen and follow AJ's leanings into academia. And your sexuality is aggressive. I mean, come-on girl. Slow down."

"Screw you. I like sex."

"Your constraints for screwing should be stricter than *if it walks and talks,*" Lilith said.

"Hey. Walking is not a prerequisite, and I sure the hell wished they'd stop talking."

"You dominated all the time."

"'Stop', 'hold on.' Nope, words you never said. Don't tell me you didn't like it."

Lilith growled. "Arrrg. This is why we aren't together. If I misrepresented your standards for sexual conduct, I apologize."

"FYI, I don't have sex with someone if they don't meet four immutable qualifications. It must be of age, it must give clear consent, it can't be an animal, and it can't be dead. If they pass those four, I go for it."

"How could you not go wrong with standards like that?"

"We're opposites. I'll screw who I want," Charlotte said. "You need the emotional attachment first. As much as my practice confuses you, yours confuses me. Not to experience sexual attraction for someone, male or female, until you've connected with them, isn't something I can relate to. Someone attractive crosses my path, and boom, my hormones rage on and clothes fly off."

Lilith sat on the edge of her chair. "I was teased in high school without end. If I didn't melt when stud boy walked by, then I must not like guys. It didn't take long to jump from 'she doesn't like guys' to 'she's a lesbian.' Between the jokes, sneers, and overreactions to anything I said or did, I was miserable. I was attracted to those who befriended and showed genuine concern for me. Their gender, or age, had no bearing on the attraction."

"Hence your self-identification in the queer community."

"Hence, my love for you. Your authentic attitude toward me in the beginning won me over. I'll always love you, but we are as different as they come. A lasting bond in close quarters would end with one of us killing the other."

Lilith sighed. "This is gonna suck."

"What is going to suck?"

"Have you been told about the Hovel?"

Charlotte paused before answering. "It is the headquarters of the Manicato I'naru' Network, and you are its chief executive officer. Which means you are moving to Barbados."

Lilith closed her eyes. As exciting as it was to move, leaving friends and family in Portland hurt. "Unexpected this is."

"Knock it off, Yoda."

"I like it down here. The challenge of helping others and setting up this division of Broken Cove Charities with Tayen's help has awakened me. I'm finding a sense of direction. Something that was never a part of me before."

Charlotte said, "We are headed down two different paths—"

"Two slightly different paths."

"Oh, honey, no. You're a queen of the Caribbean and I'm the assistant to the queen of a golf resort. I see it, but you don't. You're relocating to an island nation. ELF steals you thirty million a pop and hides you from a growing web of international spies. You're the one they're after, and you're safer there than any of us are in Portland."

Unable to continue, Lilith redirected the conversation. "Aniah won't return to Portland. She's a natural fit here and is creating her own niche. We have construction crews working around the clock. Every day it gets a little nicer."

"Lilith, stop trying to escape your feelings."

"Tayen's little black book has ELF complete attention." Lilith wasn't about to let Charlotte address her move. "They're tracing, tracking, bugging, and whatever else they need to do on her list of oligarchs. These people won't see the inside of a jail. Their business transactions are buried so deep that we can't legally expose them. They stacked the system in their favor."

"And you and ELF will steal millions from their secret accounts from right there, in the Hovel, your new home."

Lilith couldn't escape Charlotte's persistence. "I'm not ready."

"Yes, you are. There, you are in your element. You sense the call from Adela Frontera, or the secret pirate base from your great-great-granny Jade. We'll still talk and stay in touch."

"Transitions don't come without painful goodbyes."

"Failing to take an opportunity when it comes only causes more pain and suffering. A natural transition for me was college. But another natural transition brought me to a business startup in the forest of west Portland. I couldn't be happier about the people I've met, and what I am doing under Tayen's leadership."

"This is my transition. But am I ready for it?" Lilith asked.

"You don't have a choice. It is time for you to make a change."

Suspicious of Charlotte's motives, Lilith asked, "Are you encouraging me, or gaslighting me?"

"I'm encouraging you to move to Barbados."

"Oh, after weeks of subtle hints about restraints and whips, it hits me: you want to convert my room into your S&M chamber."

"Call it an idea in development."

"Time for me to go. Goodbye, Charlotte."

"Where do I send your—"

Lilith disconnected the call.

Minutes later, steps pitter-pattered up to the top of the stairwell. Aniah read a text on her phone, her face contorted in her attempt to understand it. "Why does Charlotte need the Hovel's mailing address, and why is she texting me for it?"

"Do you find me attractive?" Lilith asked.

Aniah took a step back. "Hell no, I'm not answering. Between her text and your question—Hell no, I'm not giving an answer. What did you two fight about?"

"Aniah, ignore her text. I'm serious. Do you find me attractive?"

"She texts me, and you ask if I'm attracted to you. This is an ex-lovers' quarrel."

"She's teasing about mailing my stuff here. We didn't fight. We realized I am leaving home, and that this place is my new home."

Aniah sat in a chair across from Lilith. "That fills half the blanks. Where did the question about my attraction to you come from?"

Lilith crossed her arms and smiled. "Why are you being defensive over a simple question? Did you tell someone you were attracted to me?"

"I may have let it slip that I find you attractive."

"You told Charlotte."

Aniah squinted. "Why are we discussing this?"

"Straightforward, honest, clear communication is a rule in this house. And I wanted to make sure my intentions were clear. But I would like to know when you shared your feelings about me with Charlotte."

Aniah squirmed in her seat. "Okay. Remember the night we raided Pirate's Chocolate, and you left early?"

"Oooh, the chocolate-peanut-butter cookie cake. Don't say you ate cake after I left?"

"It wasn't the only thing to be eaten that night."

Lilith cringed. "Gross. In the bakery?"

"It was a new experience. We had to clean the creamed puffs off—"

"Don't tell me where the creamed puffs went."

"—the counter."

"Oh, okay. I thought you were going to say somewhere else."

Aniah bit her upper lip. "Well, that's how the creamed puffs got on the counter."

"My god, that girl will nail anything that walks."

"No, she won't. She has a rigid requirement of age and consent."

"As well as bestiality and necrophilia."

Aniah fell back in her seat and laughed. "I added those for her. Shortly thereafter, AJ drove the *Mini Black Pearl* past the bakery on one of his late-night security rounds. Shazoo was on the kitty perch. With god as my witness, I swear the cat looked right at me. Thank god the bakery lights were out or AJ would have seen us too."

Lilith shielded her eyes.

"It's amazing how the danger of getting caught with your pants down in the bakery intensifies the orgasm."

"It was the surge of adrenaline and increase of blood flow to your nether regions."

"Yeah. That's how … Have you been reading my psychology books?"

Lilith leaned out of her papasan chair and approached Aniah. "Forget the frolic in the bakery. Are you attracted to me?"

Aniah hustled out of her chair, away from Lilith. "I told Charlotte I found you attractive."

Lilith firmly grabbed Aniah's wrist and pulled her towards her. "Please, sit with me on the couch."

Aniah tugged to release herself from Lilith's iron grip. "Since when does 'please' accompany a wrist lock?"

"Since this became important. I needed to impress upon you the seriousness of my intentions." Lilith pulled Aniah to the couch. Once there, she pulled Aniah's arm around and used Aniah's momentum to flip her onto the couch.

Lying face-up on the couch, Aniah said, "Thank you for slamming me onto a soft surface."

Lilith straddled Aniah's hips. She leaned over and propped herself up, pinning Aniah's shoulders on the couch. With her locks dangling on Aniah's cheeks, she said, "Since the mountaintop, you've displayed courage, strength, sincerity, and compassion. I haven't detected an ounce of deceit in you. Our conversations have touched me. Your genuine concern for my mental well-being surpasses a therapist's. You have earned my trust and restored my faith in the goodness of people."

Aniah gazed into Lilith's eyes. "Transference. You're reading my empathy as a romantic feeling toward you."

"I'm superb at seeing past people's façades and noticing their body language. You're displaying a defensive mechanism because you were caught unprepared to address the feelings we have for each other."

Lilith leaned to one side and pushed her leg down against Aniah's. She hooked her ankle behind Aniah's knee and pushed it up. She repeated with the other leg until Aniah's knees were spread apart.

Aniah closed her eyes and let her mouth fall open.

Lilith ran her hand down the back of Aniah's thigh.

Aniah arched her back. Her nervousness forced her to speak. "Charlotte is the dominate one in your—" she gasped. Lilith's fingers began to stroke her.

"I'm sorry. I should have asked for your consent."

"I think your fingers call tell I'm not saying no."

"Is that a yes?"

"Yes. God, yes. You have my consent. I'm of age, I ain't near dead, but your fingers are making me a bit animalistic at the moment."

Aniah leaned her head to the side, exposing her neck. "Transferring. You are assuming leadership from Tayen and AJ. The sexual relationship with Charlotte has passed, and now I am your—"

Aniah couldn't finish. Lilith had moved her hand up under Aniah's shirt and bra. The caressing of her breast cut off Aniah's thought.

Lilith spoke instead. "I didn't want to push you into a relationship if you weren't ready. After your transition from your home in the Caribbean to completely new surroundings, I figured it was too much of an adjustment. But we're on a different footing here, in Barbados. You're more relaxed and at home."

Lilith kissed Aniah's neck.

After a few kisses, Aniah pushed on Lilith's forehead with her index finger so they could make eye contact. "This isn't like you. Taking charge in intimate moments isn't your style."

"People change."

"Yeah, but your sexual appetite lives at the low end of the asexual spectrum. Are you telling me I earned your unconditional trust?"

Lilith placed her finger over Aniah's lips and

continued kissing Aniah's neck.

Aniah kissed her finger and asked, "Charlotte and I are the ones who've gained your trust level of intimacy?"

"Include AJ, and you have my list."

Lilith went to kiss Aniah on the lips, but launched back at the last moment. She pushed herself up and above from Aniah.

"Wow. I can't believe what you just admitted to," Aniah said.

"AJ has my trust. But I'm not … "

"Maybe you share a different trust. Perhaps he didn't pursue—"

"Are you saying had AJ made advances … He and I could have been lovers?" Lilith asked.

"I'm saying you and AJ share a special bond. A stronger bond than either of you know. If not lovers, what other relationship is as strong?"

27 - Masters of Art

Late into the evening of a glorious September day in Barbados, the finished computer-control room buzzed with activity. Sublevel two resembled a space center's launch control room. A tremendous leap from the original laptops ELF started with in June.

The first meeting of the Manicato I'naru' Network necessitated full attendance from the cells spread across the Caribbean. Tony stood at the computer network helm. Lilith nodded approval of his work directives to the staff. She didn't understand each person's responsibilities, so rather than saying something dumb, she kept her mouth shut and let Tony run the operation center.

"Two minutes. Take your spots, and turn on the video wall, please." Tony's orders took hold, quieting the room in an instant. The video wall popped on and multiple conference boxes lit up. The Portland cell had the honor of the top left box, which displayed AJ's vacant chair.

Tony ran down the attending cells. "Grand Bahamas, St. Thomas, Dominican Republic, Jamaica, Antigua, Montserrat, and Barbados are present. Together you total one hundred and thirty members. Welcome to each and all."

Applause and cheers came from the cells.

"Next, the Cayman Islands. I understand only the director and his assistants can attend today's meeting. Thank you for attending, Caymans."

Tony waited for the applause to end. "The last of our attending cells are Portland and New Orleans. They are online, but their representatives are elsewhere?"

Lilith shook her head in irritation. *Arguably the two most important cells, and they aren't present.*

Tony started the meeting: "At the behest of the Descendant Daughter, I call this meeting to order."

The New Orleans box came to life. Father Amare's smile displayed his delight at seeing the gathering of cells. No sooner had he appeared than the Portland box showed AJ scrambling into his tufted wingback chair in his third-floor office. He spun his chair around and faced the camera. The height of his chair's back hid most of the activity going on behind him.

Tayen and Elliott's heads rose over the chair's back. Charlotte, however, wasn't tall enough to gain screen time.

AJ talked, but no sound came. Scott's arm reached from out of the frame. "Oh shit. Thanks, Scott, I forgot the mute button."

"I say we get rid of this fucking chair and bring back the old one," Charlotte said as soon as AJ finished.

A smattering of laughter echoed from the speakers.

Lilith didn't wait and addressed them: "Portland, we can hear you. Watch the language and commentary; we're running a professional organization."

A middle finger appeared over the back of the chair.

"Charlotte, stick your finger down your throat rather than above the chair."

A second middle finger rose, giving AJ horns.

Lilith jumped straight into her questioning. "Father Amare, where have you been?"

"Hiding. Please remember, the New Orleans cell is the front line in this struggle."

"Forgive my impatience." Lilith's eyes burned with urgency. "Were you and AJ acquaintances before last year?"

Father Amare's smile disappeared, and he fell back in his chair. "You've come a long way in your research—"

"Answer the question."

"This isn't the time. I beg your forgiveness, Lilith, but I cannot speak to your question."

"Then divulge what you can. People died in the Dominican Republic, and if you withheld information that could have prevented their deaths, I'm going to be pissed."

Lilith's display of anger froze everyone.

Father Amare held up his hands. "I held nothing back. I dusted you so the interrogations to come wouldn't extract what you learned from the map room."

"Were you aware of Priestess LaTonya's work on the *Victor Visibly Vanquished* clue?"

Father Amare dipped his head. "AJ wrote the article, and I—"

"—edited it," Lilith finished for him. "You and AJ were friends."

"It is not time for me to share AJ's life prior to grad

school. He and Priestess LaTonya would be upset if we continue down this path."

"He would be upset?"

Father Amare nodded.

"AJ, are you buying this?"

The weight of the discussion had bent AJ's head down. "Father Amare saved us, so he gets the benefit of the doubt."

The stress pouring from AJ force Lilith to intercede. "Members of the Manicato I'naru' Network. My apologies for not introducing my boss and close friend, AJ de Faria."

Applause rose for AJ.

Lilith continued: "I trust AJ's opinion and follow his lead. Please give him the highest regard and deference, whatever the situation is. He's earned my devoted trust, and I hope you'll trust him as completely as I do."

Applause and cheers rose from the speakers.

"Another person I want to introduce is AJ's better half, Tayen."

Tayen stepped from behind AJ's chair and knelt next to him. "Thank you for the sparkling introduction. But let's make this clear; I'm the better half of the creative team, not his wife."

"Oops. I worded that wrong, didn't I?" Lilith scrunched her nose in embarrassment.

"Good evening, everyone." Tayen's professionalism was apparent to all. "Some of you may recognize our organization's name originates from the Taíno people. I want to thank you for giving your enthusiastic support."

Tayen muted the microphone as a scuffle broke out behind AJ's chair.

Lilith watched. Tayen and AJ stared into the camera.

A fist swung over AJ's head. Lilith recognized it was Charlotte's because of the bracelet she gave her for Christmas. Scott's glasses flew across the frame from where Charlotte's fist headed. Elliott intercepted Charlotte's wrist on the second go-around.

Tayen unmuted the microphone, but Charlotte sneaked out a yell from under Elliot's hand. "How the fuck does your dad know Taíno?"

Lilith closed her eyes and dreaded to ask. "I'm with Charlotte, Tayen. How does AJ know Taíno?"

"Can we move things along?" AJ asked in protest.

"Ladies and gentlemen of this conference," Tony said to rescue AJ, "as per instructions, we will discuss procedural matters after the Descendant Daughter addresses her immediate list of concerns."

Lilith slid into a chair. "Thanks, Tony. And thanks to those in Manicato I'naru'. I am not sure I understand why you joined us. Your lives aren't endangered as much as mine and my friends'. We weren't given a choice, but I'm giving you yours. If any uncertainty crosses your mind, get out, get safe, and get on with your life.

"If you stay, you're assuming a danger which I will do my best to protect you against. But this isn't a game. Now is the time to decide. I'll give you a minute."

After several moments, Eboni stood and spoke. "We grew up as Péchettes, hearing the folklore and aspiring to work with the granddaughter of the Great Protector of New Orleans. We'll stick around if you don't mind."

"Stick around. I am honored to lead this group."

Eboni thanked Lilith with a nod.

"Our goals are clear: Find the *Flor de la Mar* treasure and take down Ernesto Cottrell and his organization. After those, we fulfill the purpose of the Voodoo Priestess. We are a modern-day Robin Hood organization, and our Sherwood Forest is the Caribbean Sea and Gulf Coast region. AJ, tell us about the chests. I want everyone up to speed."

AJ began: "Dr. Dale Scroggins analyzed the contents of two chests. We named them the Faraday and the Marie Daly Chests, respectively."

"Excuse me," Lilith said. "This question is for anybody except Charlotte. Who is Marie Daly?"

"The first Black woman in the United States to earn a Ph.D. in chemistry."

Lilith fist-pumped to her side. "Damn straight. I love it. Continue, AJ."

"A precursory examination of the Faraday Chest showed a prototype generator and what we believe was advanced wiring. The chest was stolen from us, so we can't delve into it to determine whatever else was in it."

AJ flipped pages of paper over as he adjusted his glasses.

"The Marie Daly Chest was filled with sixty-seven boxes containing various elements found on the periodic table. Nothing new for us, but unimaginable back then. Scarier yet, Jade Péchette controlled the theoretical knowledge to predict most of the remaining elements on the periodic table. Some of you may ask, 'What can you do with the elements she found?' She created a hundred and ninety-three chemical compounds, which we are exploring.

"What modern-day equivalents can we infer to the compounds? Acetaminophen with codeine, morphine, latex, advanced burn cream, sunscreen eighty-five, special formulations in paint, medicines, and combustible materials. Dale is continuing to research them. However, without Jade's notes, we are guessing at what the original intentions were for each of the compounds.

"A few of the boxes had advanced explosives and accelerants. We escaped harm before experiment six went … awry."

"You mean blown to hell." Charlotte's voice came over the speakers to everyone's surprise.

"Two of the compounds," AJ continued without acknowledging Charlotte, "were a *teensy* bit more combustible than anticipated. The abandoned warehouse on Frontage Street is no more. The call for a five-alarm fire seemed to be excessive, but now I know a five-alarm fire includes twenty-one engines and eleven-ladder companies. We are avoiding the local news reporters."

"Is that why you have painted on eyebrows?"

AJ didn't respond.

Lilith realized this line of questioning was dead. "What about the isolated boxes?"

"We can't get into those. Dale thinks we should wait until we have Jade's chemistry notes. However, we need to discuss four compounds starting with number twenty-six. This is the precursor to Demon's Breath. Dale says it is an easy replicable base compound, but there is a ratio mixture which we don't have."

AJ stopped and stared at his monitor. "I apologize folks. I need to ask Father Amare a question."

Lilith noticed Amare's eyes had softened when he leaned forward.

"I'm here, AJ. How can I help?"

Lilith felt AJ's vulnerability as he spoke.

"We knew each other."

"Yes, my friend, we did. I am sorry I cannot divulge

more. So, believe me, you would not want me to explain anything at this time."

Lilith clutched her chest. *They were friends. God, even now you can see their friendship.*

"Did we expect this to happen?" AJ asked.

"You and I didn't."

"LaTonya did?"

Father Amare shrugged. "Maybe."

Lilith exploded. "Priestess LaTonya expected this?"

"Not this exact situation, Lilith, no. But she knew a calamitous event waited on the horizon. She kept things from me so I wouldn't divulge information at the wrong time. I'll know the conditions under which I can help AJ, but until then I cannot speak."

"Am I related to Priestess LaTonya?"

Father Amare bent his head down. In a soft voice, he said, "I believe so, but I have nothing concrete to support my belief."

"Beliefs don't originate out of thin air," AJ said. "Something as innocuous or ridiculous as it may seem birthed your belief. Share the seeds which lead to your belief."

Father Amare lifted his head and winked at the screen. "LaTonya's presence, her charisma, and her knowledge about the Voodoo Priestess. It gave me the impression she was defending her family, not a religious tradition. In her younger days, she traveled to the places which are present in this meeting. But in her later years—"

Lilith interrupted. "In her later years, she continued her family's tradition of protecting the French Quarter from the threat of Zaiaqui. She never left New Orleans once she arrived from Haiti. Or did she?"

"She left on three occasions."

"Where did she go?"

Father Amare shook his head. "I cannot say."

"New Orleans sits unprotected. Zaiaqui can roam the French Quarter at will," Tony said.

Lilith scrunched her nose and shut her eyes. "I love visiting New Orleans, but I prefer living in Barbados."

"Okay, if you don't mind," AJ said, "I think our resident Vodun expert can fill in the blanks at a later meeting."

"I agree. Schedule a meeting with Kimiko—"

AJ spoke over Tayen. "Amare, the latex material LaTonya and you covered the map room with, it doesn't work. Our replication efforts failed, and my basement is soggy. Do you have any we could use?"

Father Amare picked up his phone. "I'll set a reminder to send you what is left and the instructions for how to mix it."

"If we're done discussing home improvement … " Lilith stopped, seeing AJ had raised his hand like a student. "What?"

"The home improvement comment reminded me of our last artifact finding, the paintings from the Tampa—"

Lilith interrupted. "To bring everyone up to speed, we took a trip to Tampa and to collect evidence. Part of the evidence retrieved were two stunning paintings, which we believe Jade painted. The dating analysis reported a conundrum. AJ, tell us what you found."

"The painting of the ocean shore—we call it *Ocean Shore*—didn't contain hidden messages. We peeled the canvas out of the frame and found another painting underneath. The photoscopic tests picked up two different dating ranges. The upper layer dates from the early eighteenth century, and a hidden layer dates from the late nineteenth century. Charlotte and I framed the hidden painting, but we are exploring how to return it to its rightful owners."

Aniah stepped beside Lilith. "Excuse me, how would you know who a late nineteenth century painting belongs to?"

"It's hard to miss something which hung in the Isabella Gardner Stewart Museum."

Aniah's jaw dropped open and her face turned white.

"Why are you spazzing out?" Lilith asked.

Elliott knelt beside his father and swung the camera around so he was in view. "Hello, all. I'm Elliott de Faria. To answer your question, Lilith, *Chez Tortoni* by Édouard Manet, was stolen from Boston's Isabella Stewart Gardner Museum in 1990. That heist is the most famous art heist in the last half century. Aniah, care to share your association with this painting?"

"First," Aniah shouted as she pointed at the camera, "I never saw it in person. There is a photo of me as a child playing in a friend's house somewhere in Europe. Don't ask me where. The painting is visible hanging on the wall. Whether it is a print or the real thing, I can't say."

Elliott forced the issue. "Your reaction says something different."

"It's impossible not to know what was stolen that night. I saw my picture with *Chez Tortoni* on the wall behind me, and believe me, that impression is hard to forget."

"So, what is your impression? Fabricated or original?"

"Why the questions?"

"Because his work with the government specialized in cultural artifact thefts in both domestic and international arenas," AJ said.

Aniah ducked her head around. Lilith placed a

protective hand on her back and said, "Package it and send it back, Elliott."

"Love to, Lilith, but we can't. Someone added our business logo to the back of the painting with indelible ink. We send it back, the FBI traces it to Portland, and Dad goes to jail."

Even though Tayen stood out of the camera frame, her voice came across for Lilith to hear. "As well as those who stole it from Tampa."

AJ leaned forward. "Finding a Manet and returning it doesn't rank high on the list of things I'm worried about. Organized crime and stolen art go hand in hand. How it got behind a Péchette painting has us unnerved."

Aniah turned around, lowering Lilith's hand from her back. "What about the other painting?"

"Well. This is the perfect time to emphasize the need for the Manicato I'naru' Network's commitment to secrecy."

"You heard AJ. Mouths shut," Lilith ordered.

"Care to volunteer any other artworks you might have seen, Aniah?"

Elliott's accusatory tone set Aniah off. "You mean the big-ass Caravaggio in the bathroom?"

"Talk about a huge holy shit."

Lilith shouted, "Anybody but Charlotte. Who is Caravaggio?"

Aniah said, "Caravaggio painted religious scenes which took up the entire walls of cathedrals. A Caravaggio in the bathroom—"

"A cathedral-sized holy shit, got it. But why is Elliott nailing you with questions?"

"I stole artworks in Madrid and was part of a crew of art thieves. Our second outing didn't go well. We thought it was a pushover job. They got caught while I escaped, but authorities listed me as a 'person of interest.' Elliott ran across the report and is questioning my past."

"Have you seen a Raphael?" Elliott asked.

"Legally, in a museum." Aniah squinted after her quick reply. "What the hell did you guys uncover?"

Elliott and AJ glanced at one another.

Aniah fell back into a chair. "No way. That can't be."

Lost, Lilith spoke before Elliott could. "One person, preferably the best art historian, tells me what the hell was behind door number two."

"I don't need Charlotte swinging at my head, so I suggest Elliott take this," AJ said.

In the corner of the Portland box, Lilith could see Scott glaring at something behind AJ's chair. She guessed he was looking at Charlotte.

"Raphael's self-portrait." Elliott said bluntly. "The last sighting of it occurred at the end of World War II. The world has searched for it ever since. Many believe it was destroyed, but confirmation of that eludes us. If what we have is the original, well, hell. What do I to say to that? Regardless, someone with talent framed two masterpieces behind two lesser-known portraits. The question is why?"

Lilith covered her eyes while Elliott continued.

"Someone has the resources to procure artworks and the facilities to hide two major masterpieces. Who in the last thirty years worked with all four paintings? Who is involved outside of us and the drug cartel?"

Lilith scribbled a note on paper as she asked Elliott for clarification. "Is Priestess LaTonya involved?"

"Or did Priestess LaTonya leave a secret player in our midst?"

Father Amare said, "LaTonya worked with me, no others. I didn't come across any artwork, and with near absolute certainty, I can say no one in New Orleans worked with her without my knowledge."

"How about Kimiko?" Lilith passed her note to Tony.

"She isn't the secret player. However, she was a student of Priestess LaTonya, who taught her about Haitian Vodou," AJ said.

Lilith rolled her eyes. "Why aren't we having a serious sit-down with Kimiko?"

Tony passed the note to Eboni.

"She was taught the basics," AJ answered, "but nothing about the map wall. I think it's imperative that we return to the map room. There's another half of the room to discover."

Charlotte's voice carried over the speakers. "Shouldn't we have led with this? I mean, figuring out the clues on the wall is what we started with."

"What did he find, Charlotte?" Lilith yelled.

Charlotte continued off-screen. "He found it—excuse me—he learned it down there in Barbados. Didn't he tell you?"

Lilith gritted her teeth.

AJ spoke before she exploded. "My sailing lesson at the marina taught me about the ship's helm. Old sailing vessels utilized a ship's wheel with either eight or ten handles. The king spoke, is scored differently than the other handles, and points up when the ship is sailing straight. At nighttime, the helmsperson can determine rudder position by feeling the king spoke.

"The candles we lit didn't reveal a king spoke above the outcroppings in the map room. What I saw were faint images of the regular spokes of a ship's wheel. We must turn the wheel until the king spoke is at the center outcropping. Jade's king spoke, *Midnight's Royal Eye*, will open the other half of the map room where the journey continues."

"How do we turn a room around?" Lilith asked.

"Another set of candles should provide us with new images above the outcroppings. If done right, Jade's king spoke will appear."

"So, during our first excursion to the map room, we agreed I was *Midnight's Royal Eye*. Are we recanting that?"

"Not entirely," AJ said. "In Haitian Vodou, two worlds mirror one another. The physical surrounds us and the spiritual-ancestral plane of Vilokan resides in the Earth. What is found in one is mirrored in the other. You are the physical manifestation of *Midnight's Royal Eye*, while the mirror in the spirit world … Well, we can't say what that is."

"When my eyes go haywire with certain lighting, is that the mirrored world peeking through?"

"We need to return to New Orleans to find your answer."

"When? Immediately, or in the near future?" Lilith glanced at her chief operations man to determine a date.

Tony tapped his computer touch screen. "Our new purchase will be ready. I would suggest September nineteenth for a trip to New Orleans."

"International Talk Like a Pirate Day?"

"Chef Dean would be proud." AJ smiled as he glanced below the camera. Just as quickly, his smile disappeared.

"AJ, is something wrong?"

He looked back into the camera. "The star chart app on my computer screen shows … a total lunar eclipse on the nineteenth."

Charlotte popped her head over AJ's chair, allowing every cell to see her for the first time. For her first appearance, she was scared.

A chorus of oohs came from the Hovel's speakers.

"Manicato I'naru', meet Charlotte," Lilith said.

AJ raised his hand over the back of his chair to block Charlotte from speaking. He rushed to say, "Search the Hovel for additional clues. There is something there to aid us. Portland out."

The conference box for Portland blanked out.

Shocked by their abrupt departure, Lilith nodded for Tony to take charge of the videoconference.

Aniah crouched next to Lilith. "Why the emergency exit after Charlotte popped up?"

"I'm texting Charlotte to find out. She had her serious, no-nonsense look on her face. Something spooked her." Lilith waited a moment and lowered her phone. "No reply."

She replayed out loud what had happened just moments ago. "AJ says full moon, Charlotte shoots up, he covers her mouth, and cuts the feed."

"What's the deal with International Talk Like a Pirate Day on September nineteenth?"

Lilith placed her index finger over Aniah's lips. "Last time we were in New Orleans, we walked from the restaurant to the convent museum under a full moon and clear sky. Apparently, we'll have another full moon on this trip, one year later to the day."

"You can't have a full moon on the exact same day one year apart. Full moon cycles don't line up on the calendar."

"Excuse me, what?"

"Full moon to full moon is like twenty-eight or

twenty-nine days. I'm not an astrophysicist, so I might be off a day or so. Regardless, full moons can't occur a year to the day apart from one another."

Lilith's phone vibrated. She tapped it and angled it for Aniah to see. After reading the text message, both of them glanced over at Eboni, who winked back.

"Damn, she's good," Aniah said. "I'm gonna use her to look up some people I need to pay back."

"No, you're not. Rule number two: we don't use this facility for personal paybacks."

They had been whispering while Tony led the conference call, but he stopped speaking, which caused them to look up.

"Madam Priestess has made a rule for us to follow. Nobody may use the Manicato I'naru' Network's resources for personal use. I believe it is rule number two?"

Lilith nodded and smiled sheepishly for getting caught talking behind Tony's back.

He winked and continued with the videoconference.

Aniah whispered to Lilith, "What's rule number one?"

"Cardio."

Lilith batted her eyelashes. "Pack your bags, Wichita. We're flying back to Portland. I need to talk with the mole in The Village complex."

28 - Malady and the Scamp

Lydia pulled the spinach and cheese egg breakfast soufflés from the oven. Her crew of three baristas was late, which was atypical for her loyal wolf pack.

She lifted the soufflés out of the oversized muffin pan with her spatula, keeping an eye open for her subordinates. They didn't appear from the predawn darkness, but a familiar sight did.

Wearing black jeans and a black windbreaker vest, Lilith emerged from the darkness and entered the coffee shop.

Lydia squealed with joy. "Lilith, you're back! The girls and I have missed you over the summer. It's hard to believe you've been gone for almost three months. Can I fix your usual this morning?"

Lilith didn't answer, nor did she smile. Aniah and Elliott materialized from the dark and stood on either side of her.

Lydia read the solemnity on their faces. "Did something happen?"

Uneasy with what she had to do, Lilith slipped her hands in her vest pockets. She asked in Dutch, *"Weet je nog dat ik naar je dromen vroeg?"*

Lydia's eyes narrowed and her voice deepened. "My dreams are none of your damn business."

"We weten waarom je hier werkt."

"Bitch. Don't insult me with why you think I work here."

"I'm out. AJ gave me that much," Lilith said.

Lydia dropped her head and glared at Elliott. "Dutch too?"

Elliott didn't mince his words. "Answer Lilith. Our future, yours and mine, depends on how you answer."

"If you can't protect me, I have no incentive to comply with your demands."

Her stark reply shocked Elliott.

Lilith interceded. "We wiped out the documents Mr. Elbers used against you and handed a trove of others to the Dutch National Police. He will face a litany of criminal charges. Your parents' debts no longer exist. The bank will send an alert of their financial windfall by this evening."

Lydia listened, but couldn't believe Lilith. "You don't screw with Elbers. He can reach any corner of the world, and I don't want my parents hurt. Where is Elbers?"

Elliott flashed his phone at Lydia. "He's in handcuffs, and the rats are fleeing the sinking ship. The other guy, Daan … Shit. Dutch is diff—"

"Don't try pronouncing his name. Where is he?"

"The news says they found him under his boat?"

Lydia dropped her head. "Concrete boots."

Elliott tapped on his phone. "Ah, that explains what *betonnen laarzen* means."

"How did you learn about Elbers, Lilith?"

"I have people who can find anybody. Also, I remember you helping Holly with her grandmother's photo. Holly said the frame you built was superb. In your interview, you mentioned working as an art critic for the student newspaper. Whoever Elbers hired to build your faux digital background shouldn't have included a sample of your writing. A beautiful homage to the Dordrecht Masters—"

"Dordrecht? That's close to The Hague," Elliott said.

The hurt on Elliott's face angered Lilith.

Lydia pleaded with him. "I swear I didn't know you until Lilith introduced us in the tunnel."

"The Dordrechts Museum," Elliott was working through his visit to the museum. "Seated at the wicker tables with the blue-pebble box flooring. Your hair was tied behind your head. I suppose saying you didn't *know* me isn't a lie, but your shock in the tunnel … Your head must have exploded in seeing me with Dad."

Tears formed in Lydia's eyes. The corner of her lips drooped.

"Aw. How cute. For the second time, love at first sight. But we had the wrong location," Lilith said.

Elliott took a step forward, but stopped. Tears ran down Lydia's face.

Aniah gave Elliott a gentle push on his back. "Go. She faked her background, but not her love for you."

He stepped toward Lydia, who cried harder with each step he took toward her. They hugged, much to the delight of Aniah and Lilith, who wore the dopiest love-grins ever.

"Okay, break it up, you two. Tayen put Lydia on paid vacation. *The Black Pearl* is coming to take us up to the mansion," Lilith said.

"That's how gangsters dispose of people," Lydia said.

"We aren't criminals. If you want, you can leave. I'll have Elliott start your car to prove we didn't plant a bomb."

"What do you want from me?"

"Answers to our questions. Nothing more."

Lydia looked to Elliott.

"We freed you from Elbers and Associates. Elbers is our gift to you. You are free to walk away. But if you stick around and answer our questions, we'll see if you can keep your job as the pastry chef."

"Oh, goodie. Answers to keep my job."

Before long, the eight-seat *Black Pearl* golf cart zoomed up to AJ's back door. Lydia's missing barista crew passed them on their way back to the coffee shop. She chuckled upon entering the atrium. Her baristas had fixed breakfast in AJ's kitchen and laid out a plentiful meal on the dining room table.

Two golden retrievers bounced and barked with the unusual morning rush and the smell of food fresh out of the oven. Elliott winked at his father. "Plan A is in effect."

"Wonderful. I hope her spying for Elbers and Associates didn't cripple us too much," AJ said.

"Can you forgive me?"

AJ pointed to the chair next to him. "Elliott trusts you. We trust him, so, by the distributive property … Sorry. I've been working with our math teacher on Broken Cove Education's algebra lessons."

She plopped in the seat. "I am so sorry. I was forced to plant bugs throughout the house, the clubhouse, and The Village complex."

"What did Elbers have on you to blackmail you into doing his dirty work?" AJ asked.

"I thought you knew?"

"We're giving you the opportunity to explain your underage lingerie photos. That way we don't make any unfair assumptions as to how you got here."

Lydia leaned back in her chair and took the time to figure out how to tell her story.

"Mom secretaried for the executive next to Elbers's office. He liked the photo of me on her desk. Through their conversations, he convinced her it was time to start building my portfolio. I was photogenic and modeling could be lucrative.

"One day, Mom couldn't leave the office for a photoshoot Elbers set up for me. He assured her he would escort me and make sure I was taken care of. All she had to do was sign the contract for the shoot. He took care of it alright.

"I went to the shoot, which was supposed to be chin down shots only. I was a minor in lingerie, but he lied to me and said if my face was in the photos, he wouldn't allow it. Body shots however, who could prove who the photos were of? The shoot was good money and my face was out of it."

"Elbers kept the photos, which showed your face, and I'm guessing the contract was something else," Charlotte said.

"He forged her signature on a bogus contract, implicating her on dereliction of protecting a minor from exploitation. Or something to that effect. With that, he blackmailed both of us into doing projects for him."

"What type of projects?" AJ asked.

"Can I ask a question before answering your question?"

"Sure."

"How did you fine those photos?"

Lilith leaned forward against the table. "I have a group of people who can research just about anything you can imagine. More on how they found the photos in a minute."

"Scott found them?"

Lilith chuckled. "He's definitely my people, but no, I have others. Please, continue with the projects you were forced into doing."

Lydia leaned against the table and rested her arms on top of it. "I was forced to join a crew who specialized in stealing artwork. My job was to distract and to watch for trouble. Flirting with guards morphed into pickpocketing and eventually lock picking. I'm talented with locks now.

"But Mom was the real reason for Elbers's motives. She had framed a picture for a coworker and it impressed him when he saw it. He set her up in a tiny studio in the seedy part of town and her building frames after work."

AJ and Lilith dipped their heads while Tayen shoved away from the table.

"What is going on?" Lydia asked. "What did I say to get this reaction from you?"

"Have you heard of the Péchettes and Benningtons?" AJ asked.

"No. But I learned the identity of Code Purple's first client. Why Melody Sharpe changed her name to Aniah Clemons is a bit of a mystery, though."

"You knew who I was when I arrived?" Aniah asked.

"I saw your performance at the Grand Kadooment festival on YouTube. I thought you were spectacular."

Aniah looked at AJ. "Alas! The person who viewed the video for my dancing, not for the costume I wore."

AJ dipped his head and peered over his glasses.

"I had a minute-long solo in a sling bikini. Over fifty million views of my ass, and nobody but Lydia was interested in my dancing."

"It takes talent to dance in a sling bikini without exposing yourself more than you did," Lydia added.

Aniah and Lilith nodded in unison.

"Word in the dance community was you were desperate to escape your dad," Lydia said. "When you arrived under the name Aniah Clemons, I struggled with why you were here. You secluded yourself. A woman who dances in a sling bikini isn't someone who is afraid of social interactions. Something was up."

Shazoo pushed and clawed his way into Lilith's lap. She obeyed his wishes and lifted her hands. He jumped from Lilith's lap and ran across the table to Lydia. "Hey there, little buddy." She scratched under his chin.

His purring reverberated across the table to AJ. "Ah. I get it. His majesty didn't hear the bugs. He caught her scent and scratched whatever she touched. She's his catnip."

"Shazoo found all the bugs I planted?"

"Found, scratched out for the dogs, and for me to poop-scoop up. Oh, that reminds me—"

"Already done," Charlotte said. "Fifty pounds of dog shit and bugs shipped to Ernesto."

Aniah slapped the table, shaking her head. "I gotta be there when they open that."

"How did you get past my security?" AJ asked.

"Who doesn't have the key code to your garage door?" Lydia answered.

Tayen grabbed her phone. "Shut up, AJ. I'm on it."

"What else about the framing studio you mother had?" Lilith asked.

"Mom framed and taught me the craft. Elbers taught us packaging and shipping. If my first career choices fail, dealing in art isn't out of the question. Especially since I was smart enough to record Elbers's contact list."

"Elbers's contact list?" Tayen leaned forward. Her eyes sparkled with hope. "His list could weave into my European network, filling in the gaps. Tell us more."

Lydia put Shazoo on the floor. "Art dealers want their pieces hidden during transport. So a technique called double canvassing was employed. The master painting was framed under a lesser-known work.

"One night, Elbers had two major pieces in the studio and was waiting for us. He also brought two wonderful landscapes by an unknown artist. Mom was so nervous. The six gunmen and the creep with the knife fixation didn't help."

"Not to rush you, but by chance where those two paintings *Chez Tortoni* and Raphael's self-portrait?" Tayen asked.

Lydia's face turned white. Flustered, she looked to Elliott for help.

"Did you see Manet's *Chez Tortoni* and Raphael's *Portrait of a Young Man*?" he asked.

Lydia pushed her chair back away from the table. "Those weren't forgeries? The creep insisted—"

"Calm down, Lydia. Slow down and think it through," Elliott said as he knelt beside her.

"I double canvassed the Manet behind an unknown artist's landscape painting of an ocean shore."

"*Ocean Shore* was painted by either Tempest or Jade Péchette in the early eighteenth century," Lilith said.

Lydia struggled to speak. "Who, how ... I have questions. What I can say is I double canvassed the Manet under *Ocean Shore* with the knife creep 'helping' me. Mom did the Raphael, but I don't remember the top painting."

"The creep with the knife, he told you his constant touching of your body was incidental to his helping you." Everybody turned to Aniah. "Did he have gray eyes?"

"Elbers said his name once, and the guy impaled Elbers's hand to a crate with that knife. His name was Nico."

Lilith pushed away from the table. "Ernesto had the stolen artwork. He had it double framed and somebody stole it from him while it was in transit to the Caribbean. Who in the hell is stealing pieces of art and handing them to us?"

"You have a Manet and a Raphael?" Lydia asked.

"Yeah. In the basement."

"You have a basement?"

Lilith placed her hands on her hips. "Lydia's cleared. Onto the next business of the day. Tomorrow we will return to the map room. Tayen, help me out, please."

"Alright," Tayen said. "The original five go to New Orleans. Newbies are sidelined. Experience counts on this trip, and we have no time to dawdle. Scott and AJ have designed cameras to capture light signatures for later analysis. As per Scott's observation on the first trip, we will find everything we need in those crates."

"You're stealing more art?" Lydia asked.

"We're after the *Flor de la Mar* treasure," AJ said.

"You're going deep-sea fishing in New Orleans?"

AJ's glasses slipped to the edge of his nose. "Go ahead, Lydia. You've got our attention."

"The Elbers family company insured the ill-fated voyage of the *Flor de la Mar*. You'll need deep-sea salvage equipment and UN resolutions to rescue it from the bottom of the Straits of Malacca."

Scott chimed in. "Ah, the mystery frequency on the bugs. It belonged to an insurance company."

"What are you folks saying?" Lydia's voice rose so high it caused the dogs to bark. "The *Flor de la Mar* sunk and is unrecoverable. Portugal, Indonesia, and Malaysia will fight to the tooth to secure that treasure. Are you saying somebody salvaged the greatest treasure lost at sea?"

"Yes," Elliott said.

"That can't be. It's a myth."

Lilith sat next to Lydia. "What myth?"

"There is a conspiracy theory which had Albuquerque sailing into harm's way to sink an aging *Flor de la Mar*, while other ships under his command carried the genuine treasure. He let people believe the treasure was lost. In essence, he double canvassed an entire treasure. I can't believe you're suggesting the myth is real."

Lilith turned to AJ. "How sure are you that *DARE FROM ALL* equates to the *Flor de la Mar*?"

"Give me another word scramble that matches."

"Where was this treasure for two hundred years?" Charlotte asked. "From the sinking of the *Flor de la Mar* in 1511, to when Jade took possession of it around 1712."

Lydia objected, "You're chasing a myth."

Elliott cupped his hands over Lydia's. "Dad, Lilith, Tayen, Charlotte, and Scott are under surveillance because people believe they have access to this treasure. Their lives are in danger, regardless of the myth's veracity."

"Scott, are we clear?" AJ asked.

"Our peeping Toms are enjoying Shazoo's nap from yesterday, not this meeting."

Charlotte placed her phone on the table. "Hey. We are in possession of a Manet and a Raphael. We can't return the

Manet because of our imprint, and the Raphael's discovery would draw the world to us."

"So, how do you get out of it?" Lydia asked.

"We continue our search and apply leverage against our antagonists with what we discover," Tayen said. "On our map room visit, we need recordings to figure out Jade's wavelength frequencies. We scavenge the crates and turn the wheel for the other half of the map room. Lilith, did you find anything in the Hovel storage?"

Lilith grabbed her bag and pulled out a shot-glass-sized bottle. She tossed it to AJ.

He caught it and examined it. "The glass-like substance looks to be the same material which is covering the last nine boxes from the Marie Daly Chest."

"Tony found that tiny bottle and a half-firkin next to it."

Charlotte fell face down on the table, laughing hysterically. "You thought he said flerken. Let me guess: you thought there was half a cat in it."

"I hate her," Lilith mumbled.

AJ explained: "A firkin holds nine gallons. Half-firkin is four and a half gallons or twenty liters. It's pronounced 'firkin' not 'flerken.' And what does a cat have to do with a half-firkin?"

Tayen reigned in the chaos. "Charlotte, stop laughing. AJ, watch some movies. Lilith, what was in the half-flerken?"

"Firkin," AJ corrected.

Lilith had finished sticking her tongue out at Charlotte. "I don't know. We tried cutting it with a knife, a saw, a diamond at the jewelry store, a—"

"A jeweler let you use a diamond?" Tayen asked.

"Of course not," Aniah said. "I distracted the jewelers

by tripping over my feet and crashing into the display case. Tony and Lilith scrambled to scratch the bottle with a three-karat diamond."

"We got back to the Hovel and tried smashing it open," Lilith said.

"*You* tried smashing it open. Don't say we," Aniah corrected.

Lilith's eyes clouded over as she remembered her efforts to open the bottle. "After my sledgehammer attempt, we tried an acetylene torch, then the microwave. Nothing fazed it, and we had to replace the microwave."

"Not even the thirty-ought-six dented it," Aniah added. "The rifle wasn't a serious attempt to break it open."

AJ and Charlotte faced one another. AJ said, "Cutting, pressure, temperature, and vibration. Only one left."

Charlotte stuck her hand in the water pitcher, which was filled with lemon slices. She snapped her wrist about, removing the excess water from the lemon.

"Why is she flipping water on the floor?" Lilith asked.

Charlotte rubbed the slice over the small bottle. In seconds, a candle wax like substance formed and rolled down the side of the bottle to the table.

AJ clapped. "Acid works. Call Dale and tell them the good news."

Lilith bent over the table to inspect Charlotte's work.

Tayen pushed her chair back and stood. "I can't wait to fly in our new plane."

Elliott snapped around to his father. "You bought a plane?"

AJ deflected his son's question by tilting his head at Lilith.

"As the head of the Manicato I'naru' Network, I

figured we needed a jet," Lilith said. "Mr. Elbers might have trouble hiring an attorney since ELF emptied his bank accounts. We ordered the jet last month, and our maiden flight flew here last night."

AJ turned back to Elliott. "I didn't buy a jet, but I sure the hell am sucking up to the one who did."

***

The night's music pulsed through the French Quarter; Bourbon Street was alive.

Five dark-clothed persons scampered away from the cacophony and headed into the growing shadows. Each carried cumbersome backpacks, except AJ. He struggled in pulling a cumbersome luggage cart, which teetered on the edge of tumbling at each street corner.

Charlotte pushed Scott in the back as they entered the museum gate. "Why am I going first?" Scott asked.

"We went first last time."

"You want me on point, so if we're attacked, I'm the first man down."

"Stop it," Tayen ordered, "and put on the goggles and masks. We're not getting dusted under the gate again."

Dressed and protected, they hurried under the sheltered gate. Charlotte turned Scott around to check him for any powdery substance.

Lilith glanced up at the dim full moon as she removed her garb.

Tayen checked and cleared them one by one and permitted them to proceed to the side door of the museum. When they entered, they were found a well-lighted museum hallway, not the Halloween semi-trailer gag from their first

473

visit. Down the hallway was an opening in the floor. Its circular floor covering sat off to the side.

AJ wheeled the luggage cart next to the hole, where a piece of plywood was held in place with two five-gallon water coolers. Father Amare had attached a small winch to the plywood. AJ pulled a half-firkin barrel from the luggage cart and hooked the winch rope to the barrel and lowered it into the hole.

At the bottom of the turret stairwell, Scott and Charlotte unhooked the barrel and rolled it into the map room, where Father Amare joined them.

Charlotte bent over, resting her hands on her knees. "Every damn time we're down here, I want to throw up."

"You're not the only one." Lilith had bent over like Charlotte. "I feel sick too, and look at poor Scott."

Scott bobbed his head while leaning against the wall. "It hits you all at once and then fades away. But for a split-second, you feel you're going to die."

Tayen rose from resting her hands on her knees. "Let's not waste time. Suck it up."

AJ entered last as he struggled to catch his breath.

Father Amare stretched out his hand. "At last. We can greet each other as friends."

"We must have been hellions."

Amare laughed. "Good trouble, not hellions."

Scott connected a multi-plug outlet to an extension cord.

"Why did you ask for it in your text?" Father Amare asked as he walked toward the turret stairwell.

"If our batteries failed, I wanted a backup. Where are you headed?"

"Upstairs to turn off the lights and to ensure you

weren't followed. I'll return momentarily."

"Empty the crates," Tayen ordered as Father Amare disappeared. "When this show unfolds, I want to see what tools are available. Scott, what's wrong?"

"I have no signal. We must be too deep underground." He reached into his bag and pulled out a long cord, which had a modem at the end. "This wasn't silly to pack. Charlotte, run this up the stairs."

She returned in a flash to find Lilith texting on her phone.

"The Hovel is receiving. We have satellite capabilities," Lilith said.

Father Amare entered. "My. Look at the expensive video equipment. What is it for?"

Scott typed on his laptop. "I have two high-speed cameras to record our experience, and a special optics camera to analyze wavelength frequencies. If our time is cut short, we have recordings to study later."

Charlotte searched the room after pulling out a hand crank. "What do I stick this into?"

AJ searched with her. "Patience. As we proceed, its place will reveal itself."

Tayen directed the lighting of the previous year's visit. AJ pointed above the candles where the individual handles of a ship's wheel were visible.

After the previous year's results were confirmed, Lilith asked, "What now? Five candles, five globes, and a map with ship courses."

"Take a closer look at the candles," AJ said.

Lilith climbed on top of a crate and inspected the pedestal of the blue candle. "There are little carved channels for melted wax. Wait, no, the channels are outside the globe."

She tapped it with her finger. "Hot damn, the globes are covered in the glassy stuff. Time for the citric acid."

Tayen pulled out a glass jar from her backpack. "Gloves on. This isn't a strong acid, but let's not chance chemical burns."

Lilith used a pipette to drop the acid mixture on the globe. Beads of liquid rolled down the globe and into the channels. She reported the flow as she watched. "The stuff is flowing into a reservoir on the backside of the wall ornament."

"Genius," AJ said. "When we rotate the outcropping upside down, the liquid pours back over the globe, returning it to its original state."

Tayen offered a pipette to AJ. "Nah. If you don't mind, I'll keep an eye on the wall."

"Scott is on video, the three women are doing manual labor, and you're on the wall. Not exactly the Night's Watch, is it?"

"Nope, Maester Tayen, it isn't. But the way things have gone, I won't be surprised if *The Night Watch* appears."

Lilith and Charlotte stopped and stared at AJ.

"Figures. The one TV show I watched, and my pop culture reference flies over their heads. Jon Snow, you know nothing."

"Ooh! I get it. I call dibs on the Rembrandt if it appears," Charlotte said.

Lilith rolled her eyes. "I'll Google it later."

With the last of the globes cleared of its protective coating, they waited. When nothing changed, Lilith asked, "Why is everything the same?"

Scott pointed to his laptop. "It's not. Camera one is reading a decrease in lighting by four percent, and it is still dropping."

Several minutes passed. The light faded and the map wall changed. Three rows of gold marquees materialized over an ethereal black background. The marquees stretched from side to side, spanning the whole map wall. A woman's bare arms rest on top of the marquees. Her chin rested on her folded hands, but the wall obscured everything above her lower lip.

Lettering inside the marquees faded into view. Gold, ruby, sapphire, diamond, amethyst, and emerald lettering listed the items.

Label tabs on the top of the marquees appeared last. Charlotte read one out loud. "Chests 176-210: Gold 1900 one ounce. Diamonds, sapphires, rubies, emeralds, opals, amethysts, and spinels: eight towers each."

Lilith and Charlotte faced at one another in disbelief.

AJ dashed their hopes to the ground. "A tower is about twelve ounces in old English measurements. Eight towers is roughly five pounds."

Lilith exhaled. "Mother of God. I thought towers were going to be like your turret stairwells."

Scott said, "Twenty-seven marquees listing the same items. This is the manifest for the *Flor de la Mar*."

"I'd like to say yes, and I believe this is, but nothing here says *Flor de la Mar*," AJ said.

"Something's not right." Lilith stepped toward the wall. "The marquee design, the freehand lettering, and the colors are gorgeous in every aspect. But the centering from top to bottom?"

Tayen stepped next to her. "Everything thus far has had perfect proportions. Side to side from the walls ... Precise and equal spacing. Inside the marquees, the lettering is centered and evenly spaced. But from top to bottom, Lilith's right, something's off."

Charlotte picked up a hammer and chisel. "Things are off because of the curved ceiling. But why add a decorative feature here? Help me up, so I can knock it out of our way."

Father Amare helped Charlotte on top of the crate. She faced the center of the map wall and tapped the chisel into the plaster. With a solid whack, small pieces of the plaster ceiling fell to the floor. An ominous and the all-too familiar sound of a wall splitting open sent Charlotte into a balled-up crouch. The others stood, unaffected by her antics.

"What's the matter, darling? Is something invisible attacking you?" Lilith asked.

"It hasn't happened yet, but just wait."

No sooner had she spoken than the entire left side of the curved ceiling fell to the floor.

Scott closed his laptop and threw his backpack on top to protect it from the dust.

Charlotte placed her chisel to the right of her previous hit.

"Hold on, Charlotte," Tayen yelled as she choked on the dust. "Let Father Amare get out of the way."

Father Amare stepped back and headed toward the stairwell. "I'm going for a fan to suck the dust out."

Charlotte whacked away, and as before, the curved ceiling fell.

"There's so much dust we can't see," Lilith said.

Tayen responded, "Stand still. I don't want anybody tripping and falling. This will settle before long."

"Oh, no."

"What is it, Charlotte?" Tayen asked.

"This can't be. This simply can't be."

"It figures," Lilith said. "She's closest to the wall and gets to see—"

Several minutes later, Father Amare returned. Charlotte had climbed down from the crate and sat in the plaster debris on the floor. Scott sat motionless with his laptop before him. He stared at the wall without saying a word. Tayen crouched next to a crate, refusing to face the wall. AJ banged his head with the palm of his hand.

Puzzled by their strange behavior, Father Amare said, "The fan upstairs will pull the dust out."

With no one responding to him, he looked up at the woman on the wall.

Lilith faced away from the wall and was thumbing her amulet. "Tell me we were dusted. Tell me this is a dream. Tell me anything other than what is on that wall."

Amare wobbled his head as he stared at the image. "You're not dreaming, and no one dusted you."

She raised her arm and handed him her phone.

"Aniah took my picture two days ago. I had my hair tied back with a thin white headband scarf, and I wore opal hoop earrings."

Father Amare swung his head around to the wall.

"The scarf draped on my left shoulder and the opal hoop earrings are exact matches. The creases in the scarf and the flecks in the opals … Exact matches."

He looked at the phone and then at Lilith's chest.

"Yeah, my amulet." Lilith pivoted around and faced the map wall. The moment she stopped, the amulet's eyes—both on the wall painting and on Lilith's necklace itself—began glowing.

29 - Discovery and Disaster

Scott cut the sound feed to the Hovel.

"Smart. They don't need to hear this," AJ said. "They might wonder why the amulet on the wall is glowing, but I don't think they saw Lilith's amulet."

"So," Lilith struggled to speak, "what do I do?"

"Who else has your photo?" Tayen asked.

"Aniah took the picture on my phone and sent it to herself. Nobody else."

Tayen turned to AJ for guidance, but he threw up his hands in disgust. She took a moment to plot out her plan. "Scott, restore the audio. The rest of us will avoid discussing the glowing eyes. Nobody inside Manicato I'naru' knows about this."

"Hey, I've got two holes here in the center next to the wall." Charlotte raised her arm to point at the spot.

Father Amare joined her.

She climbed back on top of the crate and studied both holes. "I have a barbed nozzle on one, and a Robertson square head … Ah, mystery solved. The hand crank goes in hole number two."

"A rubber hose will fit on the barbed nozzle," AJ said.

"I've got your hoses over here. But they're attached to this odd contraption." Tayen held up a round, wooden, cake-shaped container. The two rubber hoses dangled from either side.

"That's a pump," Charlotte said. "We pump the acid mixture out of the half-firkin into the ceiling."

Tayen marched the pump over, and Father Amare lifted the half-firkin onto the crate next to Charlotte's foot. Charlotte assembled the pieces and stood ready, waiting for permission to crank the pump.

Lilith bent next to the wall while Charlotte worked. She traced her fingers over a narrow crevice between the wall and floor. "Here's a channel, just like on the outcroppings." Without warning, she placed her hand on the map wall.

Father Amare gasped.

"Don't worry, Father. The wall is protected with the same glass-like stuff. The oil from my hand won't harm the wall. Pump away, Charlotte."

Charlotte inserted the hand crank into the pump and began turning it. After a couple of minutes, sizzling and popping sounds emanated from above. Tiny puffs of smoke shot down from the ceiling and onto the map wall.

"I'm guessing the acid is unplugging the holes," AJ said.

The acid misted from the tiny ceiling holes, forming the familiar beads which ran down the wall and into the channel on the floor. To their horror, the marquees faded away, removing all traces of the treasure manifest.

Charlotte stopped cranking.

"The artwork may be gone, but not to worry. I have it recorded," Scott said.

Before long, lettering appeared on the black background. No one spoke as they read the wall.

"This is a log of the ships they raided," AJ said. "The conquering ships were the *Asema II,* under the command of Captain Morena Calveiro, and the *Royal Essence*, under the command of Captain Jade Péchette."

"The sixth listing down, on the far left, says Captain Andrews - *Royal Essence*. They had three captains for two ships?" Scott asked.

"The early dates are mostly in Jade's name, and the latter dates are Andrews's. As their operation matured, Jade planned the attacks and let Calveiro and Andrews do the raids?" Tayen proposed.

AJ wrung his hands together but didn't speak.

Lilith stepped in front of him. "How do two families, mine and Lydia's, get reunited three hundred years later?"

"We'll have to wait and see. For now, if Scott has this recorded, we should move on to the next phase."

"Which is?"

Charlotte jumped up on the crate and jammed the hand crank in the hole.

"Go for it. I don't have a better idea," AJ said.

Charlotte twisted and grunted, but the crank wasn't turning. Father Amare joined her on the crate and assisted. The hand crank jolted, and the slats of the map wall exploded open.

Father Amare caught his balance and said, "It had

been sealed shut for three centuries. It shouldn't have surprised us that it'd explode open."

They continued turning the crank until the backside of the slats were facing them. A new side of the map wall presented itself. Vertical burnt-umber-colored wood slats extended from ceiling to floor and the width of the room. They darkened with each passing moment, turning into the magical pure black.

They waited, but nothing else happened.

AJ shrugged. "These candles aren't for this wall."

Tayen clapped for joy when she spotted five new candles on tiny ledges to the far left. On the far right, two globes sat on similar ledges. "We have more lighting to do. Look on top of the outcroppings and match the wax colors. I remember there were two sets of waxes."

Lilith climbed onto a crate to switch out the candles. In doing so, she found a name on the wall above the outcropping.

"I have a name here." She leaned back to see the next outcropping. "Edwina is on this one. Saleem is on that one."

Tayen twisted around to the last outcropping. "Mary Ann is on the end, and Cheja is next to it."

"Tempest." AJ held his hand up to the center outcropping.

Lilith tripped as she made her way over. She righted herself and rushed beside him. "Maybe it's me, but I have a chill running down my spine."

"Turn the wheel, from daughter to mother."

AJ spoke, but he seemed distant to Lilith.

"If the woman in the market told you the truth, the new candles will turn the wheel. Jade's name will replace Tempest's."

"Then switch out the candles, and see if you are right," Tayen said.

They switched out the candles and lit them as they went.

Charlotte said, "I wish these didn't take so long to turn. I'm tired of waiting."

No sooner had she spoken than seven scalloped gold gallery frame marquees appeared in a flash.

"Okay, wish granted," Scott said.

The marquees had gold nameplates on their top center. The black-colored, cursive, French-style lettering popped out from the nameplates. A simplistic naming convention identified them as 'Master Chests,' numbered one through seven. Inside the marquees' borders were lists of what each chest contained. The gem type determined the letter coloring, which sat on the field of black inside the marquee.

Awed by the lettering's beauty, Lilith gushed, "I'd die to have handwriting like that. And those colors. The red for the rubies is so brilliant, glowing green for emeralds, the electrifying rose violet for the amethysts."

"The top center, Master Chest One. That's a load of gems. I bet those are the crème de la crème of the whole treasure," Charlotte said.

Lilith asked about the first item listed. "What are Princess Coins?"

"The night we escaped Ernesto's mountaintop mansion," Charlotte said. "In the helicopter, I showed you a humongous gold coin with your face printed on it—"

"—and the sapphire eyes. You think that is a Princess Coin?"

"Tayen, did you have the coin appraised?" AJ asked.

"The eight-ounce 18-karat gold coin with two 2-karat sapphires?"

Tayen's combative tone had Lilith ducking her head for what was coming.

"You wanted me to walk into a jewelry store with an artifact that screams 'stolen maritime treasure', and ask for its appraisal? A professional jeweler wouldn't hesitate to hit their silent alarm after I put this on the counter. I'm not spending twenty years in prison for a piracy I didn't commit."

AJ dismissed her sarcasm. "Yet you weighed it and determined how many karats the sapphires were?"

"I did a little research."

"What did your 'little research' reveal?"

Lilith cringed. *Bad move, AJ. She's gonna explode.*

"I'd estimate the raw materials are worth between thirty thousand and fifty thousand dollars per coin—"

Lilith snapped out of her cringe, not only because Tayen didn't explode, but because the value of the coins shocked her.

"—Multiply that by one hundred for the aesthetic and historical context. But without an official appraisal, my work is a best guess estimate."

Fast to calculate Tayen's appraisal, Charlotte blurted out, "Three to five million per coin. Multiply by—"

"Two billion dollars for the lot," AJ finished Charlotte's math. "Damn, that shipment was underinsured."

Tayen read out loud the other contents in the marquee. "Thirty towers each of diamonds, sapphires, rubies, emeralds, opals, amethysts, and spinels."

"One hundred- and fifty-pounds total."

"Thank you, Charlotte. I wasn't about to calculate that."

Scott interrupted. "The second to the last item? What's a seven-hundred-pound Cove Sample?"

"We'll find out when we open it. But look at the last item," AJ said.

Charlotte clapped her hands together. "Map. There's the map to the *Flor de la Mar* treasure."

"No," AJ corrected, "it simply says 'Map.' I would hope it leads to the *Flor de la Mar* treasure, but it just says 'Map.'"

Tayen pointed. "Everybody, read the list on Master Chest Two. Manufacturing manuals, plant samples, and small hand tools aren't the most exciting items. But how about compounds 106, 119-123, along with elements 9, 16, and 21?"

Lilith counted on her fingers. "That's the nine boxes from the Marie Daly Chest."

"Manufacturing manuals, plant samples, and a genius chemist. We're chasing after Walter White," AJ lamented.

"We have a problem," Scott said. "The contents of Master Chests two and four are mixed together. We have half of each of them in our Marie Daly chest."

"I suggest we move on and gather as much as we can. To your outcroppings, folks," Tayen ordered.

Scott remained with his laptop, letting Father Amare and AJ work the outcroppings with the ladies. With the globes over the new candles, the map room reverted to normal lighting.

"Let's use the two new globes; work them from the outside in," AJ said.

Scott and Lilith lowered the globes on the two outside candles. Darkness overtook the room in an instant. The map wall's luminescence brightened with new map features.

Lilith focused her attention above the outcroppings. "We have new names. Mary Ann and Edwina switched positions. Hayati,—ooh, what a pretty name—and Rija on either side of the center outcropping."

"Jade." AJ said. "Jade's name replaces her daughter's at the center outcropping. And there she be; the king spoke, right above the candle."

Tayen stepped closer to the center outcropping. "It has an eyelet. That's the way she marked the king spoke. Is this *Midnight's Royal Eye*?"

Charlotte sat on a crate. "Lilith's name means blessings which come from the midnight. Her eyes are royal colored, which is a shade of blue. And now we have a ship called the *Royal Essence* listed on the wall. It's too much of a coincidence for me to separate my girl from this."

"Should I mention the Essence Festival is held here in New Orleans each summer?" Scott asked.

AJ's pensive staring at the outcropping didn't escape Lilith. "What's on your mind?"

He spun around and faced the map wall. "I think whatever *Midnight's Royal Eye* means, it holds the key on where to find the *Royal Essence*, Jade's pirate ship, and the final resting place of the *Flor de la Mar* treasure."

A hush came across the room. Nobody commented on the new map features as AJ's words sunk in.

Light browns formed the land masses, while the faintest of blues filled in the seas, lakes, and rivers. On the far right, a rope tied in a figure eight glowed a crimson red in the middle of the Atlantic Ocean.

"Joy. One of us is headed to Seville." AJ explained before anybody asked. "A rope tied in a figure eight is the symbol for Seville, Spain. From the ship's course map, we had up earlier, one of our two ships left the Caribbean in 1724. It went to Seville."

"Ah, folks," Scott said, "we messed up. While you were working the outcroppings, I checked the previous wall, and we missed a message."

AJ peered over Scott's shoulder and onto the laptop. "Scott caught our mistake. We missed 'Turn the Wheel, Mary Ann to Edwina' at the bottom. I think it faded in so slow we missed it."

Tayen thoroughly scanned the map wall. "I'm not seeing anything out of the ordinary. However, the coastline seems wonky."

"Venezuela's coastline is way off," AJ said.

"Whatever." Lilith wasn't in the mood for a geography puzzle. She took the globe off and jumped to the next crate. After she lowered a globe over the indigo candle, two lifelike images faded into view: a lattice of small hexagons on the left, and a group portrait on the right.

A short Black woman stood in the center. Her blue eyes leapt from the wall. It was Jade Péchette. Behind her and to the left towered Captain Morena Calveiro. Her long, thick brown hair matched Lydia's, and their faces were identical. Though not as prominent as Jade's eyes, Captain Morena's green eyes were noticeable. To the right of Jade stood a man in a blue jacket. He matched Captain Morena's height, and his red hair was cut short and well-kept.

Lilith clapped her hands. "Jade looks so much like me, but Captain Morena … damn. She's a dead ringer for Lydia. AJ—" She stopped when she saw AJ and Tayen sharing concerned looks. "What's wrong?"

Tayen exhaled. "The amazing image and photo quality of this group painting doesn't strike you as odd?"

"That's a painting?" Lilith bent forward for a closer inspection. "How can somebody paint something that looks like a photograph?"

"If Ernesto gets a glimpse of this, he won't believe this is a painting from the early eighteenth century. He'll believe it is you and Lydia," AJ said.

"And they will come for you both," Tayen added. "Scott, can Ernesto crack into your transmission to the Hovel?"

"Any transmission can be intercepted. The longer we transmit, the better their chances of gaining access. I'll assign an encryption code for the laptop when we are done."

"Who's the guy on the right? Captain James Andrews or Bill Bennington?" Charlotte asked. "He looks young, and that blue jacket is naval. I say it's Andrews."

Father Amare turned their attention to the left side of the wall. "Look at the image. It seems to be alive."

The size of a full-length mirror, a latticework of small, connected hexagons shimmered on the wall. The edges of the hexagons shone a bright gold while translucent blues, reds, and greens comprised the inside of the hexagons.

"Are the colors in the center floating, or am I losing it?" Charlotte asked.

"The whole lattice work is moving," Father Amare said. "The gold edges are connecting where the slats meet."

"Connecting across a microscopic gap? How the hell would that—"

A thunderous explosion from the stairwell cut Charlotte off. Shocked by the deafening blast, they looked to Father Amare. "Head up the other turret. I'll handle this one." He ran through the door and disappeared.

Scott shoved the laptop in his backpack. Charlotte

grabbed candles and stuffed them into hers. Tayen smashed the globes on the floor to render them useless. AJ leaned toward the door Father Amare had exited.

Lilith ran to him and clamped onto his arm. "Leave him. He would've asked if he needed us."

He pulled his arm to free himself, but couldn't escape her grasp.

She begged, "Please, AJ, don't go after him. I need you with me."

AJ swung his free hand around and grabbed her wrist. Lilith saw the conflict in him: chase after Father Amare, or follow her. When he glanced at the spot Father Amare rushed to, she pleaded with him, "Please don't."

The sorrow in her voice forced him to look at her.

She saw she could use his compassion for her safety to keep him with her rather than chasing after Father Amare. She left nothing to chance and tugged on his arm with all her might. He resisted, but she persisted in baby-stepping him to the turret stairwell, where he gave up and rushed behind her.

Once they entered the turret stairwell, another explosion blasted a wall of dust and dirt down on them from above. An eerie grating sound vibrated through their bones. AJ and Lilith knelt, not knowing if what was happening would decapitate them. The horrific ringing from steel snapping in half made Lilith jump against AJ.

"Hurry up here," Tayen shouted.

They climbed the stairs and stepped onto a platform.

"What is this? We're not halfway up," AJ said.

"Our up-exit is gone, sealed shut by an enormous stone slab grinding through the stone turret walls. That snapping sound was the spiral staircase being destroyed," Scott said.

"Over here," Charlotte yelled.

They stepped toward Charlotte's voice and found her standing in a dark, round opening in the wall. Once they were with her, she led the way into the tunnel. AJ stepped in last. As he did, a stone slab rolled across the opening, shutting off the tunnel from the turret stairwell.

AJ turned to find a vertical stone slab moving to close the opening. "This is an emergency escape tunnel. The stone slab cut off the turret, and exploding this wall exposed our way out."

Scott shone his phone light at the walls. "Is it possible the stone slabs were to cut off intruders from coming down either of the two turret stairwells?"

"I think so. But did the intruders get past the other turret's slab before it sealed off the map room?"

Lilith sensed AJ's thoughts were elsewhere. She had to say something comforting. "Father Amare saved us, again."

"What's a priest for if he isn't saving you?" AJ chuckled.

Tayen bent over and threw up.

Charlotte turned her head away. "Oh, god. I won't, I won't, I won't throw up."

AJ lifted his foot. "This is a cobblestone tunnel. A favorite building style for the prohibition era. Could this be an original entrance besides the turrets?"

"Who cares?" Tayen straightened up. "We should hustle down the tunnel, unless you want to stay here and die."

They did as Tayen suggested. Several yards down, they left the cobblestone tunnel and entered a wood-framed hallway. Dust floated in the air, while chunks of plaster, wallboard, and splintered wood littered the floor.

"This office wall was blown out too. Was this a secret room for prohibition?" Charlotte asked.

Tayen opened the office door, which led into a long hallway. "Scott, could you run point?"

"Sure, why not?"

Charlotte stood next to him. "I'm with you buddy."

Together, they led the way through the dust and cobwebs.

Minutes later, the tunnel ended, and an old wooden ladder extended upward. They made the long climb up to a trapdoor. Scott pushed it open and raised his head to see they were entering an old, dank storage room. Not seeing any threats, he was the first to exit from the ladder. They hurried through the trapdoor and huddled together.

Tayen whispered, "Basements? In New Orleans?"

Before AJ could respond, the basement door opened, and two sets of footsteps pounded down the thick, rustic wooden stairs. With nowhere to hide, they readied themselves for a fight.

A young couple ran from the stairs and called out for Lilith. She stepped forward, wary of their intent.

A young lady with long, tight braids rushed to them. "You must be Lilith. We're friends of Father Amare and members of the Manicato I'naru' Network. Welcome to the New Orleans cell."

"Thank you? Care to explain where we are?"

"We're below a bar on the east end of the French Quarter. It's been kept a secret for decades."

"Okay. We're hidden. What's your name, honey?"

"I'm Candace, ma'am."

"Did you just call me, ma'am? Don't do that. We've got to be the same age."

Candace pointed behind her. "This is my boyfriend, Michael."

A tall, dark man stepped behind Candace and out of the shadows. Tayen and Charlotte swooned. Michael was wall-to-wall with muscles, and he towered over his girlfriend. A disarming smile and sparkling eyes had them spellbound.

"What were those explosions?" Lilith asked.

"I'm sorry, ma'am?"

"The explosions were underground; she didn't hear them," AJ said.

Candace looked at the trapdoor. "We need to escort you to safety. Father Amare texted you were in the basement, but he didn't mention explosions. Stay here. I'm calling my father to drive you away in his cab." She pulled out her phone as she and Michael raced upstairs.

AJ kept looking back toward the map room.

"Father Amare is fine. If he planned for our escape, he planned for his," Lilith said.

"Hope you're right. But how did they find us?"

"Ernesto has spent years looking for the map room. Eventually, he'd stumble across it," Tayen said. "And tonight's full moon won't be doing us any favors."

Lilith jabbed her index finger into AJ's chest. "We've been so busy, I forgot to ask about the curt cutoff on the conference call. Why did Charlotte flip out about the full moon, and how in the hell is there one tonight?"

AJ glanced at Charlotte. "Didn't you tell her?"

"No, she didn't." Lilith pushed her finger on AJ's chin to turn his face back to her. "You tell me."

He lowered his head. "Our Adela Frontera newspapers. One alerted Tayen to the chest in Tampa. Another gave us the transom window in the Dominican

Republic. Our invite to Barbados … All of them happened on full moons. Every month for the last year, the full moon has occurred almost a day later than it is supposed … "

Charlotte finished for AJ. "Somebody has been screwing with the moon's orbit. What has him concerned is the lunar eclipse, which is taking place above our heads as we speak."

"The full moon marks my journey. The woman in the market—"

"—Kimiko believes a loa visited you in the market. Not Marie Laveau, but the loa of the Moon Goddess, Gleti," AJ said.

Lilith shuddered.

"If Vodun's notion of a mirrored reality is true, if what happens in the spiritual world is mirrored to the physical; then our physical battle is the mirror of a spiritual battle taking place in Vilokan."

Charlotte added, "All the spirits of Vilokan permitted Gleti to realign the moon to mark your journey."

The basement door opened and Candace ran down. "Dad will be here shortly. Come on up."

Lost in a stupor, Lilith followed Candace up the stairs. The change of scenery brought her back from the abyss. The old seedy bar resembled normalcy for her. Two old-timers sat on stools in front of the beer tap.

One old-timer chuckled at them. "Boy, are you folks lost?"

The gray-haired bartender called out to Candace, "Did you sneak a party down there behind my back?"

"No, Bennie. They beamed down to the wrong coordinates. I'm taking them back for a redo."

"Oh my." Bennie pushed his glasses up from the edge

of his nose when Lilith and Charlotte came into view. "Young ladies, drinks are on the house for you."

"Bennie, quit coming on to young women."

"Hell, you're off the market since you met Michael. So, I'm offering a bit of liquid courage for this daring duo. Cute young ladies don't visit us old-timers. Tequila, ladies?"

Charlotte yanked on Lilith to follow. "Please, and keep them coming."

Lilith didn't have the will to resist.

Candace pointed to the window next to the front door. "Watch for a minivan cab while I check the back."

AJ stood next to the window. Within a minute, true to Candace's word, a minivan cab screeched to a stop. AJ, Tayen, and Scott walked out to the cab.

Lilith winced at the burning of the tequila shot. As she placed the shot glass on the counter, the screeching of the tires grabbed her attention.

Before she could take a step, Michael's muscular arm wrapped around her waist and lifted her off the floor. He swung his free arm around Charlotte and picked her up as easily as he had Lilith.

"Put me down," Lilith yelled as she tried to twist out of his grasp.

Panicked, Candace said, "Lilith, quiet. They got in the wrong van."

Before Lilith had turned to the window, Michael dropped to the floor behind the bar. He shielded the girls from the drop by lifting them before he landed. On his knees, he pushed them as far back against the bar counter as he could. He released Charlotte and spun beside Lilith.

Bennie stood next to Charlotte and glared at the door. "Sit tight, ladies. I'll take care of these jokers."

The door swung open, and two men entered. One wore a tight-fitting black T-shirt and black jeans, while the other wore black slacks and a button-up long sleeve khaki shirt. The one in the black T-shirt demanded, "Where are the two young ladies?"

Bennie feigned a glance around the room. "Ladies, in here? And young ladies too? I suggest going back to Bourbon Street if you want something like that."

"We could smell their perfume when we walked in."

"Nah. You're smelling the chicken soup from lunch."

The guy in the black T-shirt chuckled. "Mind if I look around?"

"Yes, I do."

"Old man, I don't think you understand. I am taking a look around your bar."

"Oh, young whipper-snapper, you don't understand." Bennie pointed to the two old-timers, who had swiveled in their seats and were facing the strangers. "These retired police officers will have a say in what you will see. Unless you are Billy the Kid, you're looking at eternal darkness."

Eyeing the two retired police officers, the one in the black T-shirt asked, "Where's your bathroom?"

"Paying customers only. First words out of your mouth weren't buying words, so you don't qualify."

The man in the khaki shirt said, "Leave 'em. We have what we need."

"Whatever you say, Nico."

Nico approached the bar and handed Bennie a hundred-dollar bill. "If you know about a smoking hot Latina and her equally sexy Black girlfriend, there will be a few more of these for you."

"If I see any, I'll call you."

Nico said, "You don't have my number."

"Well. That might be a good sign I won't be seeing what you want."

Nico smiled, turned, and walked out the door with his man following him.

Candace peeked over the bar counter. "Goddamn it, how did they know?"

The cab pulled away.

As the cab disappeared around the corner, Candace turned to the girls. Charlotte had curled up in a ball with both arms shielding her head. Lilith collapsed like a rag doll and whispered the same thing over and over.

Candace leaned close, hoping to hear Lilith.

"It was Nico. It was Nico."

30 - Three Graces

Kimiko's Mercedes slid on the grass field. She hopped out of the car and strained to see a plane bank to line up with Mr. Wasco's private airstrip. She had received a demanding one a.m. text, which ordered her to meet them at the airstrip before dawn. The plane landed and came to a stop. Charlotte and Lilith didn't speak to Kimiko as they stormed off the jet and rushed to the car. Slamming their doors, they told Kimi it wasn't the time to talk.

They arrived at AJ's house and marched to the back door, where Elliott opened the door for them. Aniah threw her arms around Lilith, squeezing her into a protective shell of love and comfort. Charlotte veered around their embrace and sat at the dining room table. Lydia poured hot cups of coffee and placed them in front of Lilith and Charlotte.

Elliott exercised tremendous patience, allowing Lilith and Charlotte a chance to gather their thoughts. When it seemed right, he asked, "What happened to Scott, Tayen, and my dad? Why didn't they come back with you?"

Lilith lowered her coffee cup to the table. "Ernesto sent Nico and his goons to find us and the map room. They broke into the turret stairwell under the museum, but Father Amare had … traps, I suppose you would call them. We escaped from the map room and followed the tunnel to a bar. We waited for a cab. Through dumb luck, Nico passed in front of the bar and saw Tayen, Scott, and your dad."

She bobbed her head in denial of what had occurred. "AJ, Tayen, and Scott went outside when a cab pulled up. The first cab was dropping off. That's when the second cab pulled up. It was Nico and his—"

"—Michael dragged Lilith and me behind the bar and hid us," Charlotte said. "Two men entered the bar; one was Nico. Two retired police officers stopped him from searching the bar for us. They drove away, and we flew back here."

Elliott's voice cracked. "Where's my dad?"

Lilith couldn't look at him.

"My dad has them in the Dominican Republic," Aniah said. "The chickenshit retreats to the mountaintop if his plans get screwed over. Not capturing Lilith means they failed to meet their objective."

Kimiko asked, naively, "Can we go down there and get them back?"

"No. They're after Lilith. We don't walk their dream up the driveway and through the front door."

"That ship may have sailed," Lilith replied. "They have Scott's laptop and everything we recorded. I think he kept his information about securing our phones and computers on it."

Charlotte slid her phone across the table in anger. "All security for this house, the country club, and The Village is compromised the moment they access Scott's laptop."

Aniah stopped the phone from whizzing off the table. "Good news then. It paid to have ELF and Scott collaborating. ELF has access to Scott's work, including the map room recordings. They changed the security codes after the feed cut out. Dad will be furious when he finds the laptop was scrubbed clean by ELF."

Lilith's eyes lit up. "Your Dad isn't aware of the Hovel?"

"I doubt it. But, when he discovers Scott's hard drive has been wiped, he'll assume the computer files are here in AJ's house or in the clubhouse. Nico's on his way here to get you and the files. If he can't find you or the files, he'll grab innocent BCI employees and force you to surrender."

"Why did Ernesto take action after leaving us alone for so long?" Elliott asked.

"Speaking of which, who are the Nanjing Twins, and why do they scare Ernesto?" Lilith's question caught Aniah and Elliott off guard.

Aniah leaned back in her chair. "How do you know about them?"

"Back in April, when we stumbled into your dad's mansion, AJ mentioned the Nanjing Twins as Ernesto's competitors. Ernesto wasn't as cocky with us after that."

"But how did AJ come across them?"

"Beats me."

"Oh, Jesus, Dad," Elliott said. "If the Nanjing Twins are in Portland, Ernesto will stay home. He was content to monitor us through video feeds, but entering the Twins' territory would spark an underworld war."

"But who are they?" Charlotte asked.

"Like the Bennington Crime Syndicate," Elliott began, "the Nanjing Twins are an organization out of China.

They stay in the shadows and pull the levers of power from—where else—Nanjing. The Benningtons and the twins have an unwritten agreement to stay off each other's turf."

"The Nanjing Twins Syndicate is almost invisible, but their two assassins are active and well known," Lydia said.

Everybody turned to Lydia. Disbelief and surprise were etched across their faces.

"That's how they got the name, the Nanjing Twins. She kills at close range, and he kills from far away. Together, they run an efficient and undetectable criminal organization. A Bennington Crime Syndicate/Nanjing Twin war would be a bloodbath everywhere they met."

Elliott turned to his girlfriend. "Who are you?"

Kimiko scooted next to Charlotte so neither of them would fall over and die from shock.

Aniah recoiled. "The Nanjing Twins are a brother and sister assassination team?"

Lilith slid to the edge of her chair. "Ms. Calveiro. You left a shit load of information off your resumé. How's a chastry pef—pastry chef—cook up the Nanjing Twins?"

"But the question we should be asking is how AJ learned about them?" Lydia asked.

"I'll ask him when we get him back," Elliott said.

"Well, until then, Aniah. How many targets will Nico bring?"

"We're not playing your combat video games, Lydia."

Lilith placed her hand on Elliott's arm. "Your girlfriend said targets. She didn't ask how many people were coming. She asked how many targets."

Lydia didn't hesitate to share. "Something else not on my resumé is my family's long history with firearms. We have a family tradition of—"

"—hunting with long-range rifles." Elliott cupped his hands over his mouth. "Your accuracy and precision at the gun range caught a lot of attention. It wasn't just you good looks that impressed them."

"Yeah. We can hunt too."

"How stupid am I?" Aniah blurted out. "You're a Calveiro."

Lilith raised her hand. "Sorry. I got lost on the 'hunt too' comment."

"Her family is in the business contract killing, or assassinations, depending on how you view the kill," Aniah said. "Your family hasn't made news for years."

"I didn't want to follow in my father's footsteps. I chose to pursue dance and cooking. But shooting is in my blood, and I can't shake the desire to pull a few rounds off once in a while."

Lilith gave a slow nod, as if she understood where this was leading. Shazoo jumped on the table and sat facing the back door. Lilith went to pick him up, but he hissed at her.

"Shazoo! What's got into you?" Elliott reached for the cat, but he too was greeted with a hiss and a clawed swat.

"I'm pissed too, Shazoo," Lydia said. "His majesty wants to defend this house and so do I. So, Aniah, how many are coming and when?"

"Well, if the cat's in, so am I," Aniah said. "Dad's plane carries twenty-six people. A handful of his men are okay with handguns, otherwise, it's quantity over quality of shots fired. Blade combat is their strength. Nico excels with knives and trains his people well."

"This is a home invasion. Twenty-six would be overkill," Lydia said.

"Expect six-man teams with night vision equipment,"

Elliott added. "One team each for the house and the clubhouse. The back door or garage for a silent entry into the house, and the locker room on the north for the clubhouse."

Charlotte bumped Elliott's arm with her fist. "Your National Guard duty just paid off."

Lydia closed her eyes. "Elliott spots for me, and we form the overwatch team on top of the clubhouse. It's the only place I can both cover the house and the clubhouse."

"Why all this talk about attacking people? Shouldn't we tell the police and tell them to handle it?" Kimiko asked.

"No," came a rousing chorus from the table.

"Kimi," Lilith said, "we are not in a position to—"

Charlotte cut to the chase. "We have a couple of multi-million-dollar pieces of art ... hidden away. We'd prefer to not go to jail over them."

Lilith winked at Charlotte for not disclosing the secret storage room below AJ's house.

Lydia ignored it and continued with her plans. "They'll come for the house from the south through the front nine. We might have help down by the fifth green?"

"If you're wishing for a thrashing moose charge, it ain't happening," Charlotte informed them. "Gertie is a sweetie, not a killer. If they spook her, she'll charge them, but nothing more."

"Oh, well. It was wishful thinking."

" I don't believe this," Lilith said. "You were under suspicion for spying on us. We cornered you and got you to confess to spying, and now you're planning our defense. Why?"

"You freed me and my family from Elbers. I've fallen in love with Elliott, and I adore his dad. The people dear to them have become as important to me. Three of ours are in their hands, and I'm angry enough to kill to get them back."

"How many kills have you scored?" Charlotte asked.

Elliott threw his napkin at Charlotte. "There are questions you don't ask."

"When you're employing the skills of an assassin, I think asking how many kills they have is a pertinent question."

"Charlotte, I'll handle this," Lilith said. "If Nico is coming, how do we defend ourselves?"

"Include everyone. If this isn't a Code Purple—defending the helpless from an abuser—I don't know what is," Charlotte said.

"This is the Manicato I'naru's fight, not the employees of Broken Cove Industries."

Kimiko ignored Lilith and rallied to Charlotte's side. "Fighters need a support staff, don't they? Don't include BCI employees in the fight, but let them support the fighters where they can. I say we keep the support staff out of harm's way, but use them where possible."

"Close The Village and clubhouse for today." Charlotte texted away on her phone. "We'll say there's been a death in the family."

"Stop it, Charlotte."

"I'll take body disposal and the greenskeepers. I wonder if they got the whisper-quiet drones yet? Scott made the adjustments on the heat-seeking rockets."

Aniah turned to Lilith. "*Stop* isn't in her dictionary, is it?"

"Other than Elliott, has anybody told her to stop?"

Lydia scowled at Elliott.

"It was my first day back, and Latina girl—"

"Smoking hot Latina," Charlotte corrected.

"—was auditioning to be my trophy wife. We never hooked up, so don't target me with that disapproving look."

"Gather everybody in the clubhouse amphitheater and tell them what we are doing," Kimiko said to Charlotte.

"If Lydia is shooting from the clubhouse, I'm headed to Eugene to get the rifle she loves. I can't run the meeting if I'm on the road for four hours," Elliott said.

"I'll do it," Charlotte snapped. "But I need a set of plans to present at the meeting."

"Call the meeting. We have two or three hours to generate ideas," Lilith said. "Kimiko, call Talia. She has the imagination for this."

Kimiko pulled out her phone. "Quite the planning team. Lydia, Aniah, Charlotte, me and you, Elliott, and now we are adding Talia."

"I'm sorry. What?" Lilith asked.

"Our team doesn't match up to what's coming at us."

Kimiko's statement stunned Lilith. She dropped her chin to her chest.

Lydia tapped the table. "Hey, don't forget what Deputy Castillo said: 'Pity the fool who enters Broken Cove Country Club. They have no idea what waits for them.'"

Lilith raised her head.

"Defending this place is easy," Lydia said. "Nobody is aware of our underground tunnel system. We can move undetected to wherever we need."

Charlotte added, "There are enough secret doors in The Village to make Sarah Winchester envious."

Lilith glared at Charlotte. "She must be a historical person, because I've never heard of her."

"I mentioned her to piss you off and get you out of your funk."

"It worked, bitch buddy."

Elliott twisted out of his chair. "I'm going to Eugene. Remember, these people are coming at us, so account for that in your planning."

Lydia tilted her head back and received his quick kiss on the lips. "Hurry back."

Elliott shooed the dogs away as he exited the door to the garage.

Lydia murmured under her breath. "Too much of a gun for me to handle, my ass."

Charlotte pushed her chair back and stood. "I'm taking Lydia up to the clubhouse roof. I'm taking the *Red Rum Runner* and the dogs."

Sonny and Cher jumped and barked at the mentioning of the *Red Rum Runner*. It was the four-seated golf cart which AJ used to cart them around the course.

"We'll need to check line-of-sight issues." Lydia stood. "Also, when I'm up there, I'll need you to stand in certain spots, so I can mark yardages."

Everybody rushed off, leaving Aniah and Lilith by themselves at the dining room table. Aniah poured herself coffee and took a strawberry from the fruit plate.

Lilith leaned back and stared at the glass ceiling, which she hadn't adored for months. Her early memories of this house were of spending time with Charlotte, AJ, and Tayen after Sunday dinners. She'd sat quietly during the dinners and run her hand over the table. But a year later, AJ and Tayen were gone.

She pushed her chair back. "I need some air."

Lilith rushed out the back door and jogged down the path. She believed a visit to the Gardens of Versailles would never be needed. This garden's grandeur was enough for her.

She touched the statues and the plant leaves with her fingertips. It helped distract her from what had transpired.

She entered the area of her favorite statue: a life-sized replica of the Three Graces. The sculpture of three naked women dancing. They embodied the three Graces: celebration and abundance, youth and beauty, joy and good will.

She walked to the park bench across from the statue and sat. AJ would join her and tell her the history behind the statues. He engaged her in Socratic dialog to challenge her viewing of the world. Never did he claim to have the answers, but he knew how to ask the right questions. 'Composed questions precede revelatory answers,' he told her.

If a blind man couldn't see a rose, could he still experience beauty?

Lilith answered he could through his other senses.

AJ pressed her. If the blind man had a cold, he lost his hearing and hands in war, and was incapable of taste, could he still experience beauty? Lilith didn't have an answer. 'To save our unfortunate blind man, perhaps our understanding of beauty needs to be reexamined,' he said to her.

It was time for her to ask questions.

Why is this happening? No. Compose the question; don't react to the situation.

Lilith rolled her head to the side and back.

Lives are at risk because of my pirate ancestor. So what would Jade do? How did she survive under the watchful eye of colonial powers? They sailed right in front of her, yet she wasn't seen.

A vociferous meow came from behind. She turned to find Aniah coming toward her with Shazoo. He was eager to escape and jump into Lilith's arms.

"I am sorry. I really need a moment alone."

Aniah turned around, but Shazoo objected and let out a window-rattling meow.

"Arrrg. Fine Shazoo. You can stay."

Aniah walked over to the park bench and sat down with Shazoo.

"You could have dropped him on the ground."

"No, I couldn't." Aniah lifted Shazoo, and her shirt rose. "His claw is stuck in my shirt."

Lilith took Shazoo as Aniah worked to free herself from his claw. Lilith said, "I love this place. I want to sit here for hours, enjoying Euphrosyne, Aglaea, and Thalia's company."

Aniah patted her shirt down from Shazoo's claw pulling. She glanced around the garden, unable to find the people Lilith mentioned. "Are these special friends, or have you lost your mind?"

"The Three Graces statue in front of us. You are well versed in paintings, but sculptures elude you?"

"Pretty much, yep." Aniah looked at the statue. "Tell me that is resin and not actual marble."

"What's resin?"

"It's what you make statues out of if you don't want to pay millions for the marble replica."

"Resin. AJ didn't have millions when this was made."

"Where did AJ get his money?"

Shazoo purred as Lilith scratched under his chin. "He won a diminished lottery, not the billion-dollar one three days earlier. His dream house came first, and a nine-hole golf course came next. He met Tayen, and together they created this premier 18-hole golf resort. Tonight, however, it all might come crumbling down because of your dad's business dealings."

Aniah lowered her head. "I deplore everything he does. My wish is to defeat Nico's invasion squad and put Dad in jail. If he's imprisoned, Aunt Patty can leave and get on with her life."

"Why does she stay with him?"

"Me. When my mom died, she became my replacement mom. She controls the mansion more than Dad does. At times, it feels as though Dad fears her more than she fears him. What always puzzled me is that she introduced my mom to Dad."

"Aunt Patty knew your dad before he met your mom?"

"Eh, that's always been a bit fuzzy. Family photos with Dad have Aunt Patty in the far background, and my mother isn't in the picture. Aunt Patty says the pictures were taken after Mom and Dad were married, but Mom simply wasn't in every photo."

"What was your mother's name?"

"Bristol."

"Beautiful name." Lilith brought Shazoo up to her face for a nose bump. "Thank you, Bristol's daughter. Between you two, my nerves aren't frazzled. So, any bright ideas for how to defend AJ's house?"

"A stealthy approach, whatever that may be, is our best shot. Loud bangs in the night will unnerve us. We aren't used to gunfire in enclosed areas."

"How would you know that?"

Aniah rolled her head back. "Conversations in my house tended to include hand-to-hand combat tactics. I suppose that's why I received blade combat training. Of all people, Nico trained me. He said my hand speed and accuracy were phenomenal."

"Can you train me before tonight?" Lilith asked.

"I can share some basics to give you a chance, sure. But Nico's boys are well-trained. You're not going head-to-head with any of them."

Lilith sighed. Shazoo had had enough of the close-quarters contact. He pushed her nose away. "Alright. I get it."

She twisted her face to the side and saw the Three Graces. "I told AJ once he needed to take some statues and put them on the second floor, outside the hallway. That spot always looked bare to me."

"He doesn't need anymore. Inside on the second floor? These are too big for indoors."

Lilith placed Shazoo on the ground and sprang forward to the statue. She traced the face of one statue with her fingers.

Aniah asked, "Do you want alone time with your statue friend?"

"It's how Jade evaded capture. She was in full view, but they didn't see her because she gave them what they expected to see."

"I'll take that as a yes."

Lilith spun around and faced the house. Her eyes burned with determination. "Have you ever been body painted before?"

Charlotte's Memo Pad To-do List

1.
2. # Get my people back!!!
3.
4.
5.
6.
7.
8.
9.
10.

Tayen's Notes:

"Work one problem at a time." my boss

AJ's Notes: (Clear w/Tayen first)

Follow Tayen's advice before mine.

Staff Attendance: BCI Administrative Team: ALL IN

Head Groundskeeper: Manny   Executive Chef: Dean   Sous Chef: Ladonna
BCA Designer: Kimiko   Clubhouse Manager: LaTrice   Pastry Chef: Lydia
Assistant GM: Elliott   Pasta-de-faria's Manager: James
Club Pro: Thom   Broken Cove Charities Director: Dolly

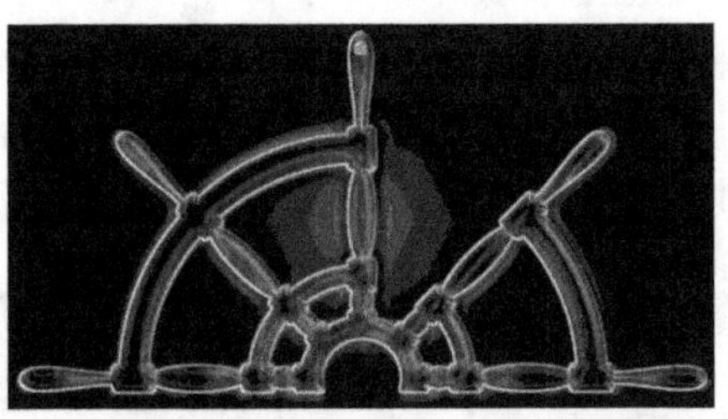

31 - Shadows Revealed

Lydia's baristas and chocolatiers joined Manny's greenskeeper crew in posting closed signs around Broken Cove Industries. Employees who hadn't read Charlotte's texts were bewildered to see the signs. Those who worked night schedules hurried to the clubhouse after they received Charlotte's emergency text.

Before long, the clubhouse amphitheater filled with concerned coworkers. Charlotte and Kimiko stood at the podium in the center of the amphitheater and waited to answer questions. Lilith and Aniah sat in the last row.

Charlotte wore jeans and a black V-neck short-sleeve T-shirt. Her attire alerted the employees that this was an entirely different type of meeting.

She decided critical mass had been achieved and started the meeting.

"To those of you we called to come in early, I apologize. If not for the extraordinary circumstances, this early morning meeting would not be happening. This is a Code Purple. What I am about to tell you cannot, under any circumstances, leave this room. I will understand if you choose not to participate. It is your choice. We aren't here to coerce your decision to our favor."

It became so quiet that the gentle breeze over the clubhouse dome seemed to echo in the amphitheater.

"Simply put, our gift shop clerk has a drug cartel coming for her, and they have taken AJ, Tayen, and Scott as hostages."

Gasps of shock filled the amphitheater.

"Calm down." Charlotte raised her hands to regain control of the meeting. "Some might be asking why we aren't contacting the police or FBI. We can't involve law enforcement. Over the last year, an old family inheritance left a bunch of historical artifacts to Lilith, and the drug cartel wants them. Unfortunately, possessing these artifacts will land us in a well-publicized courtroom trial before we are sentenced to life in prison."

Someone yelled out, "Did you steal something?"

"Yeah, well, it gets complicated. Can you steal something that was bequeathed to you, but was in somebody else's possession when you took it?"

Realizing she was speaking over everybody's head, Charlotte explained it in simple terms: "Lilith's ancestry reaches back to a pirate, and we are in possession of that pirate's treasure. We have to keep it away from the drug cartel, who is after it. But hell broke loose last night, and AJ, Tayen, and Scott's lives hang in the balance. This is dangerous. We aren't asking for you to confront those who are coming tonight. We just need your help to prepare for their arrival."

Talia sat in the front row and asked, "What are you asking from us? Being specific would help us decide."

"The biggest help will be with the greenskeepers. We have an assortment of booby traps and obstacles to set up. The vast majority of you will help them. When night falls, you folks have to leave. These are dangerous people, and we don't want anybody getting hurt. Only the clean-up crew will be close to the dangerous areas."

"What are you expecting to clean up?" Somebody shouted.

Charlotte looked above Talia's head. "Kimiko is expanding her product line into mortuary attire."

Talia waved her hand above her head to catch Charlotte's attention. "Not helpful. What is mortuary attire?"

Charlotte lowered her head. "Cadaver bags."

Gasps echoed through the amphitheater.

"Folks, if you want to back out, I get it. Lilith and I first found ourselves in this mess a year ago with AJ, Tayen, and Scott. We didn't ask for it, and here we are, outnumbered for tonight. But if we succeed, we won't be outnumbered in the future. There is a growing Caribbean network, which is like to our Code Purple. The Manicato I'naru' Network is a modern-day Robin Hood organization, and Lilith leads it."

"We are accepting members."

Kimiko's comment helped Charlotte understand how Tayen felt about a subordinate's irritating behavior.

"Lilith is the Robin Hood of an ancestral pirate den, and you're on a membership drive? I thought pirates joined or died?" Talia asked.

"Oh, no." Charlotte assumed AJ's role as the clubhouse historian. "Pirates were democratic to a fault. No one made unilateral decisions unless they were given prior permission to do so in the heat of battle."

Talia laughed. "I was joking. Where can I help?"

Lilith stood and called out, "I have something for you."

Charlotte addressed everybody else. "If anybody is willing to help, head down to the maintenance barn. I don't doubt other needs will pop up as the day progresses. Please be adaptable and ready to fill our requests. Again, if you don't want to participate, you are free to leave."

Some employees stood, others remained seated, but all were engaged in discussions.

Talia approached Lilith as requested. Chef Dean was speaking. "Ladonna and I will set up food services in the clubhouse. We don't need your busy bees wandering off campus."

Lilith nodded. "Thank you, Dean. Snag those you need."

Chef Dean strode away and Talia took his place.

Lilith read the text from Lydia. "Crap. Her line of sight only covers the front of the house."

"How serious is this?" Talia asked.

"Hand-to-hand combat where people will die."

Talia's voice rose. "Holy shit. That's out of my range of experience, and goddamn, girl, you know I've got a mother fucking range of experience."

"I can't ask you to kill someone. If the worst happens, you might have to," Lilith said. "For now, your stripper body is desperately needed to be the distraction for Aniah and me to manage our unwanted guests."

Several employees exited the clubhouse.

"That's the door to exit if you're going to Manny's maintenance barn," Talia said. "If I may ask, what is in this pirate treasure that was left to you, and who left it to you?"

"We have information they need to find a treasure. It's not simply a treasure of gold and diamonds. There are other objects of greater value. I can't say exactly what it is, because we haven't seen it."

Another large group walked toward the exit leading to the maintenance barn.

Lilith watched them leave. "I didn't expect so many to help. How did Charlotte and Kimiko know these wonderful people would join our fight?"

"Are you kidding?" Talia asked. "These people make more than the state's minimum wage. Nowhere else can they make a living doing these jobs. Plus, they love the owner, the general manager cares about them, and the tech nerd … the author of Code Purple … " Talia dipped her head.

Lilith put her hand on Talia's shoulder to comfort her. Other than serving tables, Talia spent most of her time at work with Scott. She embraced Talia. "Let's focus here and do what is needed. I'll get them back."

***

Broken Cove Country Club buzzed with activity. If the Baristas, chocolatiers, and kitchen staff weren't following Chefs Dean and Ladonna's orders, they took turns monitoring the golf course perimeter and the road into the resort. A few of the kitchen staff accompanied the greenskeepers. A hodgepodge assortment of booby traps lined the front and back nines, leading to AJ's house and the clubhouse. Old bear traps were pulled from retirement and placed strategically. Manny had sworn he would never use them again, but if a drug cartel henchman stepped in one, better him than a bear.

Charlotte pressed the nighttime security guard into Lydia's service. He stood where she directed him. She took careful measurements from the clubhouse to precise spots on the fairways and woods. The laser rangefinder gave her distances, but Ted's enormous defensive-end-sized body gave her a reference point for adjustments. Elliott returned with the rifle and accessories. He helped Lydia zero in the scope in the underground tunnel between AJ's house and The Village.

Talia's friends—once exotic dancers; now table servers—assisted in AJ's house to pull off Lilith's plans. After Nico and his men came through the courtyard garden, full of naked Greek statues, they wouldn't be surprised with statues inside the house. It took four hours, but the body paint jobs on Lilith, Aniah, and Talia made them indistinguishable from the statues outside.

As night fell, so did the lights on Broken Cove Country Club. Charlotte and Kimiko turned the third-floor sewing room into a communication center. Charlotte's laptop was linked into the security cameras and a secured mobile app, which connected her to the Hovel in Barbados.

Hours passed after sunset, and there was no movement on the golf course.

Meanwhile, an hour south of Broken Cove Country Club, a business jet approached for landing at a local municipal airport. Sheriff Musgrave leaned against a black SUV with his arms crossed. He and his deputies had driven six SUVs to the airport to pick up Ernesto Cottrell's right-hand man, Nico, and his invasion squad. Out of his county's jurisdiction, Musgrave had his people dressed in dark, plain clothes, not their uniforms.

As the business jet's wheels touched down, three additional SUVs sped around the lone airplane hangar.

Deputy Olivia Castillo walked toward the oncoming vehicles and stopped in front of Sheriff Musgrave. "Why are the feds here?"

"Benningtons aren't the trusting type, so they're checking on us. Ernesto will not be happy they're here."

The SUVs zoomed up to them and stopped. District Attorney Miller jumped out of the front door and rushed to the sheriff. "Ernesto better not be on that jet."

"He isn't. Relax and get your G-string out of your ass," Musgrave shot back.

"Who is on the plane?"

"Nico, fourteen gunmen, and computer guys."

"That maniac will leave a massacre in my county. I'll have to console bereaving families," Miller said.

"Hard to fake sympathy when you don't give a shit about the deceased?"

Miller didn't answer and turned to the jet.

The door lowered, and Nico ran down the steps with his men following in close pursuit. He wasn't pleased to see the district attorney. "Shit, Miller. Tell the Benningtons we'll take care of this."

"According to the higher-ups, Ernesto has handled this as incompetently as possible."

Nico shoved Miller against the SUV and grabbed his shirt in his fists. With his face in Miller's, he yelled, "We've scanned the entire mansion and didn't find any bugs. Who do you have spying on Ernesto? When I find him, I'll kill him myself."

Miller didn't back down. "Our person doesn't spy. They monitor Ernesto's ineptitude and judge if it is necessary to blow up the mountaintop mansion when it no longer serves a purpose. Besides, they know the ins and outs of that mansion better than you do. Should they sense any treachery from you, you'll be dead before you can approach them."

"My men can handle this home invasion without your interference, Miller. Leave retrieval missions to us. We don't need another wasted haul. What did you steal from the chemistry lab? A generator and spools of wiring?"

"We didn't think the chemistry professor would switch out the chest's contents with an old generator and wiring."

"Leave the burgling to the professionals." Nico released Miller as he turned around to the sheriff. "Which one is mine?"

Sheriff Musgrave pointed to the lead vehicle. "Deputy Castillo will drive you."

"You can't ignore me, Nico." Miller pushed himself off the SUV. "Is it clear what you need to accomplish, or do I need to clarify so you don't screw it over?"

Nico walked toward the SUV. "Find the server, retrieve the data they recorded in the secret bunker from New Orleans, and leave no witnesses. We brought a couple of dozen body bags to dispose of the accidents."

"Wrong, dumbass."

Nico spun around and held a gun in Miller's face.

Miller didn't flinch. "Find the server and retrieve the recordings, but most important, get the black girl with blue eyes. Don't harm her. No scratches or bruises. Even if you don't access the server, the mission will be a success if you snatch her. She's the key to everything."

Sheriff Musgrave stood beside Miller and said, "The amateurs at the golf course are expecting you. They closed the whole facility this morning and our occasional pass-bys show they're up to something. Deputy Castillo believes they have set up bear traps."

Deputy Castillo added, "Whatever you do, don't go into their labyrinth of underground tunnels. They created it to park and charge golf carts, but I believe it has sprawled into a complex system of tunnels. My exposure to their underground was limited, but I saw enough that I'm sure they can move around the country club with ease. It'll be a disaster if you go in blind."

"How did you see their tunnels?" Nico asked.

"I was the test subject during their Code Purple transport trials. They let me into their inner sanctum. Oh, speaking of which … the four-story building has secret trapdoors, faux walls, and hidden passageways. If you think your six is secure, think again. They can pop up behind you with no warning."

"Where are their building permits?" Nico asked. "If they are digging underground, they have to file for permits."

Miller said, "We looked the other way because of their Code Purple. We felt forcing the issue of building permits might put us at odds with these people. Better to maintain positive relationships, so payoffs come in the long run."

Nico didn't respond.

"The black girl is at the house. She arrived this morning," Sheriff Musgrave said.

Nico stepped up into his seat. "I remember that sweet thing when she was with us. She'll be pissed when she finds out what happened to her friends."

Sheriff Musgrave turned his head toward Nico. "Is one of them a nerdy computer guy?"

The inflection of Musgrave's voice struck Nico as odd. "Sheriff, are you fond of ole Scottie?"

"Scott is a good man. Regardless of our business tonight, he doesn't deserve whatever you do to him," Sheriff Musgrave said.

"Wish you would have told us earlier." Nico laughed. "Scott and his two friends are dead. I assure you, they feel no pain right now. This morning, however, they felt it by the truckload."

Nico shut the SUV door, and the five vehicles sped off.

"Shit," Miller said. "He's going to create a bloodbath. I recommend you keep your deputies away from the golf course until the call of 'shots fired' comes."

Sheriff Musgrave didn't respond. He angled his face to the ground, shielding himself from Miller.

"Sheriff?"

"I heard you."

Miller gazed toward the end of the runway. "Scott was the guy who led the Code Purple exercises. His death is an unfortunate tragedy, but he couldn't stand in our way, as I hope no one does. All threats must be dealt with."

Sheriff Musgrave lifted his head. "He was a good man and didn't deserve death. Tell me your mole on the mountaintop can take revenge. Nico's death for Scott's would help balance the scales of … Shit, justice doesn't seem to be the right word."

Miller chuckled. "It ain't right to call the Bennington spy on the mountaintop a mole, either. She can blow up the whole mountaintop with a single phone call, and nobody could stop it once she does."

***

The five SUVs headed north through Portland's western suburbs. Their tinted windows prevented any view of their passengers. Nico sat in the front passenger seat as Deputy Castillo drove. The strike team leaders sat in the back and listened to Nico's repeating of their invasion plans.

"Alpha Team, head north to the clubhouse. Security cameras are next to the seventeenth tee. Shoot them out, then follow the stream to the twelfth green. It's the twelfth fairway up to the locker room entrance."

Alpha Team leader said, "Through the locker room and up to the general manager's office. Easy."

"Beta Team, the seventh green has the same camera set up. Enter through the fourth fairway."

"Thicker woods," Beta Team leader said.

"I'll take Gamma Team up the first fairway into The Village complex. The IT office is next to the underground golf cart parking lot. The computer server is there, unless the deputy has an idea where it is."

Deputy Castillo lifted her hand off the steering wheel. "It could be anywhere. You have three strike teams to find it."

"How much further to the golf course?"

"Twenty minutes to the north side, and another ten to the south."

Nico looked at his phone. "Advance on targets at zero one hundred hours. Don't harm the short black girl, and clear it with me before you kill anyone, unless you have no choice."

"There is a new girl in the upstairs flat above the detached garage," Deputy Castillo said. "The black girl has spent significant time up there over the last six months. If you don't find our target—"

"Six months?" Nico interrupted. "They've been hiding a girl up there for six months?"

"I've caught glimpses of her. She is a pretty young thing and a talented dancer from what I overheard in the coffee shop."

Nico leaned forward. "Is she tall and has hazel eyes with long brown hair?"

"Hazel. She's taller than average and her hair is short. Brown maybe. But it's hard to tell. It looks like she shaved it off a ways back. She has a mole behind her ear."

"Which ear?" Nico growled.

Deputy Castillo leaned away from him. "Stop spitting on me. If I remember correctly, her right ear."

Nico snapped his head around to face the front window. "Beta Team, be careful. Melody may be here."

"What is Melody doing here?" Gamma Team leader asked.

"Ernesto is going to blow a gasket when he hears about this. His daughter is helping the one we are hunting."

They heard the anger and frustration in Nico's voice, killing any further discussion as they drove to the country club.

Minutes later, Deputy Castillo stopped the SUV convoy for Alpha Team to disembark and start up the cart path. All six men scurried down the path to the seventeenth green. They lowered their night vision goggles on reaching the green. Alpha Team leader used a silenced pistol to shoot out the security cameras. He nodded for them to go ahead under the overcast skies.

In single file, Alpha Team crossed two fairways and followed the creek up to the thirteenth tee. The water roared over the edge of the picturesque three-tiered weir. They stopped and crouched before crossing the bridge over to the twelfth green.

Alpha Team leader pointed to the far side of the green. "We have the woods to the clubhouse from there."

"What's that buzzing?" the point man asked.

"Kids' drones. They'll be impossible to see with this overcast cloud cover." Alpha Team leader turned to the last two men. "Holster your guns. You're the computer techs, and I don't want you shooting me in the ass." He turned to the point man. "Move us forward."

Over the bridge they raced to the twelfth green, where they stopped to hide behind the green's berm. Alpha Team leader checked on the last two men, who weren't anywhere to be found.

"Stop. Don't advance," he hissed.

The others spun around to Alpha Team leader.

"One of you with me."

The two worked back to the bridge, looking for the missing Alpha Team members. Alpha Team leader peered down to the creek below the bridge and saw an Alpha member lying motionless on the sloped hillside. A quick survey down the stream showed a hat floating away from him. He motioned for them to head back. On rejoining with the others, he explained.

"That damn weir drowned out their shots. They took out both the computer techs. One is dead under the bridge, and the other fell in the stream." He depressed the microphone on his communications pack. "Delta leader, come in." After a few seconds, he repeated his call. On neither occasion did he receive a response.

One of his men pulled out his phone. "I don't have a signal. How can our phones and comms not be working?"

Alpha Team leader said, "That damn buzzing sound is drones, which are jamming our communications. Move on to the clubhouse and be hyper vigilant. They're blocking comms and aren't shy about shooting us."

A long, cautious march through the woods between the fairways ended below the clearing of the eleventh green. Alpha Team leader gestured for them to skirt around the sand trap, where they could take the cart path up to the clubhouse.

As the point man stepped next to the sand trap, his leg was pulled out from underneath him by a rope. He had stepped in a trap in the sand trap.

The whizzing of a fast-reeling winch came from above. Leaves rustled, and the point man was yanked back through the leaves. He reached in vain for something to grab hold of before his feet rocketed from the ground. He swung up and back where he slammed against a tree trunk. The rope snapped off from his ankle and disappeared into the tree limbs. He didn't move or make a sound, but hung upside down on the side of a tree.

"Goddamn," one Alpha Team member shrieked. "Why's he stuck up there?"

"Spikes. They impaled the poor bastard to a tree."

Another Alpha Team member shouted, "Fuck this. I'm out of here." He ran a few steps down the hill and face planted on the ground. Blood streamed up from the back of his head.

Alpha Team leader dropped to the ground. "Sniper head shot. He's dead."

The last Alpha Team member rolled into the sand trap, seeking protection behind the berm. He crawled through the sand until another trap sprang.

Alpha Team leader cringed. The sound of an

uncoiling heavy-duty spring and the thump of a bear trap's teeth on a human confirmed Deputy Castillo's report. Alpha Team leader didn't have to look. His man had rolled into a bear trap. Because he didn't hear any whimpering or scream, the bear trap likely had snapped across the man's neck.

Alpha Team leader rolled over on his side and aimed his gun toward the clubhouse roof. He traced the roof line in his night vision goggles until he found the sniper. The last thing he saw was the muzzle flash from Lydia's rifle.

32 - The Third Estate

Beta Team reached the wrought-iron fence which encircled AJ's three-acre yard. They'd separated from Gamma Team at the sixth green bridge fifteen minutes earlier. Their aim was to search the home for the computer server and nab Lilith, should she be there.

Blocked comms enraged Beta Team leader. The persistent buzzing above the trees, and his inability to communicate with teams Alpha or Gamma, left him frustrated.

At zero one hundred hours, he led Beta Team through the back gate and over the open ground to the courtyard garden. They hurried onto the stone path and passed several statues of Greek nymphs, gods, and goddesses. Beta Team leader stopped and crouched behind a row of bushes, waiting for his team to catch up.

He took a moment to enjoy the classical Greek art throughout the courtyard garden. His men asked him why statues were found every couple of steps. He shrugged and butted the magazine bottom with his palm.

They rose and ran to the back door, where, to their surprise, the back door was unlocked. Beta Team leader pushed the door open and led them into the atrium. They split into teams of three. One team checked the first-floor rec room while the other cleared the kitchen, laundry room, and garage. The three-man teams reunited in the atrium after a thorough search.

Beta Team leader asked, "Nothing in the garage?"

One team member answered, "Nothing but construction materials. It looks like they were installing a garage door opener, but the spring is missing."

"Then up to the next floor," he ordered.

The six-man team ascended the stairwell with pistols drawn. They poured out of the turret and proceeded along the balcony walkway to the bedroom's hallway.

Two Greek statues of naked women stood on either side of the hall entrance. Their backs lay flat against the wall. Each had one leg raised, so the knee pointed out, while their lower leg doubled back underneath the thigh. The foot pressed back against the wall, giving the appearance of them resting against a Greek column. A third statue leaned against the balcony with her legs crossed and her arms held up.

Beta Team didn't stop to admire the statues. Instead, they split into pairs and searched the bedrooms. The last two men positioned themselves at the hallway entrance.

Beta Team leader and his partner entered the Victorian bedroom and found nothing. They reentered the hallway and checked the next room: the Moulin Rouge bedroom. Beta Team leader dismissed the provocative decor and nudged his teammate out the door when nothing was discovered.

They returned to the hallway and joined the other men. But to their horror, the men stationed at the entrance were gone.

Beta Team inched their way from the hallway onto the balcony walkway, where they discovered the three statues were also gone.

They huddled together with their backs together.

"What now?" one asked.

"Shut up and head to the third floor," Beta Team leader said.

They reentered the turret and inched up the stairwell. A clear plastic tarp covered the inside of the turret walls and stair steps. The source of a low-pitched humming eluded them.

Two of them were a step from the top, when Beta Team leader snapped his fingers. They stopped and turned around toward him. He pointed above them, where a rod extended across the turret stairwell. No sooner had they spotted it than a loud metallic click sounded in the turret.

Charlotte's evil-genius plan sprang into action.

The garage door tension spring uncoiled and swung a row of axes over the stair steps. The two men at the top of the stairs didn't stand a chance.

One ax split through a man's head, splattering blood and brains on the plastic tarp. Two axes caught the other man. One smashed into his left shoulder, while a second sliced through his right clavicle. Both bodies tumbled down the stair steps and past Beta Team leader and his surviving team member.

Covered in blood, they stumbled and reached out to grab the hand railing. It was then they learned the cause of the humming: an electrified hand railing. After a few seconds of convulsing, they too dropped dead on the stairwell.

Lilith, Aniah, and Talia sprinted to the turret from their hiding place behind a large painted tarp next to the hallway. Fantastic artwork made the rest of the balcony walkway look real in the dark.

Aniah and Lilith feared the Greek-statue-body-paint job wouldn't fool Nico's men. But when four of them ran by, all they had to do was spin around the corner and stab the men in the back of the necks.

Talia tip-toed to help Lilith drag her man behind the tarp. A couple of table servers rushed from behind the tarp to help Aniah with her kill.

The three women wore loose oversized shirts to cover their top halves, while their marble painted legs laid bare. Lilith spoke into her cell phone. "The house is secured."

Elliott's voice came over the phone. "Clubhouse secured. The drones are circling the course."

Lilith stumbled to the balcony railing.

Aniah came to her side and placed her hand on Lilith's shoulder. "It was them or us."

"I stabbed a person in the neck and killed him. I'm not feeling too good about it."

Aniah squeezed Lilith's shoulder. "You did it right. We had to hit them in the base of the neck for the quick kill. Otherwise—"

Talia stepped next to Lilith. "Otherwise, it was up to me to shoot them with those guns I sat on."

"And if she fired, the others would have run down the hall, blasting anything in sight. We saved lives," Aniah said.

Lilith's hands shook as she raised her phone. "Elliott. Charlotte said the drone flyovers showed over a dozen men coming from the south. There's only six here."

"Text her and find out where the others went."

"She isn't texting back."

"Fine. I'll run over and see," Elliott said.

Lilith nodded at Aniah. "We'll join you, but we're taking the tunnels over."

As Lilith lowered her phone, Aniah said, "I'm putting on shorts before we run anywhere."

Lilith hurried to the walkway balcony, where a greenskeeper held Kimiko's painted curtain back. Two cadaver bags were filled and zipped shut. Half a dozen greenskeepers were already in the turret stairwell, cleaning up the mess.

Aniah ran past her and picked up her shorts from the floor. "Take the knives and Talia's guns."

Lilith scrambled into her bag and grabbed her shorts. "Charlotte and Kimi are locked in tight, but nothing's foolproof."

They rushed down the turret stairwell in their bare feet. Out the back door and onto the driveway, Lilith outran Aniah to the wood pile beside the detached garage, where a set of stairs led down to the underground tunnels.

They descended the stairs and stood before the door. Aniah, who used this tunnel system when she hid above the detached garage, entered the security code, and opened the door. Both women stepped inside, and the orange lighting in the tunnel alerted them that something was amiss.

"Damn it," Lilith growled. "The other team made it inside The Village. Charlotte or Kimiko hit the alarm."

Aniah moved ahead of Lilith as they ran down the

tunnel. "I'll take the branch around Dale's chemistry lab and go to the rum house ladder. That'll give me a straight shot up to the third-floor women's locker room. You should work around the golf cart garage and up the garbage chute ladder."

"That puts us on opposite sides of the studio."

"The walls aren't solid across the top, above the drop ceiling. We can crawl over—" Aniah frowned. "Correction, you can wiggle through the crawl space. Your tiny hips shouldn't hold you back, but my hips are too big."

Lilith looked at Aniah's hips as they walked. "They aren't that big."

"Charlotte said she could squeeze through, and you two are the same size. For me, well, I'm not a contortionist. I'll try, but don't count on it."

"I won't ask why Charlotte was crawling through the ceiling," Lilith said.

They reached the intersection and northwest corner of Dr. Dale's chemistry lab. Aniah split off while Lilith hesitated to proceed.

"Fifteen minutes," Lilith said, "and I'll see you in the studio."

Aniah gave a thumbs up as she turned down the tunnel.

Lilith quick-stepped ahead to the secret door, which led into the golf cart garage. She entered the PIN code on the keypad. The four-foot-tall faux concrete wall rose off the floor. It swung back on heavy-duty hinges, allowing Lilith to step over the threshold into the garage. A quick peek around assured her she was alone.

She hurried between the carts and reached Scott's IT workshop. One of the tool panels in his workshop opened into the east side tunnels of The Village complex.

The red-handled wrench on the pegboard would open the secret door. Lilith pumped the wrench three times, waited three seconds, and pumped twice again. The panel swung back and cleared away for Lilith. The ladder for this chute was around the immediate corner. She hurried up the ladder, which went past the first-floor gift shop and up to the second-floor trapdoor.

She regretted not having put on shoes when she left AJ's house. The ladder's rungs weren't abrasive, but they were uncomfortable.

The trapdoor to the fitting room in Broken Cove Accessories required another PIN. Once inside the fitting room, a ladder popped out of the wall. From there, she climbed to the third-floor employee daycare center trapdoor, which opened with the previous PIN code entry.

She jumped off the ladder and rolled onto the carpeted daycare floor as the automated door slammed shut. The red glow of the exit sign gave her enough light to proceed to the coat rack wall. She debated if this was the way she wanted to go.

A surprise drop from the ceiling, or a direct approach to Kimi's studio? There's a good chance Charlotte and Kimi are fine. But if they aren't, I'd walk straight into Nico's arms. Damn it! Up is my only choice. Coat hooks one and four.

Lilith alternated pulling each coat hook four times, and the secret wall opened. Into the small chute and up the ladder, where another PIN code opened the trapdoor inside the hostess station in Pasta-de-faria's front lobby.

Before she climbed up through the trapdoor, movement in the dark scared her senseless. Her heart pounded through her chest. She stared at the opening in hopes it wasn't Nico or his men.

A drop of drool hit her on the forehead. Growls echoed in the chute. Relieved, Lilith growled back.

She rushed up the ladder and rolled on the floor, where two excited golden retrievers greeted her with licks. She petted them on their heads. "Why did Charlotte put you up here? You're supposed to be with her in the studio."

A peek at the bar showed the outline of a cat sitting on the bar counter. Lilith ran over to check on Shazoo. His eyes glowed blue, even though there wasn't enough light in the restaurant to produce this effect. As she petted Shazoo on the head, she glimpsed herself in the mirror behind the bar. Her eyes were glowing, like Shazoo's.

Lilith lifted Shazoo, turned him around, and positioned his darling face next to hers. In the mirror, she saw the perfect reflection of two identical sets of eyes … glowing blue.

Shazoo wasn't looking in the mirror, but at the chest AJ had hung above the bar. Lilith followed his eyes to the chest. "You hate that thing, too? I told him to trash it. But, my little friend, I have a greater concern. Why are yours and my eyes glowing?"

Shazoo kept staring at the chest.

Lilith placed him on the bar and said, "You three stay here. I'm going to check on Charlotte and Kimiko." With a few more quick pets on Shazoo, Sonny, and Cher's heads, she was off.

Lilith raced down the three tiers to the lowest level of the restaurant. She counted the tables until she reached table fourteen. Between tables fourteen and fifteen was a trapdoor, which led to Broken Cove Charities, the office next to BCA's production studio. She used her toes to feel for the creases in the floor. When she found them, she jumped back and reached under table twenty-one on the tier above. A fold-down keypad was below the table. She entered another PIN code, and the trapdoor slid back.

She entered the chute and saw what Aniah had told her. Amid the steel and wood frames were tiny openings. She crawled through one opening and realized Aniah was right. Her hips wouldn't squeeze through.

Lilith lifted a ceiling tile to peek into the studio. To her great horror, Charlotte laid in the center of the studio with her hands tied behind her back. She wasn't moving, and her long brown hair covered her face. If not for the slight movement of her foot, Lilith would have assumed Charlotte was dead.

Two people's voices carried up to her, but she couldn't see who they were. She strained to hear what they were saying. *The guy's voice is Nico's. But who is the woman's? She sounds scared.*

"How long are we going to stay here?"

It took a moment, but Lilith finally identified the voice: *Deputy Castillo.*

"We've got a hostage. They'll come to us, and when they do, I'm killing them, except Lilith. Those goddamn booby traps," Nico replied to Castillo.

Whoa. Nico. Did our booby traps get to you and your men? How do I get down there to let Aniah in?

She lifted the ceiling tile and surveyed the area below. *A twelve-foot drop to the floor. I can do it. I have to. But the landing? I'm tiny, but even my landing would make a sound.*

Lilith looked around for a solution and found nothing. She returned to the idea of jumping down. Her solution came from her shirt. She took it off and wrapped it around the support beam. Stuffing one sleeve down the other sleeve, she tied the shirt around the support beam. Her makeshift extension gave her a lower drop distance.

Lowering herself inch by inch, she waited for her swinging to stop before releasing one hand from the shirt. She released at the same time as gunfire came from outside. She landed with a thud. Even though she bent her knees, it wasn't as quiet as she hoped for.

She snuck behind the clothes rack and wrapped a robe around herself. She peered around a stack of boxes and found Charlotte sitting up with her back against a chair. Blood covered her chin and her lower lip was swollen.

Nico held a door open as he checked to see what the gunfire was about.

Lilith leaned forward for a look around the room. She didn't expect Deputy Castillo to find her. Deputy Castillo yanked Lilith's hair and pulled her across the floor next to Charlotte.

Nico limped back in the door on hearing the commotion. Grateful to see Lilith beside Charlotte, he said, "Gotcha. When we find out about the gunfire, we're leaving."

Lilith pushed Charlotte's hair aside to see her injuries.

"I'm fine. Nico's team had a rough go through the Ewok trap. The piano wire struck a chord—"

"Shut up, bitch," Nico screamed.

"The logs swung from the trees and scored two direct hits. Facial recognition software will be useless on identifying them. The piano wire we strung between the logs. Well, let's just say a cleanup on aisle one is needed. The head rolling across the fairway scared Gertie, who charged and kicked Nico in the ass. That's why he is limping."

Deputy Castillo kicked Charlotte in the face, snapping her head back and making her fall on the floor.

Lilith threw herself over Charlotte to protect her. "Stop it! You've got me. Leave everybody else alone."

"What about our other strike teams? What did you do to them?"

Lilith cupped the back of Charlotte's head and looked at her friend's swollen face. "Our drones knocked out your comms, and the booby traps eliminated them."

Deputy Castillo growled. "Damn it. You, me, and three of Gamma Team are left. Let's get out of here, Nico. We've got the girl."

"When they return from the clubhouse, we will."

"Clubhouse?" Lilith blurted out.

Nico looked at Lilith. "When we got here, I positioned two men by the windows next to the elevators. Flashes of gunfire in the trees by the clubhouse alerted us to trouble. I sent my three remaining men to investigate."

Lilith gasped. Nico's men had run across Elliott.

Nico took notice of Lilith's gasp. "How many gunmen did you have at the clubhouse?"

"One."

"I heard pistol, semi-auto, and bolt-action shots. Our guys carried pistols, no semi-autos. So, your person has a semi-auto and a bolt-action rifle, or you're lying," Deputy Castillo said.

"You asked how many gunmen. I was truthful to the letter."

"A man and a woman?" Nico shouted.

Charlotte coughed through her laughter. "Yeah, Nico. The Nanjing Twins are with us."

"She's lying," Deputy Castillo said. "They have a man and woman on guns, but there is no way in hell the twins are here."

"Que te folle un pez," Charlotte said.

Deputy Castillo cocked her leg back to kick Charlotte again, but Lilith rolled over her friend to deflect the kick.

"Stop it!" Nico yelled. "Don't touch Lilith or Ernesto will have you killed, deputy."

Lilith rolled back with Charlotte in her arms. "Touch her again, mamahuevo, and I'll kill you."

Deputy kicked at Lilith's face, but pulled it away at the last second.

"I must have said it right to get that reaction out of this malinchista," Lilith said.

Charlotte laughed. "Castillo is getting fucked three ways tonight. And good job, darling. You used both words correctly."

"Wait until we tell her a .308 Winchester Tikka A1 is waiting for her?"

Deputy Castillo spun on her heels and faced the door. "Alpha strike team never reached the clubhouse. They have a man on the ground, and a sniper on the clubhouse."

Nico placed his hand on the back of his neck. "We reached the house, but Melody helped neutralize them, didn't she?"

"What makes you think Melody is here, hijo de las mil putas?"

Nico walked beside Charlotte and bent down. He stuck his pistol against Charlotte's cheek. "Stop with the insults in Spanish and tell me about Melody before I plaster your girlfriend's face on the floor."

Lilith slid her hand under the gun and over Charlotte's cheek. "Don't, please. Melody helped neutralize your strike team. You trained your cousin very well."

Nico used his pistol to flick Lilith's hand away as he

pressed the gun harder against Charlotte's cheek. "Where is she?"

"She's here. Where, I have no idea. But she is looking for you."

"Wonderful." Nico stood and turned to Deputy Castillo. "Call Sheriff Musgrave and have him get his vehicles out of here. We're taking Lilith with us."

"How d'you find Charlotte?" Lilith asked.

"I don't answer you," Nico barked. "But you tell me how you got in here."

"Secret passages throughout The Village."

Nico tilted his head back and found the hole in the drop ceiling. "Is that how we leave?"

"No, the charity office's trapdoor goes up, not down." Lilith was protecting Kimiko, who was scared and hidden somewhere in the restaurant.

"Then where is the nearest secret passage that leads down?"

"Next door. Through the women's locker room."

"Whoa, slow down," Deputy Castillo said. "She's being too helpful, and I told you, Nico, stay out of those tunnels."

Nico rolled his head back. "Relax, Deputy. They don't have a Minotaur targeting us in their labyrinth."

"I don't care which gun model—Smith and Wesson, Ruger, or Minotaur—is used to shoot me in the head."

Lilith and Nico stared at one another.

"Ten bucks says she hasn't heard about the Roanoke Colony," Lilith said.

Nico replied, "Not John White's best outing, for sure."

Deputy Castillo stomped her foot on the floor.

"Whatever. What about the men we sent to the clubhouse?"

"They're dead. The last shots were from an assault rifle," Nico said.

Lilith squeezed Charlotte's hand; Elliott had eliminated Nico's men.

Deputy Castillo grabbed Lilith by the arm and pulled her up and away from Charlotte. "You and me, sister. Take us through the locker room."

Nico picked Charlotte up off the floor and used his knife to cut the ropes tied around her wrists. "You're mine, sweetie. When I get you back to the mountaintop, I'm making you a permanent member of my harem."

Charlotte stumbled forward but kept her balance thanks to Nico's iron grip on her elbow. "Not if our Minotaur works. Then again, a local company here in Portland makes a spectacular twelve-inch blade—"

Nico shoved Charlotte forward. "Melody's my concern."

They left the studio and hurried down the walkway to the women's locker room, where Lilith entered her pin. She pulled the door open, and the motion detector tripped the lights on. Deputy Castillo held the scruff of Lilith's robe and pushed her forward at arm's length. She pointed her pistol around the locker room, ready for any surprises.

A long row of fitting rooms on the right caught Nico's eye. "Why the dressing rooms?"

"The service staff need a place to change into their pirate regalia. Some outfits require more privacy to fit into than others," Lilith said.

"Why not solid doors instead of these curtain partitions?"

Deputy Castillo also didn't like what she was seeing.

"Somebody can hide behind these curtains."

"God, you're both paranoid," Lilith said. "I'm the only one who came up the chutes."

Deputy Castillo pulled Lilith beside the fitting rooms. "Open them."

Lilith yanked the first one open. "There. Nobody home."

"Next." Deputy Castillo yanked Lilith to the next fitting stall.

Nico stepped in front of Charlotte and scrunched her top in his hand as he faced backwards.

"Afraid of that long blade I mentioned." Charlotte said.

Nico ignored the comment and walked backwards, pulling Charlotte after him.

Lilith opened the fitting rooms until they reached the lockers at the end. She turned the locker dial and entered the combination. A pair of handles popped out, and she pulled them until an opening appeared.

Deputy Castillo peeked inside the dark chute. "There aren't any lights in here."

"We don't light the chutes," Lilith said.

"Fine. I'll go first, and you're behind me, Lilith."

Nico pulled Charlotte against him. "I'll go after Lilith, and you come last."

Deputy Castillo climbed into the chute and onto the ladder. "Damn moose."

"Why are you mad at Gertie?" Lilith asked.

"Gertie, as you call her, trounced on my night vision goggles when she stampeded us."

"Good Gertie. But one moose doesn't make a stampede."

Nico's patience evaporated. "Stop it and go down."

Deputy Castillo descended, followed by Lilith and Nico. Charlotte entered the chute and pulled the locker wall closed, casting them into pitch darkness. Nico reached up and felt Charlotte's shoe.

"Watch it, buddy," Charlotte squealed. "You almost pulled me off this ladder."

"Making sure you're there, darling."

They descended a few rungs when something fell down the chute.

"Sorry. My shoes are slippery and I'm taking them off. Watch out, one more falling," Charlotte said.

The second shoe hit Deputy Castillo on the head and bounced away. Nico reached up to feel for Charlotte's ankle.

"I'm still here."

"What's wrong with your feet? They're freezing."

"Haven't been with many women, have you? We always have cold feet," Charlotte said.

Lilith clenched her fist. *Charlotte's voice is different.*

They continued their descent. Deputy Castillo reached the floor and found herself in an alcove. She stood next to the ladder and waited for Lilith. The moment she was on solid ground, Deputy Castillo resumed her tight grasp of the scruff of Lilith's robe and pushed her into the orange-lighted tunnel.

Charlotte's not jabbering. She gets chatty when she's nervous.

Nico's foot was on the last ladder rung. With his head down, the back of his neck and head were exposed.

A marble-painted foot poked out of the chute above his head. Lilith understood what was about to happen.

Aniah dropped from the chute and over Nico's shoulders. The twelve-inch knife Charlotte scared Nico with was in her hands. Aniah's momentum helped to plunge the knife into Nico's neck and through his throat.

Charlotte and Aniah had switched spots when the door closed. Aniah hid above the locker room chute entrance in the dark. Nico didn't realize he had been checking Aniah's feet, not Charlotte's.

Deputy Castillo turned around. Lilith swung her arm back, knocking Castillo's grip from her robe. Castillo brought the gun around, but Lilith punched her arm, which caused the gun to fall. Castillo fell on her back after Lilith swept her legs out from under her.

Lilith fell on top of the deputy, pinning Castillo's arm to the ground with her leg. She lunged across Castillo's chest to pin the other arm down. With her free leg, she repeatedly kneed Castillo in the face. Unfortunately, her position didn't allow for full blows, but rather quick jabs.

Nico had fallen backwards and over Aniah. She rolled his dead body off of her and ran over to help Lilith.

Castillo, bloodied by Lilith's repeated kneeing to the head, made a desperate lunge for the gun. Lilith made the mistake of getting off balance, and the deputy succeeded in grabbing the gun. A single wild shot was all Castillo could manage.

Lilith and Aniah jumped on Castillo and removed the gun from her hand. Lilith whirled around and held the gun under Castillo's jaw.

"For your information, deputy. Our chutes are lighted, but Aniah turned them off before we entered," Lilith said.

She inhaled and heard a body hit the floor behind her. She whipped around to find her greatest fear coming true. Charlotte had slumped over and lie motionless on the floor. Castillo's desperate gunshot had found Charlotte.

33 - Unfair Trade

Blue and red lights lit up the predawn night sky. Deputy sheriffs cordoned off Broken Cove Parkway. One of the eight county patrol cars pulled back to allow an ambulance through. The siren wailed as the ambulance raced away. Minutes earlier, another ambulance left with Charlotte in it.

Lilith had crumpled to the side of the road, watching the paramedics administer medical assistance to Elliott and Charlotte on the parkway. Kimiko sat next to her in quiet support.

Half an hour earlier, Deputy Castillo had taken a wild shot and hit Charlotte in the face. She was alive, but severely wounded. The bullet shattered the left cheekbone. Traumatized by the sight of Charlotte's gaping face wound, Lilith froze. She didn't know how to stop the bleeding.

Manny and his greenskeepers poured into the alcove and cared for Charlotte. Aniah stood with her foot on the back of Deputy Castillo's neck. She used both hands to aim the gun at the deputy. Manny ushered Lilith out of the alcove to make room.

After a minute, a greenskeeper gave Lilith the news. "She'll live, but she needs a hospital now," he said.

"Is there time to create a story for her injury?" Aniah asked. "Take her into a hospital with a gunshot wound, and our defense of The Village comes to light."

Lilith placed her foot on the back of Deputy Castillo's neck, pushing Aniah's foot away. She slid her hands down Aniah's wrists and took the gun. Aniah took a step back, letting Lilith stand over the deputy.

Lilith pulled the trigger.

Aniah whirled away in horror. Olivia Castillo was dead.

Lilith dropped the gun on Olivia's chest and walked away.

Aniah couldn't look. Olivia was defenseless, but it didn't stop Lilith from killing her in cold blood.

She didn't chase after Lilith, and while she stood in place, she heard the greenskeepers talking about Elliott.

Elliott was on his way from the clubhouse toward The Village when Nico's men emerged from the parking lot. A gunfight transpired on the street with Elliott killing Nico's men, but he was hit by three bullets. The greenskeepers saw the battle and ran to help him.

"I've got it."

Aniah snapped out of imagining the event on the street with the greenskeeper's shout.

"The story for the police. Take Charlotte and put her

beside Elliott on the parkway. He rescued Charlotte and killed her attackers. It explains Elliott and Charlotte's wounds and the three dead men on the parkway."

Aniah twisted around and rushed down the tunnel to Lilith. "It's not over, honey. I've got to take you up on the road. This is what you have to tell the police … "

***

Lilith sat by the road, numb to the world. Kimiko joined her to keep her company.

When Charlotte's ambulance sped away, her attention shifted to a voice which seemed directed at her. The shock she was living in created a thick fog around her. Words lost their meaning. Colors turned gray. Sounds were muddled together. A sharp tap on the arm broke through to her. She turned toward Kimiko, who pointed for her to look up. She lifted her head to find a man towering above her.

"Lilith Daisy Peters. I am Sheriff Musgrave. Can you answer some questions?"

Lilith didn't respond.

Kimiko had her arm around Lilith. "I'm here. Can you talk with the sheriff? Or do you want to go home? Let me know, honey."

"Kimi, why does he want to talk to me?"

"Ms. Peters—"

"He's not talking to Manny, or you. You're an admin member. Why does he want to talk with the gift shop clerk?"

"Ms. Peters. Where were you before the attack?"

Lilith slowly rose to her feet. "Deputy Castillo … Olivia … She was yours, wasn't she?"

"What do you mean by *was*?"

"Which one do you work for: Ernesto or the Bennington Syndicate? She was with Nico. So, you work for Ernesto."

"I don't know what you are referring to."

"We have surveillance footage of Nico's SUVs. Is your SUV by the entrance? Same make and model—"

"You're delusional. This morning's attack has you imagining things."

"We took out nineteen men and one woman last night."

Sheriff Musgrave placed his hand on his sidearm.

"You think you're intimidating me? We have a sniper, and I'm guessing they have you in their sights."

Sheriff Musgrave scanned The Village for a rifle barrel. "You'll return to the Dominican Republic for your friends."

The memory of AJ, Tayen, and Scott's kidnapping infuriated her. "Tell Ernie to meet me tonight at nine at Adela Frontera. If he can't find it, tell him it's where the helicopter landed beside the curved road."

"The meeting will take place tomorrow night. Only you, and you alone, are expected at the mountaintop."

She took a page from AJ's playbook. "He isn't stupid enough to endanger twenty-billion-dollars. Adela Frontera, tomorrow night at nine, just him and me. Unless he wants twenty body bags dumped in his office."

Sheriff Musgrave trained his eyes on Lilith rather than searching for a sniper. "You killed everybody?"

"Why do you think I said *was* in reference to Olivia?"

Lilith turned and walked away.

Kimiko ran to keep pace with her. "Where are you going?"

"Up to Pasta-de-faria's. Shazoo and I need your help."

"Did one of them hurt his majesty?"

"He's not hurt. But he is carrying a mystery, which I believe you are aware of."

"I only transported him from New Orleans to Portland for Priestess LaTonya. I'm not privy to her enchantments."

A minute later, the elevator doors opened. Sonny and Cher greeted them with barks and wild tail wags. Lilith marched past them and proceeded to the bar, where Shazoo sat. Lilith picked up Shazoo and lifted him next to her face for Kimiko to see.

"Ooh! Your eyes … and his eyes? His and her … funky ethereal blue eyes? This might be a problem."

Lilith turned toward the mirror behind the bar. "I suspect Voodoo is involved with our eye color, so figure it out, sister."

Kimiko stepped next to the bar. "Shazoo is staring at AJ's two-dollar piece of shit pirate's chest."

"Yeah, that thing. He said the shipping cost more than two dollars."

She lowered Shazoo and walked behind the bar. It wasn't difficult to climb, and in seconds she straddled over a beer tap. AJ's plastic decorations were plucked and discarded with a vengeance.

"Careful. You're making a mess."

"Son of a bitch." Lilith placed her hand on the deflowered chest. "The protective sealant we keep running across is covering this chest."

Kimiko clasped one hand over the other. "That means … What?"

"Hand me your phone. I need your flashlight."

Kimiko turned the light on and handed it to her.

Lilith shone it in the crevice between the chest and the wall. "Nothing." She hurried around the chest's far side and repeated her search. There, she found it.

"What's wrong?" Kimiko asked after Lilith rested her forehead on the chest and closed her eyes.

"Priestess LaTonya taught you about Haitian Vodou, and she enchanted Shazoo, right?"

"She placed protective enchantments on Shazoo. The enchantments are supposed to be bonded to a person."

Lilith opened her eyes and faced Kimiko. "Did she say if Shazoo and AJ were the bonded pair?"

"I assumed they were."

"What did Priestess LaTonya say?"

Kimiko's eyes darted back and forth between the chest and Lilith. "'Protect this treasured heirloom. The bonding preserved, from Hayati to the daughter marked by Buddha's eyes.'"

"Wonderful. My eyes came from Buddha. But who is Hayati?"

"I practice Louisiana Voodoo. I can't tell you about all the loa from Haiti or Africa. What did you find on the chest?"

"Oh, the name carved into this chest. Master Chest One."

Kimiko gasped and held her hands to her mouth.

Lilith pressed her forehead back onto the chest. "Jade Péchette's chest arrived minutes after I walked in for the interview with Tayen. This ain't a two-dollar piece of shit. It's a twenty-billion-dollar treasure covered in two dollars' worth of AJ's plastic shit."

***

Two nights later, Lilith drove with reckless abandon through the winding darkness on the narrow Dominican Republic road. She drove fast enough to nearly outpace the car rental's headlights. Midway through the long bending curve, sat Adela Frontera.

She skidded the car to a stop near the walkway to the patio. The shadows of the knee-high stone wall confirmed she was in the right place. The gas lamps shone, and the bluish haze appeared like a dome.

She launched herself from the car and ran to the empty patio. Gone were the tables and chairs from her first visit. Behind the tent-sized room, a shadow grew from the surrounding darkness into a form she knew, the caretaker of Adela Frontera.

"Greatest granddaughter of Tempest." His features, as well as the large white dog, became more defined as they came closer. "Examine your heart. What lives within lights the path or leaves you in darkness. I know which thrives within you, but if you enter with hate, darkness will reign."

"My anger is justified," Lilith said.

"Sadness and anger are temporary stages on life's way, and my girl, you are stuck in an eddy where a stream has nowhere to flow. It will take an act of courage for you to escape the trap you are in. The protection of Adela Frontera will not extend to you if harming Ernesto is your intent."

"I am in no position to hurt him. It's just me and nobody else."

"But physical harm isn't your intent. You are ready to deceive and lead your enemy astray."

Lilith tilted her head to the side. "My friend, Kimiko, she was taught by Priestess LaTonya on Haitian Vodou. She believes you might be Papa Legba, and this place could be an open crossroads between the living and the dead. Is she right?"

The caretaker rested his hands on both of Lilith's shoulders. "Kimiko, LaTonya's student, has wonderful insight. Adela Frontera is an open crossroads, and assuming I am Papa Legba is not without merit. But I am not the great and honorable loa of the crossroads of the living and the dead. Kongo, however, belongs to Papa Legba, but they are currently separated."

The caretaker reached down to scratch the dog behind the ear.

Lilith couldn't resist and lowered her hand for Kongo to sniff. "Who are you, and why do you have Papa Legba's dog?"

"I am a steward of the island. Those who come for fair trades are in my care—"

"—Because when you lived here, the fair trade was betrayed, and your people—your aunt, Queen Anacaona—were brutally massacred."

The caretaker winked. "If you discovered who my aunt was, then you know who I am. Determine now which is in your heart. Fair trades are protected."

Headlights from Ernesto's approaching vehicles appeared in the corner of Lilith's eye. She turned her head to find a convoy of lights speeding down the road. When she turned back to the caretaker, he had disappeared.

In rapid succession, the vehicles pulled alongside the road with their headlights beaming at Lilith. A panel van pulled parallel to the patio with its side facing Adela Frontera.

Ernesto rumbled his motorcycle onto the walkway and stopped short of the blue haze. He shutoff the engine and removed his night riding motorcycle glasses.

"The blue haze of Adela Frontera. I encountered it once before." Ernesto rocked the bike back, letting the kickstand secure it in place. "God, what a horrible night that was."

He pulled out a revolver from underneath his leather jacket and fired.

Lilith flinched. Unsure of what happened, she asked, "Did you shoot at me?"

"I aimed right at your chest, baby doll. It sucks when the local folklore becomes reality. I had to see if it was true. While you stand under that bluish dome, I can't harm you."

Lilith felt her chest and stomach to see if she had been shot.

Ernesto holstered his gun. "You want a fair trade?"

"We give you the treasure, and we get to stay alive."

"Forget the finder's fee."

Lilith fought back the urge to yell. "Those were AJ's terms; I have mine. Where is he, and the others?"

"In the van. I'll release them after I have the treasure, and you tell me where Nico and his men are."

"Before we make the trade, I should tell you a story. Otherwise, you won't understand what the treasure is."

Ernesto didn't move or make a sound.

"If you're not ready—"

"GO!"

Lilith flinched. "Jeez, moron. Normal people give a sign it's okay to continue speaking. Idiotic silence or imbecilic shouting aren't great signs."

"I'm listening."

"Afonso de Albuquerque conquered the Sultan of Malacca in 1511."

Ernesto sighed and rolled his eyes.

Lilith ignored him and continued. "Over a three-day period, his men raided the city and stole a vast array of riches. Albuquerque sailed the *Flor de la Mar* from Malacca, but the ship sank, along with the greatest treasure ever lost at sea. Or so legend says."

"Why the history lesson?" Ernesto asked.

"You don't understand what the treasure is. Yesterday, I learned about the history of the treasure from a pile of old journals … " Lilith stopped herself from revealing the journals' location in the Hovel in Barbados.

Ernesto walked over to the knee-high stone wall and sat.

"Um," Lilith cleared her throat.

He pulled his revolver out and pointed at the sky. "It won't work here."

Lilith saw the gun's hammer cock back and spring forward. But no shot occurred.

He returned it to its holster. "What did the journals tell you, Lilith?"

"The Sultan of Malacca had a big family—all girls and one boy. One daughter was gifted with blue eyes. So pure a blue that the locals said it was given to her from Buddha. Suitors from far and near offered treasures and personal fortunes to have the girl. But the Sultan waited for a bounty worthy his inflated ego.

"A ruler in a kingdom to the north, who was hopelessly infatuated over the girl, produced a collection of awe-inspiring coins etched with the daughter's likeness. Each handcrafted gold coin contained two multi-karat Kashmir sapphires which matched Princess Hayati's eyes.

"Albuquerque's covert invasion of Malacca occurred

at the same time as the coin shipment. Princess Hayati ran down from the palace to see the coins. Albuquerque's invasion focused on controlling a bridge in the city's center. His men evaded detection, captured the bridge, and unknowingly surprised Princess Hayati's greeting party. Smitten by her beauty and filled with greed by the coins, Albuquerque kept both. The coins were for Portugal's King, and Princess Hayati would go to the highest bidder.

"Albuquerque's ill-fated and decrepit ship, the *Flor de la Mar*, no longer was suitable for hauling cargo. The Lion of the Sea, a title given to Albuquerque for his prowess in navel superiority, knew it. If the *Flor de la Mar* sank, he didn't want to lose the coins and the girl."

Ernesto's head remained still and his eyes never focused on anything but Lilith's face. She didn't doubt he was taking it all in.

"The question is, Ernesto, did Albuquerque sail his ship into harm's way and trick everyone into believing the treasure was lost? Did four hundred of his men die in the ultimate shell game? The *Flor de la Mar* sailed from Malacca as a lone vessel, but Albuquerque returned to Portugal with five ships. A once-in-a-lifetime treasure ship sailed alone … and five treasureless ships sailed in a convoy?

"Nah. Albuquerque sailed from Indonesia with many ships and the *Flor de la Mar* treasure. And I am proof that one sunk on the way home, off the coast of Benin, the land where my ancestry extends to."

"Your ancestor, Princess Hayati, was the girl from Malacca," Ernesto said.

"The coin is the spitting image of me."

Ernesto lowered his voice. "You have the coins?"

"I'll show you in a moment. For now, back to the

sunken treasure. Did it sink in the Strait of Malacca, or did Albuquerque split the treasure on the ships which sailed for Portugal?"

Ernesto added, "Did the Voodoo Priestess steal the *Flor de la Mar* treasure, or did she intercept the coins?"

"The coins, for sure; the bulk of the treasure, no," Lilith said. "The ship which sank next to Benin carried the girl. I'm proof of it. The coins, rescued and hidden from Albuquerque by parties unknown, accompanied the girl on her journey up the Niger River. Two hundred years later, someone discovered the coins—God, don't ask me where—and sailed for the Caribbean with them in tow. The Voodoo Priestess raided whoever had them, and they remained with her until now."

Lilith pulled her phone out. "Come, look."

Ernesto rose and stepped next to Lilith. He studied the picture on her phone. "It is you."

She swiped the screen. "And this is the space above the bar in our rooftop restaurant where the chest sat until Nico invaded our business."

Ernesto stepped back. "Nico took it?"

Lilith frowned. "He hasn't returned here with the chest?"

"Sheriff Musgrave told me you and your band of misfits killed off Nico's teams."

"Hold on, Ernesto. You sent two dozen men with guns to steal from us and kidnap me. How could we withstand an attack like that?"

"Stop lying to me. Melody is with you in Portland."

"She was there, but no longer. I haven't seen Melody in months." Which was true for Lilith. Melody became Aniah the day after they arrived in Portland.

"Melody isn't with you in Portland?"

"No. Has Sheriff Musgrave teamed up with Nico? Have you found the secret operative the Benningtons have on the mountaintop? Is Nico that spy?"

Ernesto's eyes shot open. "Melody told you? You've talked with District Attorney Miller?"

Lilith played it cool. Aniah had prepared her well to get under Ernesto's skin and ignite his paranoia. "I haven't talked with Miller. But your daughter did say you feared a mole was in your organization. There might be more like Nico in your mansion."

Ernesto raised both hands to the back of his head. "Goddamn-it. Nico has the chest and is keeping it from me." He bolted toward his bike as he screamed his orders to his men, who stood by their vehicles. "The hostages are of no value to us. Discard them and head back to the mansion."

The van door opened, and AJ fell to the ground. He laid lifeless while cadaver bags thudded next to him. Ernesto's bike roared to life, and he peeled off down the road. The van's tires squealed and then chirped as they grabbed the pavement.

Lilith stepped forward, though she wasn't certain her feet were touching solid ground. Her legs felt like lead, and she struggled to move. AJ wasn't moving. The gas lamps' blue glow reflected off his eyes, but signs of life failed to present themselves to her. She saw a blink from AJ, which spurred her to his side. She cradled his bloodied chin and called for help on her phone. "Stick with me. I'm not leaving you."

"The chest. I heard you found the chest." He whispered.

"Help is coming. Stay with me. Manicato I'naru'

Dominican Republic will be here in a minute." Lilith felt the back of AJ's shirt. What she feared had come to pass: Ernesto had inserted a knife in AJ's back and cut his spinal cord.

AJ gazed into the night sky. "I love the night sounds. A thousand screaming parakeets one is rarely privileged to hear."

The menacing screams of an army of parakeets drew Lilith's eyes from AJ to the encircling darkness.

"Owls, the shrill screams," AJ said. "The múcaro veiled by the night, the harbinger of death boasts a kill."

Lilith didn't understand his babblings, nor did she care. Hearing his voice was enough for her.

A van pulled up and Manicato I'naru' Dominican Republic cell members streamed out, hurrying to aid AJ. Lilith stood and walked to the first cadaver bag, unzipping it enough to identify the face. She zipped it up, not allowing herself to fall apart at seeing Scott's face.

She moved to the second bag and unzipped it. It never occurred to her this bag would contain Father Amare's body. The explosion in the turret stairwell under the convent museum had cut his face in several spots. She zipped up the bag and said a prayer for the dead priest.

She came to the third body bag and fell to her knees. It would take a strength she didn't possess to open this bag.

Tony had rushed to Lilith's side. Her collapse over the third forced him to kneel beside her. He unzipped the bag, keeping the opening from Lilith. He closed his eyes and said, "Rest in peace, Manicato I'naru' - Tayen."

Lilith crumbled to the ground. Devastated beyond grief.

***

Late the next day, Lilith dedicated herself to AJ's care, refusing to leave his side at a Santo Domingo hospital. Doctors confirmed what she already knew. AJ was paralyzed from the waist down.

Exhausted and nodding asleep, she sprang up when he held out his hand. She held the water below his mouth and slipped the straw between his lips. After a few sips, she pulled it back.

"The cab dropped off a passenger, sped away, and we assumed the next cab was Candace's father," he said.

"You don't have to tell me what happened."

AJ's need to explain kept him speaking. "Nico jumped out and shoved a gun at us. I figured you saw it and ran. He laughed. For years, they'd suspected the bar held a place of importance to the Péchettes. When they spotted me outside the bar, he couldn't believe it.

"They flew us back and took us in the mansion. They had Scott's laptop, but couldn't access it. I guessed ELF had wiped the hard drive after the feed cut with the explosion. Tayen refused to disclose the Hovel's location. Nico stair-stepped the knife up every vertebra until, on the sixth puncture, she died. He tortured her for over an hour.

"Scott didn't speak, cry, or scream. After three inserts and no reaction, Nico's patience ran out, and he slammed the knife through the top slot. If you gotta go, that's the way to do it. Scott never felt the last insertion.

"Ernesto said I was his message to any who dared to interfere with his operations. He pushed the knife in my back himself."

AJ stared at the ceiling. "They took me to a bedroom and attended to my wound. Apart from the occasional beating, they wanted me alive. Live reminders inspire fear better than dead ones."

He closed his eyes and squeezed Lilith's hand. "The third body bag they dropped."

She squeezed back, assured that the name she spoke would devastate him. "Father Amare."

His hand went limp.

She waited for him to open his eyes before she spoke again.

"Did Nico kill—"

"He killed no one." Lilith didn't allow AJ to finish. "Nico hit us, and we suffered some injuries, but no one died."

"Is Elliott safe?"

"Thanks to Ms. Calveiro, yep. She is going to make an excellent daughter-in-law. Embrace her without worry. And for god's sake, don't piss her off."

"They're engaged?"

"She proposed to him before the ambulance arrived."

AJ's eyes popped open. "Ambulance?"

Lilith braced herself. "Elliott was shot three times in the leg. Nothing serious after they stopped the bleeding. Charlotte will need extensive reconstructive surgery. Her face …"

AJ squeezed Lilith's hand to comfort her.

Lilith wiped her tears away. "We staged their wounds as Elliott coming to Charlotte's rescue by armed men. Elliott heard her scream and responded with deadly force. Sheriff Musgrave isn't challenging the story since we can connect him to Ernesto."

"Shit. People we trusted were spying on us," AJ said.

"He and Deputy Castillo were under Ernesto's orders. District Attorney Miller is a Bennington. I'm betting Miller stole the chest from Dale's chemistry lab. Now for some good news.

"Amateur pirates cleaned the area of Nico's failed invasion. Manicato I'naru' - Portland is the largest cell in our network. I'm using a couple million from our Robin Hood holdings to pay bonuses for their heroic acts and support. In particular, the body disposal."

AJ's question had formed on his lips and disappeared with the last bit of information from Lilith. He blinked, then asked, "You found the chest above the bar?"

Lilith nodded and frowned at him. "Master Chest One. Jade Péchette's chest, and you didn't bother to tell us?"

AJ rolled his head away from Lilith. "When it came, I didn't understand the significance it held. How did you find it?"

"Shazoo and Priestess LaTonya. She enchanted the three of us into a three-way bonding. When Shazoo and I stand next to the chest, our eyes glow that ethereal blue, which freaks everybody out."

"So, you got the chest out of the wall?"

"It took five hours for Kimiko, Talia, Aniah, me, the expensive tequila, and Athena to work through your passwords and designs to bring it down. Talia said it would have taken a few minutes had Charlotte been there. Only she would have worked through the Star Trek trivia and eighties movies without delay."

AJ closed his eyes.

"The chest harness didn't take long to put together, nor did taking it out of the wall and lowering it on the floor. Manny isn't happy about our dismantling … hell, our complete destruction of the bar. It'll take a week to make it as good as new."

"Where is the chest?"

"In the garage. We layered blankets on top, don't worry."

AJ moaned. "A twenty-billion-dollar chest, and you laid a two-dollar POS blanket on top?"

"I deserve that. You weren't lying when you said the shipping was more than two dollars. And talk about being underinsured!"

"Ya think?"

"Aniah prepared me to work under Ernesto's skin. He's ransacking his own organization, trying to find those disloyal to him," Lilith said.

"How did you learn about the story of Princess Hayati?"

"The Hovel went full steam ahead after your kidnapping. They devoured all the artifacts in the basement storage. One journal, author not cited, told the story of Princess Hayati and the coins. Another journal by an unidentified author proposed those questions about Albuquerque and if the treasure sank for real."

Lilith patted AJ's hand. "After they lifted you in the van at Adela Frontera, once the nurses took care of you, the caretaker appeared and whispered in my ear. 'Two and one-third parts 26, one part 27, one half-part 28.'"

AJ gasped. *"If you know how.* Now we know how to be impervious to demons."

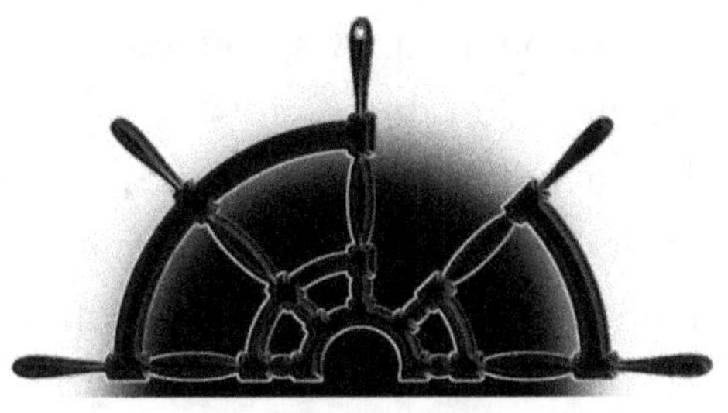

34 - Memorial

AJ listened to the doctor as he laid in his Portland hospital bed. Days earlier, he had been transferred back home from the Dominican Republic.

The doctor stood by AJ's bedside. "I'm sorry about your unfortunate incident, Mr. De Faria. We found no infection in the wound. The knife was razor sharp and perpendicular to the spine. But the wound you suffered will keep you paralyzed from the waist down. Physical rehab will help with your adjustment. The emotional and psychological effects require adjusting too."

The doctor's words didn't register for AJ. Nothing had for the last few days. He had lost three close friends and his legs. The abyss-wide emptiness left him disconnected and depressed.

The hospital sat on a hill which towered over the city.

Lofty clifftop views served as a distraction for patients. Bald eagles soared above the trees. Down in the valley, boats traveled up and down the river, hauling their wares. In the far distance, a halo of clouds crowned the many peaks of the Cascade Mountains.

Well-wishers brought cards, flowers, and candy, which filled the hospital room's counter. The overflow of gifts had uncovered underlying secrets.

Over the past year, Lilith had grown close to AJ and slid into the role of a concerned, caring daughter. This relationship dynamic unfolded without notice to either of them until Lydia and Elliott were engaged.

The daughter-in-law in waiting visited her future father-in-law with loving frequency and predictability. Whenever Lilith returned to AJ's room, her arrangement of cards, flowers, and candies had been rearranged. It didn't take a genius to figure out it was Lydia's doing.

Lilith rearranged the arrangement. When she returned from a bathroom break and a stop in the cafeteria, she found Lydia rearranging Lilith's rearrangement. Lydia left for a quick trip to the hospital cafeteria, and Lilith jumped to the counter to rearrange Lydia's rearrangement of Lilith's original arrangement.

Minutes later, Lydia returned to find her arrangement, rearranged. Lydia glared down range at her deranged counterpart, who pretended to be reading a store's flyer about kitchen ranges.

Lilith glanced above the flyer. Lydia's perturbed appearance didn't escape her. Like a teenager who played dumb as to why mom was angry, Lilith lowered the flyer and shrugged.

Lydia nudged a vase to the right.

This would not be tolerated. Lilith rose, stepped to the counter, and nudged the vase back to the left. Both women raised a brow. The sound of the vase sliding on the counter alerted Lilith. Lydia had nudged the vase while they stared into each other's eyes. But she was pleased to see Lydia's irritation when the sound came again. This time, it was Lilith who nudged the vase.

AJ coughed but remained asleep in his bed.

Both turned to check on him. Seeing he was asleep, they resumed their battle of the vase. This time, however, Lydia had lost her combative stare.

Lilith noticed. Lydia was the rightful heir to be AJ's daughter; she had to yield. Lydia found her adversary's combativeness gone. What each woman saw in the other was the pain they shared from their mutual losses. Reservoirs of tears were pooling in their eyes.

They embraced, lending comfort to each other.

***

A couple of days later, Manny closed Broken Cove Industries for the employees to grieve. The greenskeepers placed Kimiko's tiny flags around the clubhouse and village complex. Blue flags for Scott and white flags for Tayen. The ground rolled like ocean waves when a breeze blew through the country club.

The waterproofing material Father Amare had promised to send to AJ arrived. Dr. Dale followed the mixing instructions and handed the water sealant to Manny's paint crew. Intrigued by a formulation which included hydrochloric acid, Dale asked to watch the application process. Dale's phone signal vanished with the last brush stroke on the subterranean storage room wall. Manny and Dale bent over when a wave of nausea overcame them.

In the clubhouse, memorial portraits of Tayen and Scott sat on easels as lines of mourners filed through. Many questioned how the two tragedies had unfolded at the same time. AJ, Tayen, and Scott's attack occurred on the same day Elliott heroically came to Charlotte's rescue. Some mourners insisted there was a connection.

Chef Dean and Chef Ladonna kept the kitchen staff busy. Idle minds needed busy hands, and the chefs did their part to heal wounded souls.

Servers followed Talia's lead and forewent the playful banter for which they were known. They presented water, soft drinks, and finger snacks for the mourners.

The morning passed with well-wishers complimenting the outstanding informal memorial. When the crowd thinned, the afternoon formal memorial service began.

A low-rise stage faced rows and rows of chairs on the clubhouse's ground floor. The members'-only memorial service waited for the final attendees' arrival.

As the clock struck two, Scott's younger sister, the inspiration for Code Purple, walked down the center aisle accompanied by Lilith. Mourners stood and bowed their heads. Tina wore a mourning veil to hide her tears. Lilith wore a veil to help Tina not feel out of place.

Heads pivoted, and eyes strained at the next pair.

Elliott limped into view with the aid of a petite woman, who wore a black and dark gray niqab. With the deep purples and inflamed reds around Charlotte's left eye, no one questioned the reason for the veil which covered her head. Elliott guided her, and she helped him walk. Retired military personnel saluted him as he passed.

With Elliott and Charlotte seated, heads turned back up the aisle. Lydia wore a mourning veil and wheeled AJ down the aisle. A tribal blanket covered his legs. Turquoise-colored patterns dominated the varying shades of oranges, yellows, and reds.

AJ had asked Tayen's elders for the blanket, which they made for the service. He would attend her memorial on tribal land the next day.

With AJ rolled next to Tina, Lydia scampered out of the way.

A tribal elder spoke first, eulogizing Tayen. Top of her high school class, double major in college, heavily involved in tribal education programs, a grant writer, and a skilled equestrian.

Lilith's jaw snapped down. *Tayen rode horses, but equestrian jumping?*

Her phone vibrated, causing her to jump in her chair. She jammed her hand into her pocket and stopped the buzzing. AJ leaned forward, and she cringed. *He's pissed.*

A minister stood and eulogized Scott. Quiet, loyal, reliable to a fault, and committed to exploring geology.

Rocks? Scott was into rocks? Because his head was always down, I thought he had low self-esteem. Turns out, he was looking at rocks.

A phone buzzed in the row behind her. A slow turn of her head gave her a view of those in the row. It didn't surprise her to find Aniah scrambling to silence her phone. It also didn't surprise her to see AJ leaning his head back to give her the evil eye.

One more vibrating phone and he's going to pull a Jesus and walk from that wheelchair to strangle the one who didn't silence their phone.

The video memorial highlighting Tayen and Scott's lives shone on the hanging screen. Tayen stood an inch taller than her sister and equaled her brothers. One image showed her jumping a gate wearing the proper attire for an equestrian; Lilith was impressed. The barrel-riding montage took her by surprise. The pictures from after Tayen became vice-president of the Fortune 500 company showed the strain she endured. Gone were the gleaming smiles and bright eyes.

The video turned to Scott. Pictures showed his incessant digging in the river. In family photos, he was always holding a rock, or scuffing the ground with his shoe. One photo showed him struggling to push a small boulder from a bridge into the river below. The rocks vanished by the time he hit his college years. The replacement: computers.

A phone vibrated to Lilith's great horror.

AJ reached into his jacket pocket and silenced his phone.

I should lean forward and give him the evil eye.

The last photo shocked and delighted everyone. A chorus of aahs filled the room. Scott leaned on a fence, smiling as the cool dude enjoying the equestrian event at the county fair. Lilith guessed it was a photo from his high school years. But what a strange picture to close out the memorial with.

The background of the photo snagged Lilith's attention. Over Scott's shoulder, a horse had extended for the gate jump. The rider, dressed in her typical elegant fashion, was Tayen.

She slapped her hand over her mouth. A chance photo of her two friends at a fair years ago. She understood why the memorial had ended and paused with this photo.

The video tribute faded, and the minister prayed to

close the ceremony. Respecting the sentiment, Lilith bowed for prayer. Not silencing her phone irritated her to no ends. *Who'd call during a memorial? And Aniah ... then AJ?*

Lilith snapped back to New Orleans in the previous year. Two police officers questioned Tayen, Charlotte, and her about the business logo on the street. Each of their phones vibrated. Scott had tried to warn them of a police visit.

She snuck her phone out and cupped it with the other hand. With her head bowed, it didn't look disrespectful to read her phone during prayer. The message was from the Hovel, but it made no sense. She turned to Aniah, who was reading her phone. Aniah darted from her seat and disappeared around the corner.

Lydia jumped behind the wheelchair after the minister finished praying and rolled AJ down the aisle.

Lilith broke with decorum and jumped beside Lydia. "Take him to the office, now."

Lydia pushed the wheelchair with more energy than a jazz funeral march, which left AJ a bit disconcerted. Lilith apologized to Scott's sister and jogged to the office.

Lilith scooted through the waiting room and to the general manager's office. Aniah stood next to the oval table, clenching her phone in exasperation. "The Hovel is reporting the St. Thomas cell was attacked."

Lilith didn't believe what she heard.

"ELF can't reach the Caymans or the Jamaica cells," Aniah said.

"Whoa, slow down. Why do you say it is an attack on St. Thomas?"

Aniah disconnected the Bluetooth and put her phone on speaker. "Eboni, tell her."

"Our cell in St. Thomas reported explosions and

suppressed gunfire in their office building. Those we spoke to said they were fleeing the area. Fred noticed a massive uptick in communication signals to the Dominican Republic after the attack."

Lilith looked worried, but didn't know what to make of the news.

Eboni's voice trembled with fear. "The Caymans and Jamaican cells aren't answering us. We contacted the remaining cells and told them to find somewhere safe to lie low. Several are headed to Barbados. Tony is out securing food and supplies we'll need for the refugees."

"Ernesto couldn't find Nico," Lilith dropped her head back, "and he's attacking unprotected Manicato I'naru' cells."

"After the failed raid on Portland, he won't try us again," Aniah said.

AJ clenched his wheelchair's arm. "We must take the battle to him. Sorry, Aniah. I know he's your father, and—"

"I'm sick of his path of destruction." Aniah's eyes burned with rage. "Kill him, and I'll deal with the grief later."

"Take it to Ernesto?" Lilith asked. "Nico came to us. We don't have home field advantage, and we don't have the people to attack him."

"It may not be your home turf, but it sure the hell is mine," Aniah said. "I know it better than anyone, except Aunt Patty."

"You can get us past security and into the house? And then what?"

"I can get in without a problem. Give me something and I can create a lot of trouble. Maybe enough to deter more attacks. A little show of force can't hurt."

Lilith raised her hands, palms up, in protest. "What

could we hit them with to stop Ernesto?"

"Go small, infiltrate, and surprise them," Lydia said. "I can hit targets to secure an exit for Aniah if need be."

"Slow it down, ladies," Lilith howled. "I'm not letting two people head off on a suicide mission. Regroup and refocus our efforts elsewhere."

A knock came on the office door, and Dale poked their head in. "Am I disturbing this war conference?"

"Shit. They can hear us in the hall," Lilith said.

"I figured something was wrong when the leadership team ran away. There are a lot of freaked out people in the clubhouse," Dale said.

"Wonderful. Chaos runs unchecked here and in the Caribbean."

"I heard something about another invasion team?"

"Sorry, Dale. Two of us are floating pipe dreams about invading a drug cartel's fortified mountaintop mansion."

"Oh, well, I am here to report my findings—"

"Not the best time for your report." Lilith felt things slipping out of her control.

"Under the circumstances, I'd say my timing is impeccable," Dale said. "From the sounds of it, you need a disruptive force against Ernesto. I have the stuff to do it. I think we can go much further than a simple disruption of his operations. *Destroy* is a better word."

"Our Frontage Street debacle gave us something positive," AJ said.

Lilith whirled her arms in the air, encouraging Dale to explain.

Dale smiled. "The proportions you gave me for the compound mixture work. You have Demon's Breath. In the dust form, the way you received in New Orleans, it induces a twilight amnesia, a minimal state of awareness, and blocks memory formation. The one who ingests this compound is susceptible to suggestions and can function at half capacity. You could grocery shop and remain on task if no one talked to you.

"The aerosolized form works faster and without the sluggishness of the non-aerosol variety. Minimally reduced motor function, heightened suggestibility, hindrance of memory formation ... You could sail a ship with the aerosolized version of Demon's Breath."

"How would we counteract it? How do we make ourselves impervious to demons?" Lilith asked.

"Replace compound 28 with compound 29, use the same proportions, and be prepared to sleep for a day. However, using this continually might prove catastrophic. This is cutting-edge neural science, and I can see potential harm down the road. More testing is needed, plain and simple. I am in the front hall of a thousand-room mansion with what I explored."

Eboni's voice came from Aniah's phone. "Hey, folks, Leonard says if you have a TV close by, you need to turn it on."

Lilith jumped to Tayen's desk, pulled out a remote from the desk drawer, and turned on the TV.

Eboni appeared on the screen in quick order. "I could hijack the clubhouse office TV once it was powered on. As for Leonard's video, you wouldn't receive this local Caribbean feed in North America."

The screen blinked to the scene of a fire consuming a city block. "This was the building the Jamaica cell used."

Everybody in the office groaned in pain. Lilith fell in

Tayen's chair, overwhelmed by the sight of towering flames consuming the building. "What about the Caymans?"

"No contact. But police were called to investigate the report of a mass suicide. The address belongs to one of our members."

Nobody spoke.

Eboni broke the heavy silence. "I hate to bring this up, but if we lose the Caymans, we lose access to every bank account we traced through Tayen's black book. We'll be blind, deaf, and without funding."

Exasperated, Lilith asked, "What else, Eboni?"

"In three hours, we take in fifty Manicato I'naru' members … with more headed here as we speak."

"Can Ernesto find the Hovel, or are you secure?"

Eboni exhaled. "I don't see how he could find us. Then again, if you told me this morning that two cells would disappear and the others had to abandon their locations to flee—"

"—Do have any reconnaissance data on the mountaintop mansion?" Lilith asked.

Fred's voice replaced Eboni's. "With Aniah's help, I constructed models of the inside of the mansion. These are incomplete, but it's better than nothing. Plus, a full 3D rendering of the grounds, with a two percent margin for error. Some underground halls … Never mind. Without a full picture of the mansion, some halls are very weird from an engineering point of view."

Lilith turned to Aniah. "Don't look at me. I don't know what Fred is referring to. We used my photos and sketches. If he sees something, I'm not aware of it."

"Don't sweat it. It's just big picture stuff that looks weird to me," Fred said.

"Dale. How does Demon's Breath destroy that mansion?" Lilith asked.

"It doesn't. But our Frontage Street experiments helped me understand the chemical composition of two of the compounds."

"Scott was right. Just like I said he was," AJ said.

"On that fateful day on Frontage," Dale worked to downplay their delight, "Scott asked what would happen if we combined compounds #9 and #21. I told him nothing significant. Alone by themselves, both were extremely flammable. However, when combined, the resulting compound burns at temperatures reserved for Hell. It is the most explosive formulation I have ever seen without going nuclear."

"Can you reproduce it?" Lilith asked.

"By morning, I can whip up a couple of kilograms."

"I don't believe it. We are going to blow up an island mountaintop," Lydia said.

Lilith ignored Lydia. "Is a couple of kilograms a lot?"

"Two kilograms of the compound will produce a five-hundred-meter concussive blast area with a KSI of … "

Dale saw AJ shaking his head; it was too technical for Lilith. "Ah, to put it another way, be two or three city blocks away when it explodes … And have ear protection."

"Ear protection?"

"Miami will hear it."

"Well, it'd be the second time we made the news in Florida," AJ said.

"Fred … " Lilith stopped for a second to figure out what AJ meant. "Oh, the Tampa Heist. Fred, put your 3D rendering on the screen, please. We have an invasion to plan."

"Is there a month where you folks haven't made the headlines?" Aniah asked.

Lilith shoved Aniah in the back. "Work on the invasion, please."

AJ sat and watched. Aniah, Lydia, and Lilith worked together, pointing to guard towers and tunnels. One idea flowed into the next, where the plan was accepted or rejected in unison.

Lilith twisted her shoulders around to stretch her back and caught sight of AJ. "What's on your mind?"

"You three, you're the invasion force?"

"I don't see anyone else. If Elliott weren't hobbled, he would be an enormous asset. It is up to us, or more and more people will die. It ends on the mountaintop, or we die trying to take control of our lives."

AJ shook his head. "That's not what I'm getting at."

Aniah and Lydia turned around.

"What hit me is you three: protecting those who can't protect themselves, fulfilling the Voodoo Priestess's mission. Captain Andrews's journal listed the organization he worked for as BCP. Aniah is the Bennington, Lydia is the Calveiro, and Lilith is the descendant of Jade Péchette. A daring attack from Aniah, Lydia, and Lilith … A dare from *ALL*."

35 – DARE FROM A.L.L.

Three white limousines sped through the gate entrance and drove down the parkway to the mansion's front door. Protected from the sun under the immense porte-cochère, a dozen women spilled out of the limousines and stood behind the limos. Guards opened the trunks and lifted the sex workers' designer suitcases out.

Kimiko had dyed Aniah's hair platinum to conceal her identity at the mountaintop's monthly party. Aniah matched the sex workers' attire by wearing an oversized white T-shirt and dark gray leggings. Extra-large sunglasses ensured nobody would recognize her as Ernesto's daughter.

The guards performed their detailed, invasive visual inspections of the sex workers—not of the bags—as Aniah prayed they would. It meant the devices in her bag wouldn't get confiscated, and her cover wouldn't be blown.

The women filed into the mansion and proceeded to their boudoirs. Aniah peeled away from them at the end of the hall and headed upstairs.

A guard spotted her slinking down the hall and yelled, "Get your skanky ass downstairs!"

"Skanky? I make more in an hour than you do in a month. Besides, Patty sent me up here to grab Melody's things from her room." Aniah held her room key up for him to see.

"Patty doesn't hand that key to anybody."

"If she handed it to me, then you know I have permission to be up here."

He sneered and moved on.

After unlocking the door and stepping into her room, Aniah pressed her back to the door, so it closed. This was her room, her escape from the hell of her Father's business. But the solace she had once felt here … was gone.

She shook off the ghosts of the past and headed for her closet. Underneath her pile of shoes laid a box containing the knives Nico had trained her to use. He feared when the day came and all hell broke loose, her training in knife fighting would give her a chance to survive.

The box laid deeper under the pile than she expected. Lilith's complaint about her being a slob suddenly made sense.

She opened the box and took out two long blades. Wrapping her palms around the handles, she took comfort in how they seemed to remember her. As much as she detested Nico, she appreciated the training he'd given her. She slid one into her bag.

The next thing she needed to retrieve was the gun Aunt Patty told her to hide for emergencies. Aunt Patty hadn't been warning her about external threats, but the internal ones. Danger would come from someone she knew, not a stranger. Should an imbecile make an advance on her, she was to use the gun.

She pressed her finger over the wall, finding an indentation. With the knife, she sliced into the drywall. A quick punch left a hole, where she stuck her fingers in. A couple of tugs broke the drywall away and allowed her to pull out a gun tote bag.

Out from the closet and dashing to her dresser, she didn't need to turn around when her door opened. "Hi, Aunt Patty. I suppose the idiot asked if you sent someone to my room. If he calls me skanky again, I'm shooting him."

Silver highlights hinted of Patty's age. Her voice echoed her sister's voice, Aniah's mother. It fell between anger and love when she spoke.

"There are two keys for this room. One in my pocket, always. And then I'm told a sex worker had the key. As per my arrangement with Ernesto, not even he has a key to this room. Only one other person has a key: my niece, daughter of my beloved sister."

Aniah didn't want to look in her aunt's eyes. If she did, her anger would dissipate, which she didn't want at this moment. "What deal did you make with Dad after he killed Mom?"

"You don't know he killed your mother."

"He had Nico do it?"

"You don't know that either."

"Who else straps people in the paralysis chair and severs their spines?"

Aunt Patty marched beside her niece. "Why are you here? Why the gun and the knives?"

"What I do with them is my business. Go tell him I'm here. He promised to kill whoever helped those fugitives back in April."

"You don't know that either."

Aniah whirled around. "Goddamn it, Aunt Patty, you gaslight me every fucking time! Dad promised to kill me at Adela Frontera after I flew the helicopter there to help innocent people escape him."

Patty recoiled. "He threatened to kill you? In front of the caretaker?"

Aniah took the time to read her aunt's face. "I wasn't aware you knew about the caretaker."

"Did the caretaker hear Ernesto at the crossroads?"

Aniah pushed her hand down like she was pressing on a table. "The caretaker was standing with us when Dad screamed he would kill the one who flew the helicopter."

"You were under the blue fog?" Patty sat on the bed, lost in her thoughts. "Was there a white dog?"

"Oh, Jesus Christ. Yes, there was a big-ass white dog."

Aunt Patty stared in the mirror. "The black girl with the blue eyes. Is she the true descendant of Tempest and Jade Péchette? Does she have a friend with green eyes that glow in the dark?"

"Damn it, Patty. Have you been sampling the product?"

Patty sprang from the bed. "I don't use drugs and you don't have time to listen to our family story. Know this though: as despicable as your father is, his love for you and your mother is sacrosanct."

Aniah whirled her hands in the air, doing a respectable impersonation of Lilith when she was flustered.

"The Bennington bloodline runs deep in our heritage. The Bennington Syndicate is widespread and your father is nothing but a powerless, numb-nutted fool who does their bidding. They, not your dad, put your mother in the chair. You were to be sold into sexual slavery … "

Aunt Patty paused. The strain on her face told Aniah her aunt was reliving something horrible.

"Ernesto took your mother to Adela Frontera for the bonding ritual. She was suffering from the knife puncture in her back. Paralyzed and refusing to allow you to be sold, she entered the ritual and died, mercifully. A shield extended around you. Her life for your safety. Bristol believed it was a fair trade.

"In the morning, your buyers retracted their offer, and the syndicate lost interest in selling you. The trade was made. Ernesto's part in the ritual was the promise to protect you from all harm, including any threats from him. The bond also extended to your home: this mansion.

"With his threat to kill you, he broke the bonds. The curses are coming and the mountaintop—you included—are no longer protected from our enemies. The barrier which prohibited the descendant of the Voodoo Priestess from exacting her revenge, is gone. Enriquillo, the caretaker of Hispaniola and Adela Frontera, is sending the angel of death to us."

***

The sun set, and darkness fell on the mountaintop above Lake Enriquillo. Two shadowy figures approached the electric fence on the southeast side of the mountain. The canopy of trees shielded them from the full moon on their approach to Ernesto's compound.

Lilith pulled a voltmeter from a duffel bag and tested the electric fence. A quick read showed there was no current. Aniah had successfully disarmed the fence to allow her and Lydia to cut through the chain-link fence.

Lydia snipped the chain-link fence with her wire cutters while Lilith placed the voltmeter in the duffel bag. Lilith crawled through the opening and took the duffel bags from Lydia. After Lydia climbed through the opening, they tip-toed to the command tower's mammoth, faux tree trunk. It only looked like a tree, but it was a cylindrical chute big enough for a ladder.

They knelt beside the faux trunk. Lilith grabbed a pistol from a bag and gripped it like Lydia had taught her. Lydia swung an elongated duffel bag over her shoulder. With a pistol in her hand, Lydia entered the pass code Aniah gave them for the chute-ladder doors. The door unlocked, and they slid it open.

Up the ladder they went, stopping at the top before they entered the command tower. Lilith straddled one side of the ladder with Lydia on the other. The guards were too busy watching the parade of vehicles entering the complex to notice two women aiming pistols with silencers at them.

It took Lilith five shots to down her first target, but by the time she searched for her second, Lydia had finished shooting the other five.

They climbed off the ladder into the command tower.

"You're sick. Five shots to my one."

"I've had a little more practice than you." Lydia crouched below the open gallery window, which overlooked the entire mansion compound, and began assembling her sniper rifle. "Set up our comms link to the Hovel. I'll feel better with air cover."

Lilith plugged a data-streaming stick into the computer console and waited. "I never thought the drones from the country club would be our air defense. Crazy. The groundskeepers are linked through the Hovel, and the drones are waiting for the connection."

A green light flashed on the data-streaming stick. "The Hovel is connected to the tower. Our drones are connecting."

"I can't believe they fit on the plane." Lydia stopped working on her rifle and confronted Lilith. "I also can't believe you own a customized jet."

"Hello?" came Eboni's voice over the comms.

Lilith pushed her comms further into her ear. "Roger. What's your status, Santa's Workshop?"

Lydia laughed. "Charlotte and her naming conventions. ELF is Santa's Workshop."

"At least we didn't get Sasquatch, Mata Hari, or Princess Leia," Eboni shot back.

"Enough. Status, Santa's Workshop," Lilith said.

"Link established on comms. Drones are connecting to Portland. Ready in fifteen. We're on the verge of breaking into the computer core, but the secured server ... The encryption is tight, but Mata Hari's data-streaming stick is giving us a good chance."

Lilith dropped her shoulders and sighed. Aniah's infiltration had succeeded.

"Thanks, Santa's Workshop. Princess Leia, changing clothes."

Lilith unzipped her black top and let it fall to the floor. Underneath it, she wore a burgundy lace-up strapless corset. Just as fast as she lost the black top, she stepped out of her sweatpants, under which she wore a matching burgundy micro skirt and lace up over-the-knee boots.

The first mountaintop mansion visit had shown how salacious the party attendees dressed. Kimiko remembered Charlotte's descriptions of the attire and put her mind to it to design a killer outfit for Lilith. However, Lilith wasn't prepared for the lace up over-the-knee boots.

Lydia couldn't stop peeking at Lilith. "Over-the-knee boots without heels?"

Lilith reached in a bag and pulled out two detachable heels. "From flats to stilettos in a simple click, by Kimiko."

"I've worn nothing that provocative before. At least not in public."

"I haven't worn anything this provocative in private, let alone in a party setting. I feel as though if I pull one thread, this thing will fall on the floor."

As she straightened her clothes, Lilith looked over the sprawling mansion complex. The fountains sparkled, and the gardens were lush with blooming flowers. Accent lights animated the flower's colors. The marble driveway glittered like a Hollywood movie premier.

"Damn, this is beautiful. As big as the clubhouse and as long as the first hole."

Lydia adjusted the rifle's scope. "Just shy of six football fields."

"Can you reach the guard towers at the far end?"

"With this? Yep."

Lilith surveyed the guard towers, which lined the perimeter of the mansion compound. But something was wrong. "Ah, Lydia. How many guard towers are there?"

"Nine, including this one and the front gate."

Lilith counted them again. "I think they added two

guard towers. I'm seeing nine besides this one and the front gate."

Lydia poked her head up and clicked on her comms. "They added two towers?"

Lilith pointed at the recent additions. "One is next to the helipad wasn't on Aniah's sketches. And there is another way, way down on the corner. If there are two guards per tower, your shot total increased by four."

"I'll have to change the shot order, but I can do it." Lydia attached the suppressor. "Where's the music to the towers, Santa? My suppressor muffles the shots; it doesn't drown them out."

A second later, music could be heard coming from the towers.

"Excellent. Thank you, Santa."

Lilith checked the streaming stick and depressed the comms button in her ear. "Are we ready?"

"Five of the drones aren't working, but we have twenty headed your way. Sasquatch, we have confirmed you have two additional towers," Eboni said.

"Those drones better do their job and knockout their comms. If these guys talk to one another, they could coordinate an attack on me," Lydia said.

"You'll be protected, and don't turn off your comms."

Lilith picked up a duffel bag. "I'm headed down to the tunnels. You gonna be okay by yourself up here?"

"If the drones create confusion, like we planned; if Aniah did what she's supposed to do; and the dumbasses don't figure out this tower is the center of the attack. I'll be fine. What scares me is you going into the den of lions. You're going to be rubbing shoulders with them."

Lilith shrugged. "What other choice do I have?

Everything is dangerous tonight."

She left the command tower and climbed down to the underground tunnels. At the bottom of the ladder, she took out a gas mask out of her duffel bag and fitted it around her face.

"Princess Leia in. Where's the intake vent?"

Fred's voice came over the comms. "Above your head and down the hall."

"Oh, I see it."

Lilith jogged to the intake vent for the air-duct system. She pulled out a flask from the duffel bag. Dale had designed a small fan and nebulizer for the flask. It was going to aerosolize Demon's Breath and dust everybody in the tunnels.

She lifted the flask and flipped on the fan. The powder zoomed into the vent, to Lilith's joy. Depressing her comms, she asked, "How long before everybody in the barracks is down?"

"When the flask is empty, you can go," Eboni said.

Lilith waited. Seconds felt like minutes. She kept watching down the tunnel, hoping the dust was doing the job. If a guard confronted her, at least she could say she was lost. After all, she was dressed like one of the sex workers.

The small fan petered out. Lilith rattled the flask, but it was empty. "Demon's Breath delivered. Princess Leia moving on."

"Roger," Eboni said.

She lowered the flask to the floor and stepped forward with the last remaining duffel bag. It took her what seemed an eternity to reach the underground kitchen, where no guards were in sight.

The door next to the kitchen was the sleeping quarters. She cracked the door open and peeked inside. The lights were on and the men laid on their bunks, sound asleep. "Santa, startup the suggestion playlist."

Aniah's voice came over the speakers. In a warm, relaxed tone, her prerecorded message began a lengthy list of hypnotic suggestions. The first was to seek law enforcement agencies and expose the inner workings of Ernesto's organization.

Lilith proceeded to the munitions room, the last room before entering the mansion basement. It was filled with enough weapons and explosives to make a small country envious. She pulled two bladders from her duffel bag and hid them behind a gun rack. A quick flip of the switch on top of the first bladder turned on a signal transmitter.

"The bladders are in place." The computer on the desk by the door distracted her. A streaming stick protruded from a USB port, and it was blinking green. Aniah had been here.

Fist pumping into the air, Lilith gave her order to Eboni. "Inform Sasquatch. She is in the clear."

Lilith hurried to the basement door. She removed her mask and held her breath as she entered the basement. If any Demon's Breath floated around, she didn't want an accidental dose to put herself to sleep.

Once inside, with the door shut, she learned her comms weren't working. She depressed the comms button. "Santa? Mata Hari?"

No reply.

Crap. No time to panic.

She climbed the stairs up to the ground floor. Men approached her with cash in hand. Most flashed the money in her face, which she flat out ignored. A couple tried stuffing money down her corset. She wasn't turning tricks, but she was body dropping perverts. With their hands at her chest, she turned and stuck out her hip as she pulled their arms forward and down, slamming the would-be groper to the floor.

After the second body drop, she caught sight of herself in a wall mirror and was impressed. Not only did she look sensational in a martial arts pose, but she body dropped a guy in heels.

Her path to Ernesto's office sent her through the parlor room, where she witnessed the murders of three people. She attempted to block out the memories, but it came flooding back to her.

The guests huddled against the wall, scared and trembling. Charlotte's face was covered with blood, and the man beside AJ didn't sneeze. The gunman pulled the trigger—"

Lilith shuddered and jerked her head to the side to dislodge the memory. She faced straight ahead and made a beeline for the hallway leading to Ernesto's office.

She rounded the corner and stumbled into a man in a wheelchair. She froze for she knew him. It was Greg, the man Ernesto paralyzed in front of her.

Their eyes met. His face had deep wrinkles and blotches of discoloration. It was the face of a life ruined and filled with despair.

Greg recognized her, but didn't say a word. She expected he would at least give her the once over considering what she was wearing. But he didn't. His eyes never broke contact with hers.

Lilith's heart went out to him. She bent over with her face close to his. "I'm so sorry, Greg. If you can leave, do so. Get off this mountaintop now and get as far away as you can."

She hurried around him without saying more.

"4-7-2-8-1."

She stopped, realizing what he had said. He had given her the pass code to Ernesto's office. She repeated to him, "Get off this mountaintop, now."

Armed with the pass code, she marched to the office. It worked. She hurried inside and shut the door.

The sole light source to the room came from the computer monitor. She rushed to the desk and untied a corset string below her breasts. She pinched inside her corset and pulled out a flash drive, which she inserted into the computer's USB port. A series of flashes on the drive ended in a solid green light.

"Lilith? Are you there?" Eboni's voice echoed her fear of losing Lilith.

"I'm okay. What happened to comms?"

"A signal in the mansion cut us off. The origination point is a mystery, but I see you're in the office. Our program is working … and working … and piddles."

"Piddles?"

"We have a blocked file. Leonard's on it. But … "

After waiting for Eboni to finish, Lilith asked, "But what? What's happening?"

"Leonard's right. The mansion has construction oddities. I suppose we can figure those out later?"

Lilith's attention diverted away from construction details to the chop-chop sound of a helicopter outside the window. "I hear a helicopter. It's getting louder."

The monitor blinked. "I'm streaming the helipad camera to you," Eboni said.

A man ran from the helicopter that had landed.

Lilith studied the monitor. "I'm almost certain that's

Ernesto. I've got to get out of here."

She jumped from the chair and before she reached the door, an explosion from outside shattered the windows. Glass shards turned into lethal projectiles and shredded the chair she'd sat in. She dropped to the floor and leaned against the wall.

Partygoers shrieked, blood-curdling screams, and shouts pierced the office walls. A brilliant yellow flash gave way to a thunderous explosion, where the tower outside from the office had exploded.

The door burst open, shattering the door frame, and four armed men entered. The lights flashed on, and the men aimed their guns at Lilith.

Another explosion thundered in the background as Ernesto marched into the office. On seeing Lilith, he yelled, "Whoever you have out there, tell them to stop or you're dead!"

"I'm here for the party—not to attack your gorgeous home, Ernie."

Ernesto grabbed Lilith's arms below the shoulders, picked her up, and hurled her into a chair. "It's time I taught the leader of Manicato I'naru' a lesson after lying to me about Nico."

"I didn't lie. I omitted precise details and asked questions, which your paranoia converted into a conspiracy."

Ernesto twisted and swung his open hand to slap her in the face.

Lilith saw it coming, blocked his hand, and twisted his wrist, bending it back to his forearm. She slipped down off the chair and locked her leg behind his. Wrenching his arm forward, she pulled Ernesto to the floor. Before she could wrap her arm around his neck, the four guards pulled her off of him and threw her back into the chair.

A guard wound up and threw a vicious punch, which broke her nose and sent blood gushing over her mouth. Lilith tried to cover her face, but they had pinned her arms and tied them to the chair. She went to kick, but they had strapped her ankles too. She tilted her head back, which left her face exposed. The guard took the shot and nailed her under the eye. Had her arms not been tied down, she would have spun out of the chair and fell on the floor.

"Stop it! They don't want her harmed," Ernesto yelled.

A series of explosions pulsed through the air.

"Tell your people to stop, Lilith, or I swear, we will kill everybody in your Manicato I'naru' Network. I got a couple dozen last time."

Lilith struggled to sit upright. Blood flowed from her nose and her eye began to swell. "Fuck you. It ends tonight. Touch my people, and I'll kill you."

A guard reported, "Nobody is answering in the command tower."

"Go. Get it under control. I can handle this twat."

Lilith's comms earpiece had dislodged after she took the punches. It was dangling from her ear and about to fall when Eboni's voice came through. "We're in." The earpiece fell.

The fog of a concussion left Lilith feeble and groggy. "Trouble, Ernie? Your command tower doesn't answer, your computer is hacked, and … Shit, I forget what else we did."

"If you hacked our computers, you could only breach the lower operating systems. The server is shielded from outside attacks."

"How about inside attacks?"

Ernesto stared at Lilith.

"Yeah. That's what I forgot. Inside attacks, which your daughter started this morning. She posed as a sex worker and snuck in this afternoon."

"She couldn't access the restricted files."

"No, but with her help, we didn't waste time on the first firewall, which gave us time for the next fire-thingy."

Ernesto faced Lilith, but his eyes were glued to his computer monitor.

"Lots of gunfire, wouldn't you say? Are your men hitting anything? It's like they're shooting blanks."

Ernesto leaned forward on his desk.

"Your daughter and the sex workers exchanged live ammunition for blanks. Had your guards checked the suitcases, they'd have found hundreds of blank rounds. Whatever RPGs are, we did those too. Plus, we did a fourth, or fifth—I've lost count—thing. A transmitter in the munition room terminal let us in your computer files."

"RPGs. You're using them on the towers."

"And those cute whistles," Lilith tried to right herself from slumping over, "are mine. Our drones are firing heat-seeking missiles. Teeny little missiles which are shitting all over your parade."

Ernesto swiped the monitor off his desk, sending it crashing against the far wall.

"We pulled your teeth without you knowing. No bullets, no computer shield, and a sizzling hot professional sniper is wrecking your shit up."

"You have a girl sniper?"

"Yeah. Sizzling hot. I should tell her I find her attractive. Damn. Concussions and Demon's Breath make me chatty."

"Who's the woman sniper?"

"Oh, yeah. `bout that. Do you remember the family who framed your stolen art a few years back?"

"The Calveiro girl assumed her dad's profession?"

"Hell yeah she did."

Ernesto pulled a gun from his desk drawer. "I'm not sticking around here while your people shoot this place to hell. We're going to the helicopter."

Aniah burst through the door and pointed a gun at her father. "She's with me." Aunt Patty stepped in behind her niece and strode up to Ernesto. She jabbed her pistol under his chin.

"Melody," Ernesto said.

"Game's up. Your time is over, Dad."

Aniah lowered the gun and began undoing the straps on the chair to free Lilith.

Aunt Patty took the gun out of Ernesto's hand and pushed him back into his chair.

"Patty, we can work this out."

"Your time is over, Ernesto. You broke the bond in front of the caretaker, and the curses are your reward. The Bennington Mansion is no longer under protection."

Ernesto pleaded. "Patty, don't do this. Melody can fly us off the mountaintop."

"My niece's name is Aniah, not Melody."

Aniah placed her arm around Lilith and helped her stand. "My god. Look what they've done to you."

"The guy with the mole on his nose. He hit me."

"Oh, good. I didn't waste four shots on Bart for nothing. I killed him on our way here." Aniah replied.

Lilith pointed to the outside. "Hey. Do you hear that? No gunfire or explosions."

Patty looked at the broken monitor on the floor. "Madam Priestess, did your people shutdown the computers?"

Lilith pressed her ear, having forgotten her comms earpiece had fallen out.

Aniah used her comms. "Mata Hari to Santa's Workshop. Do you have the files?" She nodded her head and addressed Aunt Patty. "We got what needed, but is there a problem?"

Patty dipped her head. "Take your friends to the helipad and leave."

"Aren't you coming with us?"

"No, my dear. I have to stay. This is my station, and I have to close it down."

Shocked, Ernesto asked, "Your station? You … you are the Bennington mole?"

Aunt Patty said, "This mansion belongs to my family. It was built three hundred years ago by Bill Bennington. We let you run your cartel from here so we could keep watch over you. God, I had to change your plans so many times. You functioned as a lightning rod to keep authorities focused on you, not on the Bennington Syndicate. But this is done. You're exposed and the planes are on their way. Time for the Bennington daughters—or Syndicate Sisters—to move on without you tying us down."

Lilith planted her foot to stop her and Aniah's progress to the door. "Hello, what? Syndicate Sisters?"

"Madam Priestess, please. Order my niece to take you away from here."

Ernesto moved toward Aniah.

Aunt Patty shot a warning shot in front of Ernesto. "Don't move. You're staying with me. Madam Priestess—"

"We're leaving. But explain this sister syndicate thing."

Aunt Patty gripped the gun tighter. "Aniah has more aunts. We form the governing body of the syndicate and stay behind the scenes to defend our namesake's fortune. A fortune which is both realized, and forgotten."

Aniah stared at her aunt. "You already have an abundance of wealth and control: the realized fortune. But you're after the forgotten … the lost treasure."

"Jade Péchette didn't have exclusive rights over the entire *Flor de la Mar* treasure. Others have a claim to it."

"Bill Bennington," Lilith said.

"And his daughters," Aunt Patty added.

"Jade Péchette's War." The pieces of the past were coming into focus for Lilith. "Jade versus the Bennington daughters. Where does Calveiro fit in?"

"Who do you think bore Bill Bennington's children?"

Lilith slumped in Aniah's arms. The news of Captain Morena Calveiro and Bill Bennington being Lydia's ancestors was another punch in the face. "Get me out of here."

Aniah put her head down and assisted Lilith down the hallway. Neither spoke as they worked their way to the helipad.

Lydia stood next to the helicopter, holding the door open. "Success?"

Neither responded to her.

Aniah helped Lilith in. She slipped into the pilot's seat and powered up the helicopter. Lydia sat in the back with Lilith, bewildered by the silence and estranged looks Lilith and Aniah gave one another.

Aniah banked the helicopter hard over the ridge and

descended rapidly from the mountaintop.

Lydia grabbed her seat. "What's the hurry?"

"Others are coming, and Aniah's getting us the hell out of here," Lilith said.

An explosion shook the helicopter.

"Eboni. Wait until we are away," Lydia screamed.

A series of massive explosions erupted on the mountaintop. Aniah banked the helicopter hard, knocking Lydia and Lilith to their sides.

"What are you doing?" Lilith yelled.

"I'm getting low to avoid the concussions from the blasts and staying out of sight from the fighter jets firing on the mountaintop."

"Fighter jets? Those aren't Dale's explosives?" Lydia asked.

Aniah pointed at the full moon.

Lilith pushed up beside Lydia to look out the window. The silhouette of a fighter jet passed in front of the moon.

"Who the hell sent fighter jets?" Lydia asked.

An enormous explosion lit up the sky and rocked the helicopter.

"*That* was Dale's," Aniah said as she managed the flight stick.

Lilith rolled back to sit in her seat. "Aunt Patty had fighter jets? Call Eboni and find out what Leonard suspected."

Lydia pressed her comms. "Santa's—Hell, we're done with code names. Eboni, what did Leonard discover?"

Aniah flipped on the cabin speaker for them all to hear.

Eboni's voice burst through. "Is everybody okay?"

"We're fine, but what is Leonard's surprise?" Lilith

asked.

"Through their internal monitoring system, Leonard recorded most of the mansion. Two sets of stairs continued down below the basement level. Also, a bunch of electrical conduits ran into the floor. There was something underneath."

Aniah's voice came over the speaker. "Tunnels below the tunnels? We may have popped the zit, but failed to get rid of the underlying infection."

"Thanks, Eboni," Lilith said. She leaned away from Lydia and pressed herself against the door, with her back to Lydia. Aniah turned off the speaker without saying a word.

Lilith and Aniah's silence flustered Lydia. "We are alive, and a drug cartel is crippled, if not decapitated. Yet, you two are acting like we lost."

Lilith reached above the door and grabbed a headset. Lydia did the same.

"We are the direct descendants of an ancient feud, and our families are on opposite sides," Lilith said.

"You and Aniah?"

"We mean the three of us. Me against you and Aniah."

Lydia trained her stare in the mirror, expecting confirmation from Aniah.

Aniah turned the mirror to keep Lydia from seeing her face.

36 - The New Team

From late September until mid-December, life returned to normal at Portland's premier golf resort. A national golf magazine touted Broken Cove Country Club as one of the finest golf courses in the world. The country club's popularity soared to new heights, and the influx of new customers kept everyone busy.

Charlotte preferred a solitary corner in the general manager's office. A navy-blue veil stretched from ear to ear and concealed the gunshot wound, which had left her face disfigured. Reconstructive surgery was progressing, but restoration was far away.

The new general manager adhered to his rehab. Elliott's limp lessened each day. He removed the bolts from the desk and sent his father's portrait to storage.

Construction neared completion on his and Lydia's new home. The three-acre lot beyond the ninth green suited their needs. An early wedding gift from AJ sat in their backyard: two customized golf carts. *The Commodore* for Elliott, and *The Revenge* for Lydia.

Lilith planned on moving from Portland to the Hovel in Barbados after Elliott and Lydia's wedding. Aunt Patty's revealing of the Bennington Syndicate meant Manicato I'naru's work did not conclude with the mountaintop's destruction. Tayen's black book held the secrets needed to collapse the syndicate.

On New Year's Eve morning, Lydia dangled a breakfast bag over the counter for Lilith. Since the mountaintop's destruction, they—along with Aniah—had agreed to form a partnership, not a rivalry. Regardless of what had transpired centuries ago with their ancestors, they would share equally in the spoils, whatever the spoils might be.

Lilith took the bag from Lydia and lifted the beverage carrier from the counter with the four man-o'-war sized coffees. They did whatever small favors they could for AJ to help reduce the stress of adjusting to life as a paraplegic.

Elliott helped in the mornings. He cleaned the kitty-litter, exercised the dogs, wheeled his dad downstairs, and opened the door for Lilith and breakfast.

Lilith's arrival at the back door had conditioned Sonny and Cher to a familiar routine. They sat still through the distribution of breakfast. With everything in place, they raised their begging eyes to Lilith, who couldn't say no and fed them bacon treats.

Lilith pressed her fork into the spinach and cheese soufflé and noticed AJ focused on the eastern turret stairwell. "Is the elevator finished?"

"Completed last night," AJ said. "We're waiting on the inspections this afternoon. When the turrets were built, little did we know we left enough room for a two-person elevator. Elliott and I cheated this morning and took it for a ride."

"What a great feeling." Lilith forged ahead to create a positive affect into their morning. "You're regaining the freedom to roam the house. We're getting back to normal."

"Alright, Pollyanna," AJ said. "If there's a positive to the elevators, it's that Elliott no longer has to drag me up and down the stairs."

Elliott lowered his coffee. "I won't miss it, but if you think I was inconvenienced, think again."

AJ turned to his son. "It hurt to watch you struggle during rehab. But now, with your limp barely noticeable, I feel like things are getting back to normal."

Charlotte opened the back door and greeted the dogs. They had taken a special interest in her over the past months, as if they knew she was injured. Lilith sprang up and hugged her. Afterwards, she stepped in front of AJ and bowed her head to him. He kissed her on the forehead, and she took the seat next to him. This was their ritual, which no one questioned.

"Dale worked on our chests and reported to me last night. They have really worked hard to understand the Marie Daly Chest," AJ said.

"You want to talk about this now?" Lilith protested.

"We four are the new inner circle." AJ's voice cracked, which forced Lilith to look away.

"We were hit hard. Two of us are gone, and a tremendous ally … A great friend from New Orleans no longer graces us with his presence. For their sake, we must finish what was started. If we have cause to celebrate, it's because your nose and cheek bone have healed."

Lilith twisted her head around so fast her hair whipped over her face. "Look who's doing the Pollyanna crap."

"I want us to review Dale's report," AJ winked at Lilith, "before dragging significant others in."

"Fine. But I want to share my news first." Lilith scrolled on her phone.

"Look at you. Tayen wanted you in management, and now you look and sound like her."

Elliott answered Charlotte's text. "Don't call her Princess Madam or Madam Princess. And Madam Lilith may carry connotations she may not want."

Lilith laughed. "Her new angle to work under my skin is this international brothel title. Since I read everything about the Roanoke Colony, she hasn't been able to tease me."

Elliott folded his arms and eyed Charlotte.

"Recruitment numbers for Manicato I'naru' are through the roof," Lilith began. "College grads with accounting and banking backgrounds are flooding in. Family and extended family want in on this fight.

"Next, construction will give us a five-story underground command center. The money we siphoned off Ernesto's accounts with Aniah's help is covering the expenses."

Elliott twiddled his fingers.

Lilith caught his action out of the corner of her eye. "Hundreds of millions, Elliott. We confiscated hundreds of millions."

"Yep. She adopted Tayen's habits," Elliott said.

"I'm directing the investment of every penny we can

into building facilities for the Manicato I'naru' Network and Broken Cove Charities Caribbean. There is a tremendous need for public assistance throughout the area."

Charlotte knocked on the table and pinched her earlobe while pointing at Lilith.

"The sapphire earrings are a onetime indulgence. With an unlimited expense account, it just looks like I'm rich."

Charlotte touched her chest, questioning Lilith's sapphire silk designer top.

"Come on, girl. Fire earrings demand a matching top. Don't tell me this ain't dope. And the skirt and boots were on sale."

"When speaking with Charlotte, anyone's last sentence always starts with the word *and*. We've been trained to guard against her getting the last word," Elliott said.

Lilith laughed. "I'm done. Who's next?"

Charlotte texted her news.

AJ read it and commented. "Patience is the key, and you're making excellent progress. I'm sure you're counting the minutes before they unwire your jaw. Your doctors are the best, and they aren't cheap."

Charlotte pointed back and forth between Lilith and AJ.

"I'm paying for your plastic surgeons. Lilith wanted to, but you're my responsibility. I had to pay for it," AJ said.

Lilith looked forward, remembering their bitter debate after Halloween over Charlotte's surgery expenses.

All eyes turn to Elliott. "Sales continue to grow, Code Purple has eight successful passages, the wedding is on schedule, and the contract for a women's professional golf tournament is under review by our attorneys."

AJ clapped his hands together. "Yes."

Sonny and Cher barked at the hand clap, sending Shazoo onto the table next to Charlotte.

"Sorry, sorry. My excitement got the best of me."

Elliott calmed Cher with head scratches. "That is my present to you. Although Tayen greased the wheels for us."

Lilith cupped her hands under Sonny's floppy ears and kissed his nose. "Your turn, AJ."

"Very well."

AJ's tone alerted Lilith of what was coming. She gritted her teeth and drew her shoulders up, shielding herself from him.

"Lilith lost the fight over Charlotte's surgery expenses, but she got even by paying off my bank loans. How she got the bank account numbers is not a mystery. My suspicions are unconfirmed, but it sure the hell ain't a mystery."

Charlotte held Shazoo in her arms. Her indifferent shrug warded off AJ's stare.

"Our understanding of the compound boxes," AJ gave up on staring Charlotte into a confession, "is limited without Jade's chemistry notes. The glassy sealant material has Dale baffled. Other than melting it with acid, it hasn't revealed its secrets. But Dale uncovered something else.

"Dale watched Manny apply the water sealant to my underground basement. Adding hydrochloric acid to plastic beads to form a water sealant was too fringe for Dale, so they had to see the stuff in action. When Manny spread the mixture on the concrete walls, he covered the surfaces with our mystery-glass substance. That's when Dale discovered the last property: resistance to electromagnetic radiation."

Lilith waited for more.

AJ tapped his phone.

She realized he wouldn't proceed without her permission. "Go ahead with technical stuff."

"I learned to wait for you before launching into technical stuff with your history on science."

Charlotte snorted.

"Electromagnetic radiation resistant means cell phone signals won't penetrate. Not infrared, not microwave, ultraviolet radiation and x-rays … Nothing on the electromagnetic spectrum can penetrate it. This baffled Dale because they could see through it."

Charlotte texted furiously.

As she did, AJ continued: "This material reflects whatever is closest to it. When it's on the concrete wall, we see the reflection of the wall beneath the surface."

AJ read and addressed Charlotte's long text. "Dale and Manny threw up after they finished the water sealant. Just how we felt when we first stepped in the map room. Dale performed another test and found this material is also resistant to magnetic fields.

"Enclose a room with this material and you eliminate the earth's magnetic fields. When we transition into that void, we experience a mind-numbing nausea for a split second. Recovery doesn't take long, but for that one gut-wrenching second, you want to die."

"So, when we enter the storage room, we'll be sick every time?" Lilith asked.

"Every time. We have scheduled tests in—"

"Will the test explain how my picture ended up on the wall instead of my great-grandmother Jade?"

AJ pointed at Lilith's amulet. "The eyes on your amulet and the eyes of your face on the map room wall glowed in sync."

"They are linked?"

"Possible. They're covered in the same stuff. Is the wall getting a signal from your amulet? It's a fair question."

Elliott and Lilith glanced at one another.

"I suggest we come back to the amulet." AJ frowned as he turned from staring at Lilith's amulet. "Charlotte reviewed the Tampa Heist records. We know the museum sent documents to an astrophysicist in Oxford, Ohio, but we don't have them, nor do we know what they contained."

"Why consult an astrophysicist?" Elliott asked.

"Someone in Tampa ran across an anomaly and had enough of a science background to realize something unique was at work. They weren't messing with something above their expertise, so they sent the documents to Oxford."

"Speaking of which, we have a Master Chest to open. A pirate's legacy waits for us in your garage," Lilith said.

"It would have been nice to open in the bar."

"Not with the increase in business," Elliott said. "Since *Golfer's Paradise* ran the rapturous review, we haven't had a moment's rest. Customers hang around here until midnight, and they're here when Coffee Cov*fefe* opens."

Charlotte texted.

Lilith read it out loud. "Today's the first day a line didn't form at opening, and only two deep at the busiest point half-an-hour ago." She turned to Charlotte. "Do you have the wolf pack reporting to you minute by minute?"

Charlotte texted.

"Oh. They're bored and texted how slow things are."

AJ turned his wheelchair around. "Let's open it before too many people come for lunch."

He led them to the garage. Lilith nudged and teased Shazoo with her foot as they went. Elliott pulled the canvas bags off the chest as Charlotte kept the dogs out of his way. Shazoo jumped on top of the chest after Elliott yanked the last canvas off.

"Shazoo is sitting there like he owns it," Lilith said.

AJ smiled. "Priestess LaTonya had the chest for years. Shazoo was a kitten when Kimiko brought him from New Orleans. Both gifts to me from Priestess LaTonya, who bonded them together in one of her religious rituals."

Elliott bent over the chest. "How do we open it?"

Charlotte stepped forward and pulled a pipette and a small vial from her bag. She used the pipette to spread the liquid along the crack between the chest lid and its side.

"Dad, what is Charlotte doing?"

"Breaking the glass seal with an acid." AJ leaned forward as beads formed and dropped to the floor. "It's like a fast-acting candle wax falling down the chest."

The wax-like substance hit the floor and formed into perfect circular beads of assorted sizes. As they formed, they rolled toward the drain in the floor. Elliott scrambled to throw a canvas bag on the floor before the beads entered the drain.

"Thank you, Son. We don't want those floating out to the ocean."

Charlotte circled the chest and bent down to survey her work.

Elliott stepped forward to open the chest, but Lilith stopped him. "In the movies, the person who opens the chest receives the curse."

Elliott retracted his hand. "I defer to a senior partner."

AJ rolled in front of the chest. "Chickenshits. Scott wouldn't have hesitated."

He lifted the lid. Unable to push it open, Elliott and Charlotte took the corners and finished lifting it.

"Uh oh, you're all cursed," Lilith teased.

They ignored her.

She stepped forward to find a pair of leather boots laying on top. "Is this a joke? Jade placed leather boots in a treasure chest?"

"Charlotte, use rubber gloves and put them in a garbage bag. Add a DNA test to Dale's to-do list," AJ said.

Elliott turned to his father. "Did Jade unlock DNA in her research?"

"If we find her journals, we can answer that."

Charlotte lifted the boots from their tray and held them up. As she did, they unfolded, causing Lilith to gasp.

"Over-the-knee leather boots?" Lilith spun around, excited over the discovery. "I'm a fashion queen because my ancestor was one first. It's genetic, not a personality flaw."

AJ shook his head. "I'm done underestimating that woman. Her expertise ranges from DNA and astrophysics to women's fashion. And I'll ask before Charlotte mentions it. Why did Lilith receive the fashion gene rather than the one for science?"

Charlotte wobbled her head; he had predicted her thoughts.

She handed the boots to Elliott, who placed them in the garbage bag. She bent over the chest's edge and lifted out the tray insert. After she placed the tray on the floor, she jumped beside Lilith, who was as quiet as a church mouse.

Pristine gold coins with hundreds of sapphire eyes twinkled in the light. Nobody spoke. The sight was too overwhelming for any words to capture.

Lilith broke the silence, confirming the chest's first treasure pieces. "Princess Hayati's dowry coins." Her eyes reflected the golden light and the sapphire sparkles.

"Jesus," Elliott remarked, "that is you."

Charlotte and Lilith stood silent.

AJ lifted a coin for a closer look. "It's heavy, and the artistry is astonishing."

Elliott picked one up and studied it. After a minute, he said, "The coin's edge doesn't have a uniform pattern."

Charlotte picked up a second coin and compared the edges. Elliott did the same.

"What have you two found?" AJ asked.

"The edge markings appear to be random, but randomness doesn't mirror uniformity."

"What?" Lilith asked.

Charlotte banged her coin's edges together.

Elliott said, "She sees it too. The tiny slits are perpendicular to the coin's rim and parallel to the other slits. There isn't any error in the angles. Also, there are tiny pinhead circles in the direct center of the edge."

"As in the space above and below the circle—"

"—Is equal," Elliott finished.

Lilith said, "Uniform markings but the pattern—"

"—Is random."

AJ put his palm on his forehead. "It's a damn jigsaw puzzle. We have to piece it together, and then we'll have a map."

Lilith lifted her head. "The map to the *Flor de la Mar?*"

"Put the coins back and put the tray insert on the floor. I want to see what else is here," AJ ordered.

They put the coins back in the chest and lifted the tray insert out. They struggled to lower it to the floor without tipping it over. Once on the floor, they stepped back to look at what was next.

Inside the chest were compartmentalized sleeves. Each sleeve had a specific gem type. Oppenheimer blue sapphires, diamonds, Burmese rubies, emeralds, amethysts, opals, and spinels twinkled in the light.

Lilith's phone buzzed. She read Charlotte's text. "She is wondering if we pour these in your tub."

"So she can bathe in luxury. Not today, Charlotte." Realizing what he said, and who he said it to, AJ added. "Nor any day in the future."

"How 'bout me?" Lilith asked.

AJ shook his head and kept shaking it until Lilith gave up looking at him.

"Fine. I won't either."

Charlotte had felt along the edge inside of the chest and found a strap. Elliott ran his hand opposite hers and found a second strap. Together, they lifted the emerald sleeve out.

"Kind of shallow, don't you think?" Lilith asked.

Elliott agreed. "Not as deep as the chest, that's for sure."

They extracted each gem sleeve from the chest and laid them on the garage floor. With the last sleeve out, they stared at an orb at the bottom of the chest. Charlotte tapped on the side of the chest and pointed at the pipette.

AJ understood. "This is a small boulder of our glassy mystery material. The sickly yellow color must be its natural form."

Lilith bent into the chest and ran her hand over the orb. "Cold to the touch. But you must be touching it to feel the cold."

"Isostatic equilibrium," AJ said. Charlotte and AJ began texting one another.

Lilith pushed herself up and sat on the chest's edge.

She waited for one of them to speak, but when they didn't, she said, "Spill it, whatever you are on to."

AJ pointed at the ground. "The beads on the floor, the melted glassy stuff. When it reconstitutes itself from liquid to solid form, it does so in these spherical structures."

"Sorry. You did not have me at hello."

"When the wax-like beads fall to the ground they should puddle up. But they don't. Instead—"

"—It does that *Terminator 2* thing, and gathers itself into a sphere," Elliott said.

"Yeah ... that thing." AJ had been amped to tell Lilith, but Elliott stole his thunder.

"Isostatic equilibrium is the cyborg thing?" Lilith asked.

"Isostatic equilibrium happens at the planetary scale, not the marble level. We are out of our field of experience."

"Whose field of experience is it in?" Elliott asked.

AJ closed his eyes. "An astrophysicist's field of experience. The Tampa Heist."

Charlotte sat on the floor. Cher sniffed her face, but she didn't raise a hand to dissuade the dog.

"Okay," AJ said, "I'm breaking a long-standing rule, but I don't have anywhere else to start. What if—"

"Oh my. Right past the Powhatan Slide and into piercing the giblets on that tradition," Lilith said.

AJ gave her a dirty look.

Lilith looked at Charlotte. "Add the Urban Dictionary to languages he knows."

"What if," AJ continued, "Jade discovered something that eclipsed her scientific abilities?"

"Or maybe it led to something she couldn't control," Elliott added.

"Control. Thpppt," Lilith said. "We never had control from the outset. My world hasn't been the same since that first trip to New Orleans. You had cause to be suspicious with the fifty percent discount."

Charlotte texted Lilith.

Lilith shared Charlotte's concerns. "She corrected me. We entered another world when we stepped into the map room. But one of us had been there before. Somebody has been hiding what they know."

She lowered her phone and stared at AJ. "Did you know about the chest before you hung it above the bar?"

"Not its contents, no."

"How about entering another world? We've endured too many coincidences to believe a force wasn't behind it."

AJ hunched over in his wheelchair. "Tayen entered a half-filled coffee shop, which she claimed was packed. She chose my table when the next table next to mine was empty. We argued over the coffee shop crowd until the day she died.

"In New Orleans, the Broken Cove logo error was a shock. I checked the file before sending it to Kimiko. Shazoo spilled my drink, and when I returned with towels, he batted the mouse around like a toy. I clicked send, never considering a cat playing with a mouse could change a file.

"Lilith pulls the shirt out of the box, and the Broken Cove Industries logo wasn't on the sleeve. BCP was. If that error didn't occur, would this adventure have happened?

"Priestess LaTonya dies, and I crash through a rusted platform. Weeks later, I—sporting a blue shirt with a broken wheel logo—am broadcast worldwide because snakes swarmed over Beagle's Bluff. Ernesto saw it and lured us to New Orleans."

"Damballa's legions," Lilith said.

"Our encounter with Damballa led to the old woman in the market. Gleti, the Moon Goddess, talked with Lilith at the French Market to inform that her journey would be marked by the full moon. For over a year, the full moon cycle shifted each month until two full moons occurred exactly one year apart. What hit me, but apparently nobody else, was Tayen's name. It means 'New Moon.'

"Along with all of this was that damn lunar eclipse on our return to New Orleans. Voodoo belief says when a lunar eclipse occurs, it is because of Gleti's husband passing between her and the Earth. It's a time when she can't extend her protection. A time when she can't see danger, and we walked in the darkness without her.

"Adela Frontera. How did the light from the gas lamps protect us? Ernesto and his men walked right by us on the first trip. On the second, Ernesto shot Lilith in the chest, but the bullet didn't touch her. All thanks to the caretaker, Enriquillo, the defender of Hispaniola."

AJ waved his hand indiscriminately out of frustration. "Father Amare and I were friends before my mysterious head injury. Was it a head injury, or did Priestess LaTonya dust me with Demon's Breath to hide my past in New Orleans? I don't know. But Priestess LaTonya crafted the *Victor Visibly Vanquished* clue for me. Father Amare said I would be upset if he revealed things before the time was right."

Lilith closed her eyes.

"We go to Barbados and our hosts at the Hovel find journals, which point to Maman Brigitte. Upon reading about her, we remembered the dance club where Lilith froze everybody with her dance. But it wasn't her, it was the Goddess of Death. History's most erotic and skilled dancer, who drank a rum too spicy for men. She danced in the flames after Lilith spit alcohol over a candle.

"But one encounter has escaped me until now. The woman who entered your stepmother's hair salon and sent you here … "

Lilith's eyes sprang open. "Oh, yeah. About her."

"We never finished our food court discussion," AJ said.

"Well, about that. Tayen's mystery woman, the one who gave directions to your coffeehouse … She was the woman who handed Mama-Titi the envelope for my job interview."

"Who was she?" Elliott asked.

AJ closed his eyes. "Priestess LaTonya."

Lilith clasped her hands over her mouth.

AJ swayed his head from side to side. "Priestess LaTonya, a Vodou Priestess, enchanted Shazoo. Papa Legba guards the crossroads of life and death. Somebody related to Jade Péchette, or Jade herself, opened the crossroads at Adela Frontera and left a caretaker to guard it. Crossroads are under the care of Papa Legba. Yet he wasn't there, but his dog, Kongo, was. Papa Legba speaks every language under the sun … and I haven't heard a language I don't understand or can't speak."

Elliott, Lilith, and Charlotte stood motionless.

"My secret is my mystical connection with Papa Legba. But like you, I'm lost on where this is headed.

"Those in Jade's time called her discoveries Voodoo. Perhaps it was their way of wrapping their prescientific minds around her discoveries. Regardless, somehow I am bound to her journey."

He turned to Lilith. "And so are you. I opened this chest, and now it is your turn to open the lid."

Lilith looked past him. "There's a compartment in the lid?"

"Center top, on the edge. My vantage point from this wheelchair allowed me to see from a lower angle. There is a slot, just like the one Charlotte destroyed in Tampa. They couldn't open the lid without the key, and no locksmith could pick the lock. Rotted wood splintered, and you retrieved the contents. But Charlotte's butter knife wasn't the solution. The key to the chest lid was inches away. Your amulet is the key to unlocking the upper lid."

Lilith raised her hand to her amulet.

"When we come across a chest with a slot like this, we know you can open it."

She stepped forward and unclasped the amulet from her neck. Too scared to speak, she slipped the amulet in the slot. Nothing happened.

Shazoo jumped up and recklessly balanced himself on the chest's edge. He let out a loud meow.

"I'm trying, Shazoo. It's not like I can say abracadabra and the thing opens."

Tiny clicks like tumblers ticked from inside the lid. A final loud ping of metal ended the clicking.

AJ pulled out his phone. "Reminder to self. Research the history of *abracadabra*."

Charlotte helped Lilith remove the panel. As they did, the weight of hidden objects pushed the plank out of their hands. Rectangular boxes the size of books crashed into the bottom of the chest.

Charlotte pointed.

"Yep," Lilith cringed, "I'm not touching that one."

"What's wrong with the one Charlotte pointed to?" AJ asked.

Elliott pushed the dogs back. They had their noses high in the air, sniffing above the chest's edge. "Shazoo pooped in the chest. He thinks it's a new litter box."

Lilith held a box up. "It's got the glassy stuff on it."

Charlotte picked up the pipette and dripped a few drops of acid on a seam. She waited a moment before pulling a journal free. She gave it a cursory examination and handed it to AJ.

Lilith's patience vanished. "Are these Jade's notes?"

AJ took a deep breath and read out loud.

"'This is a refugee story. If you are reading this, you are searching for the amulet, which unlocks Broken Cove Palisade. My name is Jade Péchette, and I was born in the year 1691. The daughter of a Chetimachan woman and a—'"